For Hannah, Gabe, and Sarina.

Many thanks to Hawthorne Books, Jay Ponteri, Meg Daly, the Cougars, and the editors of the publications in which the following stories originally appeared:

"The Cantor's Daughter" : *Ellipsis*
"Half a Day in Halifax" : *Carve Magazine*
"Model Rockets" : *Del Sol Review*
"Return" : *Arts & Letters*
"Lego" : *Gobshite Quarterly*

THE CANTOR'S DAUGHTER

Stories
Scott Nadelson

 HAWTHORNE BOOKS & LITERARY ARTS
Portland, Oregon | MMVI

THE CANTOR'S DAUGHTER

The Cantor's Daughter

HER NAME WAS NOA NECHEMIA. SHE WAS SIXTEEN NOW, a junior in high school. Her narrow face was too somber to be called pretty, with deep-set eyes and a hairline that started low on her forehead, not much more than an inch above her heavy eyebrows. Her lips were full and well shaped, but she had a habit of sucking them between her teeth and chewing them during school, and they chapped easily. At night, with the bathroom door closed, she practiced putting on lip gloss, so in the morning she could get it straight even as the bus jolted over potholes. She kept extra tissues in her purse to wipe it off before coming home. Her father didn't disapprove of makeup—but seeing it on her would have brought out that oppressive, mournful expression that meant he couldn't believe how fast she was growing up, couldn't believe how much she was beginning to look like her mother.

Her father sang Ashkenazi services for Temple Emek Shalom in Chatwin, New Jersey, though he'd grown up on Sephardi tunes, first in Tangier, then in Netanya, where Noa had been born and where a car accident had killed her mother when Noa was eight. But Cantor Nechemia could sing anything—he had a rich, powerful voice and enormous range, and his ear was flawless. At home he listened only to opera, Mozart, Verdi, Janacek, anybody but Wagner, and when a record ended he often sang several measures from memory. "Yes, maybe I could have made a tenor, a passable one," he sometimes said, massaging his windpipe through the taut skin of his neck. But then he shook his head and shrugged, adding as he did whenever an uncomfortable thought entered his mind, "But for me, God wanted something else."

"This is the worst music ever," Noa said, lifting the needle from a record in the middle of an aria. "If God existed, he'd set fire to all the opera houses in the world."

God was a sore subject for them. For years her father had explained her mother's death by talking about God's will—divine reasoning, he said, was beyond the grasp of human understanding. As a little girl she'd accepted what he told her without question. She hadn't known any better. But now she understood that talking about God was an excuse for her father not to face the guilt he still felt, an excuse not to get over his grief and move on with his life, and the mere mention filled her with rage. "It doesn't make any sense," she said. "He's God, right? He could make things understandable if he wanted. What's the point of believing in something you can't understand?"

"Question all you want," her father said. "But in the end, all we can do is trust."

"Trust what?" she said. "Why should I trust something I can't see? Where is he? In here?" She opened the hall closet and pushed aside coats and rain jackets. She was being dramatic, she knew, making a big act of peering under shoe boxes and behind an umbrella stand. "Come on out," she said. "Show yourself."

Her father didn't get angry. He never did. He just watched her sadly, as if he'd lost not only his wife in the accident but his daughter as well. All three of them had been in the car, her father fiddling with the radio while he drove, Noa in the backseat. All she remembered of the impact now was a strange sound that had stuck with her all these years, that still sometimes surprised her in the middle of a waking dream—a slow splashing, like water poured from a pitcher, or small waves hitting shore, though they'd been a mile from the sea, heading home from an excursion to Tel Aviv. She guessed later that it had been gas spilling out of the tank beneath her, or water from the radiator, though an irrational part of her still believed it was the sound of her mother's life draining away. Noa had walked away with nothing more than a bruise on her cheek—God's will, her father said. He hadn't been so lucky. He'd broken an arm and two ribs, and lost his left eye to a flying glass shard. He wore a patch now, and on several occasions she'd overheard one of his congregants say he looked like a young Moshe Dayan. Those that didn't know about the accident probably imagined he'd been wounded in Sinai or the Golan. It was true, he had fought in Sinai in 1973, a few months before Noa was born, pulled out of Yom Kippur services, hustled onto a convoy, thrown into combat within minutes, it seemed— but at that time, he said, God had chosen to keep him from harm.

Noa knew the statistic: more Israelis were killed in cars every year than in all wars and terrorist acts since 1948. But she sometimes told friends at school other versions of her mother's death—a bomb in a crowded market, an ambushed bus in the desert, a rocket lobbed from southern Lebanon. She confused her stories, never remembering whom she'd told what, but no one ever called her on her lies. Why did she do it? To seem exotic, she supposed, to make the sorrow she felt only vaguely now, if at all, more present. As much as her father's sadness infuriated her, she envied the respect it brought him, the careful way people treated him. If she ever wanted to believe in God, these were the times, hoping He pitied her for the shame she felt as she told each lie, for the disgust that overshadowed any satisfaction she might have gotten in the telling.

She and her father lived in the same two-bedroom apartment he'd found when they'd first come to the States, a year after the accident—finding the job and moving them across the world was the last assertion he'd made in his life, the last, she thought now, he'd ever make. The apartment was two blocks from the synagogue, so they stayed. Not because he couldn't drive on Shabbat—Emek Shalom was a Reform shul, and most congregants drove in from distant neighborhoods and surrounding towns, in Cadillacs, Mercedes, BMWs—but because he wouldn't drive at all, wouldn't even ride in a car unless absolutely necessary. Noa was stuck riding the bus downtown and then catching another bus to school. She stopped for food at the small convenience store across the street, paying twice as much as she would have at a supermarket, buying only what she could carry. The neighborhood, a mile north of downtown Chatwin, had been shabby when they'd first arrived and was even more so now—weathered houses had been left unpainted, stores boarded up, apartment buildings demolished and abandoned as empty lots. She heard as much Spanish on the street as English. The convenience store had begun to advertise Kool and Colt 45 in its window, and when she came out with her groceries, black men drinking from paper bags clicked their tongues at her and called, *"Como estas, chica?"* She was dark enough to be taken for Puerto Rican or Dominican, and she learned to move her hips the way girls in the neighborhood did. She kept her eyes forward and held her chin at an angle that meant she heard everything the men said but didn't care one way or another.

The apartment had been cramped from the start and had only gotten worse as Noa grew, as her father filled the living room with plastic crates crammed with records, all opera. Books on opera, too, from which he sometimes read aloud to her, recounting in an amazed voice some detail in the life of Jussi Bjorling or Franco Corelli. His obsession was absurd, she thought—he hadn't trained as an opera singer, had never even listened to the music until they'd come to the States and he'd watched a production of *Norma* on PBS. In truth, Noa didn't hate the music so much as the way it affected her father, bringing that mournful look to his one exposed eye, a slouch to his shoulders, a silence that would drag on hours after the final note had faded away. He was indulging himself in the doleful tunes, the tragic stories—it was one more way, she thought, for him to avoid imagining any other possibilities for his life, or for hers.

At the synagogue he was a different person. As his voice filled the sanctuary, his body seemed to stiffen and reach out across the bimah, and when he was silent his eye scanned the pews and rested on anyone who met his gaze. Noa understood why congregants were in such awe of him. There was power in his voice and his bearing, mystery in the eyepatch and the woolly hair that had gone gray prematurely, the boyishly smooth skin that needed shaving only once a week, the reluctant smile that showed itself infrequently—whoever brought it out felt the swell of accomplishment, and this, too, gave him power. She understood why women flocked to him during kiddushes, holding their cups of punch in both hands, shunning the trays of brownies and freshly baked rugalah, smiling too brightly and talking too fast—divorcées, single mothers, old women with unmarried daughters in tow, all crowding around him, not seeming to notice how he leaned away, one foot creeping behind the other. None of them knew how he shrank into himself in the apartment, at the same time getting in Noa's way wherever she turned, his stool too close to hers when they ate dinner at the kitchen counter, his smell—meaty, she thought, like overcooked brisket—lingering in the bathroom an hour after he'd been in.

Some days the desire to punish him nearly overwhelmed her. Exactly what she wanted to punish him for she couldn't have said. Driving the car that killed her mother? Failing to own up to his guilt and anguish? Expecting her to share in the suffering he refused to acknowledge? All this and more. At times the impulse to hurt him came to her with the force of simple need. Some things she only imagined doing—converting to Christianity, to Buddhism, to Islam, changing her name on her eighteenth birthday to Noelle Nicholas. Other things she did more than imagine. She smoked cigarettes and drank sweet wine. She shoplifted items she didn't need or even want—silk underwear, cucumber soap, a rhinestone-studded change purse. She let boys kiss her, touch her, drive her off to secluded parking lots and quiet residential streets. Three so far she'd let take off all her clothes and plunge themselves between her legs, two of whom eventually told her, breathlessly, but with obvious reluctance, as if carrying out a tedious but necessary chore, that she was beautiful, that they loved her.

She thought she would let things slip discreetly, to have her father discover for himself the person she'd become, the cigarettes, the stealing, the boys. But when the time came, she always held back. Even when she spent two hours with a boy after school, she made it home to the apartment first—her father taught bar mitzvah lessons until dinner time. He came in while she was cooking, the chicken already breaded and in the oven, the broccoli steaming. His heavy briefcase made him lean to one side. His overcoat was too warm for the day, and his brow was sweaty. His nose lifted, eye squinting, "Have you been smoking?"

She could have admitted it then, thrown it in his face. She knew how he would have reacted—a deep breath, a slow shake of his head in disappointment and shame. He would have immediately blamed himself, for neglecting her, for not paying attention to her needs. Wasn't that what she wanted? Didn't she dream of the day he'd recognize she was worth living for, even if his wife had been lost? "I burnt the bread," she said.

"It smells like cigarettes."

"I said it was bread, okay? What do you know about cigarettes?"

He went straight for the record player, lifted the cover, and then stood puzzled in front of the crates, rubbing his throat. He dropped the briefcase at his feet but didn't bother taking off his coat.

"Is it sore?" she asked. "Do you need some tea?" He didn't answer, but she put the kettle on. "Who was today?"

"Todd Rosen," he said, flipping quickly through the records, the first two fingers of his right hand jogging, then pausing, then jogging again. "Hopeless."

"How much longer has he got?"

"Two and a half weeks."

"You'll get him into shape."

"Not if he doesn't practice. What can I do? How does he expect to learn?"

"Maybe he thinks God'll put the melody in his head."

To this, she knew, he wouldn't reply. He kept shuffling records, moving from one crate to another. Sometimes it took him almost an hour to decide what he wanted to hear. Noa grabbed a loaf of bread from the refrigerator, stuck two pieces in the toaster oven, turned the heat up too high. He wouldn't have thought to look in the trash for burnt toast, but as much as she'd wanted him to know the truth earlier this afternoon, now she was desperate for him to believe the lie.

"Well, it's not your fault if he doesn't learn it," she said. "His parents should make him practice."

"Sometimes," he said slowly, "the words. They make no sense to me."

"Aren't his parents divorced?" she said. "Maybe that's the problem. Bobby Rosen's in my psychology class. He never does his homework."

"Hopeless," he said again.

"His mother's the good-looking one, isn't she?" She said it casually, pulling down a mug, fishing in the cupboard for a tea bag. "The one who always wears pink sweat suits and a diamond brooch? She likes you. Bobby told me she does. Doesn't she always want to talk to you after the lesson?"

"Noa," he said.

"She'd go out with you in a second," she said. "I could handle Todd Rosen as a step-brother, I guess. I don't know about Bobby."

"Please," he said.

"Don't you think it would be good for you? You know, get out once in a while? You can leave me alone. I don't need a babysitter." He was silent now, but they'd had this conversation so often she could answer for him. "I know, I know. 'If God wills it.' But how do you know God doesn't will it already? How do you know he doesn't want you to screw every woman in the congregation?"

He lost patience with his search, instead pulling out the first record he could find. It was Puccini—she'd heard them all enough now to know after the first few notes—not his favorite. He turned up the volume loud, so even if she had more to say he wouldn't hear it. From the toaster, smoke began to rise, and from the kettle, steam.

THE BOY WHO CLAIMED TO LOVE HER NOW WAS ANDREW Cuirzcak, a senior at Chatwin High, two months from graduating. He was tall and lanky, with long freckled arms and a broad smile in a face that, at eighteen, had already taken on a manly shape, with a sharp jaw and prominent forehead. He used his gangly body to good purpose, getting laughs in school with clownish, slapstick gestures, and on the soccer field snagging balls that seemed destined for the back of the net. He was starting goalie for Chatwin's varsity team and often came to class with a bruise on his temple or cheek—he was fearless, diving on balls even when he knew he'd take a cleat to the face. In junior high she remembered people calling him Andy, but now he went by Drew. Everyone, including teachers, said the name with a certain reverence, as if addressing royalty.

He told her he loved her without her having taken her clothes off yet—though she would, as soon as he asked. When he first said it, it shocked them both. She'd been riding home in his car only a week by then, taking the same detours other boys had taken, not bothering to jump in the backseat when they parked, kissing instead over the gearshift. She never knew what to do with her hands when they kissed—the way Drew's arms went around her made it awkward to reach up for his back or his hair. This time she put them against his chest. She could feel his stiff nipples beneath her thumbs and rubbed them the way other boys had done to her. It seemed to work some kind of magic on him—until now his kissing had been too gentle, tentative, but suddenly he ground his mouth against hers, forcing his tongue past her teeth, his breath coming fast through his nose. Though it hurt her chapped lips, she preferred this kind of passion—even if she didn't feel it herself. She counted the moles on his face, six small brown ones on his cheeks and chin, a reddish-peach one above his left eyebrow, puffy and only slightly darker than his skin, though the more excited he grew the closer the color of his face came to matching that of the mole. When he came up for air, he was already muttering, "God, I think I love you. I think I do. Is that okay?"

Since then he'd said it every day. He loved her and wanted to have sex with her, but not until the night of the prom. This was a fixed idea for him—sex after the senior prom. To Noa the whole idea was ridiculous. Why wait? How would the back of his car be any more romantic on prom night? What would it matter if they were stripping out of an expensive dress and a rented tux rather than their ordinary school clothes? She knew their first time together would be awkward—if he really wanted to make the night special, they should practice for the next two weeks.

Mostly she doubted what he felt was really love. She told him as much, but only in a playful way, in order to make him protest and reaffirm his feelings. She could guess what attracted him to her—her dark skin, her exotic name, her husky voice that, after seven years, had lost all but a hint of its accent but still sounded foreign even in her own ears. He wouldn't have proclaimed his love to Noelle Nicholas, of that she was certain, so for now she gave up the daydream about changing her name. Her body wasn't much to look at—skinny and not terribly strong, her breasts small and far apart and pointing to the sides, hips still narrow as any boy's, no matter how much she tried to swing them like those of the Dominican girls in her neighborhood. It was hard to believe that if she were still in Netanya she'd be entering the army in two years. She wondered if the atmosphere in America had changed the way she'd grown. If she were still breathing Israel's salt air and desert wind, would she be tougher than she was now?

Drew's grandparents had come from Poland, and in his mind this somehow bonded them. He was deeply troubled by what had happened to the Jews there, though his grandparents had left long before the war. "Don't you think it makes things better, me and you going out? A Polish kid and a Jewish girl? Healing, or whatever?"

She shrugged. "Maybe, if I were a Polish Jew. But I'm not."

She was tempted to laugh at his sincerity, to mock him, but something kept her in check, the same thing, maybe, that kept her from wounding her father at those moments she wanted to most. As he drove her home late in the afternoon, after they'd spent two hours groping and straining against their clothes while parked on a private road in the hills south of town, his face grew very still, his eyes fixed ahead. "So you miss your mom a lot?" he asked.

"That's a stupid question."

"I mean, you think about her every day?"

"Sure," she said.

"I mean, aren't you pissed? Don't you just want to go fucking kill those fuckers who planted the bomb?"

She looked out the window. "They blew up, too."

He drove fast. Trees whipped by, then houses, then the old brick buildings downtown. She hadn't said she loved him back. He'd told her not to, not until she truly meant it. She knew he was waiting for it every day, hoping. But when the words didn't come he said, "It's better that you don't fake it." His voice was full of uncertainty, but he tried to force confidence into it. "It'll happen. I know it will." When he looked his saddest, she said, "Maybe after the prom," and he was instantly cheered—this fit with his vision for the night. If there was anything she did love about him, it was the way he drove. The car was a Hyundai, not built for speed, but somehow he made the most of it, pushing each gear to its limit, gunning the engine downhill to give extra momentum on straightaways. His parents had offered to buy him a more expensive model, but he'd wanted something he could play around with, without worrying about scratches or dings, though he did put in a new stereo and was considering custom hubcaps and a spoiler. He steered with one hand at the top of the wheel, the other hovering above the gearshift, fingers clenching and unclenching, ready to grab on if needed. He hardly braked around curves, and often the car felt on the verge of flipping. Noa kept her seat belt on, her door locked, her hands tight on the armrest. She was afraid, but the fear exhilarated her, her heart racing faster than when they were kissing and groping. She knew, too, that this would have horrified her father more than anything—smoking, drinking, sex were nothing next to such recklessness, and she decided if she were ever truly going to punish him it would be to tell him about the car, and the way Drew drove.

He slowed after they left downtown. Where Russell Avenue became Martin Luther King Jr. Boulevard, he pressed down his door lock with an elbow. He was as fascinated by where she lived as by her name and history. She didn't tell him her father made enough money now that they could have moved whenever they wanted to, could even have bought their own house. Not up in the hills where Drew lived—his parents were both biologists, his mother a consultant to a pharmaceutical firm, his father a professor at an expensive, if not prestigious, private college—but at least in the modest neighborhoods just east of downtown, where most of her friends lived. Drew took in the liquor store, the methadone clinic, a lineup of haggard people out front of each. When Noa had first come to live here, the neighborhood had still been called the Bottoms, for purely historical reasons—until late in the last century the stretch of land between the original colonial village and the ridge to the north had been filled with reeking swamps and a slow-moving, muddy river. But with a name like that, what chance did the place stand? The neighborhood had always struggled, since the swamps were first drained and German immigrants built rickety, foundationless houses on the still-settling sediment, quickly abandoning them to the Irish who followed. The Bottoms had been Jewish for fifty years, though now only Temple Emek Shalom remained as proof. Two years ago, a coalition of African American and Latino groups had protested against local newspapers for using the name—it was racist, they claimed, intended to hurt the community's self-image. The mayor had agreed, and officially renamed the neighborhood North Chatwin.

"You don't mind living here?" Drew asked.

"What other choice have I got?"

"I'd think you'd get scared walking around at night."

"Are you supposed to be my boyfriend, or my dad?" she said.

But the truth was, her father never worried about her this way. He never asked where she was going or with whom. And in fact she *was* scared to go out at night by herself, instead keeping to the stuffy apartment, struggling to pay attention to her homework, blocking out the sound of her father's records with stolen Black Sabbath or Guns N' Roses tapes turned up loud on her headphones. On Friday nights, until she'd first refused to go to services a year ago—"Why should I pray to something I can't see?" she'd said. "I'd rather worship the TV."—she'd stuck close to her father on the walk home from the synagogue, shivering even on warm nights when they passed an abandoned house or shadowy alley. She partly admired the way he tilted his head in greeting to a group of Puerto Rican boys leaning against an old Lincoln with holes rusted in its frame, all of them in sleeveless undershirts, tattoos covering their arms, but was also made more afraid because he didn't seem to notice the way the boys eyed her, close to leering. Once, he paused when a woman spoke to him without warning outside the convenience store: "How about a date?" She wasn't dressed like a prostitute, and maybe that's why he stopped— she wore a baseball jacket and cap, and had an oversized backpack slung over one shoulder. Her face was free of makeup, and she was far from young. He seemed to consider what she'd said, in a way he never did when Noa suggested he find someone to go out with. Finally, he smiled and said politely, "Thank you. Another time, maybe. I have my daughter with me now."

In front of Emek Shalom, Drew slowed even more, letting the yellow light change to red without tearing through. He lowered his head to get a glimpse of the building through the passenger window. The synagogue was eighty years old, a yellow-brick box with oak doors in the shape of stone tablets and an oxidized copper dome that towered over buildings on either side: a sooty concrete apartment house whose shades were always closed and an abandoned turn-of-the-century firehouse whose bell had been scavenged, along with its brass poles and all its leaded windows. A high fence separated the parking lot from an empty yard, which over the past seven years had steadily gathered broken furniture, car parts, hundreds of shattered bottles—no matter how often the Temple Sisterhood swept the blacktop, brown and green shards crept through the chain links, and at least once a month a congregant came out of services to find a flat tire. Across the street an evangelical church had sprung up in a former electronics storefront—the old sign, Sammy's Stereo's & More, was only partially hidden behind hand-painted banners declaring *No Salvation for Sinners!* and *Your Soul Belongs to Jesus!*

"I'll get out here," Noa said.

"Can't I come in?" Drew asked. "I want to meet him."

"Not now."

"Doesn't he want to know who you're going to prom with?"

"I doubt it."

"I understand," he said. "You don't love me yet."

It was hard to keep herself from laughing. "Afterward," she said. "You can meet him after prom." The light had turned green, and the driver behind them laid on his horn. "I'd better go," she said, but Drew reached for her, mashed his lips against hers, pulled her hands up to his chest so she could touch his nipples again. He was in no hurry, no matter how many times the other car honked. She tried to open the door while he was still kissing her, but couldn't manage the lock with her body twisted and caught in his arms. He let her go only when she pinched a nipple hard enough to make him gasp. Then he lingered at the light, even as the driver behind began to shout, stayed until she'd run up the sidewalk all the way to the oak doors. Only when she opened them did she hear the screech of his tires, the whizzing of that tiny engine.

Inside, the squawk of her sneakers' rubber soles echoed under the hollow dome. On Friday nights, with all the heels and murmuring, the lobby could be deafening, but during the week,

when no one was around, she sometimes made bird noises or
farting sounds, or called out, "Hare, hare, Krishna," just to hear
the strange sound of her voice reflected back at her. As a girl
she'd felt such peace in this building, its airiness a relief from the
claustrophobic apartment, the old passageways providing
abundant mystery. One wound behind the sanctuary and ended
abruptly in a solid brick wall; another led to the original boiler
room, no longer used, with its skeleton of iron pipes and gears, all
rusted and frozen now. She'd found a staircase once, in the back
of the ballroom, that led to a door with an old-fashioned lock
whose keyhole she could peer through—behind it were piles of
yellowed books and big black cases of some kind, steamer trunks,
she thought, or caskets. No key on her father's chain matched the
lock, so instead she tried for years to fashion a pick from bobby
pins and work her way inside. But then, three years ago, the
ballroom was refurbished, and the door disappeared altogether,
along with the staircase. Was that when the building lost its
appeal for her? Was that when she began to associate it with her
father's notion of God—a falsehood, unconnected to the reality
beyond the dome, the oak doors, the marble floors, the flickering
eternal flame?

Her father's office was in the basement, a small room as
crowded with books as their apartment was with records. The
confined space made him feel safe, she supposed, but knowing
this didn't bring her any closer to sympathy. Instead it made
her want to shake him, to grab hold of his head and force his good
eye to see something beyond these walls, beyond this neighborhood, beyond his memory of the accident. Today it wasn't her
father's voice she heard when she came down the stairs, but a high-
pitched, scratchy whine. The sound wasn't like singing at all, or
even chanting, and the words didn't resemble Hebrew or any other
language she recognized. The voice rose and fell and slurred and
then suddenly cut off. Then her father's voice: "Again."

If he saw her lingering outside his open office door he
didn't acknowledge her. His attention was focused on Todd Rosen,

an undersized thirteen-year-old in a red- and blue-striped rugby shirt that puffed out where his shoulders didn't fill it and came down far past his waist. The boy squirmed in his seat and checked the face of his digital watch, a gaudy thing with a built-in calculator, wider than his wrist. His crewcut made the back of his head look soft and lumpy, and the huge woven yamulka sat on top like the end of a plunger. He sighed and started to sing, rushing through the portion, this time not even trying to follow the accent marks. "Again," her father said. Todd glanced at his watch once more, and her father said, "Still time. Again."

She hadn't been waiting long when Mrs. Rosen appeared, taking the stairs to the basement lightly in her running shoes, a dainty silk purse slapping against her hip. Her sweat suit was white this time, her jewelry ruby—necklace, rings, earrings, and a dragonfly pin over her left breast. Her hair was cut in a lopsided bob, cropped above the ear on one side and swooping in a kind of bird's wing on the other. She didn't care if people knew it was dyed—most of it was blond, with two brown streaks that framed her eyes. Her lips were thin, but she tried to make them bigger by spreading rust-colored lipstick in a half-inch swath around her mouth. When she spotted Noa she broke into an exaggerated look of surprise and pleasure and mouthed a drawn-out "Hi!" Then she whispered, "How's he doing in there?"

"Coming along, I guess," Noa said.

"My God," Mrs. Rosen said, her whisper getting louder and raspier. "Only two weeks left. I don't know if we'll make it. I just keep imagining getting to the party so I can have a drink and forget how much it's all costing me."

She'd been married to an orthopedic surgeon, a decade her senior, and the divorce had left her with a house near Drew's in the hills south of Chatwin, a condo in Sarasota, a maroon Jaguar with only a handful of payments outstanding. Noa heard about her from Bobby Rosen, who lived most of the time with his father and called her, as his father did, "The Vampire." She drove the Jaguar with her shoes off, Bobby said, so she could feel the pedals against her instep. Then he added, "She'd fuck that car if she could." Noa tried to imagine what her life would be like if her father really did marry someone like Mrs. Rosen, if they moved into the sprawling near-mansion with columns out front and Fu dogs guarding either end of a circular driveway. She could picture the luxury, could even picture her father smiling and talking to the Rosen boys over breakfast, but she couldn't see herself among them, couldn't imagine Mrs. Rosen opening her mouth without wanting to burst out laughing in her face.

Mrs. Rosen's expression changed suddenly, her eyes narrowing in concern, a finger rising to either side of her chin. This time her whisper came out low and breathy. "Is your pop doing okay? This is a hard time of year for him, isn't it?"

"I guess so," Noa said, though she didn't notice any difference in her father's moods from one day to the next. The anniversary of the accident had recently passed, and they'd marked it with a yahrzeit candle and a day without opera, nothing more. "He's fine."

"If there's ever anything I can do," Mrs. Rosen said, her whisper growing louder again. She pressed both hands to her chest, covering the ruby dragonfly. "You know I think the world of you two."

Noa's vision of a new life had already faded. She didn't want this woman anywhere near her father. "We're fine," she said again.

Todd came out of the office in a huff, hands stuffed into his pockets, the collar of the rugby shirt bunched around his ears. He looked too young to be a bar mitzvah boy, not even close to puberty. Mrs. Rosen didn't whisper now, her voice brash and honking, coming out, it seemed, through her tightly pinched nostrils. "Well? Did you learn it yet? We're not wasting any more time, mister."

"I don't care," Todd said.

"I'll cancel the party right now. You can say goodbye to all your presents."

The boy kicked at something invisible on the ground. "Fine," he said. "I don't care."

"You'll care when I get through with you." Her father took his time coming out of the office, but Mrs. Rosen lingered, waiting for him. "Tell me, Cantor. Is it even worth it? Is he going to be ready?"

"There's only so much I can do," her father said.

"I can pull him out of school," Mrs. Rosen said. "I can bring him to you every day."

"No," her father said quickly. "No need for that. He'll do fine. He'll manage."

"I'd really like to sit and have a talk with you about him," she said. "Sometimes I don't know what to do. He doesn't listen. And his father, forget it. He's never heard the word 'discipline.' He already gave him his present, a computer, and now all the kid does is sit around playing games all day."

Her father seemed to notice Noa for the first time then, and smiled at her, gratefully, she thought. "My daughter and I have to be going. She needs help with her homework."

"What do I need a bar mitzvah for anyway?" Todd said, kicking again at the invisible ball on the floor. "I don't even *want* to be a man."

Noa didn't know which she found funnier, the words, or the boy's expression, so serious and full of worry, but she broke into giggles. Mrs. Rosen joined in after a moment, cackling. Todd put his hands behind his back and shuffled his feet, uncertain, she thought, whether to be angry that people were laughing at him or pleased with himself for causing such a sudden stir. "Don't worry," her father said. "You can stay a boy awhile yet. For now, learn the portion and collect your gifts, and that will be plenty."

THE PROM WAS ON A FRIDAY NIGHT, THE NIGHT BEFORE Todd Rosen's bar mitzvah. A year ago her father might have objected to her going, but now he didn't say a word. She was disappointed. She wanted a fight. But even if he had objected it would have been in his sorrowful, resigned way that suggested no heartbreak now could match what he'd already suffered. She waited until he'd left for shul before showering and taking the dress out of her closet, and almost immediately she regretted not having shown it to her father. She didn't know what she would have wanted him to see in it—that she really was growing up, that she really had begun to look like her mother? or that she was her own person, not just the shadow of someone who'd died?—but she had the nagging feeling that if he did see it, something, anything, between them might have changed.

In fact, the dress had been Drew's choice, not hers. She hadn't liked it at all when she'd tried it on—she hadn't even wanted to try it on to begin with. But Drew had pictured her in pink or salmon, though she'd insisted she would have looked better in forest green or violet, something that would complement her dark skin. "That's what you always wear," he'd said. "This is a special night." He had a complete vision, had already picked out a tux with a pink cummerbund, had chosen the flowers she would wear on her wrist. And of course he was paying for everything. The dress fit as it was supposed to but was far from comfortable. The straps cut into her shoulders, the fabric constricted her ribs. Only when she stepped out of the dressing room and saw Drew's face did she know she'd have to get it—he gawked at the exposed parts of her skin, knowing how soon he'd be seeing it in its entirety. One night of discomfort was worth giving her body the illusion of curves. By the time they left the store she believed the dress was the most beautiful thing she'd ever owned, something that transformed her completely, from the hard, knobby, foreign girl she saw in the mirror most days, into something soft, voluptuous, strangely American.

Now she put it on and took it off three times to watch the surprising transformation, imagining the disappointment Drew might feel when he saw her curves disappear. When he came to pick her up, she still hadn't put her shoes on or finished her makeup. "Your father didn't wait?" he asked, and already a disgruntled look had settled onto his face, his smile strained. A fresh bruise from last Sunday's game covered the left half of his jaw. "I'm surprised he didn't want to see you off." This was part of his vision, shaking her father's hand, having him hand off his daughter into Drew's care. He was ready with compliments, trying to make them sound original, though in essence he'd already said the same things in the store. He flipped through her father's records and again seemed disappointed in his first view of the apartment. She followed his eyes as they wandered over the spare furniture, the secondhand couch and armchair, the wooden stools at the kitchen counter, the water stains over the sink. He expected greater squalor, maybe, or not so much. He made an elaborate ceremony of pinning the flowers around her wrist, saying, "I've never seen anything so beautiful," but then he wouldn't kiss her. "Your lipstick," he said. He wouldn't touch her at all, wouldn't even take her hand. "I'm not a piece of fruit," she said. "I won't spoil." She didn't feel half as precious as he wanted to make her, partly because she had trouble walking downstairs in the heels he'd bought her, even though she'd been practicing all week, pacing her bedroom carpet every night after her father had gone to bed.

Outside, she saw it first: the shattered passenger window, the batteries wrapped in duct tape still on the seat, the empty hole where his stereo had been. The glass had broken into thousands of jagged beads, most of them scattered across the car's floor. She could have told him what a mistake it would be to park where he did, in the alley behind the apartment building. But she couldn't tell him anything now, couldn't even try to comfort him as he raged, shouting, "Motherfucker! Motherfucker!" so loudly she glanced up to see if blinds were opening above. The display embarrassed her—despite its decay, the neighborhood was usually quiet, and his shouts ruptured the tranquil evening. "How can you live in this shit hole?" he asked, but instead of answering she started brushing glass beads off her seat. "Don't," he said. "Your dress. I'll do it."

He tried to calm himself, to at least swallow his anger for
the moment, but as they pulled away from the apartment she
could see how it shuddered through him, the bruise on his jaw
twitching, his eyes wincing shut, then a quick shake of the head to
push it away. He could no longer manage even his strained
smile. Both hands were on the wheel, knuckles white, eyes set on
the road. All his careful plans were being foiled, and she knew
he blamed her. "I don't see how you can live in that place," he said.
Wind whipped through the missing window, and she held her
hands to her head to keep the bobby pins in place. "Your hair," he
said, but drove the way he always did, gunning the car through
yellow lights, passing anyone who slowed in front of him, never
keeping to a lane for more than half a mile.

He'd planned everything. On the dashboard was a mixed
tape with all her favorite songs—"Mr. Crowley," "Kashmir,"
"Sweet Child o' Mine"—and even though they couldn't listen to it
now, she said, "This is so nice. Thank you." If he had softened
the slightest bit, given her just a mere hint of a smile, she would
have felt a surge of affection for him as she read the carefully
printed titles. She wanted to make him feel better, at first trying
for conversation, shouting over the wind, and then singing
some of the songs on the tape. She hadn't inherited her father's
voice—she couldn't carry a tune at all, and purposely butchered
the songs in what she hoped was a comical way. Drew did smile
then, reluctantly, with an impatience that made her realize
she was better off being quiet. He started to relax only when they
made it to the hotel. They sat in the parking lot for half an hour,
Noa fixing her hair, Drew sipping from a flask of Seagram's 7 and
7-Up he'd hidden in the glove compartment. "Good thing
the motherfucker didn't find this," he said. "I'd've really lost it."

He danced with her only during slow songs. The rest of
the time he sat with his friends at their table, telling the story of
his car and the stolen stereo. "You should see the shit hole
she lives in," he said. She stayed out on the dance floor as much as
possible, bouncing and shaking with a group of other girls. As

soon as she started to sweat the dress began to itch, under the straps, at the waist. The shoes cut into her toes and heels, and after half an hour she had to take them off. Several girls told her how good she looked, but now she only half believed it— whenever she glanced back at her table, expecting to see Drew watching, he was huddled up instead with his teammates. He might just as well have been on the soccer field, Noa out of sight on the bleachers. Another boy, Mark Filene, danced up beside her. He was the first who'd told her he loved her, after she'd slept with him a dozen times in the tall grass at the edge of the baseball field. His jacket was already off, his bowtie loose around his neck, his eyes bloodshot. She remembered him most for the long, carefully filed fingernails on his right hand—he'd grown them out to play a guitar he hadn't yet bought, and they'd stabbed her more than once, in the back, the belly, close to her throat. He'd wept when she'd told him she didn't want to see him anymore and said he was sorry they'd ever met. A day later she found a note in her locker: "Your cunt smells like dead camels. I'm glad I never have to go near it again." Now he looked her up and down and whispered, "I'd still fuck you, camel jockey."

"Only in your wet dreams," she said, and turned her back on him. She managed to keep dancing through the rest of the song, struggling to hold back tears, and then ran to the bathroom in her bare feet. But by the time she got there she no longer felt like crying, so instead leaned in close to the mirror, pulling flakes of dried skin off the edge of her lower lip. She wanted a cigarette but had promised herself she wouldn't smoke tonight, wouldn't soil her dress with the smell.

Later, Bobby Rosen danced with her. He was short and beefy and had a sparse goatee that made his face look unwashed. His breath reeked of whiskey, and his voice was slurred. "I don't know why you go out with that goy asshole," he said. "What's wrong with Jewish guys?"

"Don't you have to go to your brother's bar mitzvah in the morning? You're going to be totally hungover."

"Only way I can handle it," he said. "The little shit. You know how bad he'll embarrass us?"

"My dad's a wreck about it."

"You better warn him. My mom? She'll be all over him. Bloodsucker."

Drew fetched her when their dinner arrived, overcooked chicken and Cæsar salad. He ignored her as they ate, still talking to his friends, now about the kind of stereo he would buy to replace the one he'd lost. She didn't want to be alone with him. She wanted to stay here as long as possible, to be in other people's presence. But he'd planned their exit the same way he'd planned everything else—during the next slow song he pressed close to her for the first time, his thighs gripping one of hers. When the music faded he whispered, "Go get your purse."

They didn't have to use the backseat of his car. He'd arranged to borrow a key from a friend whose parents were out of town, had already made up the bed in the guest room. He popped the cork on a bottle of chilled champagne and lit candles around the room. He had trouble with the hooks on her dress and muttered in frustration—nothing was going his way. Noa wondered if the bruise on his jaw had been planned as well, a part of the vision he had for himself, his ruggedness and manly appeal. She wanted to be attracted to it, but it was unsightly, as much a blemish as the mole above his eyebrow. She unhooked the dress for him, pulled it over her head, folded it neatly on a chair, her bra and underwear beside it. She didn't look up to see whether or not his expectations had been met. Why did it occur to her only now that her own expectations had never come into consideration? He'd never asked how she pictured the night, how she wanted everything to go. When she finally faced him she didn't care anymore what he thought of her body, didn't care how much he might be disappointed. Her bottom lip, chapped as it was, had found its way back between her teeth. But now his face was pitiful, cheeks flushed, smile hesitant and twitching at the corners. She went to him boldly, took his hands, and led him to bed.

Afterward, they were back in his car. There was a party across town, at the house of another soccer player, where they would spend the night. She'd brought a change of clothes but had put the dress back on anyway, in order to feel her body reshaped by the impossible arrangement of fabric. At the party all the girls would disappear into a bedroom to change and talk about where they'd gone in the dark hour after the prom was over, and what they'd done. She'd felt little pleasure with Drew, no more than she'd felt with any other boy. He'd been too gentle at first, and then too hurried. Her lower back was sore, and so were her lips. When he'd collapsed on top of her he'd whispered, "I love you. I do, really. If I didn't before, I do now." And because he'd expected it, because he'd been waiting for her to say it, she answered, "Me, too." He hugged her then, not with joy, she thought, or even gratitude, but simply in confirmation. She didn't feel guilty for lying, not even mildly. More than anything she was struck by how long it had been since she'd thought of her father, hours, maybe. She didn't imagine telling him what she'd been doing with Drew, or how she'd lied to him. Sometime during the night the mess of her life had suddenly become all her own. What was she doing, if this were for no one but herself? "Andy," she said, glad to feel how he bristled at the name. "Your knee. It's digging into my leg."

Now Drew's face had settled into an ugly bliss, all color drained from it, except for the dark bruise and the red mole. He drove lazily on the quiet highway, as fast as ever but without the usual urgency, two fingers draped on top of the wheel, his other hand a dead weight around her shoulders. He wasn't worried about her hair now—she'd lost most of the bobby pins, and loose strands whipped against her eyes. He talked about graduation, all the parties they'd go to this summer, how she'd visit him at Penn State in the fall. "I don't know, maybe one weekend a month? I'll probably have a lot of schoolwork. And practice. I'll come home for Thanksgiving. And Christmas." He was already getting rid of her. She should have been glad for it—the sooner the fantasy he'd created for them was over, the sooner she could come up with one for herself—but instead she wanted to cry. She pretended a hair had gotten in her eye and leaned forward, pulling out of his grip. He let her go without a struggle—even if he saw the tears she was wiping away he wouldn't have wanted to comfort her or known how to.

She felt it before he did, or at least before he acknowledged it—the swing of the back tires as they came around a sharp curve, a skid on loose gravel, her body straining hard against the seat belt, the weight of the car heaving beneath her. Her first thought was of her dress—despite everything, she wanted to keep it, to remind her of the night and how she'd never have to relive it. And then her father's words: God's will. But even as she thought it, as the folded metal of the guardrail sped toward her, she knew it was nonsense. This had nothing to do with God. Nothing to do with coincidence, either. This was her own will, no one else's. She'd chosen to ride in the fastest car she could find, the one most likely to flip, the one with the most reckless driver. She'd always wanted to know what her mother had felt, to discover if it was easier than the grief she and her father had had to suffer. But even before the impact she knew easier wasn't the word, if there was one. She knew she would suffer just as much for the suffering she would cause her father. She couldn't remember her mother's face, though she passed her picture every day, propped on an end table beside her father's record player. She couldn't remember what her father had been like before the accident, if he'd really been joyous and full of life, or if she only now wanted to imagine him that way. She waited to hear the noise from that first crash, the watery sound that until now had been so distinct in her mind but was suddenly abstract and hard to recall. The only sounds she did hear were a grunting noise from Drew and the hollow roar of the wind smack in her ear. She saw nothing now that her eyes were closed, and waited, too long, it seemed, for the pain to arrive.

But it didn't. The car had straightened and was moving forward again. "I got it," Drew said. "I got it. Fuck. I got it, it's okay."

When she opened her eyes they were speeding down an incline, Drew hunched forward, both hands on the wheel. "Take me home," she said.

"I got it," he said. "No big deal."

"I want to go home."

"The party," he said. "We're supposed to go."

"I just want to go home."

He slammed an open hand against the dashboard. "Fuck! We're *supposed* to—" He cut himself off, sighed deeply, dropped the hand to his lap. "What's the point?" he said. "You don't love me anyway." He kept his eyes forward, waiting for her to object. When she didn't, he put his turn signal on, checked his mirrors, pulled slowly onto a tightly curving exit ramp. "This fucking night," he said. He thrust his chin at the broken window, the missing stereo, wires still dangling out of the gaping hole. With another sigh, he said, "I guess I got laid." Noa rolled the fabric of her dress between her fingers and wondered what she'd gotten and what, if anything, she wanted.

HER FATHER WAS STILL AWAKE WHEN SHE CAME IN, sitting at the kitchen counter. He was in pajamas, no shirt, the hair on his chest still black though there wasn't a trace of color left on his head. His patch was off. She'd seen the scar recently enough, but it still surprised her, the mottled ridge that started in the middle of his eyebrow and cut diagonally across empty, sunken flesh almost to the bridge of his nose. For a moment she thought he'd waited up for her, out of concern, even worry. But then, from his confused glance from her to her bedroom and back, she guessed he'd forgotten about her altogether, hadn't even realized she wasn't home. "Your dance," he said after a moment. "You had a nice time?"

"It was okay," she said.

"You look—" he started and then hesitated. She waited for him to say she reminded him of her mother, that she was the spitting image. "Very nice," he said. "Pink. A good color for you."

"What are you doing up?" she asked.

"The Rosen bar mitzvah tomorrow. A disaster waiting to happen."

"You did all you could," she said.

"Such bad music was never supposed to enter the world."

"Bobby Rosen's going to puke all over his mother's dress. No one'll even notice the singing."

"She offered to pay extra, for all the trouble."

"You don't have to go out with her," Noa said. "I know I said you should, but you can do better."

He laughed, a sudden, conspiratorial chuckle, so startling that she joined in without knowing exactly what was funny. "Thank you," he said. "I think so, too."

She filled the tea kettle, turned on a burner, and said, "How about some music? It'll help us both relax."

He went to his crates, started flipping through the stacks. She had the strange feeling that more than just a few hours had passed since she'd last seen him this afternoon. But nothing about him had changed in the interval. Of course not. Why should she have expected it? He was as puzzled in his search through the records as ever, as pained. She knew he didn't see any life for them other than the one they were living, and never would. He hadn't been waiting for God to present him with something else—most likely he hadn't been waiting for anything at all. Above the kitchen sink, the small window was open a crack, a sliver of darkness showing—how could she tell if some mysterious future was out there, or just the squalor of the neighborhood? The only life she'd ever truly envisioned for herself was the one she couldn't have, the one that was lost to her for certain—a life with her parents together, alive, happy, in view of the beach and the sea. "I want to learn how to drive," she said. "I want you to teach me."

Her father stiffened but pretended not to hear. "What should we listen to?" he asked.

"I'm going to learn," she said. "You're going to teach me."

"Something light? Or serious?"

She tried to remember albums she liked, or ones she could at least tolerate, but her mind was tired and nothing came to her clearly. She could have sung from memory any of the songs on the tape Drew had made her. She could recall snippets of the Sephardi tunes her father still sang sometimes, and prayers from Friday night services. He was waiting for her to answer, his fingers ready to jog through the records. "*Tosca?*" she said, the only name she could come up with. She couldn't remember the story, or the sound of it, or even the name of the composer, and her father gave no sign to indicate whether or not the choice was a good one. But she said it again, with confidence this time, "*Tosca,*" and waited for the music to start.

Half a Day in Halifax

NEITHER OF THEM BELONGED ON THE BOAT. THAT WAS what they shared. Anything else was purely circumstantial, a matter of coincidence. They were so relieved to find each other that first night, at the edge of the disco, as far as possible from the dance floor without leaving the room. The music had been bad in the '80s and was worse now. Roger's eyes, already bleary from two and a half Dewar's, burned in the haze of cigarette smoke. His ears were numb with noise. He leaned against a chrome table and tried not to catch his reflection in its surface, glistening with spilled drinks. His face hurt from the smile he'd held all through dinner, telling strangers about his consulting business, explaining that yes, this was his first cruise, yes, he'd come alone, listening to advice about where he could get food in the middle of the night, which slot machines paid off best, where he might find likeminded young people without attachments. He scowled at himself in the chrome, his features distorted hideously as thumping bass made a puddle of cranberry liquid shimmer across the table's surface. Then, beside him, a woman spoke unexpectedly. "I think I had this deejay at my bat mitzvah."

She was taller than him by at least three inches, and broad-shouldered, with a squarish face and heavy eyebrows. He was startled, and without thinking, replied, "He was at my wedding, too." He couldn't help himself from adding, "No wonder it didn't work out," and regretted it immediately, reading pity in the woman's expression.

But if Beth felt pity then, it was only for herself. She'd tried out the bat mitzvah line on two other people, a man and a woman. Not as a pick-up—she was hoping only for a laugh, a recognition of shared absurdity. From the man, young, attractively scruffy, sweaty and breathless from dancing, she'd gotten only a blank, semi-attentive look, as if he were waiting for a punchline. The woman, as old as her mother, in a dress whose neckline came down almost to her nipples, had squealed, "What a coincidence!" and asked whether she'd told the deejay the news. Finally, from this man, with dark bristly hair and the beginning of a paunch, a carefully cropped mustache that, strangely, made him look younger than he probably was, a boy in costume, she'd gotten the response she'd wanted, the touch of irony, but with it came a sadness she'd hoped to avoid. Lightness had never been her strong suit, and she supposed she couldn't fake it. Her irony would always have an edge of loneliness to it, but she tried again for levity. "I thought silver lamé went out with moon boots," she said.

"Maybe this isn't a cruise ship after all," Roger said. "Maybe it's a time machine."

"I hope it keeps going back, then," she said. "There's got to be a better era than this."

He suggested trying a different bar—the ship boasted fourteen, the most on the high seas, the catalogue touted. In the Caribbean Lounge, a dreadlocked, olive-skinned kid—he might have been Latino, or even Israeli, but certainly not West Indian—played the steel drum for a cheering group from the Bronx, all in shorts and flowered shirts, though it was mid-September, fifty degrees and drizzling on deck, the ship heading north up the Atlantic coast. In Paddy's Irish Pub, a circular counter surrounded a revolving piano, at which an emaciated college girl played Elton John songs and sped-up, frantic standards. She had talent, it was clear, and clear, too, that she knew she was wasting it here. She was separated from her fans by only two feet of polished wood but didn't speak to any of them—requests were typed into keypads on the bar, and she read them from a small monitor propped on the piano.

"How Irish," Beth said.

"Didn't you know?" Roger said. "The revolving piano was invented on the Emerald Isle. Right after the revolving cello. Which, of course, didn't catch on so well."

The pianist threw her head back, ending "My Funny Valentine" with a flourish of trills. "Poor girl," Beth said. "Hell of a way to pay off student loans."

"Beats prostitution."

"Maybe."

In the Comedy Corner, a skinny Hungarian told jokes about life behind the Iron Curtain. One obese man cackled hysterically, slapping a meaty palm against a table that seemed suddenly rickety, several empty glasses jumping. "How many years ago did the Berlin Wall come down?" Roger asked.

"He couldn't have been more than eight," Beth said.

Through the bright reflections in the nearby windows, Roger could just barely make out the dark, sloshing water below. "I guess it's too far to swim to shore."

"I hear drowning's not the worst way to die."

"What about hypothermia? Or sharks?"

"Who was it who said, 'Fear death by drowning'? Pound? Eliot?"

"I couldn't tell you," Roger said, quieter now, scratching a freckle on his arm.

"Whoever he was," Beth said quickly. "I bet he never booked on Carnival."

In the casino, Roger lost sixty dollars in fifteen minutes, twenty at blackjack, twenty in the slots, twenty in one spin of the roulette wheel. He described the euphoric feeling of losing, the relief of it, like chopping off unused limbs.

"Like drowning, from what I've been told," Beth said.

"You should try it."

"What? Drowning?"

"No, losing."

"Afraid I'm on a budget," Beth said.

"Not me," Roger said. "Here." He handed her a twenty, and when she objected, said, "If you refuse one more time I'm jumping overboard. Sharks be damned."

She sat at one of the five-dollar tables, and he stood behind her, giving advice she mostly ignored. She won two hands, three, four. She doubled down, and Roger winced. She won. "Wow," he said. "That looks like even more fun than losing."

"Like gaining extra limbs," she said.

"Like getting saved from drowning."

When she was up a hundred and twenty and beginning to yawn, she quit. She tried to hand him the stack of chips, but he waved them away. "I'll only lose it," he said. "And now you've got a bigger budget."

"At least take your twenty back," she said. He did, and feeling lucky, tossed it on the roulette table, on the line between numbers 17 and 18. He lost. "How many limbs can you do without?" Beth asked.

They were too tired now to be drunk. They hadn't exchanged names, and aside from Roger's remark about his wedding and divorce, hadn't traded any personal details. In the elevator they suffered their first awkward moment, pushing buttons for different decks, Roger the seventh, where the rooms were large and luxurious, with couches and balconies, Beth the first, the bowels of the ship, just above the staff quarters, close to the roaring engines, with a small porthole only a dozen feet above the churning waves. Roger's stop was first. He stood in the elevator doors to keep them from closing. "Nice to meet a fellow cynic," he said, and put out his hand noncommittally, in a way that could have been taken as a wave or an invitation for a shake.

Beth reacted slowly, reaching out only as his arm was falling, her fingers brushing his wrist. "See you overboard," she said, berating herself all the way down to her room for not saying one honest thing, one serious sentence—how hard would it have been to say, "I hope we run into each other again," or "Would you like to meet for breakfast?"

SHE WOKE FOUR TIMES IN THE NIGHT, MOUTH DRY AND sour from the wine she'd drunk, hands aching as if they'd been clenched, breath short. Each time she had the panicky sensation that the rhythm of the engines had shifted, the movement of the ship changed—they were lost, heading straight out to sea now, or into some dark, frozen, forbidden bay. The fourth time, she got out of bed, peering through the condensation on the porthole, scanning the horizon for icebergs. The waves had grown higher in the night, crashing now just below her, spray fanning against the thick glass. For a moment she thought the sky had cleared, and that moonlight glittered on the black water—but no, it was only a spotlight on the side of the ship, shining from several decks above. Along with the spray was rain still. Craning her neck, she could make out the solid ceiling of clouds.

She was naked. It was the first pleasure she'd discovered about being on a boat, soon after they'd pulled out of New York Harbor. Where else could she do this? At home she had roommates, women who'd put an ad in the paper, still nearly strangers after more than a year. Her bedroom had been meant as a common room, and would have stayed that way if rents in Williamsburg hadn't skyrocketed in recent years. It had no real doors, just curtains, and had to be crossed to reach the kitchen. Her roommates—two recent college graduates, living on daddy's money while exploring the city and taking occasional service jobs—were careful to knock on the wall before entering, but their boyfriends, often changing from one week to the next, were slow to learn the rules. She undressed only in the bathroom, one hand holding the door closed because the lock was broken. Even when her roommates were away for the weekend, taken by one boyfriend or another to Fire Island or the Finger Lakes, she kept at least her robe on—her window faced another apartment building across a narrow alley, and her blinds covered the glass imperfectly.

But here no one could see, and it was exhilarating to stand bare before a window in the middle of the day, or at night with the lights on, shades opened all the way, her pale body exposed only to the unlikelihood of a passing ship. Not that anyone would want to look, she thought, hearing the words in the husky, sarcastic voice she'd used all evening on deck with the boyish, bristly-haired man. It was her voice and not her voice, and she only half-believed it. She was a big woman, that was true— big was the first word, she knew, that people used to describe her when she couldn't hear. She wasn't heavy, except maybe in the hips and thighs, but her shoulders had a thickness to them that most women's didn't, and her arms were muscled though she did little to make them so. Her blocky face would have been better served by long hair, she'd been told, but she kept it short, for the sake of convenience, mostly, and partly in defiance of people who gave advice when they weren't asked. By age eleven she'd known how her body would grow—it started with her feet, flippers by the time she entered junior high, even now dispro-portionate though her legs had stretched to match them. Only her breasts had never caught up with the rest of her—adequately sized on a smaller woman, they were sad and clownish on her broad chest.

But it was self-pitying and dishonest to say that no men were attracted to her. She'd had lovers, not a small number, either—half a dozen in college alone, though only one in the last two years. She knew how easy it was to get men into bed, even ones who weren't drawn to her looks. She'd learned how thin the line between attraction and repulsion was, crossed easily in either direction. There were men she could sleep with now, men in her office, in offices on the floors above and beneath her own, men in her apartment building, men she met in bars, men—she was sure—on this boat. She'd had several aspiring writers— one a true beauty, with long eyelashes and sensitive lips—nearly panting over her when she mentioned she worked in publishing. It didn't matter that she could do nothing to advance their careers.

They wanted her simply because she revolved in a world that was mysterious and intimidating to them, a world they didn't understand. The actuality of her job would have quelled their desire: she edited a series called the Books of Wisdom, cheaply printed pocket editions that featured out-of-context snippets of religious or philosophical writing beneath paintings whose rights cost the company little or nothing. At the moment she was working on the Russian Book of Wisdom—she'd brought the manuscript with her but now had no desire to look at it—which paired quotes of Tolstoy with those of Rasputin, Catherine the Great with Lenin. Her readers—like the people on this boat—had no sense of irony, and she despised them. She consoled herself only by remembering that her books made the company enough money that it could publish quality literary works, books of poetry, which made nothing. She didn't tell the writers she met what she did, but neither did she go home with them, hoping instead to leave them with a longing she knew she sparked in few people.

No, the problem was not finding men to sleep with. Nor was it finding one to love and marry, as her Aunt Fran believed— Aunt Fran who'd bought Beth this trip as a surprise for her thirty-first birthday, who hadn't asked if she'd be interested in a cruise or even if she could take vacation time on the chosen dates, the reservation nonrefundable, her Aunt's face bullying with its fragility, its obvious fear of rejection. So what did she want, if not sex and not love? It was easier to say what she didn't want, what she'd gotten from Ben Glasser, her most recent lover—a hesitant tenderness, a relationship that fizzled for two years before dying completely, a sympathetic smile, disingenuous tears.

She wouldn't fall back asleep tonight. It was after four. Her stateroom was tiny, and after pacing several laps, she knew she'd have to leave. Even the thrill of being naked had begun to wear off, though a giggling part of her wanted to run through the rest of the ship this way, through all the lounges and the casino. What did it matter? Who knew her here? Instead she slipped on a pair of loose linen pants and a cotton sweater, no underwear, no bra. Her giddiness revived momentarily, until she stepped into the hallway, under the buzzing glare of fluorescent lights. Here she felt only exposed—not intimately, but as if she were being judged. Her awkward body, her serious face that made her look older than thirty-one, purple circles under her eyes no matter how much she slept, a few dark hairs on her upper lip that she'd once made the painful mistake of waxing. She'd rather have been naked, the shock of it a distraction from what was really there to see.

The main decks were still crowded, the bars raucous, the slots in the casino jangling. The pools were full, the Jacuzzis jammed. A buffet was still spread in one lounge—she snatched a slice of pizza that had been sitting too long under a heating lamp, the cheese dried out, the pepperoni brittle, ate it in three bites, and immediately wished she hadn't. Out on deck the wind cut through her sweater and pants, stung her crotch and belly, and drove her back inside. She took a seat at a blackjack table, and again began to win. But without the bristly-haired man there to urge her on, giving bad advice, her gains felt empty. She had two hundred dollars now, but what was there to spend it on, other than more blackjack? All her expenses were being charged to Aunt Fran's credit card, which made her want to spend nothing. She would have pocket money when she returned to normal life, though now, in the confusion of noise and lights, the swirl of bodies, she had the uncomfortable sensation that there was no normal life to return to—this was now her permanent existence, and all she had to look forward to was walking naked in front of her porthole.

By the time she made it back to the elevator, she'd finally admitted to herself that she'd been hoping all along to run into the bristly-haired man, admitted that she'd left off her underwear thinking of him. So, okay—tonight she would take sex or love or anything, anything at all. She'd looked into every lounge, every public space she could find, half-expecting to see the skimpy mustache, the sagging cheeks, the paunch that had seemed sad to her earlier tonight now somehow appealing. She'd imagined him at the end of a bar, head propped on knuckles, giving a wink when he spotted her, saying in his dry voice, "I thought you'd never come." Wasn't it supposed to work this way? Both of them unable to sleep, drawn to each other as if magnetized through the maze of this enormous floating tub?

She stopped on the seventh deck, still hoping, walking slowly past each door, waiting for one to swing open, and then a sarcastic snip—"Ready to make the leap?" But all the doors were closed and stayed that way. She took the stairs the rest of the way down, embarrassed now at her neediness, remembering the way Ben had looked at her the last night they'd spent together, after their final, conciliatory lovemaking and a long shower, his pitying expression not matching the vigorous way he toweled himself off, stripping the water from his hairy legs. "You're going to do so well," he'd said. "I'm just sorry I'm not going to be there to see it happen." She hated him then, and realized she'd hated him for some time before that. What had kept her going to him was imagining there was something illicit about their meetings, that the reason he called her so infrequently was that he was secretly married, that he was leading a double life. But in truth, once a month was as often as he could bear to be with her, to be with anyone, she guessed, though that was little comfort.

Back on her own deck she was confronted by the steward's cart, stacked with fresh towels and cleaning solutions. Then the steward himself, springing from the supply closet with an armful of toilet paper rolls. He was Indonesian, a frail-looking little man with pocked cheeks, oily hair, and a sparse beard. He'd introduced himself yesterday afternoon—Ahmed or Muhammad, she couldn't remember which. Her waiter was also Indonesian, also had a Muslim name, though he was taller and almost handsome, his face clean-shaven. The steward's eyes were on a level with her chest and stayed there, out of deference or because he could spy her nipples through the stitching of her sweater, she wasn't sure. He greeted her in a delighted, whispery way, thin eyebrows arching. "Ah, Miss Kaufman," he said, and she was stung with shame for not remembering his name—she had only one steward and one waiter, and he had how many guests? "And how was your evening? I trust you have experienced the Triumph's many excitements and amenities? May I freshen your room with new towels?"

She hadn't showered yet, hadn't even washed her face when she came in last night. "Thank you, no," she said, and then struggled to find some polite thing to say before ducking into her room. Whatever charge of energy had kept her awake for the last hour was gone now, and she felt ready to collapse. Her mind worked slowly. "How long have you been on this ship?" she asked.

He seemed delighted still, one clump of hair bouncing over his left temple as he nodded. "One month, twenty-two days," he said.

"And how much longer will you stay?"

"My home away from home," he said.

She had more questions now. Where was his home? Who lived there? Would he ever go back? She chose the least personal item from the list. "Do you ever get seasick?"

"May I freshen you with a new soap?" he asked.

His life was closed to her, as she should have known it would be. Why did it make her so sad? She was tired, very tired. "Thank you, no," she said again.

"Please," he said, suddenly desperate, as if another refusal would break him. "Take with you a mint from my tray."

She ate it on the way back to her room. Inside she stripped and stood in front of the porthole for only a moment before crawling back into bed.

ROGER WAS AWAKE AT SIX, BUT IT WAS ANOTHER HOUR before the Dramamine let him get out of bed. Then it wasn't so much his stomach as his head that was queasy, his balance thrown off, not quite dizziness but a loss of depth perception, like a cat whose whiskers have been cut off. The ship's roll didn't bother him as much as its forward pitch, the sinking feeling as the bow dipped, the sudden increase in gravity as they rode up a wave, a pressure rising through his feet to his knees and into his chest. He managed to make his way to breakfast, where again he smiled and nodded as the older couple to his right—a different one than he'd sat next to last night, but wearing the same knit golf shirts, the same parental expressions—asked where he was from, what he did for a living, and with a wink from the woman, if he was here to look for a special someone. "Just getting away from work for a while," he said, pushing the remains of an omelet around his plate, his appetite, shaky to begin with, now completely gone. He had to stare out the window, finding the horizon through the fog, steadying himself before he could go on. "Haven't had a vacation in two years."

"Retire early, that's my advice," the old man said through a mouthful of sausage. His nose was large and pitted, cheeks splotched with burst capillaries. "Retire and sail around the world."

"That's great advice," the woman said, "coming from Mr. I-Want-To-Work-Till-I'm-Seventy-Five. He thought he'd feel useless," she said to Roger. "Thought he'd get bored sitting around with me all day."

"If I had it to do over again," the man muttered, but the woman was already shaking her head.

"We've been cruising for the past three years," she said. "Alaska, Greece, three times to the islands. Trust me, the food on this one, the worst by far."

"You get what you pay for," the man said.

The woman winked again. "But you're not here for the food," she said. Then, lowering her voice, she added, "The singles gather after dinner in the Irish bar, I hear."

He escaped as soon as he was able to excuse himself without seeming rude. In the Internet Café he paid a dollar-fifty a minute to check his e-mail. There were more than a dozen already, mostly from vendors, one marked urgent from a panicking client who'd received an unannounced visit from the FDA. The last was from Angela, his assistant. "You shouldn't be checking this, but

I know you will anyway," she wrote. "I took care of the Marshall freak-out. DON'T WRITE THEM BACK! It'll only confuse things. You're on vacation. Quit thinking about work." Then there was a two line break and a single additional word. "Well?????"

He knew what she was asking, could picture her winking the same way the old woman at breakfast had. It was Angela who'd urged him to go away. For months she'd been nagging him, telling him he'd drive himself crazy if he didn't take a break— then she'd switched tactics and started saying, "You're driving *me* crazy. Get the hell out of here." She'd been working for him six years now, and though he often joked that he regretted keeping her on after the first week, she was indispensable to him. He *had* considered letting her go that first week—from the start she'd been pushy and overbearing, a small, bony woman two years older than himself with a voice that carried from room to room and a habit of smacking the nearest object when she laughed, her desk, a wall, Roger's shoulder. But she'd quickly ordered his files, arranged his schedule, made the business run smoothly just when it had grown large enough to start feeling unwieldy. He soon knew too much about her personal life—she and her husband had married right out of high school and now slept in separate beds, agreeing to stay together until the children were out of the house. The kids were both ADHD, neither college-bound, and Angela had talked Roger into finding them summer jobs with clients, the boy on an assembly line, monitoring a machine that bottled pills, the girl as a receptionist's assistant. Angela's younger sister was a diabetic and a pothead who couldn't hold onto jobs or boyfriends, and she and Angela often had screaming bouts on the office line.

And now Angela knew too much about his personal life as well. A year and a half ago, three weeks before his divorce was final and two days after he knew for certain it would be final, she came into his office to find him sobbing into his sleeve, his wedding photo propped in front of him, the twenty-six-year-old version of himself in a ridiculous top hat and cane, his wife,

Emily, planting a kiss on his chin. Angela patted his back, rubbed his shoulder, hugged him to her chest. She turned the photo face down on the desk. In another minute she was in his lap, unbuttoning her blouse so his hand could slip inside. Then she was straddling him, skirt around her waist, tights around her ankles. "Life isn't over yet," she whispered. "Don't you worry. You're not finished yet." It happened four more times over the next two weeks, the first three gifts, he felt, and was overcome with gratitude. The fourth time he took notice of her pleasure, and tried to heighten it—and afterward he felt sick to his stomach, shameful and base. Angela caught his expression as she was straightening her collar. "No way," she said. "I'm not losing my job over this. We're done now."

Since then she'd been instantly aware, even before he was, the moment he began looking at her with something approaching desire or longing. "Gotta find you a girlfriend," she'd say, pinning up her hair if it was loose or draping a sweater over her shoulders if they were bare. She tried to set him up with friends and then with her sister, the diabetic—the date reminded him too much of being in college, with Emily before she was his wife, pulling onto dark side streets to share a joint. The next day at work his head was fuzzy, his mouth dry, his eyes red, and Angela said, "We'd better try something else." Early last spring she'd begun dropping brochures on his desk, every vacation idea she could come up with—a month-long bike ride across southern Europe, a two-week safari in Kenya, a five-day raft trip down the Colorado, all designed for "the single professional." She talked about the cruise she and her sister had taken two years ago, from Miami to St. Thomas and Aruba, the food, the drinks, the flings they'd both had. Roger found himself growing furious as she described the young German she'd seduced, losing herself in the description, forgetting her reason for telling him to begin with. "God," she said. "I don't think we left my cabin for three days. I don't think I even saw Aruba."

"All right, already," he said, blind with anger now, snatching the newest brochure from her hand. "I'll go on a goddamn cruise. Can we please get back to work now?"

That afternoon he booked his berth, choosing this trip because it was the shortest he could find. "Nova Scotia?" Angela asked when he told her. "Who the hell wants to go there?"

"I can go to the islands anytime," he said. "This sounds more interesting. More culture."

"Culture!" she cried. "Jesus, I thought you wanted to get laid." She threw up her hands and headed out of the office, bony hips sashaying in a way that immediately aroused him and made him ashamed to be alive. "I don't know why I bother," she said, and slammed the door behind her.

And now her waiting question, "Well?????" What could he tell her? That he'd met a clever, husky girl, not attractive in the least—not at all, really, though now he couldn't stop picturing her sarcastic smile, the shallow crinkles around her eyes—but more interesting than anyone else on the boat? That he'd made an ass of himself, following her around all night, throwing money at her—God!—and then didn't even ask her name or if he could see her again? That he was lost without Angela, that he'd never be with another woman again unless she took pity on him the way Angela had?

Or the way his wife had, for that matter? Why else would she have taken up with him in the first place, as beautiful as she was, as desirable and desired? True, she'd recently come out of a relationship that had ended badly, and Roger was safety, comfort, stability. He was a senior in college then, and she'd just graduated, unsure what to do next, waitressing in a café where students met after class, mocking her, it seemed, with how useless she was now, how inactive her mind. Roger had been her friend and confidante since sophomore year, when she'd dated his roommate for two months—he never told her, even after they were married, that his fantasies at the time often revolved around the noises he'd heard late at night, coming from the bed across the tiny dorm room. Now she was cut off from most of her old friends, who'd gone off on various adventures abroad, or gotten married, or moved back to their hometowns. Roger told her about his plans to return to New York after graduation. At the time he still thought he might be able to play music professionally—he'd been in half a dozen bar bands, had recorded two records in a basement studio, was still collecting forty dollars a year in royalties. His chemistry degree was a fallback, nothing more. Emily's eyes widened as he spoke of the city, the possibilities. She'd been a journalism major, and the idea of so many newspapers and magazines in one place fed her imagination. They started to make plans to move together, they'd be roommates, but before the year was up she was already living in his apartment in College Park, sharing his bed. What else had he offered her but escape, pure and simple? What else had she done but latch on for the ride, getting off when she'd arrived at the right destination?

He shut off the computer without replying to anyone, surprised by the sudden freedom he felt as the screen went blank. He couldn't remember the last time he'd been out of touch with everyone, entirely out of reach. He enjoyed the image of himself adrift at sea, incommunicado.

He took a seat by the indoor pool, the most central location he could find, with a view toward the casino and the early lunch buffet line. What could he do but hope the husky girl would pass by, that he could call to her, "Ready to swim for shore?" Above him the glass ceiling was steamed on the inside, spattered with rain above. He hadn't checked the deck chair before he'd sat, realizing it was wet only when he leaned back, the plastic slats cold through his shirt. The pool was full, of children mostly, leaping off the edge in cannonballs and belly flops, while one old woman in a bathing cap and goggles tried to swim laps between them, pausing every few strokes to terrify someone else's child with her raspy scolding. He couldn't read. The heavy, chlorinated air brought his nausea back and stung his eyes. This was the most unromantic place he'd ever been, and suddenly he was sure this had been part of Angela's plan—her revenge on him for having sex with her in his unromantic office, for not thinking of her as someone he could fall in love with, not before or after she'd sat in his lap. It took all the restraint he could muster to keep from going to the nearest bar—there was one just over his left shoulder—and beginning his day bitterly. He wouldn't be the only one. There was a line already, the bartender pouring one Bloody Mary and mimosa after another. His will was helped along by his stomach, which rolled with a new pitch of the ship, rebelling at the thought of juice combined with booze.

And then he saw her, running with a small group, out of the casino, past the pool, up a short flight of stairs to the door leading out on deck. Her loose slacks flapped around her legs, her big sandaled feet surprisingly nimble, arms crossed awkwardly over her chest. They were going overboard! She'd found other people to join her. His jealousy propelled him out of his chair, despite his nausea. He cut in front of two boys getting ready to dive into the pool, and the old woman in the bathing cap shouted at him not to run on the tiles. The wind made it difficult to open the door to the deck, and then it hit him full in the face, nearly blowing his glasses off his nose. But it also seemed to blow away his seasickness, and the icy rain somehow made him bold. The running group was headed toward the stern, the husky girl trailing a little behind. He would have thrown himself over with her now, would have followed anywhere she led. He slid twice on the wet boards, once nearly fell. The group was at the back railing, leaning out, the wind to their backs, hair blown forward. The husky girl's sweater lifted in back, exposing a solid waist, the blue band of her underwear digging into the soft flesh above her hips, a line of dark fuzz rising into the small of her back. "Don't go without me," he said breathlessly, hearing the desperation in his voice, though he tried to find the sarcastic note that had worked so well last night, helped along by the several glasses of Scotch.

She blinked down at him, and her smile held no irony. Her words seemed to catch in her throat. "A whale," she said. "One of the waiters said he saw one. God, wouldn't the whole thing be worth it if we saw a whale?"

"I'm Roger," he said, and this time put out his hand in an unambiguous way.

"Beth," she answered, and returning his grip, added, "Good to finally meet you."

They leaned over the railing, scanning the dark water. A man beside them pointed to every white crest, shouting, "There! There!" and then muttered, "Fucking wave. Just a fucking wave."

They stayed after everyone else had trickled back inside. They were soaked to the skin. Beth hugged herself. Roger shivered. They agreed they should go in and change, but kept standing there, neither wanting to move, to lose sight of each other again. Only when Beth suggested they meet for lunch in an hour did Roger let go of the railing.

THEY COULDN'T JOKE ANYMORE. ROGER'S QUEASINESS had something to do with it, and so did Beth's lack of sleep. Now everything they saw was tinted with a disgust that made irony and sarcasm sound jaded. In line ahead of them for the buffet were seven obese people, three in wheelchairs. Beth whispered, "They giving out insulin up there?" and immediately Roger thought of the date with Angela's sister, the lazy way she'd stuck the needle in her arm before they left her apartment, relishing Roger's squeamishness.

"Welcome to the horse trough," he said. "Time to put on our feed bags." He took an apple, one tong's worth of salad, a spoon-ful of cottage cheese.

"Small horse," Beth said.

"Sick horse."

"You poor thing. The motion's not so bad on the lower decks. You can come down to my room. Later. If you need to lie down." She hoped he didn't hear the tremble in her voice, the thrill of for-wardness undercut by embarrassment. It was the ship that made her want to throw herself at him, the fact of their being trapped together. She wanted to cling to him, to scratch him, to pull his hair—they same way she'd felt as a gradeschooler, when she had no other expression for an attraction she didn't understand. There was one boy she'd tortured in third grade, punching him in the jaw, kicking his shins, pinching him until he cried and the teacher called her parents in for a conference. She tried now to recapture the lightness in her voice. "My window's so low we'll be eye to eye with the whales."

They had the whole day at sea, and the night, and they agreed without saying so that they would spend as much of it as possible together. After lunch and a few more hands of black-jack—Beth up $220, Roger down $180—they searched for a quiet place to talk. They grew shyer with each passing hour, more polite. The library, a glassed-in nook with two tables, a couch, and magazine racks but no books, was occupied by a family playing Monopoly, a nine-year-old boy cleaning up on his parents and two older sisters, hands full of paper money, property cards stacked up on his lap, his hotels scattered across the board. The cigar bar was momentarily empty, but as soon as they settled into the soft leather chairs—the most comfortable they'd come across on the entire boat—the group from the Bronx came in together, six couples, all still wearing their Hawaiian gear. They were practicing for tomorrow night's guest talent show, singing an *a capella* "America the Beautiful," in tribute to the firefighters who'd died beneath the Twin Towers, one of whom had been a brother-in-law. They couldn't figure out whose brother-in-law, because the woman who told them spoke too fast, gesturing sloppily over her shoulder, speaking of Tim and Bob and Ginny as if they knew exactly who she was talking about. She wanted them to stay and be their audience. "We need feedback," she said. "It's two hundred bucks if we win."

At first they exchanged funny faces, Roger cocking an eye-brow, Beth scratching her nose to cover a smirk, but by the time the song was into its second verse they both found them-selves getting choked up, not at the performance so much as the inevitable memories it inspired. The two-year anniversary of the attacks had just passed, but Roger still clearly recalled the sinking sensation he'd felt as Angela came running into his office, shouting the news. He'd picked up the phone immediately and started dialing Emily's cell phone number, dialing for more than an hour before getting through. She'd gone into the city that morning, searching for an apartment—she'd told him a week ago that she was moving out and wanted to find her own place by the end of the month. Every time he heard the busy signal he cursed himself for having moved them to Jersey, even though it made the most sense for his business—that was why she was leaving, the boredom of suburbia, the mundane life, none of it what he'd promised. When she finally answered he was frantic, and all he could do was repeat her name, three or four times before she could reply. "Relax, Rog," she said, in a kind way he hadn't heard for months, which instantly reduced him to tears. "I'm uptown," she said. "I'm fine."

Beth had been late for work that day, waiting in the Metropolitan Avenue station, heat pouring out of the tunnel as usual, but no train. She'd been furious, impatient, but also somehow pleased by her annoyance, finally a true New Yorker after four long years of faking it. Later, hearing the details, watching the news reports, listening to her roommates who'd run all the way to the Esplanade as soon as they heard, she felt ashamed of her pettiness, and even more ashamed at the self-pity she felt now—that she'd never be anything other than the suburban kid she'd always been, lost among the towering buildings, some of which could collapse on her in an instant, without the slightest warning.

They caught the serious looks on each other's faces and might have talked about their experiences, but the Bronx crew was already singing their second round. When they finished, Roger and Beth clapped again, less enthusiastically than after the first. "Well?" the fast-talking woman asked. "We on pitch, or what?" They both assured her that the performance was excellent, that they were sure to win the prize. When the woman insisted they stay for a third try, Roger stood up quickly and said, "We told friends we'd meet them in the Jacuzzi. We'd better get going."

They felt the group watching as they walked away, assessing them as a couple, Beth half a head taller, Roger trying to straighten his back, pulling himself up to his full height. On their way through the rotunda, where glass elevators rose to the upper decks, a photographer, one of dozens on the ship, stopped them and gestured for them to stand together. Neither was sure if they should put arms around each other's waists—instead they stood shoulder to shoulder, heads tilted slightly together. A quick flash, and the photographer waved them impatiently away. "I blinked," Beth said.

"That's okay," Roger said. "I almost puked."

They felt closer now, as if they'd been brought together by tragedy, even though they hadn't said a word about the singing or what it had recalled. Some of the awkwardness between them had gone, and it was clear that the only place to go now was to one of their cabins. Beth thought better of bringing him to hers, remembering the clothes she'd left draped over the room's single chair, the clogged hairbrush she'd left in plain sight in the bathroom, the roar of the engines. "I want to see what I'm missing," she said, and though Roger answered, "Don't get too excited," she could tell he was pleased, in a less self-conscious way than when he'd handed her the twenty-dollar bill the night before.

It didn't matter what he said—she *was* excited by what she saw. A king-sized bed to her double, sheets recently turned down, a mint on each pillow. A leather sofa with reading lamps on either end. A sliding door leading to a balcony large enough for two deck chairs. "I have to check this out," Beth said, and went out without inviting Roger to join her, closing the door in part to keep out the wind, in part to give herself a moment to let loose the breath trapped in her chest. The waves were impossibly far below, made more distant by the fog that had gathered around the ship in the last few hours. The ship rolled, tilting her toward the water, and though there was no chance of her falling, she gripped the railing tightly. The rain was lighter now, a mist on her cheeks. She had the pleasurable sensation of losing control, not of herself so much as her future, each moment dictated by forces unconcerned with her will. It made her sad only to remember that she'd felt this way with Ben once, the night they'd met at an inter-office party, on the wild taxi ride downtown, every light green, the heavy-lidded driver accelerating faster and faster, not once touching the brake. They'd left streets she knew for ones she didn't, some cobbled, others broken by old streetcar tracks, unused for fifty years or more, almost all the way to the river, where the city's meatpackers lined up near the wharf. She hadn't known anyone lived this far west, and the darkened buildings gave Ben a mysterious, even dangerous air. Only a few weeks later did she learn he wasn't so dangerous or even original—most of these warehouses were being turned into lofts, with trendy restaurants popping up in converted garages. Nothing lasts, she thought, nothing, and she fought to take back the direction of her life. She tried to imagine each moment ahead of her—another three seconds of looking out to sea before she'd turn and open the door. Then she'd march straight to Roger, reaching for him, the buttons on his shirt. Or her own clothes—they'd be off by the time she reached him, scattered on the floor from the balcony to the bed. No—she'd walk in, shake his hand, head out the door and down to her room, stay there until it was time to get off the boat. She wouldn't see him again, would quickly forget she'd ever met him.

But she didn't do any of the things she'd imagined. He was waiting for her when she came back inside. In each hand was a puffy terrycloth robe on a hanger, the ship's insignia stitched on the left breast. "This is my favorite part," he said. "Worth the extra four hundred bucks."

"You get to keep them?"

"No. I can buy them when I leave. But we get to use them for the rest of the ride."

She heard the "we," and though she tried to ignore it, couldn't help feeling warmed by it. "I get to wear one?"

"What am I going to do with two? You can put it on out here. I'll go change in the bathroom."

Now she couldn't get all the way naked. She left her underwear on, her bra though the straps dug into her shoulders and back, her socks. She did stand in front of the glass door for a moment before putting on the robe, catching a faint reflection of her legs, wishing she'd shaved them this morning, and immediately chastising herself for thinking like a teenage girl. The toilet flushed, an uncomfortably intimate sound, and then Roger called, "All clear?" She was relieved to see he wasn't naked under his robe, either. He had on flannel pajama bottoms and a T-shirt, only his feet bare, small, hairless toes with closely clipped nails. "It's crazy," he said. "I love wearing robes, but I don't own one. I don't think I've had one since I was a kid."

He sat on the couch, and she took the bed, lying on her front, arms propping her head and shoulders so she could look at him. He wished she were closer but at the same time was glad to have some space between them—his nausea had given way to jittery nerves, and he kept crossing and re-crossing his legs. Her legs were in the air behind her, the robe gathered around her knees. Why did he feel himself so drawn to the large feet, the thick ankles, the long calves that didn't match the width of the thighs? Was he desperate? Pathetic? Would he have been attracted to one of the obese women in the buffet line if she'd given him a kind smile, a friendly word?

There was nothing to do now but talk about themselves. "Publishing," Beth said, and watched Roger's impressed nod. She considered clarifying, then thought better of it, and felt only the mildest guilt. Roger tried to explain his business. His card read, "Quality Assurance Consultant," which could have meant anything. He gave a few details, and was surprised by her stern, puzzled look. "So basically you help drug companies cut corners," she said. "You help them cheat."

"I prefer to call it streamlining," he said uncertainly. "Smoothing out inefficiencies."

Her smile was slow to form but sly. "Don't worry. I won't report you to the authorities."

"You won't think too badly of me?"

"Just don't tell me if my Prozac isn't safe." He was silent a moment, and she burst out laughing. "Just kidding. No anti-depressants for me. Just some Xanax when I have to fly."

Their lives had crossed paths in a way. He'd grown up in Flushing, she in Jersey, not far from his office. His parents had moved to Florida two years ago, but hers still lived in Morristown, on a street he drove past every day. "God, I hated it there," she said. "The suburbs. They were so stifling. It was like living in an airtight box. We had this toy chest in our basement, with big metal hinges, and I used to close my eyes and imagine myself inside, choking."

"I guess I would have hated it as a kid, too," he said. "I don't know, as an adult, it's not so bad. Comfortable. That's why people live there, right? Close enough to the city when I need some culture. Shit. I'm getting old."

"But you were married," she said. "That makes a difference. It's easier to be anywhere with another person."

"True," he said softly.

"Was it recent?"

"Almost two years."

"Recent enough," she said. "I'm sorry."

They didn't speak for a minute, and Roger worried that something had been ruptured, the growing bond between them suddenly snapped. They could be intimate only as strangers— the more they knew about each other, the more distant they would become. But then Beth rolled to her back, the robe flapping open to mid-thigh. "I don't feel like jumping overboard anymore," she said.

He closed his eyes and opened them slowly. "Me neither."

"I don't think I can face the dining room, though," she said. "That might be too much. What about you?"

"Not unless I can wear my robe."

They ordered room service. The attendant was a tiny blonde woman with an Eastern European accent, pretty except for a blackened front tooth. She came in carrying an enormous tray, took in their robes, Beth's clothes folded neatly over a chair, and gave a suggestive smile before going out. When they lifted the covers off the food they saw that the portions were skimpy compared to the size of the plates. Roger was famished now, his nausea gone entirely, and he ordered a second round, this time remembering a bottle of wine. The attendant was clearly annoyed on the second visit, her hair suddenly frizzed, her eyeshadow smeared—this time she didn't smile at all.

"Let's never leave this room," Beth said after they'd eaten. "Not until we're back home, anyway."

"We dock tomorrow," Roger said. "Halifax might be interesting."

"Okay. But while we're on the boat, we stay right here."

"Deal."

There were movies on the TV's three channels, and they flipped between them, a children's cartoon they could make no sense of, a romantic comedy in which the protagonist was humiliated over and over in his feeble attempts at wooing, a documentary on the whaling industry of New England and Nova Scotia. Roger joined Beth on the bed, which was large enough for them both to lie comfortably without touching. They sipped Chardonnay. Beth's eyes grew heavy. She let them close. She knew they were supposed to make love now. She wanted to. It sounded wonderful, really. But she was just so tired. "I didn't sleep much last night," she said. "I think I might conk out on you."

"You should get some rest," Roger said.

"We have time to spend together, right? Two more days?"

"Plenty of time."

She felt the blanket slide out from under her legs and drape over her hips. Then the bristle of his mustache against her forehead, the pressure of dry lips. She heard the balcony door slide open, the roar of the ocean, and then silence. She hoped he'd wake her if he spotted a whale.

IN THE MORNING, NOTHING HAD CHANGED. THE ROBE was twisted around her waist, tangled in her legs. The bed was empty. Roger was still standing on the balcony, pressed up against the railing. Had he been there all night? No. The pillow beside hers held the imprint of his head. The blankets were rustled all the way across the wide mattress. And he was no longer in his robe and pajamas—he wore khaki pants now, and a striped, button-down shirt, what he wore to the office, she guessed, when he didn't have to meet a client. His hair was wet. She was reminded, sadly, of mornings in Ben's apartment, waking up alone in the bed, Ben having slipped out early to shower and eat breakfast and read the paper silently at a metal counter that served as his only table. He never looked up when she joined him, rarely even grunted in response to her greeting. She'd learned quickly to match his silence, making herself coffee—he never brewed an extra cup—sliding a section of the newspaper carefully from the bottom of the stack. Why had she settled for this? Why did she see herself continuing to settle, with Ben or Roger or any other man who happened into her life?

Roger turned to her as soon as she opened the door to the balcony, smiling shyly, his eyes resting first on her feet—those flippers—and then slowly rising to meet her own. "I thought you'd never wake up," he said, genuine delight in his voice. She wanted to be distrustful—after all, they hadn't made love yet—but couldn't help returning his smile. She didn't know whether or not to step forward and hug him, so instead she reached out a hand to touch his shoulder. He stopped it halfway there, taking it in his hands and squeezing the fingers.

"Have you been up long?" she asked.

"A while," he said. "Hard to sleep.

"Oh God. Did I snore?"

He laughed. "No, you didn't snore. You hardly moved. I had to check to see if you were still breathing."

"I'm sorry you didn't sleep," she said. "You should have woken me."

"You needed it. And there's plenty of time, remember?"

He said this last gently but with an urgency she felt herself now—time was moving quickly whether they liked it or not. And now that she was beginning to come awake she saw what was different—the water below them was perfectly still, except where the ship made it ripple, and not far in the distance was a low ridge of land, black rock topped with tufts of yellow grass. And even more incredible, the sky itself, clouds still thick in spots, but broken apart now, patches of blue showing through. Sunlight struck the water a hundred yards from the ship's hull, illuminating dust and bits of trash and a shimmer of oil. "Where are we?" she asked.

"In the mouth of the harbor, I think. We're supposed to dock in an hour."

"I should go change, then," she said. "I have to give you back your robe." She was prepared to take it off right here, to bare herself to him on the balcony, in full view of the shore. She didn't care about Halifax now, didn't want to leave this room, not ever.

But he waved a hand. "Don't go, not yet. I ordered us breakfast. And you're keeping that robe. A gift. Don't even try to turn it down."

"I won't," she said. "Thanks. I can't remember the last time I was so well taken care of."

"I can't remember having taken care of anyone so well. It was never my strong suit, I'm afraid."

"People change."

"I hope so," he said, doubtfully.

She wore the robe through breakfast, taking it off only afterward to shower. She hoped he would come into the bathroom before she'd finished, or while she was drying her hair—but he didn't, and she put the robe back on, this time with nothing underneath. When she came out he had his hands in his pockets and was rocking from heel to toe. "I hope I haven't been pushy," he said. "I mean, if you wanted to go and explore the city on your own, I'd understand. We could still get together for dinner—"

"Shut up right now," she said, and swung one end of the robe's belt in his direction. "Don't you dare say another word. I'm going down to change, and you're going to meet me by the gangway in fifteen minutes." He opened his mouth to speak, but she held up a finger in warning, and then she was out the door, slapping down the hallway in bare feet, holding the robe tight at her waist and chest. Her hair was still damp, and so were the spaces between her toes. She was aware of people watching as she passed and did her best to ignore them. She looked straight up in the elevator, at her reflection in the brass ceiling plates, and the reflections of other passengers' crowns, all their hair thinning, it seemed, a plague of baldness.

The door to her room was open, and the steward—Ahmed? Muhammad? she still couldn't remember—leapt out of the bathroom with the same springing motion, squinting and nodding his oily face, his mustache seeming wispier now with sunlight coming in through the small porthole, his teeth yellower. "Ah," he said. "Miss Kaufman. I trust you had an excellent evening."

"You trust correctly," she said.

"I have freshened your towels," he said.

"I've met the loveliest man," she said, needing to tell someone, anyone, needing to use the word "lovely," maybe for the first time in connection with a man.

The steward's smile was strained. "Is there any other way I can be of service?"

"Lovely," she repeated. "On this ship. Can you imagine?"

"I am at your service," he said, ducking out.

The ship was turning. Out the window bare rocks gave way to industrial buildings of some kind, mills she guessed, spewing chunky white smoke into the confusion of clouds and clear sky. They were coming underneath a bridge, and soon a city came into view, sprawling up the side of a hill. She hadn't known how glad she'd be to see land, thrilled at the prospect of soon touching it. How could sailors stay away for months at a time? Along the docks were other ships, small ones with sails, rusted fishing boats covered in filthy nets, another cruise ship, as big as this one or bigger, but clearly more luxurious, with newly whitewashed sides, green-tinted windows, a long, snaking water slide visible on its highest deck. And suddenly there were people in view, close enough to see into her porthole. She drew the shade before taking off the robe.

HE WAS WAITING FOR HER AT THE HEAD OF THE GANGWAY with a surprise. Two copies of the photograph they'd had taken the day before, only Roger had cut out little scraps of paper and taped them on above their heads. Thought bubbles. Above his, the words, "I'm going to hurl," and above hers, "There's no place like home, there's no place like home … " Her eyes were shut, her smile crooked. She towered over him, especially because he'd been slouching, his paunch protruding. She laughed when he handed it to her, but not as hysterically as he'd hoped. "It's almost too hideous to be funny," she said. "But I'll keep it anyway."

She wore a light dress, short sleeved, calf-length, with sandals and no tights. As much as he enjoyed seeing her skin— nice skin, he thought, a pinker tint than his own, with small brown moles here and there—he wanted to tell her she'd be cold, that she should bring a sweater, but was afraid of sounding paternal. He had a sweater on and carried a jacket. The gangway led them into a covered wharf where they were met by a hundred vendor carts, locals selling *Canada* T-shirts, fake leather purses, beaded necklaces. Their fellow passengers swarmed over the carts, buying everything in sight, amazed at the purchasing power of the U.S. dollar. They spotted the Bronx crew looking over carved wooden eagles and bears. The fast-talking woman waved for them to come over. "We've got to get out of here," Beth said, and Roger agreed, though he couldn't find the exit—each turn led to more carts, more cruise passengers waving bills. They found a man in a kilt, holding up a sign that read, "Info?" Before he gave them directions, he catalogued the city's history, the original British fortifications, the loyalist settlers, graves dug for *Titanic* victims, the tragedy during the First World War when a munitions ship collided with a merchant vessel, the most devastating explosion on the planet before Hiroshima, half the city destroyed. A long history of struggle and despair. Finally he pointed them toward the waterfront, and they escaped into the sunlight a little gloomier than they'd anticipated, their excitement dampened.

Walking felt strange to Roger. His knees were wobbly, and the ground seemed to fall away from his step. "I feel like I'm still on the goddamn boat," he said.

Beth squinted in the brightness. "I wish I'd brought my sunglasses."

"I bet they have them in there," Roger said, gesturing behind at the wharf. "We can go back if you want."

"I'd rather go blind."

They passed half a dozen stalls offering trips on historical schooners, charged by the half hour. College girls dressed in colonial garb rang cowbells and handed out flyers. "No more boats," Roger said.

They passed the Maritime Museum, which advertised special exhibits on the *Titanic* and the Great Explosion of 1917. "No sea disasters, either," Beth said.

But then they came to a stretch of old stone buildings, ware-houses of an earlier century, and between them narrow streets winding away from the harbor. They were in a different place, far enough from home to feel as if they'd been let loose from ordi-nary life. Their moods lifted as Roger read out loud from the guide-book he'd picked up a few weeks ago, in order to prove to Angela that he truly was interested in Nova Scotian history and culture. After studying the map he tentatively held out his arm for Beth to take. She slipped her hand through and let him lead her from one street to the next, across a busy thoroughfare, and up a grueling set of stairs on a green hillside. Here was the Old Town Clock, not much more than a white wooden box on stilts, and above it the Citadel with black cannons trained on the harbor. "Why does 'history' always mean 'war'?" she asked, but she was less troubled than she made out. This was war long past—the guards at the fortress gates in their bright red uniforms with brass buttons seemed more make-believe than historical, something out of fairy tales. They walked the ramparts, took in views across the harbor and all the way back out to sea. One cannon pointed directly at their ship, and they took turns pretending to fire it. "There goes the casino," Roger said.

"The buffet line," Beth said.

"The revolving piano."

"That goddamn photographer."

Clouds were gathering at their backs, and they could see now that the breaks of blue sky were only part of a narrow wedge between two storms. As soon as the sun slipped away, Beth began to rub her arms. "I didn't plan for this," she said. Roger draped his jacket over her shoulders, expecting her to protest. She didn't—she was giving in to being taken care of. "I wasn't thinking at all."

By the time they left the Citadel the downpour had started. Roger's sweater was cotton, as was the T-shirt beneath, both soggy now and useless. He pulled her into a doorway, where they huddled shoulder to shoulder. He felt her breath on his cheek and ear. Droplets clung to her eyebrows. He edged as close to her as he could. Her lips were too far away to kiss without pulling her down to him. Her chin was almost in reach, but he dreaded it moving away. He felt the opposite of paternal now, a fumbling teenager with a crush. Before he could determine to put his arm around her, she started laughing. His heart seized up. This was the worst thing he could have imagined, his greatest fear in all those years with Emily, that he was making an ass of himself, that she was making fun of him behind his back. But Beth wasn't laughing at him—he hadn't noticed the name of the shop whose doorway they'd occupied. The Juggler. In the window were brightly colored balls of various sizes, bowling pins, long metal torches. She couldn't have said why it tickled her so much, the culmination of three absurd days, she supposed, along with the nervousness she felt at having Roger stand so close. "Haven't you heard about those famous Halifaxian jugglers?" she said.

"Haligonian," he said uneasily. "At least according to my guidebook."

"All right, then. Haligonian." The shop didn't open for another half hour, but she made him promise to come back before they left. "I've just decided. I'm going to learn how to juggle. My new calling in life. Answer to all my problems. Want to give it a try?"

"You learn first and then teach me."

"I'm not talking about balls, either," she said. "Torches. With flames on either end."

"Maybe I'll pass," he said.

They waited for the rain to let up, but when it didn't they braved the street again, darting from one storefront overhang to another, then pausing to wring water from their sleeves. Across from a stone church and cemetery was a café, and Beth said, "Looks like a Halifaxian kind of place, don't you think? No cruisers in here."

"Haligonian," Roger said.

"Right. Haligonian."

They drank hot tea and ate hot soup, but Roger couldn't stop shivering. Neither could he shake the sinking sensation that had overtaken him when Beth had burst out laughing. Why did he suddenly fear that she could see straight through him? What did it matter? What was there to see through, anyway? "Well? Now what?" he said.

"Anything but the boat."

"Back to the juggling store?"

"I think I've given up that dream," she said.

"How about a movie? We could find the listings."

"Okay," she said. "As long as it's not another cartoon."

In the booth beside them was a couple, older but not old, the woman pretty, her blonde hair very subtly turning gray at the roots, the man distinguished by dark bushy brows over bright blue eyes. He leaned across his seat and spoke to them. "Caught by the rain, are you?" His accent was English, Yorkshire, if Roger remembered correctly from a semester abroad his junior year of college. He'd been in Durham, ostensibly to study polymers, though he'd spent most of the three months sampling beers, perfecting a wink that finally helped him seduce a girl in his lab, marveling at the cathedral, the sheer size of it, the strength of the ancient arches, the years of labor that went into its construction. He'd never again felt as free as he had that spring, as indifferent to the forces or whims pulling him in one direction or another. He wanted to feel that way again now, with Beth, to let the strange circumstances that had brought them together lead them where they would. But somehow he was too conscious of his body, the way his skin prickled against his cold T-shirt, how heavy his water-logged shoes felt against the floor. "Us too," the man said. "The closest cinema's ten blocks or so. Not much playing. Not that interested us, anyway."

"That interested you, you mean," the woman said. She didn't share his accent—hers was nasal, Midwestern. To Roger and Beth she said, "He's a film snob."

"Are you on holiday?" the man asked. "Were you here for the beautiful weather we had yesterday?"

"We just got in this morning," Roger said.

"Too bad, too bad. Wonderful day, yesterday. Spent the whole morning at Point Pleasant."

"Sorry we missed it," Beth said.

"Quiet yesterday, too," the man went on. "Today, those cruise ships. You've seen them? Pulled into the harbor this morning. Now the waterfront's crawling with bloody imbeciles."

"You're not on one of those, are you?" the woman said, her small nose suddenly wrinkled, her lips tensed, prepared to be mortified. "He insults people everywhere we go."

Roger hesitated, but Beth answered quickly. "Don't worry. We drove up. From New York. We spent a few days in Maine."

"Never been to Maine," the man said. "Hear it's quite lovely."

"Beautiful," Roger said, though he'd never been, either. Where had he been? Except for his honeymoon in Cancun, this was the first time he'd left the country since that semester in Durham, nearly fifteen years ago. Since then he hadn't even thought to recapture the aimless bliss that had seemed the whole point to being alive at the time. He'd talked about it nonstop that year he'd come back, the year he'd walked Emily home every night after her waitressing shift, recognizing her loneliness and preying upon it, employing his wink when her resistance was at its weakest. Why hadn't he seen it before? With his newfound confidence, he'd taken advantage of her need. He'd known he was doing so even as he went forward, inviting her to move in with him, suggesting, ever so casually, that they spend their lives together. It made sense that she'd leave him as soon as she realized what he'd done—he deserved all the harm he'd caused himself.

"You have to get down to Point Pleasant," the man said. "You'll be here a few days, yes?"

"At least," Beth said.

The couple was from Toronto, their son in graduate school in Halifax. "We just dropped him off," the woman said. "Tomorrow we're heading on to Cape Breton. Will you have time to make it out there?"

"We've got plenty of time," Beth said quickly, and reached across the table for Roger's hand. Her touch clearly surprised him, though he didn't pull away. She tried to read his startled look, but how could she when she still knew so little of him, their history together still so brief? She wanted to believe the lies she'd told the couple, that they'd driven up from New York, that they'd been together at least long enough to plan a trip and carry it out, long enough that she might be able to guess his thoughts. But no matter how much she might want it, there was still this stranger across from her, his cold hand in hers.

They lingered in the café until the couple was gone. Outside the rain hadn't relented at all. They flipped through Roger's guidebook, reading about Cape Breton and Prince Edward Island. "We could rent a car," Beth said. "We can use my blackjack winnings. They won't miss us on the boat."

"What about work?" Roger asked. "Could they spare you a few more days?"

"If I didn't give them a choice, they could."

They discussed details, who they would have to call, where they could find a car, what kind of hotels they would stay in, but the more enthusiastic Beth became, the more Roger questioned practicalities. All their clothes were on the ship, he reminded her. He had four meetings scheduled for next Monday. His mail was being held only through the weekend. He saw what he'd done wrong with Emily—mistaken need for devotion. Or rather, believed that need was good enough, that devotion would come with time. He wouldn't make the same mistake again.

Back on the street they were soaked in an instant, shivering again. They might never have been warmed at all. The enormous exhaust pipe of their ship, the tail of a terrible fish, rose above the nearest buildings, churning out black smoke. "We don't have to go now," Roger said. "We can plan a trip. For next month. Or next spring. I bet it's nice here in spring. We've got plenty of time."

"I guess you're not so far from Brooklyn," Beth said quietly. Roger wished he didn't hear the disappointment in her voice, but it was impossible to ignore. He steeled himself against it. "I come out to Jersey to see my parents all the time."

It was just after noon when they found themselves back in the wharf, the vendor carts still mobbed, the racket of voices against the low roof nearly deafening. Beth bought a *Halifax* T-shirt for Aunt Fran, Roger a purse for Angela. The line to get back on the ship was long and slow-moving, everyone passing through security, passports checked, bags scanned. "I'd better return some e-mails this afternoon," Roger said, and then started telling her about his panicking client, how most of consulting work was psychology, easing people's fears.

His hands were in his pockets. His voice sounded different— Beth couldn't have said how, exactly, only that it was. She wanted to turn off the part of herself that needed to question how things could change so quickly, the part that still wanted to remember the first taxi ride to Ben's apartment, to recapture the thrill that had begun to disappear even as she'd felt it most acutely. The part of her, too, that still wanted to run fingers through Roger's bristly hair, though she knew he was far from her now. It was possible that he'd come back, true, but it was better not to hope. Better, too, not to wonder where he'd gone and why, though why was the only word that came to mind. He was craning his neck to see the front of the line now, this short, boyish man racing toward middle age, impatient to get away from her. She followed his gaze and then scanned the side of the ship, trying to guess which porthole was hers. She would be in front of it soon, the shades open, her clothes scattered across the floor. She'd watch the waves casually, ready to be surprised by the sudden spout of a blow-hole, the arch of a great gray back, but she promised herself she would expect nothing. She wouldn't be disappointed, she swore, if waves were all she saw.

Model Rockets

THIS TIME STEVEN BROUGHT A KNIFE TO SCHOOL. NOT only brought it, but showed it to kids beside him in history class, clicking the blade in and out to the rhythm of the teacher's chalk beating the green board. But the boy had no rhythm—it was stifled by Berkowitz blood, not Benny's—and the teacher soon turned, saw the knife, and began shouting about police and juvenile court. Steven was tall for his age and bulky, with a round, formless face and blond hair shaved so closely it gave his head the appearance of having no boundaries—but he knew how to make his eyes water at will. Benny could imagine his son dropping the knife to the floor, pointing to a boy across the aisle, and bawling, "It's his! He told me to hold it." If there was anything Benny had tried to teach him, especially as he got deeper into trouble, it was to take responsibility for his own actions. But the boy had inherited from his mother the habit of blaming someone else for each of his own problems.

It was Merna, of course, who first heard from the principal and immediately called Benny at work, sobbing. "Your son's a gangster," she said. "He threatens little children into giving their lunch money. Did you teach him about knives?"

"You're blaming me for this?" Benny shouted. Sure, he'd told the boy stories about growing up in Crown Heights, about the Hasids moving in, and then the shvartzas, when ordinary Jews had to do things maybe they should have been ashamed of to keep from being run out of their own neighborhood. But this wasn't Brooklyn. These were Jersey suburbs, with lawns and driveways between each house. No other family lived upstairs or behind a thin wall. A playground with real grass and dirt baseball fields sat just off the highway, around the corner from fast food joints and gas stations. Nobody needed a knife here. "Calm down, Merna," he said, calmer now himself. "It must be those hoodlums from the lake. The ones he plays hockey with. You should never have gotten him that stick. Only crooks and Canadians play hockey."

He came home from the press too late that night to have a talk with the boy but made sure to wake Merna and remind her that Steven's suspension was to be a punishment and not a vacation. But just after lunch the next day came another hysterical phone call: Merna had stepped out, just for a minute, just to pick up some onions for the roast, and when she came back, Steven was gone. An hour later the police brought him to the front door. They'd arrested him and another boy in the 7-Eleven parking lot, where they'd begged anybody over eighteen to buy them a pack of cigarettes and then finally gave up and stole one instead.

This was too much for Benny. It would be their second trip to juvenile court in two years. Though he almost never left work before seven, today he packed into the five-thirteen train from Penn Station, sitting for an hour and a half beside a man in a three-piece suit who stunk with the same sourness his own father used to bring home from a day of installing kitchen cabinets and custom doorframes. He tried to imagine how his father would have handled the boy. But he couldn't picture the hairy, stooped man doing anything but sitting in the worn leather chair beside their sixth floor window in Crown Heights, staring down on the avenue constantly roaring with traffic, muttering, "Who needs this? I should retire already and move to Florida." His father was no help and never had been. He'd learned nothing from the man. By now Benny was furious and couldn't form his thoughts into sentences. And this made him angrier still, knowing he would have nothing prepared to say when he sat the boy in front of him.

The house was quiet except for the sound of Merna sniffling in the kitchen. The door to Steven's bedroom was locked. He told himself he wouldn't kick the door down, he wouldn't, but he stood outside it, holding a box of cigars, shouting, "You like tobacco! I've got some for you. Come out here, Steven, and have a smoke with your old man."

He could picture the way the boy's eyes would widen— dark eyes like Benny's, the one feature that didn't come from his mother's family—as he stuffed the cigar between his lips, wedged it past his teeth and down his throat. He kicked the door once and stepped back to kick it harder. Merna touched his arm and said, "Please, Benny. You're scaring him."

"He better be scared."

"You'll make him act out again."

"You're blaming me?" He glared at his wife's fleshy face, framed by the silly squarish fluff of gold hair that always tilted to the side at the end of the day. She had the same face as her father—Benny's boss—only with extra fat in the cheeks and below the chin and a pathetic sag to her lips. She dabbed at her lower eyelashes with a tissue. He walked past her into the kitchen and said, "You can't stay home one single goddamn day?"

"Onions—" she began.

"I know. Onions." He opened the refrigerator and rooted through the vegetable crisper. There were onions everywhere, white ones, red ones, giant yellow ones, the long green ones Merna called scallions. "Who needs this many onions?" he said, and though he didn't know which she'd bought today, picked up a red one the size of a baseball and threw it across the room. It bounced with a loud clang against the oven door, behind which the roast was browning, and rolled beneath the table where he'd later have to strain his knees to pick it up. "You're worried about onions, and my son's becoming a gangster."

BENNY'S FATHER-IN-LAW, LEO BERKOWITZ, HAD A HABIT of rising on his toes with the lift at the end of his sentences. As the only blond Jew growing up on East Broadway—he often told Benny, in the nostalgic, condescending voice of a veteran or retired school teacher—he'd been taunted constantly by neighbors who would call down from third story windows, "little goy," or "Swede bastard." So from a young age he'd learned to act tough—tougher than he looked, Benny translated silently—and this was what had allowed him to climb from a printer's assistant in a newspaper sweatshop to the owner of the second-most successful screenprinting business in Manhattan.

But even on his toes, Leo didn't top the bulge of Benny's shoulder. As long as they both stood, Benny could always be sure of looking down onto the old man's shiny red scalp. Wispy white hair still looped over Leo's ears and ringed the back of his head, but the rest had begun to fall out by the time Benny married Merna, more than twenty years ago. This view was a comfort when Benny and Leo stood together on the printing floor in front of the production crew. Leo was forced to shout above the hiss of compressed air if Benny didn't lower his head. Leo might be boss, but on the floor, surrounded by the whirling arms of the automatic presses, the crew could see it was Benny who was in control. He often walked among the presses, a finger in each ear—he was convinced the noise would eventually deafen him— and imagined that every T-shirt was being printed for his profit alone.

But now, in Leo's sound-proof, mezzanine office, the old man looked down on him from behind his high wooden desk polished to a greasy shine. Benny would have preferred to stand, but Leo motioned twice to a low cushioned chair in front. From this angle, Leo's gray eyes were shadowed by his brow, so his pupils, ordinarily pinholes, had widened into dark pits.

On the wall behind the desk hung two enlarged photographs in gaudy silver frames. Both had been there for years, Benny knew, but still he had the uncomfortable feeling that Leo had arranged them for this particular meeting. The first was a color shot of Leo with Steven riding on his shoulders, laughing and innocent at age six. The other, black and white, pictured the whole Berkowitz clan, Leo and his five brothers, all blond and smiling, arms around shoulders, except for one, Morty, who sat apart with a hat pulled low on his head. Morty had been production manager at the press until Leo fired him to make way for his new son-in-law. When Benny glanced at either photograph, he felt equally accused.

The old man pointed to a bowl filled with candies wrapped in yellow cellophane. Benny shook his head, and Leo leaned forward. "Merna says you can't keep the boy out of trouble," he said.

Benny stood, placed a hand on the desk, and quickly took it away, leaving a smudge. Leo's eyes followed him, pupils narrowing in the light. "Who's home with him all day?" Benny asked. "He's suspended, and she knows he's not supposed to leave his room. But she can't keep herself from going shopping."

"Sit, sit. This isn't a trial. What good does it do Steven when you defend yourself? Your fault, Merna's fault, it doesn't matter."

Benny sat slowly, watching with a chill as pinholes widened again to pits. "The boy's rotten," he said.

"A fine thing for a father to say."

"It's a father's business what he says about his son. What is it you want, Leo? I have orders coming in and a schedule to write."

Leo reached two fingers into the candy bowl and swirled them until they brought up a small disk in a brown wrapper. "Coffee," he said. "I always keep two or three at the bottom. You sure you don't care for one?"

Benny knew the old man was about to propose something he wouldn't like. Leo could be direct when it suited him, when he didn't risk being contradicted. But last month he'd spent nearly twenty minutes making small talk before telling Benny to fire a printer who'd been with them for eight years but was too slow to keep up with the new automatics. "What is it you're after?" Benny said.

Leo unwrapped the candy and held it for a moment between his teeth before sucking it into the pocket of his cheek.

"You're a good manager, Benny. And I'm not saying you're not a good father. But you're a dedicated manager, and you work long hours, and you probably don't have enough time to spend with Steven. Not the kind of time you'd need to keep him out of trouble."

Benny was about to stand again but instead gripped the arms of the chair. "I'd give him my arm if it would do any good."

"Of course you would."

"I'd cut off my arm tomorrow."

"I know you would."

"What am I supposed to do? Stay home from work and take care of him?"

"Of course not," Leo said.

"His mother doesn't work. Can't she stay home from shopping one day?"

Leo made a long slurping noise, and the bulge of the candy moved from one cheek to the other. "Be reasonable, now. What can a woman do?"

Benny realized he'd been holding his breath and let out a long sigh. "You want me to take a vacation?"

"No, no!" Leo said and began to cough. For a moment, Benny thought the candy had lodged in the old man's throat. It would be a difficult and welcome decision whether to let him choke to death and take over the business or to put the old man forever in his debt with a pump of fists beneath the ribcage. He could imagine Leo having to declare him a hero in front of the entire staff, could almost picture himself with his feet on the wooden desk in the mezzanine office Leo would finally give him to replace his closet on the production floor. But before he could move, the old man hit his chest twice with the flat of one hand and spat the candy into the fingers of the other. The hand with the candy disappeared beneath the desk and returned a moment later, clenched. "Goddamn things," Leo said. "They've got that soft chocolate in the middle, I always forget. No, I don't want you to take a vacation. What would I do without you here? And Merna, she'd never forgive me if I let you stay home a week. Bring the

boy here. Let him spend his days with me. Until he can go back to
school."

So this was it. Benny couldn't bear Leo's waiting smile, and
instead found himself facing the photograph of Steven, which
seemed sadly ancient, a relic from a forgotten world. In it, the boy
gripped the collar of Leo's suit jacket, swinging his heels against
the old man's chest. It was hard to recall the last time he'd seen his
son laugh so genuinely, with such absolute trust. But back then,
Steven's future had been open to every possibility. Now he was
embarked on a direct and indivertible course toward a tragic life.
Benny, of course, would try every means available to save his
son. But wasn't it already hopeless? Wouldn't Leo do more harm
than good? He stared hard at the photograph, shot in a park
during some family reunion or other, and tried to remember what
he'd been doing while his son sat laughing on Leo's shoulders.
Most likely he'd been commiserating with husbands of other Berkowitz daughters, or else getting a hot dog for Merna. Or maybe he'd
been swamped with work and had stayed behind at the press.

Quickly, he turned to the other picture. Unlike the family
reunion, the day he'd replaced Morty as production manager had
never left him. That entire morning he'd kept himself out of the
way in a corner of the production floor—so much quieter in the
days of manual printing—watching his wife's uncle pack and
then lug a battered cardboard box from the office, his hat under
his arm. Morty called, "So long," and several printers answered
back, "Good luck, boss," or "Take care, pal." Benny told himself
this had nothing to do with him. It was Leo's business if he wanted to throw his own brother out on the street. Maybe the old man's
obligation was greater toward his daughter, whose husband
had been slaving for less than peanuts on the shipping docks. Or
maybe Morty was just a lousy manager.

A few feet from him, Morty stopped, placed the box on the
floor, and without glancing at Benny, pushed his hat down on
his head until it touched the tops of his ears. After a long moment,
he picked up the box, straightened, and headed for the exit with

his head held high. Until now Benny had felt pity, but at this he fumed. It wasn't his fault the man had lost his job. If Morty needed to be haughty with anyone, it should be with Leo. On his new office desk Benny found the stub of a pencil with a ring of teeth-marks in its yellow paint. His anger flared. Pencil in hand, he ran across the printing floor, out the doors, onto the street. He would show who deserved to be haughty. Morty was almost at the entrance to the subway. "You forgot something," Benny said, dropping the pencil into the box and crossing his arms. Morty blinked twice, swallowed, and let the box fall to the sidewalk as if it suddenly weighed eight-thousand pounds. One corner of the cardboard burst and several paper clips skidded across the side-walk. "Good luck, Benny," Morty said, and hurried down the stairs to his train. Benny carried the box back to his office, pinch-ing closed the ripped corner, and emptied its supplies into his desk drawers.

Now, Leo cleared his throat. "So? What do you say?"

Benny tried to think of all the reasons he hated the old man's idea. But the only words he could manage were, "I don't want him to see me at work."

Leo paused a moment. He moved his hand toward the candy bowl, then, shaking his head, drew it back. "What's to see? He won't even notice you. He'll be up here with me. It'll be good for him, trust me. I have a way with children."

"Funny, Merna never mentioned that."

Leo frowned. "With boys. Daughters belong with their mother."

"He's not a child anymore. He's almost sixteen. What'll you do with him here? You won't get any work done."

"I'll teach him the business," Leo said, leaning back in his chair and folding his hands with satisfaction over his belly.

"He's supposed to be punished," Benny pleaded. "He should stay at home."

Leo closed his eyes. "You'll bring him tomorrow."

DESPITE THE BUSINESS WITH THE ONIONS, BENNY KNEW Merna wasn't responsible for Steven's behavior. No, it wasn't her fault, not directly. It was these suburbs, with nothing for the kids to do. His brother and sister-in-law lived only two exits down Rt. 80. Their daughter had always been a relatively smart girl and was now in college part-time. But during high school, she'd come home from her weekend dates with dress rumpled, bra dangling or missing. She reeked of booze, slurred her speech, and laughed at her mother who stomped her feet across kitchen tiles and pulled her own hair in anguish.

"In the city you didn't go looking for trouble," he told Merna now, the night after his talk with Leo, as she lifted a slice of pink meat onto his plate. Steven was locked again in his room, playing loud music. "There were always things to keep you busy. Not a minute for messing around."

"That was a different time," Merna said, wiping her eyes with the back of a hand. "A different city."

He would have preferred to raise Steven in Brooklyn, but when the old neighborhood went to rot, Merna insisted they move to Jersey. He'd agreed at the time, because too many cars got stolen in Queens, and unless he borrowed money from Leo he couldn't afford uptown or Long Island. And he would quickly admit, for the first few years, while Steven was an infant and toddler, he'd felt more comfortable than he'd ever imagined possible, sitting in a plastic chair in his backyard without grimy brownstones or apartment buildings towering over him, without an upstairs neighbor in a black hat who would lean out a window and curse him in Yiddish for driving on Saturday.

And as the boy grew up, it wasn't as if Benny didn't try to find things to catch his interest. He'd enrolled Steven in every sports league the township offered, paid for his uniforms and equipment, driven him to games on the Saturday mornings he didn't work. But even though Steven turned out to be a decent soccer player—he was slow and though he never learned to pass, had a powerful kick that would occasionally score a goal—he quit after two seasons. Benny tried to introduce him to hobbies, chemistry sets, coin collections, jigsaw puzzles, but the only time the boy would sit still for more than five minutes was when he lay prone on the couch watching TV.

But then, about two years ago, Benny discovered a new hobby, one that he'd never heard of before. It was a suburban pastime, unsuitable for the city. On Sundays, in the grassy lot at the end of their block, a handful of neighborhood kids launched model rockets they'd built from cardboard tubes and balsa wood. A number of parents stood by the road and cheered. This was the perfect activity for Steven—it combined the conscientious attention that would keep him out of trouble with the excitement of flames and mild explosions. It was both dangerous and approved.

And for several months, Benny actually believed model rockets would save his family. Steven seemed indifferent until he saw the first rocket scream from the wire launcher and rise black against a backdrop of white clouds. After the plastic capsule burst from its tube, Benny noticed Steven's pudgy red hands pressed together at his waist, wringing as the rocket glided to the ground beneath its cellophane parachute. Then, for the first time, the boy asked to go to the hobby store, to buy cardboard, wood, paint, and gunpowder boosters. Benny and his son worked side by side on the dusty ping-pong table in their basement, cutting wings, painting tubes, and tying improvised napkin parachutes with dental floss. Every week they launched a larger and more elaborate rocket to the cheers of other neighborhood kids and parents.

Once, Benny even consented to help Steven build a rocket that dropped a soft-boiled egg when its capsule popped hundreds of feet in the air. As the egg fell out of sight behind a cluster of trees, he watched his son's soft hands clasped together in exhilaration and decided these didn't have to be a laborer's hands, the hands of a factory worker. The boy was slow, but he might still have some chance to make use of his hands, as a cabinet maker, maybe, or even, if Benny pushed him hard enough, a dentist. Not the type of dentist who charged outrageous prices and didn't remember his patients' names, either, but like those Benny remembered in Crown Heights, who always wore thick mustaches and patted him on the shoulder, giving regards to his mother, before he left the office. Several times while they worked together in the basement, Benny bared his teeth and asked Steven if he could see anything caught between them. But Steven was always more interested in gluing wings on straight or painting bloodshot eyes on his nose cone than in staring into his father's mouth.

And who could blame him? There would be time for teeth later. Benny was enjoying the hobby so much he even started a rocket club at the printing press. At the annual picnic on Long Island, the production crew, the art department, and the sales team would compete for the highest flight, the most elaborate design, and the loudest take-off. Despite the long-term damage it might cause him, Benny found himself savoring the sharp roar of the launch and never once covered his ears.

But then one day Steven refused to let Benny use a square of his balsa wood to make extra tail fins for the production crew's rocket, which he'd designed to look like a shark. The boy carried his materials to the far end of the ping-pong table and worked in silence. Benny mumbled, "And who taught you to be so generous?" but said nothing more as he left for the hobby store. Two days later, when Benny broke the blade of their X-acto knife cutting the shark's last dorsal fin, Steven threw a box of boosters onto the floor. Benny shouted, "What's wrong with you?" but then calmed himself and said, "We'll go get a new one."

"I want my own," Steven said.

"We'll share."

They drove together to the hardware store. Benny picked out a new knife, showed it to Steven, who shrugged, and went to look for some glue. Steven said he'd wait in the parking lot, by the car. But as Benny began reading the instructions on a small tube of rubber cement, he heard a loud ruckus by the front door and felt something in his chest grow heavy and sink. He dropped the knife and glue and ran outside. There was his son, face down on the pavement. A fat, bearded man wearing a Yankees jacket knelt on the boy's back. A few feet away, another X-acto knife, larger than the one Benny had chosen, lay on the concrete, torn from its packaging, glinting in the sunlight. Steven was flailing beneath the man, crying, "I did it! I want to go peacefully."

Benny approached slowly, not willing to believe what was happening until he saw the man's handcuffs and laminated badge that read SECURITY. "Get off my boy," he said. "This must be a mistake."

The fat man said, "No mistake, pal. Your son's a thief." He managed to get one of Steven's wrists into the cuffs, but the boy was lying with all his weight on his other arm. "Quit squirming," the guard said, and then shouted, "Someone call 911."

Steven cried, "No handcuffs! I want to go peacefully." He kicked his heels at the guard's back.

Benny came closer and bent to Steven's face, which was scraped above the left eye. Spittle dripped from the boy's mouth, but his eyes were focused on the knife. His face was red, and his cheeks were puffed with air, seeming to swell far beyond the limits of ordinary skin. Benny barely recognized him. "Did you steal that?" Benny asked.

"I did it!" the boy cried. "No handcuffs!"

Benny pulled his son up by the shoulder and wrenched his other arm from beneath his body. Steven went limp as his father held his free wrist for the guard to cuff. The boy's plump hands, a criminal's hands, were pinched tight in the metal rings, and Benny worried a moment the circulation might be cut off. But then he sat on the curb and waited for the police to arrive, telling himself he'd done nothing wrong, that almost every father had to watch his son taken to jail once in his life, and at least now it would be over with.

But tonight, at dinner with Merna, and later in the dark of their bedroom, after Steven's second arrest in two years, he began for the first time to imagine the possibility of his child's violent death. With his eyes closed, he pictured a steel table in a sterilized room, and on it a stiff bundle covered by a white sheet. Quickly, he pressed his face into the pillow. But before he could sleep, the image of his own father rose to his mind. In the vision, Benny was only a boy. He and his brother sat at the dinner table as his mother took away their soup bowls and served plates heaped with meat and boiled vegetables. Their father stood by the window, staring down at the street. He glanced once over his shoulder and said, "The way you people eat, I'll never afford to go to Flor-ida." Now, Benny cursed his father for denying his duty, and then, briefly, wondered if he had the courage to do the same.

IN THE MORNING, BENNY ROSE WELL BEFORE DAWN AND made his way to the train station in the dark, alone. Merna would bring Steven on a later train and spend the day shopping in the city. She'd surprised Benny by accepting Leo's proposal without hesitation. She'd never had a good word to say about the old man as a father. He'd worked almost constantly while she'd grown up, rarely spending more than one evening a week at home with his family. But he'd still managed to so terrify Merna's mother with stern glances and reproves that all day she drifted from one room of the house to the next waving a feather duster or pushing a vacuum, shrieking at the sight of mud dragged in on her daughter's shoes. Benny had hoped to hear Merna argue against bringing the boy to Leo. "Are you crazy?" he'd expected her to say. "Isn't he bad enough already?" But instead she'd only shrugged and said, "Maybe it's for the best."

Steven's reaction troubled him even more. Benny had put the matter to him as if it were a choice: stay locked in his room all day or come to the press. The boy had seemed almost excited, though excitement for Steven meant nodding, then tilting his shapeless head skeptically to the side, and saying, "I don't have to get up at five, do I? Can I bring my walkman? Will Grandpa get me lunch?" Immediately, Benny wanted to take the offer back.

Why should the boy seem so fond of Leo? He'd certainly never showed a similar affection for Benny's father—on every winter visit to the steaming Ft. Lauderdale condo, Steven did nothing but stretch out on a couch in front of the TV, chin in hand.

But it was true: with Steven, Leo seemed to become an entirely different person. Even Benny had to admit this. Around the boy, the old man no longer rose on his toes or puffed out his chest. He lowered his head, nodding, listening with a gentle grin. He looked astonishingly like an actual grandfather. And Steven was another boy altogether. Benny remembered watching them at some family function two years ago, not long before the boy stole the knife from the hardware store. Steven had momentarily lost his sour, vacant expression and become almost cheerful, describing to Leo one of the rockets he'd made. He spoke in such a hurry he had to gasp for breath between his sentences. But when Benny piped in, something about how the next rocket they were planning had enough boosters to send it to the moon, the boy returned to scowling.

Now he felt somehow trapped, drawn into a danger he didn't quite understand. He was glad to have two hours to prepare himself for whatever might come. But even this early, the noise of traffic on the highway, the honking of cars fighting for spaces in the train station parking lot threatened his eardrums and made thinking difficult. By the time he made it to work, his mind was in a frenzy, and he believed one thing for certain: the boy hadn't agreed to come because he liked Leo. He wasn't coming out of guilt for all the trouble he'd caused or in order to appease his father. No. He was coming with the strict intention of humiliating Benny in front of his crew. He'd steal a box of personalized pens or smear a T-shirt before it could run through the dryer. He'd knock over a rack of solvents. From the mezzanine balcony he'd accuse Benny of teaching him to be a criminal, while Leo looked on, arms crossed, shaking his head.

A heap of order slips waited on Benny's desk, and stacked boxes of unprinted shirts leaned precariously just outside his office door. But for an hour he could do nothing but pace, tapping the desk, the chair, the file cabinet with the end of a pencil. When someone knocked on his door, a chill rippled through him so suddenly it was almost painful. The door opened a crack. One of the newer printers, whose name Benny hadn't yet learned, stuck in his head and asked about the artwork for a job that should have been finished last Friday. "Do I look like the fucking art department?" Benny shouted. "Can't you people do anything for yourselves?" The printer's head vanished and the door shut quietly. Benny slumped at his desk, already exhausted, and forced himself to write up the day's job schedule.

Out on the production floor, automatic presses hissed and whirled all around him, and printers scurried from one machine to another. Instantly his ears began to buzz. The first of ten thousand T-shirts for a computer company—bearing a reddish eight-pointed sun with a serene woman's face and the slogan, "Let Our Icons Guide You!"—was sliding on a conveyor belt through an electric dryer. High on the mezzanine balcony, Leo's office door was closed, and behind it the old man was plotting, plotting. To what end, Benny had no idea, though he suspected it would be to turn Steven even further against him. Benny's only comfort was that this computer job would take all day and half the evening. He'd have to stay well past seven to make sure all the shirts were properly packaged and ready to ship. Merna would take Steven home on the five o'clock train, while Benny would eat dinner alone in his office, in peace. He couldn't bear to be present when Merna questioned the boy about his day with Leo.

And that was when he saw them: Merna, Leo, and Steven, standing together on the balcony, all eyes on him. He waved feebly. Merna waved back, her heavy coat, her scarf, the loose skin under her chin, everything jiggling. Leo nodded once, slowly. The boy, leaning against the railing, stared. Steven was taller than his grandfather, but the way he crouched forward with elbows splayed made him look short and squat. Even from far away his face was pinched and dark with anger. Benny felt sweat forming on his forehead as he watched his son and the old man turn and disappear into the office. What could they possibly do in there? Eat coffee candies and talk about business? Steven wouldn't sit still for five minutes. Merna, who might have been reading his mind, shrugged. Benny motioned for her to come downstairs, but she only touched both hands to her shell of hair and headed for the exit.

He tried to go about his business. But once he'd sorted the new orders—most of which still needed Leo's approval—and sent them to the art department, he was at a loss. Half the sales team was out with the flu, and the other half took its time bringing in new accounts. For once all the presses were working properly, and he didn't have to spend his day on the phone, shouting at repairmen or their managers. But to have nothing to do was worse. What would the boy think if he saw Benny idling? This was why he spent six days of every week away from home? All he could do was walk from one press to the next, testing the cure of the ink, the alignment on multi-colored jobs. He wanted desperately to talk to someone, not about anything in particular, but simply for distraction, to keep him from glancing up to the balcony. But the printers all gave him a wide berth, stepping carefully out of range of his voice. And anyway, to have a conversation meant straining above the noise of the air-compressors. Already, the ringing in his ears was beginning to scare him. Sometime soon he would have to buy earplugs, no matter how frail they might make him look in the eyes of his crew.

He stopped off at the desk of the production secretary, a young black woman he'd hired only two weeks ago, one in an endless string who could never get along well enough with Leo to last more than a year. She was reading a paperback and twirling a pen in one hand. In Crown Heights, he would have called her shvartza, but now that he lived in Jersey, he could admire her full lips and large, white teeth and think of her as a young black woman. She had a son, three or four years old. Benny remembered because the boy had a Jewish name, which had made him laugh when he'd first heard it, though now he couldn't recall what it was.

Because she lived in Newark and must already have envisioned her son hauled away to prison or murdered by gangs, Benny felt they had something in common. "How's the boy?" he asked.

Only her eyes moved to find his face. The pen kept twirling between her long, slender fingers. "I know," she said. "But I don't have any work to do."

"Excuse me?"

She held up the book. "Didn't you tell me not to read again? I'm on company time and all that?"

"Your boy," he said. "Your son. I asked about your son. What's his name?"

She shifted in her chair and observed him sideways. "Isaiah. He's fine, thanks."

"Mine's here today. With Leo. That's why I'm asking."

She smiled and pointed over his shoulder. "That him?"

He swiveled and nearly tangled his own legs. On the balcony Leo held his clipboard, scanning the floor and making notes. The boy leaned against the rail, gaping at Benny. Benny waved again. Behind him, so close it made him jump, the secretary said, "He doesn't look like you."

Was the boy smiling? This was how he'd take his revenge. He'd spend the day spying on his father and tonight would report to Merna about Benny's flirting with a shvartza. He could already picture her yanking suitcases hysterically from the closet, crying, "Bad enough another woman, but a colored one!" She'd always wanted to believe he had affairs, had once accused him, when, for a whole week, he came home every night after eleven o'clock. With tears pooling around her swollen nostrils, she'd said, "Tell me now. Tell me who it is." He'd laughed too heartily, told her not to be silly, asked her how they were supposed to live if he didn't work. But she snapped, "Don't tell me it's work. Tell me it's a woman. A woman I can handle. Don't tell me I'm second to T-shirts." He kissed her and blamed Leo for keeping him late, cursed the old man until she nodded, sniffling, and said, "First he took my mother from me, and now he takes my husband."

But now it was hard to tell whether Steven's lips formed a smile or a sneer. His eyes, it seemed, were focused somewhere above Benny's head, and when Benny turned his heart sank. Above his office door hung the enormous, gray-blue rocket he'd made for the company picnic, with its three detachable stages, its asymmetrical arrangement of fins, its flattened nose cone painted along the sides with fearsome shark's teeth. He'd passed beneath it so often he no longer noticed it, but now he could have kicked himself for leaving it there. He'd meant to destroy it soon after Steven's arrest, after it had won the contest for original design, but somehow he hadn't been able to. A reminder, he'd told himself then, a reminder of the good times he'd had with his son. But Steven, he knew, would never see it this way. The shark's black eyes flashed resentment, hatred. Benny determined to destroy it right now, stomp it to shreds while the boy watched. But before he could move, the secretary said, "I think Leo's calling for you."

The old man was beckoning him to the stairs with a mena-cing sweep of an arm. Steven was already on his way back into the office. What was coming now? With each step forward, Benny wanted more and more to run in the opposite direction. His discomfort confused him and he couldn't banish the one consist-ent thought from his mind: Leo was trying to take his son away from him. On his way up the stairs he tried to prepare an argu-ment, whispering to himself over and over, "I'm his father, and I love him no matter what he does."

In the office, both Leo and Steven stood formally behind the desk, arms at their sides. Between them was the photo from the family reunion, Steven riding happily on Leo's shoulders. The double vision made Benny nauseous. His ears were numbed, throbbing dully with his pulse. The old man pointed to one of the low chairs. Benny sat and took a deep breath. "You aren't going to sit?" he said, his own voice sounding distant and hollow. He worried that he wouldn't hear what Leo would try to put over on him.

"How's the 'Icon' job coming?" Leo asked, rising to his toes and slowly descending.

The old man's voice was louder than Benny expected and clear enough. "Almost finished," he lied. Leo didn't care one way or the other, but Benny wouldn't give away the upper hand so easily. If the job was late, he could blame the shipping company that had been giving him trouble for months.

"Your son and I have been talking," Leo said. Steven was swaying, shifting his weight from one foot to the other.

"What else would you be doing?"

Leo leaned forward and placed both hands flat on the shiny desktop. He didn't seem to mind if he smudged it. And why should he, if someone would come in to polish it as soon as he left for the night? Benny looked away from the old man's pitted gray eyes. "He's almost sixteen, isn't he?" Leo said.

"In twenty-two days," Steven said.

"Sixteen in twenty-two days," Leo repeated, nodding absurdly, as if he'd never before heard of such a thing.

"Hard to believe," Benny said. "Where's the time go?" He wanted to stall long enough to remember the argument he'd prepared, but it didn't seem to fit what Leo was saying. The noise on the production floor must have numbed his brain as well as his ears. Or if not the noise, then the fumes from the ink and the chemical stencil. Why hadn't this occurred to him before? It now struck him with a dizzying certainty: he might or might not go deaf, but those fumes would be his funeral.

"In twenty-two days Steven can work," Leo said. "He can drop out of school."

Benny sprang from the chair and glared at the boy. "Did they expel you? Tell me now."

"School's a waste of time," Steven said, lowering his head.

"They expelled you! I'll kill him," Benny said, stepping forward.

"Listen to what you're saying, Benny," Leo said, waving his arms. "They already suspended, how can they expel him?

Schools have to have reasons for punishing. I'm talking dropping out on his own."

"They hate me there," Steven said, eyes still set on his shoes.

Benny lunged. Leo held him back with surprising strength. The old man's shiny scalp flushed, and the wisps of white hair flared over his ears. The pinholes of his upturned pupils now seemed fiercer than the pits, the gray irises vast and dominating. "Steven, please," Leo said. "Wait for us outside."

The boy edged along the wall and slipped out the door. "My son won't be an idiot," Benny shouted after him.

"Of course he won't be an idiot," Leo said. "He'll work for you. You'll teach him everything you know."

Immediately, Benny's energy left him. A weight in his guts dragged him back into his chair. He reached for a yellow-wrapped candy and glanced at the photo of the Berkowitz brothers. Once more he heard Morty's parting words, "Good luck, Benny," and for the first time wondered how a man would spend the rest of his day after being fired by his own brother. From stories he'd heard he guessed Morty had gone to a bar—but had he drunk in depression or in celebration? He asked quietly, "You want Steven to work here?"

"Doesn't matter what I want," Leo said. "It's what he wants."

Still Leo refused to sit. Everything the old man said came clearly through Benny's clogged ears, but the sense of the words escaped him. "He wants to print T-shirts?"

"He wants to work for *you*," Leo said. "You'll start him washing screens, just like anybody else. But of course, I won't be around forever. Someday the two of you will run the place together. He's my heir, after all."

Father and son. Partners. They'd take the train together in the morning, come home together at night. They would share this mezzanine office and wooden desk when Leo was stiff in a box. They might even launch rockets again, at the annual company picnic. Was this supposed to excite Benny? Now he'd never have the chance to run the business on his own. He might, one day, even be fired by his own son. He tried to feel angry, for lack of anything else, but his anger, too, failed him.

"Let's go tell him the good news," Leo said.

Steven wasn't waiting outside the door. Benny turned frantically in every direction. He half-expected to see his son sneaking out the back door with Leo's bankbook, or the company safe. But there he was, down on the production floor, surrounded by automatic presses and printers who dodged him to keep up with the mechanical arms. Even from above, Benny could make out the boy's pudgy hands clasped behind his back, hands that would soon scrub screens and fold T-shirts, hands that could so easily be crushed in all that metal, those grinding gears. The boy's mouth hung slightly open, and in went toxic fumes. Benny suddenly conjured an image of his own father, sometime around his twelfth birthday. During a punchball game in a vacant lot, Benny had stepped on a two-by-four hiding a nail that went deep into his heel. Another boy had fetched Benny's father, who carried him into the apartment, swabbed his wound with wads of cotton, and wiping his eyes, muttered in a trembling voice, "Who needs this? Do you think I need this?"

Leo's arm went around Benny's shoulder. "Look at him," the old man said. "He was born for this place. He reminds me of myself when I first started out."

Benny nodded, but he didn't believe it. He watched Steven turning one way and then the other, startled by so much noise and commotion. The boy wasn't ready to be here. He stood with the same helpless confusion Benny had felt that first day watching Morty clean out his office. One of the printers, shirt tied around his head, bare back sweaty and tattooed, slid around a dryer to where Steven loitered. The boy took a step backward. An arm of the press behind him grazed the fleshy crown of his head. He whirled, fists balled before his face. Benny's, too, were already clenched and throbbing.

Walter's Girls

ALL THREE OF WALTER LANN'S DAUGHTERS BLAMED themselves for their father's suicide, but only Jamie, the youngest, kept it to herself. Two days after the funeral, her sister Andrea was typically dramatic, holding her head in both hands, muttering, "I should have called more often. I should have listened to him. Maybe I could have seen the signs."

"You live in Oregon," said Karen, the oldest, from the kitchen sink, where she was washing the last of the dishes from the elaborate dinner she'd insisted on making, no matter how many times the other two protested. "What could you do from out there? I'm the one who saw him every week. I should have known what was going on."

"That's what I *mean*," Andrea said. "I live so far away. I just wasn't *there* for him."

"I was the one who should have seen him that day," Karen said for the third time in an hour. "He sounded so excited to see the kids. Who knows what would have happened if I hadn't canceled."

"I don't think he ever forgave me for moving," Andrea said. "He never understood how much my career means to me. He never respected it."

"He didn't kill himself because his daughter's a chiropractor," Karen said.

"I didn't *say* that, did I? I'm talking about the larger picture. It's one more way he felt alienated from the people around him."

"Alienated," Karen said disdainfully, with a hiss of air between her teeth. "The man was sick. He had a disease, and I should have gotten him help."

Jamie hadn't said a word for twenty minutes or more, but neither of her sisters could have been surprised. She'd always been the quiet one, the one who disappeared during dinner conversation. "The sensitive one," they'd said dismissively when she was a girl. Since she'd grown up, they'd continued to explain her in the same offhand, condescending way, now saying sarcastically, as if exposing not only Jamie's pretension, but all the pretension in the world, "the artist in the family." To prove it they'd point out her clothes, always casual and slightly frayed, her pale complexion, her closely cropped hair. She never bothered to remind them that her schedule didn't allow her much time in the sun, or that she had to wear a uniform to work so that when she was off she only wanted to wear what was most comfortable. Tonight she had on a black dress, sleeveless and too short for the occasion, bought a year ago for a cocktail party. She'd purposely avoided the clichéed wardrobe full of black clothing, and now the only mourning clothes she owned were a wool suit she'd sweated through at the funeral and a pair of slacks she'd worn last night. They wouldn't have listened if she'd told them her haircut was fashionable in the city and quite expensive, the one thing she always splurged on. It had always been easiest to keep quiet.

Since dinner had ended, she'd focused her attention on a thread that had come loose from the edge of the tablecloth, rolling it between a finger and thumb. The inside of her mouth was pasty and sour, but she couldn't get up to refill her water glass. Even the thought of stirring made her queasy. Karen couldn't cook anything that didn't require a ten-step recipe from the *Kosher Gourmet Cookbook*, an hour of preparation, seven different spices, a sauce so rich that three bites made Jamie full. She'd finished her whole plate tonight, two chicken breasts in a sopping ginger glaze, a heaping side of wild rice, a mound of curried yams, ate every last crumb only to keep her jaws working, to prevent any words from spilling out of her lips. Karen had been pleased enough to say, "About time you're eating like a human being. I swear, one day I'll go looking for you, and you'll just vanish, gone without a trace." Andrea had raised her eyebrows and smirked but hadn't said anything. Jamie knew what she'd been thinking— Karen's image of a human being was distorted, her husband a shapeless tub, both her children round and soft and soon to be asthmatic. She could hear them now, walking around upstairs, their heavy footsteps rattling the ceiling fixtures.

Karen herself still had the bony shoulders all three sisters had inherited from their mother, the protruding collarbones, the deep hollows behind them, but her hips had rounded to nearly twice their original width, her ass bulbous and out of place, jutting so suddenly away from her back it looked fake, a prosthetic she put on to show solidarity with her obese brood. She'd turned thirty-three a few weeks ago but looked at least ten years older, her hair thinning on top and otherwise hanging in a loose fringe over her ears. Her skin was sallow and blotchy around her neck and chin. Jamie had never once commented on her looks, but several times, catching her stare, Karen had talked without prompting about the ravages of childbirth, how hard it was on the body, how she'd started to recover after having Ariel, but then Noah—nine pounds, six ounces—had done her in. "You'll see," she'd say. "The same thing'll happen to you." Jamie knew plenty of other women who'd given birth, most of whom were still thin and fit, but she always managed to hold her tongue.

She didn't have to worry about listening to Karen's predictions today. Karen knew better than to talk about childbirth in front of Andrea, who'd miscarried twice during her brief marriage, which had ended eight months ago. Without Andrea around, Karen wasn't shy about giving her opinion—that Andrea had never struck her as nurturing enough for motherhood, that her hips were too narrow for a natural delivery, that the reason the pregnancies didn't take was because a Jew's genes didn't do so well trying to mix with those of an Irish Catholic. She also complained to Jamie about how much they'd all paid to fly out to Portland for the wedding, the gifts they'd hauled across the country, all the time she'd spent searching for a dress—why didn't stores carry anything that fit anymore?—the trouble she'd gone through getting Will's tux tailored. "All for nothing," she said, waiting for Jamie to agree. When she didn't, Karen repeated, "Nothing."

Now Andrea sat cross-legged on her chair, shoes off, back perfectly straight, the length of her neck exposed before her hair flared out from her skull in a spiky duck's tail. She looked more like their father than either Karen or Jamie, her features blunter, her skin a shade darker, her flat chin identical to that of the man most people called Dr. Walt, a handful Major Lann. She took a deep breath and crossed her hands over her belly, as if she were trying to hold her guts in place. "I just don't know what to *do* with this," she said, lifting her head briefly to face the ceiling and then thrusting it back down. "How are you supposed to get over it?"

"You don't get over it," Karen said, slamming the door of the dishwasher closed. "You just live with it."

"How do you know?" Jamie said before she could stop herself. Her voice was raspy and pitched too high. "What makes you such an expert?"

"That's it, honey," Andrea said. "Let it out."

"I never said I was an expert," Karen said, a touch of doubt and injury creeping into her voice. "I was just talking."

"It's not about you," Andrea said. "She can't keep all this anger and pain bottled up. She's got to express it somehow."

The thread was now wound several times around Jamie's finger. She pulled it gently and enjoyed a faint pleasure in watching it strip away from the rest of the fabric. "What are you doing?" Karen cried. "That's my good cloth!" She rustled around in a drawer and came out with a pair of rusted scissors. Jamie pulled harder, unraveling as much as she could before Karen grabbed her wrist and held it still. "What's the matter with you? Why do you have to ruin other people's things?"

"It's just a tablecloth," Andrea said.

"It's mine!" Karen shouted. Then a quick snip, and the thread was free, dangling from Jamie's knuckle.

JAMIE HAD BEEN IN KAREN'S HOUSE FEWER THAN A dozen times in the last five years, even though it was less than an hour's train ride from her downtown studio. Karen, of course, had made an open invitation. "Come whenever you want," she said. "I'll make you a copy of the key." She called specifically to tell Jamie there was a free seat at the table for every holiday— not only the standard ones, Rosh Hashanah, Hanukkah, Passover, but also Sukkoth, Purim, Shavuot, and others Jamie didn't remember learning about during her few years in Hebrew school, Tu B'Shvat, Tisha B'Av, Simchat Torah. Karen clearly enjoyed saying each name on Jamie's voice mail, her accent exaggerated, the words nearly gargled in the back of her throat. Jamie found every excuse possible not to come, just as her father did. Luckily, her job—assistant banqueting supervisor at the midtown Sheraton—gave her most of the excuses she needed. Her hours were long and unpredictable, and often she was on call all through the weekend. Her father hadn't had the same luxury— he'd run a private cardiology practice and set his own hours. When he ran out of excuses—a weekend fishing excursion with colleagues, a date with a beautiful nurse he couldn't possibly cancel on now—he lashed out at the whole concept of Judaism. "Don't you think I get enough of this from my patients?" he'd say. "You know how many people invite me to their synagogues and Shabbos dinners? Can't you all get it through your heads that I'm an unredeemable heathen?" Other times he'd grumble, "What have I got to give praise for? A wife who left me and three daughters who judge my every move?" No matter what he said, Karen still called and left chiding messages. "Don't do it for me," she'd say. "But you know, you've got two grandchildren who might really love you if they saw you once in a while."

It was the familiarity of Karen's house—on the western edge of Essex county, in the heart of the Jersey suburbs—that troubled

Jamie most and kept her away. She suspected the same was true of her father. The house might have been a replica of the one they'd all lived in until Jamie was eight, when her parents decided they'd been living a life they didn't want—a two-story colonial on eastern Long Island, with a pair of bay windows, a swing set in the backyard, pine trees that dropped dozens of cones into the driveway. She remembered the pine cones best, especially the ten or so that Karen had once hurled at her in a fury over a borrowed pair of socks that went missing. The way Karen had decorated, too, was eerie, an updated imitation of the domestic aesthetic her mother had accepted without question early in her marriage and now openly scorned—paintings of sailboats and red barns, shadowy mirrors in gilded frames, silk flowers in colored glass vases, ceramic lamps etched with butterflies. The only difference here was the added Jewish flair, the prints of the Western Wall, the dozen menorahs of various design scattered throughout the house, the mirrors all now covered with bed sheets. There were two of them in the living room, ghostly shapes on the walls where the sisters now sat waiting for the first of the evening shiva visitors to arrive. This was the last night of it for Jamie, thank God—tomorrow they would take Andrea to the airport, and she would catch the Path back to the city, leaving Karen to sit the last four nights on her own.

Now Jamie was sunken into a couch whose cushions had been removed, fingering an antique mortar and pestle on the end table beside her, the one thing that came for certain directly from the Long Island house—she remembered a bitter argument after her father had once absentmindedly flicked his cigar ashes into the brass bowl instead of a nearby ashtray. She didn't know how Karen had ended up with it, and until now hadn't cared—but tonight it was comforting to hang onto something so familiar. On the floor, Andrea sat yoga-style, bending slowly forward until her forehead touched her feet. "You don't have to rub it in my face," Karen said. "I don't think I've even seen my toes in two years."

"If I don't do this my hips spasm all night, and I can't sleep," Andrea said.

"Some people are too busy to worry about their bodies all the time," Karen said.

"If you don't take care of yourself now, you'll regret it."

"I've got too many other people to take care of."

"Thanks," Andrea said. "Rub *that* in my face."

"That's not what I meant," Karen said.

"Sure. What did you mean, then?"

"I was just talking about myself."

"Well, you're not the only person in the room," Andrea said.

Jamie's apartment had her father's post-marriage décor, or at least as close to it as she could come without any money. Copper and stainless steel kitchen ware dangled from hooks above her stove. Her bed was a black futon she kept folded up during the day. No other furniture except a pile of floor pillows in front of her single, grimy window. The stark white walls she'd hung with her own meager imitations of Franz Kline paintings—she'd dipped a sponge mop in black paint and smeared it across heavy posterboard. Her father had had a real Kline, bought at auction that first whimsical year after the divorce, and now she wondered, with a good measure of shame, whom he'd left it to. Not her, she guessed, though she wouldn't know for sure until the will was read next week. The MoMA, probably. Dr. Walt had always felt guilty about owning it, such an important work on display for only his few visitors—but he'd never felt guilty enough to part with it while he was still alive. He justified keeping it by noting that most museums had too much work for their limited wall space, that whatever wasn't being shown collected dust in midtown basements or Queens warehouses. Jamie had made an effort to stare at the painting when she was a girl, not because it captured her imagination but because she knew how much it had cost. She was the only one of the three sisters who'd lived in the Murray Hill apartment for extended periods of time, the only one who didn't mind sleeping on the leather couch or ignoring the little hairs her father never bothered to rinse from the sink when he finished shaving. "You're the only one I'd want around here," he'd said more than once, though he'd offered the same invitation to both Karen and Andrea and hadn't hidden his hurt feelings when they'd turned him down. "You're the only one who understands that people have to have their quiet times once in a while." He took great pride in the apartment, the view onto Second Avenue, the way the wind whipped off the river and whistled around the building's stone cornices in winter. Most mornings he talked to her from the bathroom while he shaved, Jamie still slowly waking, peeling her cheek from the sticky leather where the sheet had pulled away. He told her how much he'd loved riding the subways in from Brooklyn as a kid, how he'd never once felt overwhelmed by all the noise and traffic and crowds of Manhattan. "And all the women," he said, winking at her in the mirror. "I've never minded all the beautiful women." He told her how stifled he'd felt during his years in the suburbs, how there was no other place in the world to live but this city.

She'd taken his words to heart, though sometimes it felt as if she were living in two different cities—the one where she worked, directing a ragtag group of recent college graduates and dropouts, most of them sober for fewer than six hours a day, through a circus of weddings and bar mitzvahs and corporate Christmas parties; and the other in her room above Elizabeth Street, the corner beside the kitchen with her miniature easel and her tiny paintings on scraps of scavenged plywood. Her father had had two of her pieces hanging in his living room, too small for the space and dwarfed by the Kline and a series of lithographs by one of his patients, who wasn't so much talented, she thought, as savvy and calculated, with his shocking close-ups of raw meat and the innards of fish. Maybe all of them would go to the MoMA, her paintings included—but even as she thought it she was disgusted with herself, even more ashamed than when she'd wondered if she'd get the Kline. Why couldn't she focus on the thing itself, the fact of her father at his dining table, a sleek black design from Sweden, with a built-in center vase—a steel tube he filled with utensils rather than flowers, a pair of tongs, a spaghetti spoon, an unused spatula—why couldn't she picture him there as he'd been most recently, slumped face down, the army-issued pistol they'd all forgotten he owned still gripped in one hand, blood pooling on the slate tile floor, no note, no hint of explanation in sight?

They were waiting for the doorbell, but the phone rang first. Their mother, Jamie knew, calling for the third time in as many days. She hadn't made it to the funeral, though she did send an enormous bouquet—pink peonies, giving off a stench her father would have hated. "I *am* sad," she'd said the first time she called. "But you know, he's been gone from my life a long time already." She lived in California now, a faux Frank Lloyd Wright bungalow with a flat roof and windows facing the ocean. It was far from her ideal—she'd talked for years about her dream of living in the mountains, near a lake, an approximation of her childhood summers in the Catskills, the happiest days of her life. Again she was married to a doctor, again living a life she didn't entirely want—but now she was sharing it with a man who, unlike Walter Lann, made her happy enough to go on living it with only the mildest regrets.

After the second ring, Karen was still struggling her way out of a deep armchair, which, without its cushions, nearly swallowed her. Andrea leapt up from the floor with a sudden limber movement, rocking from her rear onto her feet without using her hands. She ran to the phone in an almost cheerful way, kicking her heels up behind her, but then answered solemnly, "Wexler residence. Can I help you?" She tilted her neck slowly to one side and then the other. "Hi, Mom. Yeah, we're all here. Day number three. It's still surreal." Her face was sad but also somehow pleased and indulgent, as if all this sorrow brought with it a secret satisfaction. Jamie didn't doubt that Andrea was partly enjoying this, the same way she'd somehow enjoyed her miscarriages, her divorce, the drama and chaos that had consumed her during each. When wasn't there some upheaval in her life? Jamie couldn't remember her ever being at peace, not since high school when she had a new love or breakup every three weeks. All her yoga and acupuncture aside, she felt alive only in the midst of elation or tragedy—everyday, mundane emotions were death to her. "The thing I can't get a handle on is how we're supposed to *live* with something like this. It'll never go away, will it?" Yes, she was enjoying it—and this tragedy would get her a long way. She could carry it forward as long as she needed it, until the next chance for elation took over. "I know," she said. "I worry about her. She's too much like him. Everything bottled up. I'm trying to get her to let it out."

"She's talking about you," Karen said.

"I never would have guessed," Jamie said.

"I'll put her on," Andrea said. "The more of us who try, the better."

"I'm not here," Jamie said.

"Just don't tell her she should cry," Andrea said. "She almost bit my head off."

She brought the phone to Jamie and dropped it in her lap. For a moment Jamie let it lie there. Her mother's voice came through faintly, "Jamie? Sweetheart?"

"Be patient with her, Mom," Andrea called.

Karen said, "For crying out loud, pick it up already."

"Hi, Mom," Jamie said. Her voice had that scratchiness to it still, and a quiver she hadn't noticed before. "Don't listen to Andrea. I'm fine."

"Sweetheart, you don't have to be fine. You don't have to be anything you don't want to be. Don't cry if you don't want to. Don't talk to anyone."

"Thanks," Jamie said. "I won't."

"Do you want to come out here for a while? Stay with me and Jim? We won't bother you. You can sit on the beach all day. The bar down the street makes the best margarita I've ever had. A change of scenery might do you some good."

"I've got to get back to work tomorrow."

"They'll understand. They'll give you as much time as you need."

"It's the hotel business. They can't afford to wait around for people. It's just the way it works."

"Well, screw them!" her mother cried. "Quit. Who cares, anyway? It's not your dream job or anything."

"I've got to make a living," she said. "I'm not married to a doctor."

"Look," her mother said. Her voice had altered in an instant, all the compassion gone, a familiar hardness in its place. Soon she'd be incapable of sympathy—when she was angry, her mother couldn't hold any other feelings in her heart, not sadness, not pity, not regret, not even love. Right now, Jamie preferred her this way. "I know you feel terrible. I know this is awful, and you want to blame me for it."

"I never said anything about you," Jamie said.

"Well, goddamn it, I've been gone a long time. He didn't kill himself fifteen years ago."

"I don't think it's your fault," Jamie said. "Not at all."

"If you want to know the truth," her mother went on, hearing nothing. "If you ask me, I saved that man's life. For all the good it did me. He would have done this years ago. You think he wasn't a miserable bastard all the time I knew him? You know how many times I had to pull him out of that dark place he loved to dwell in? If it weren't for me he wouldn't have seen thirty."

"Karen wants you, Mom. I'll talk to you later." She didn't wait for an answer before passing the receiver on. Karen squeezed her arm as she took it, and all of Jamie's muscles clenched at once.

"Mom, calm down," Karen said. "No one's blaming you. Of course it isn't your fault. It isn't anybody's fault. The man was *sick*. If anybody should have seen it coming, it's me. *I'm* the one who saw him every week."

AS FAR AS JAMIE KNEW, SHE WAS THE LAST PERSON TO see her father alive. Or at least the last who knew him—her neighborhood wasn't often quiet, and certainly not at 3 a.m. on Sunday morning. Who knows how many indifferent people he passed on the street and in the subway station, how many people looked him in the face without seeing someone who would soon be dead. His building's doorman told the police he hadn't seen Dr. Lann that night—he must have come in through the garage, on Third Avenue. No one saw him again until Monday at noon. He didn't show up for three morning appointments, didn't answer his phone, so his partner, Dr. Koniff, sent a receptionist around at lunchtime. The poor woman still hadn't recovered, Jamie had overheard at the funeral. The building manager had opened the front door for her and followed her in tentatively, letting her come upon the terrible scene and scream her throat raw for two straight minutes without even attempting to comfort her or pull her away. Jamie, thank God, had been at work by the time the police finished their business and started making calls. It was Karen they found first, Karen who had to call Will and drop off the kids at a neighbor's, who had to come into the city and identify the body. Jamie felt for her, truly, having to live with that image forever.

But she had an image, too, that would never leave her. Her father's face, at the door of her apartment in the middle of the night, the familiar sardonic smirk on the same side of his mouth where he stuck enormous Honduran cigars after work every evening, his bald, bullet-shaped head red from drink and glowing from the glare of the hallway's fluorescent lights. He hadn't knocked loudly, but she was up from bed, peeking through the spyhole while his fist was still raised. She hadn't fallen asleep yet, and the door was thin—but also, she'd been half-expecting to hear his knock since the last time he'd shown up this way, a month earlier, unannounced, half an hour after she'd come home from work. She'd been alone that night and had opened the door for him after snatching a robe from a nearby stool. He weaved into the room, knocking against a counter before finally dropping onto the pile of floor pillows, legs sprawled, feet splayed.

But even this wasn't entirely unprecedented. Jamie guessed he'd broken up with another girlfriend—she could count at least two dozen since he and her mother had split, and probably as many that she didn't know about. Sometimes he called her after a fight, desperate to tell his side of the story, to explain how this woman, too, had gotten him all wrong. The first time she'd still been in college, and as he revealed intimate details of his life—"I just wanted to sleep," he'd said. "But she had to have her goddamn leg draped over me all night"—she'd felt both titillated and disgusted, and hung up without saying much more than, "Don't worry, Dad. You'll find someone else." Afterward she joked with her roommate about *Electra*, which they'd both recently read in Western Civ., but her roommate's laughter was nervous and forced. Since then she'd gotten used to hearing more about Dr. Walt's life than she wanted to know, not only about his current romances, but also about his marriage to Jamie's mother—how she'd withheld sex to punish him, how he'd been convinced she was having an affair while he was in Vietnam. Once she'd asked if he didn't have anyone else in his life to talk to, and his first reaction had been anger and defensiveness. "What," he snapped. "You think I'm some pathetic old man, I don't have any friends?" Then, after he'd calmed himself, he said, "You're the only one who really understands me. You always have. Remember, when you used to stay with me and I talked to you about everything?" She didn't believe what he said and didn't think he believed it, either. She didn't understand him at all, though she'd been trying hard since she was a little girl. She didn't know what he wanted in life, or what made him happy. She knew that he loved her, but didn't know what he loved, exactly, or why. Didn't he realize how confused she'd been as a ten-year-old, watching him in the mirror as he shaved, pulling his nose up so the razor could slide beneath it, wondering what went on inside that pointy head beneath the already thinning hair?

So his showing up on her doorstep in the middle of the night seemed like a natural next progression, even if it did surprise her.

What she didn't expect was the way he stared at her, judgmentally, scrutinizing, even as he sprawled on the floor pillows. She thought again of *Electra* and her college roommate's nervous laughter, but that felt less than honest—his expression wasn't sexual so much as severely parental, in a way she didn't remember seeing since they'd all left the Long Island house. She was suddenly embarrassed by the coffee cups littering the sink, the dust on top of the microwave—as much as she tried to live like him, she could achieve no more than a poor approximation, no better than the imitation Klines. Instead of talking about a girlfriend—if he had one at the moment, Jamie hadn't heard about her—he said, "I worry about you." His voice was hoarse, his words slurred. "I haven't been keeping close enough tabs on you."

"What's to worry about?" she said. "I'm fine. And who says I need anyone keeping tabs on me. I'm twenty-seven years old."

"You're a fucking kid," he said. "You will be until you're fifty. Just like me."

"Oh, so you're not a kid anymore?"

"Finally," he said sadly.

"Well, I'm telling you I'm fine. There's nothing to worry about."

"That's for me to decide."

"You want a drink or something?"

"I want to look at the merchandise," he said, pulling himself up from the floor with difficulty, nearly losing his balance when he straightened to full height. He staggered to her easel. There were only two paintings finished, still propped against the wall to dry, though they'd dried two weeks ago, and two others barely started, nothing terribly inspired. "What are these, flowers?" he said, with a good measure of disgust.

"Of course they're not flowers. They're abstractions."

"Flowers. Jesus. You wouldn't know abstractions from iconography."

"Since when did doctors know anything about abstraction?" she said. "Just because you can buy a painting doesn't mean you can make one. Or tell anyone else how to."

He ignored her. "Now this one," he said, picking up the smallest piece of wood, a ragged square the size of his palm. "Here's something interesting."

It wasn't much more than a sketch, something she'd done in a moment of boredom, sitting in her underwear, staring down at her crotch. That's all it was, the two white lines of her panties meeting the black line between her legs. There was nothing interesting about it, nothing even erotic, though it was sex she'd been thinking about when she'd made it. She'd planned to paint over it as soon as she picked up her brushes again, which hadn't happened for more than a week. But her father held it up now, examining it in the light from a hooded reading lamp. "Clean lines," he said. "Fresh perspective."

"It's not finished," Jamie said.

"That's your problem. You always overdo things. Let well enough alone." He carried it with him back to the window and flopped down onto the pillows again. "You need more guidance," he said. "I'm sorry I've been slack on the job." He laid his head down and closed his eyes. They didn't open again. In five minutes he was breathing heavily, the painting hugged to his chest—but in the morning it was back on the easel, as lifeless and unfinished as she'd originally believed. Her father was already leaning against the kitchen counter when she woke, a steaming mug in his hand. His scalp was pale and wrinkled above the eyebrows. "I know you don't make much money, but you've got to be able to afford better coffee than this."

"I took it from the hotel," she said. "None of our guests ever complain about it."

"That's because people are used to getting rooked when they travel."

"Well, next time you decide to invite yourself over, bring your own goddamn grounds."

His smile was back, a little sheepish now. "Yeah," he said. "Sorry. I was in a state. I guess you know that. Did I start talking about your mother again?"

"Not this time."

"Good. Maybe I've finally gotten that woman out from under my skin." He had an unlit cigar in his mouth when he was ready to leave, and it bounced as he spoke. "Sorry again," he said. "That's what you get for living in the city, I guess. Your crazy old dad showing up in the middle of the night. It won't happen again, I promise. No, I shouldn't promise. But I don't think it will."

And now here he was, a month later. This time she wasn't alone. There was a man in her bed, naked, asleep. Could she call him a man? A twenty-two-year-old with thick shoulders and a flat stomach, one of her weekend bartenders. It wasn't the first time he'd come home with her, but the first time in a couple of weeks. She could have him any night she wanted—what twenty-two-year-old wouldn't jump at the chance to sleep with the boss—but she made sure never to let him get too comfortable or expectant. At most once a week she put her hand on his hip during a shift, let her breasts brush against his arm, asked him if he wanted to share a cab. She usually waited until the night before her day off, so she could fuck him silly for twenty-four hours before sending him on his way. It not only made going to the hotel bearable, but filled her need for companionship well enough that she could spend the rest of her free time painting. At least this was how things were supposed to work—but she hadn't made a singe stroke since the last time her father had shown up.

The bartender, Rory, had been asleep fewer than ten minutes, but the knocking didn't wake him. His mouth was open, his lips squashed against the pillow. The dimple on his chin was folded into a full crease. He didn't move at all when Jamie slipped out of bed. She grabbed her robe again, this time in a heap on the floor. There were even more coffee mugs in the sink than last time. She opened the door a crack and said, "It's a mess in here. You can't come in."

Her father had that stern, paternal expression again, but his eyes were swimming, his face puffy. His breath was sour and sharp—he'd been drinking something Jamie stayed clear of, vodka, maybe, or tequila. "I came for my painting," he said. "I forgot to take it last time."

"I thought you weren't going to do this again."

He pulled a roll of bills from his shirt pocket and held it too close to her face. "I'm your patron," he said. "I've come for my commission."

He tried to push past her, but she held her ground. "I'll get it for you."

His eyes widened. "Oh," he said. "I see. You've got someone in there. Good for you."

"He's asleep," Jamie said.

"I want to meet him."

"It's almost three in the morning."

"I let you meet my girlfriends," he said. Then he added, "Some of them."

"Not very many," she said.

"I want to know if he's good enough for you."

"Dad."

"It's not a girl, is it? You're not munching rugs in there, are you?"

She set her feet and her jaw. "You're not coming in."

"Okay," he said. "Okay. I won't wake him. Just let me come get my painting."

"I'll bring it to you," she said again.

She started to close the door, and as she did his face contorted, reddening even more, his one visible eye bugging. "Let me in," he whispered, and put a foot against the door.

"I'll be right back," she said. Behind his drunkenness was some kind of pain, she saw it clearly—or at least remembered seeing it now, if she hadn't recognized it at the time—but she didn't let up her pressure on the door. After a moment his foot retreated. He backed all the way off then, leaning against the hallway's opposite wall. Sweat stood out on his forehead, but his desperate expression was gone—the sardonic smirk had suddenly returned, as if all of his insistence had been an act, a test, his expectations confirmed. When the door latch clicked, Jamie let out a long, stuttering breath she hadn't even been aware of holding in. She hurried across the room, grabbed the painting from the easel, nearly tripped over Rory's jeans on her way back. Rory stirred but didn't wake. She opened the door onto an empty hallway, the fluorescent bulbs buzzing faintly, the grimy wall where her father had been leaning hazy and far away. She felt more anger than guilt, furious that she should feel any guilt at all. This time she slammed the door closed, and Rory rolled over, blinking. "You feel like having another go?" he asked, and she went to him, dropping the robe on the way.

EVERY NIGHT THE GROUP OF VISITORS CHANGED. THE evening after the funeral the house had been crammed with relatives Jamie hardly knew, people who asked if she was still painting and then said how lovely it was to have an artist in the family, though none, she was sure, had ever seen her work. Two old women spoke only Russian and Yiddish and looked offended when Jamie didn't understand them. Last night it was her father's colleagues and army buddies, two of whom she'd overheard whispering about the pistol her father had used—they couldn't imagine trusting a rickety old piece like that with something so important. "If you're going to do it, you better do it right," one said. The other shrugged and said, "I guess it worked right enough."

Only one person showed up all three nights—Aunt Diane, their father's sister, who rang the doorbell twice, and then waiting no more than five seconds, rang again. Again Karen tried to rock herself to her feet, without any luck. Andrea was reluctant this time, but since Jamie didn't make a move, she pulled herself up from the floor with effort and went to the door. She was a full head taller than Aunt Diane but seemed suddenly diminished in the older woman's presence, dwarfed by the frantic energy, the mass of hair, the solemn, breathy way Aunt Diane said, "Hi, dear. This doesn't get any easier, does it."

Aunt Diane had shown up at the same time each night, carrying a box from a wholesale bakery on the highway between Karen's house and her apartment in Montclair. Danishes, coffee cake, éclairs. It didn't matter that Karen reminded her each time, "We can't have those in here." Aunt Diane only huffed and said, "Not with that kosher nonsense again. This cost me six-fifty." Now she shoved a white box into Andrea's hands and said, "Brioche." Then she pulled Andrea's face down to hers, kissed her on both cheeks, and left finger marks on her jaw. Aunt Diane was six years older than their father and shared his square chin, his black eyes that had always seemed too close to the surface of his face— though now Aunt Diane's chin was tucked down toward her chest by the beginning of a hump in her spine, and her eyes were hidden behind bifocals, the split in the lenses cutting straight across her pupils. She and their father had never gotten along, had avoided seeing each other more than once a year though they lived only twenty miles apart. "That woman," Jamie had often heard her father say. "I don't see how we could have come from the same womb." Now Aunt Diane claimed him as her lost baby brother, claimed them all as the family she was obliged to take care of, since she didn't have one of her own.

She came into the room in a flurry, flinging her purse and coat ahead of her onto the couch before dropping heavily next to Jamie. "Couldn't you put at least one cushion back?" she said. "These springs aren't good for an old lady's butt."

Karen was studying her hands. "You know, Aunt Diane," she said. "I really meant it when I said I didn't want you to bring anymore—"

"You're not going to throw out perfectly good brioche, are you? You know how much it cost me?"

"Will isn't happy about it."

"He doesn't have to eat any," Aunt Diane said. "God knows, he doesn't need any."

"I'll put them on a paper plate," Andrea said, carrying the box into the kitchen.

"That's right," Aunt Diane said. "You wouldn't want to ruin the china with fine French baking."

"If you can't respect the rules of the house—" Karen began.

"I'd have the sitting at my place, only it's not big enough," Aunt Diane said. "Some people's husbands aren't patent lawyers." Andrea came back with a paper plate piled with pastries and set it on the coffee table. "Some of us don't have husbands at all. Some of us do just fine without them, isn't that right?"

Andrea straightened and ran her hands down her narrow hips but didn't say a word. Karen said, "Napkins."

"What, you're not going to cut them?" Aunt Diane said.

"Plastic knife," Karen said.

"Got it," Andrea said.

Aunt Diane huffed again, gathered the loose frizz of her hair in one fist, and held it for a moment against the back of her neck. "That's right," she said, and then released the hair, which sprung violently in front of her eyes. "No goy flour on your cutlery."

Jamie had felt herself sinking into the couch for minutes now, the springs tightening beneath her, her pulse beating fiercely in her ears, her veins, it seemed, straining against her skin. She still had her hand on the mortar and pestle and now drummed the brass knob softly against the inside of the bowl. Aunt Diane followed the sound and waved a hand in its direction. "That's really mine, you know."

"What do you mean, yours?" Karen said.

"You can keep it," Aunt Diane said. "But it's mine."

"Dad gave it to me."

"Well, it wasn't his to give. My grandmother left it to me. But I don't care. You can have it."

"It's mine," Karen said firmly.

Jamie suffered a terrible moment then—she was suddenly certain it was Aunt Diane who would inherit the Kline. Wouldn't it be just like her father to leave his most precious possession to the person who deserved it least? Wasn't it just like Jamie, too? The morning after her father had come to claim it—the morning

he'd carefully cleaned his pistol, loaded it, and unloaded it into
his skull—she'd given the unfinished painting of her crotch to
Rory, the bartender, the man—no, the boy—she slept with every
week or so. A boy, that was the only word for him—he talked like a
boy, dressed like a boy, fucked like a boy, and clung to her at night
with a boy's sense of propriety. She'd given the painting without
thinking, or thinking only vaguely of getting back at her father
for knocking on her door in the middle of the night. Rory was still
naked, padding around her studio in his bare feet, twice sloshing
coffee onto the floor, once onto his long, hairy toes. He paused in
front of the easel and glanced at the painting only casually.
"You like it?" Jamie asked, admiring the way his shoulder blades
moved beneath his skin when he shrugged. "If you want it, it's
yours." He shrugged again, tipped his head in thanks, and picked
it up in his free hand. He held it a moment, looking for a place
to put it down, and then propped it back on the easel. Later, when
he was dressed and heading for the door, he shoved it into
the back pocket of his baggy jeans, where it fit, barely, bulging
the seams and, she guessed, splintering the edges of the wood.
At the time she thought she'd tell her father she'd painted over it,
that she was planning to make him something better, as soon as
she had time to concentrate and get some work done.

She didn't deserve the Kline any more than Aunt Diane did.
She took her hand away from the brass it had warmed and made
sticky with sweat and buried it in her lap. Aunt Diane turned to her
then. "You know, you don't have to keep quiet all the time. You
can say something every once in a while." Andrea stopped cold
in the doorway, a stack of napkins in one hand, two plastic knives
in the other. Karen suddenly found her strength and pulled
herself to her feet. She took the knives from Andrea and started
cutting furiously into a brioche, not worrying that flakes fluttered
off the edge of the plate onto the coffee table, some even onto the
carpet. Aunt Diane went on, "This isn't about you, you know.
Your dad's dead, remember? He shot himself, and now he's dead."

Jamie was as far from hungry as she could have been, but

she reached for a brioche anyway, a whole one, and stuck the end in her mouth. She chewed slowly, letting the flakes dissolve against her tongue, knowing how hard it would be to swallow.

IN AN HOUR THE HOUSE WAS FULL. TONIGHT THERE WERE Karen's co-workers and Will's partners and people from their synagogue, all of whom mumbled condolences and then sipped wine from paper cups, discussing work and exchanging gossip. The brioche was gone. Any remaining crumbs on the carpet had been ground underfoot. Jamie caught a woman lifting the edge of a sheet from one of the mirrors to check her make-up. Will himself was downstairs now, in a specially tailored suit that seemed designed to show off his full enormity, lumbering from room to room with more cups and more wine. The tubby kids were in a corner, stuffed into their dress clothes, coloring with crayons and nibbling cookies. Andrea was with them, trying to prove what a good mother she'd make, Jamie guessed, telling a story, making exaggerated faces, stomping her feet. Noah, the two-year-old, gazed around in boredom, and four-year-old Ariel looked terrified and on the verge of tears. Aunt Diane had cornered a young lawyer in front of the fireplace, wagging a finger in his face. Karen, the queen of the evening, sat in her armchair again, with women crouched on either side of her, patting her arms, nodding as she repeated, "The man was sick. I should have known it. I should have seen it coming."

Jamie had given up her seat on the couch and was standing close to the door when there came a tentative knocking, not on the door itself but on the window pane beside it, a softly insistent tapping, all knuckle. She had no excuse not to open it. The woman on the stoop was her age, maybe a year or two younger. Her skin was darker than Jamie's and pinker, her hair only slightly longer and just as black. Her dress was similar, too, cut low enough for a cocktail party, only it was wool, and a sheen of sweat covered the woman's neck and the exposed triangle of her chest. Her black clogs didn't quite match the black of her tights. "Is this—" she started, her voice high and quivering, and then taking in the room, the shaded mirrors, all the people in dark clothes, she finished for herself. "I guess it is." Jamie knew who she was almost instantly, without her saying a word. Her nose was the small, goyish kind her father had come to like, her lips thin like Jamie's mother's. Her hands were too large at the end of dainty wrists, the fingers red, nails unpainted and bitten down to the cuticles. "Can you tell me—which are Dr. Walt's daughters?" she asked. "I was—a patient of his. I just want—"

"Over there," Jamie said, pointing to Karen. "And there, with the kids."

"Aren't there three?"

Why should the woman have recognized her? Why should she be so disappointed—no, not disappointed, heartbroken—that she hadn't? "The other's not here, yet," she said. "She's on her way, I heard." If the woman had been her father's lover for long, surely she would have seen family photos in his apartment. Surely her father would have spoken of Jamie, would have described her, his favorite daughter, the only one who even attempted to understand him. Surely there was still some resemblance between them, enough for the woman to acknowledge, though her chin was finer, her skin paler, her eyes deeper set. Surely whatever grief showed in her face was more profound than that of a distant relative, a friend, even another lover. "I'm waiting for her, too."

She watched the woman approach Karen haltingly, her clogs moving two steps forward and then one to the side. In the end she came around the back of Karen's chair and leaned forward, holding the neck of her dress closed, though her chest was relatively flat. Her free hand hovered above Karen's shoulder, not touching, the ragged fingernails raking air. Jamie came close enough to hear the trembling voice. "I can't tell you how sorry I am," she said. "I can't— I don't know what else to say."

Karen craned her neck around and blinked a few times, trying to place her. She seemed annoyed for a moment to see someone she didn't know. But sympathy was sympathy, wherever it came from—she nodded, and her eyes welled up. "You don't have to say anything else," she said. "This is the hardest thing any of us have ever had to do."

"Dr. Walt," the woman said. "He meant— He was—"

"I couldn't have done anything," Karen said. "Even if I'd wanted to."

"He was very good to me," the woman said.

Andrea turned her back on the kids when the woman introduced herself, took one of her oversized hands in both of hers, and said, "It's so good of you to come all this way."

"I've been going to see Dr. Walt for years." Her name was Gwen, she said. She had a heart murmur. Everything about her was familiar, her sad smile, her narrow hips, her bad posture, even her name. There had been another Gwen, ten years ago, maybe, when Jamie was still in high school. That Gwen had been the same age as this one, with the same nose and lips. "If it weren't for him, I don't know where I'd be now."

"We're all going to miss him," Andrea said. "I wish I'd lived closer. I wish I could have spent more time with him." Then, as if she couldn't help herself, she added, "He was such a hard person to be around sometimes."

Aunt Diane accosted Gwen behind the couch, told her how she'd helped raise Walter, how she was like a second mother to him, how she knew him better than anyone else in the world. What he'd done, she said, unfortunately hadn't surprised her at all. "He was always such a selfish person," she said.

"He never mentioned he had a sister," Gwen said.

"Why should he?" Aunt Diane adjusted her glasses, peering first through the upper half of her bifocals and then the lower. "Since when do doctors talk about their families in the office? I'm sure he was busy examining your chest."

Soon Gwen was by herself, lingering near the kitchen, watching the front door. Jamie followed. She could still smell the remains of dinner drifting from the trash can under the sink, the tangy ginger sauce that brought her back to the edge of nausea.

She swallowed hard and said, "He told you you were different, I bet. And I bet you believed him."

Gwen pulled at her wool sleeves and scratched her neckline. Then she didn't seem to know what to do with her hands; they hung awkwardly at her sides for a moment and ended up grasping her bony elbows, forearms hugging her belly. She could have been one of Jamie's co-workers, a fellow supervisor at the hotel, or one of her college friends. Her earrings were cheap silver teardrops, her chapped fingers free of rings. She would have been as out of place in her father's apartment as Jamie had been, as intimidated by the Kline. "You said she was coming soon? There's a cab waiting for me. I can't stay long."

"So where'd he find you? Working at an art gallery? The coffee shop at the MoMA?"

"I really was his patient," Gwen said.

"You don't have to lie to me," Jamie said. "I know who you are."

"Really," she said. "I've had a heart murmur since I was in high school. My aunt sent me to him when I moved to the city."

"So that's where he was finding them now. Not even bothering to leave the office."

"I guess I know who you are, too," Gwen said. "I know all about it. Dr. Walt and his girls. I heard about plenty of them." Her voice lowered and so did her eyes. "And yes, he told me I was different. And yes, I believed him. Didn't you?"

She hadn't planned this, pretending to be something she wasn't—but she fell into the role so easily, the rival, the former lover, and she couldn't help recalling her college roommate's giggling after that first drunken phone call from her father, and the shame it brought. "You weren't at the funeral."

"I wasn't—well," Gwen said. "It's been so hard."

"Not just for you," Jamie said.

"I was the last one to see him."

"I don't think so."

Gwen nodded and went on as if she'd heard wrong, finding encouragement instead of warning in Jamie's voice. "That morning.

I was there, in the apartment." She didn't raise her eyes. They'd had a terrible night, she said. He ended things. Again. For maybe the third or fourth time. Jamie could see the white scalp through a part in Gwen's hair, and against her will, pictured her father's stubby finger tracing the line from forehead to neck. Gwen's own fingers were picking at loose fibers on her sleeves, and Jamie recalled the strange elation she'd felt earlier as she'd stripped the thread from Karen's tablecloth. "Whenever he wanted to break up he called me 'kid.' 'You're a great kid,' he'd say, and I knew what was coming. Usually I'd get hysterical and make him feel guilty. One more notch on Dr. Walt's belt, I'd say. And then he'd take me back. I thought it would be the same—I'd go home and he'd call by noon to tell me he was sorry. I didn't hear from him all day. He was so drunk, I thought maybe he'd slept in. *I* was the one who'd threatened to take all my pills. But I never would have done it. Never."

She shook her head but still didn't look up at Jamie, who'd stepped away now and leaned against the kitchen doorframe. The smell of ginger chicken was too strong—she had to breathe through her mouth, and even then it seemed to coat her tongue. Andrea had returned to entertaining Karen's kids, all three of them sitting cross-legged on the floor, running their crayons over colored construction paper. Karen whispered to a woman whose body matched hers, narrow at the top, bulging in the middle. Aunt Diane watched Will filling her cup with wine, giving little waves of encouragement as he tilted the bottle, and then held her thumb in the air. Jamie's father had taken her to dinner with that other Gwen ten years ago, in a filthy downtown Thai restaurant that had smelled of seafood beginning to turn. She was a sculptor, struggling, living in some East Village hovel. The whole time her father kept winking at Jamie and touching Gwen wherever her skin was bare—her shoulder, the back of her neck, her earlobe, and under the table, her thigh. Jamie ate three bites of a red curry that singed her lips and throat, and then took the train alone to her mother's, feeling aroused and humiliated and close to despair.

"When did he do it?" this new Gwen asked. "An hour after

I left? Fifteen minutes? Why couldn't he have waited a few days? A week? Why couldn't he have been with someone else first?"

"It's not your fault," Jamie said faintly. She said it mostly because she didn't believe what Gwen was saying. She couldn't have been the one to see him last. Not when Jamie was stuck with the image of her father at her door, his eye straining as she shut him out of her life. That had to be the last thing, the thing that sent him over. How much could she have meant to him if this woman—this girl—had caused him to pull the trigger? "He was sick," she said, and then shook her head. "He was troubled."

"It *isn't* my fault," Gwen insisted, as if she'd heard wrong again. She faced Jamie then, her eyes red, her mascara clumping and beginning to run. "*He* was the one who broke up with *me*."

Her voice had grown loud enough for Andrea to glance up from her drawing, for Aunt Diane to adjust her glasses and glare at them. Jamie said quietly, "He wasn't with you the whole night."

"How do you know?" Gwen asked.

"He came to see me," Jamie said.

"That's not true."

"About three in the morning."

"I don't believe you."

"I sent him away. I told him to go back to you."

"He stormed out," Gwen said. She was crying openly now, wiping her eyes with the heels of her big red hands. "To get drunk. That's what he always did. When he came back he said he'd gone to his daughter's. He wanted to give me something to remember him. A painting of hers. I'd always loved the ones in his apartment. He said there was another I'd like even more. He kept calling me 'kid.' Do you know how awful that is?"

"We killed him," Jamie said, without guilt, or anger, or even accusation. As soon as the words were out, she knew there was no truth to them. But they didn't bring any relief, only more sorrow, more pain. The well was bottomless.

Gwen's hands were at her throat. "He was troubled. You said so."

"It wasn't much of a painting. You wouldn't have wanted it."

A shudder of recognition, and the last of Gwen's compo-
sure crumbled. "Oh God, you're— I should have—" She reached
out a hand and this time managed to touch Jamie, two rough
fingers on her wrist. "Oh God, I'm so sorry. I can't tell you—" And
then she was heading for the door, a hand over her eyes. The
room had gone silent. Everyone was watching Jamie. She didn't
care about the lawyers, Karen's co-workers, the strangers who
could judge her all they wanted. But she hoped to find understanding in her sisters' expressions, though even on Andrea's face all
she saw was confusion and concern. Wasn't this what they'd asked
for? Didn't they want to see tears streaming down her cheeks, all
of her feelings on display? Ariel started to cry, and Noah quickly
joined in. Karen whispered something to the woman crouching
beside her. "The artist in the family," Jamie guessed, though it
wasn't true—she was the waitress of the family, nothing more, a
waitress in charge of other waitresses. Andrea said, "That's it,
sweetheart, let it out," but her voice was uncertain, and she didn't
come any closer. It was Aunt Diane who came at her, arms outstretched, fingers clawed with arthritis.

The front door was still open where Gwen had flung it wide.
Through it Jamie saw her, cutting across the lawn. And then she
was hurrying after her, snatching the mortar and pestle from the
end table on the way. "Hey," Karen called. "That's mine."

"No it's not," Aunt Diane said. "Not really. But I don't care."

"Just let her go," Andrea said.

The hardest part wasn't picturing her father slumped over
the kitchen table with the gun in his hand, or even picturing him
pulling the trigger—it was imagining him the moment before,
when the pistol was oiled and ready, when he believed himself so
lonely and lost that nothing, no one, could help him. How could
he have gotten to such a point? How could anyone? The real trouble
was she *could* imagine it, all too easily—for her father, for her
mother, for her sisters, for herself. Just one moment, that's all it
would take—one moment of utter desolation, absolutely

terrifying, no matter how fleeting. The air outside was warmer than she'd expected, and she felt sweat spring to her skin, replacing whatever had spilled from her eyes. Here the grass was covered with acorns instead of pine cones, and they crunched under her sandals as she ran. Gwen was across the street now, climbing into the waiting cab, her dress, too short already, riding high on her thighs. She couldn't have the painting, but she would have something else to take home, whether she wanted it or not. Behind, Karen cried, "Bring it back! It's mine!"

Return

SINCE THEIR FIRST DAYS TOGETHER, THOMAS HAD TALKED of bringing Audrey to Scotland, where he'd spent eight months in his early twenties, bartending, hitchhiking, trudging through sopping bogs and scrambling over wind-scarred ridges. Now half a year had passed, and except to go to work, they'd barely left her three-room bungalow, barely even left the disheveled bedroom facing a neighbor's overcrowded English garden, a tangle of bright colors and cloying smells that blurred in his mind with the tangle of their bodies and the heavy scent of their mixed sweat.

They'd taken the time to get to know each other, to immerse themselves in one another's presence. They could talk for hours, forgetting food, sleep, sometimes even sex. Why should they go anywhere? They made a conscious effort to be honest, to open themselves completely, to reveal everything. He told her stories, mostly about his college days and the few years following, when he'd taken extreme measures to avoid becoming serious about anything, not his education or his career goals, not his family or his future. He told her about his travels, his bizarre assortment of short-term occupations, his difficulties with various substances, his descent into the often amusing but sometimes dangerous underworld of college towns, Bloomington, Madison, Ann Arbor. Sometimes when he recalled a run-in with police or described a sleepless, speed-charged night in a Polish train station, she'd lean away and gaze at him with an expression half suspicious and half amazed. "I don't believe it," she'd say. "That doesn't sound like you at all." Other times she'd shake her head and pull the sheet to her neck. "God. I've never done anything. I've never gone anywhere."

At thirty she was still girlish, fresh-faced, with high cheek-bones and an open-hearted smile that seemed incapable of masking any hurt. Even upset or angry she looked pouty and inno-cent as a child. But she wore flashy, revealing clothes bought in vintage stores—short velvety skirts, shiny synthetic blouses whose buttons started halfway down her chest, thick-soled ankle boots whose pitch seemed to thrust her forward into the world— that somehow, when they were dressed at all, complemented his drab outfits, all black or shades of gray. Her own stories were of relationships, one after another since she was seventeen, more than a dozen men and several women, terrible fights and break-ups, lengthy depressions, unanswered letters, phone calls in the middle of the night, awkward, fumbling attempts to recapture lost passions. "You've been so adventurous," she said. "I've played everything so safe."

Safe wasn't the word that came to mind while he listened to her describe numerous flirtations, the thrill of a first touch, the rustle of clothes flung onto dusty floors, strangers' bodies quickly becoming familiar, sliding over hers in this bed and others all over town. He listened with a measure of excitement tempered by a sickening feeling somewhere between jealousy and dread. The same mixture came over him when he caught other men's eyes on her in public—the pride he felt with her arm around his waist always undermined by knowing it had been around so many others. He'd slept with only a handful of women before Audrey— he could, in fact, count them on one hand, with a finger to spare— and the thought of any of them brought on such agitation and overwhelming regret that he had to distract himself by turning on the TV or playing a favorite album. He didn't tell her any of this, instead reassuring her: "Don't worry. You'll get your fill of advent-ure. I haven't given it all up yet."

On their six-month anniversary, he surprised her with a

pair of plane tickets to Edinburgh. It would be their first trip together, not counting an attempt at camping on the beach for Audrey's birthday—two hours in a steaming tent, sweatshirts pressed over their ears to block out the raucous laughter of teenagers drinking around an enormous, threatening bonfire, and then the silent drive home along black, winding roads. Now she scanned the dates on the itinerary and asked hopefully, "Will we be there for the Festival?"

"Festival's overrated," he said. "Tourists everywhere. All the hotels jack up their prices. It'll be quieter when we're there."

She tried to hide her disappointment, but he saw it plainly in her strained smile, her distracted flipping through the guidebook she bought one day on her way home from work. He could guess at her idea of traveling—checking off a list of attractions, wasting rolls of film on stained glass windows, men in kilts, long-haired cattle. On the plane she read to him about sights he'd never seen or didn't remember. Even then she was dressed in a tight-fitting satin blouse, a skirt that bunched under her thighs, the clunky ankle boots wedged beneath the seat in front of her, and he was momentarily irritated by her naïveté—how could she not anticipate the need for comfort on the long flight? *"After decades of deterioration and neglect,"* she read from the guidebook, *"the Royal Mile has once again become the vibrant heart of the modern city."* Her excitement made him ashamed of his irritation, and he put a hand on her bare knee.

He wanted to make her happy, so he let her spend the first two days of the trip staring in wonder at the narrow alleyways, the blackened churches, the cobbled streets and solemn cemeteries. She snapped dozens of pictures of the castle, of St. Giles, of Holyrood Palace and Arthur's Seat. She dragged him through John Knox' House, the National Gallery, the Museum of Antiquities. But he also wanted to show her the real city, the one he'd come to know so well. He pointed out his former flat, the two-hundred-year-old building with its original stone steps now nearly worn away, the single-paned windows that barely cut the wind whipping down Rose Street, behind which he'd huddled in a thermal sleeping bag and all his clothes and still couldn't keep his teeth from chattering. He showed her the back entrance to the North Bridge Hotel, where he'd had his first job scrubbing pots and pans, hosing down the broth vats that bubbled all day with bones and gristle, so much fat spilling onto the floor it clogged the treads of his boots and made him slide backward into a rack of canned tomatoes, nearly splitting his skull.

Then the myriad of pubs and nightclubs—the Queen's Crescent, the Vault, Whistler's. He would have taken her to every one that first night, but after the second pint her eyes began to glaze, and she stifled a yawn. When he offered to take her back to their room, she shook her head and forced a smile. "Of course not," she said. "I want to stay up all night." They got up to dance, though the floor was only sparsely occupied, the real dance crowd not showing up until midnight or later. Audrey moved too fast for the languid, spacey rhythm, her arms chugging like a jogger's. It was the first time they'd danced together, and their bodies collided more than once. In order to find the beat and stay with it, Thomas had to close his eyes on her awkward bobbing, her bright smile flashing in the blue and green strobe. When the song ended she yawned again, and again he suggested heading back to their room. This time she asked, "Are you sure you won't be disappointed?" and when he told her of course he wouldn't, she said, "You're so good to me." A familiar feeling came over him as they made their way to the street, the apprehension that had always crept up at the end of a long night hunched over those same tables sticky with spilled beer, eyes scratchy from smoke and strained by the dim light, when his friends had all disappeared and the girl he was after had gone off with some other guy—when he knew he'd have to trudge alone back to his dark, freezing room, wrap himself in two woolen coats, and lie awake listening to the wind hissing through the closed, useless drapes.

The next day he tried to find those friends, the people he'd bought drinks for, the ones he'd stayed out with all night, sometimes for several nights on end. There were the two Valeries, one from Paris, the other from Lyon; the Roman, Carlo, masquerading as a university student to avoid his mandatory army service; Roger, who sold them all hash and speed and descended into depression when the mad cow panic cleared shops of the ground beef he ate for every meal; Traci, who worked in a candy factory during the day, boxing bon-bons in a white apron and hair net, and then danced till dawn in hip-length boots and see-through blouses. None of them now lived where he'd last seen them. Why would they? He'd moved on to a more comfortable life, quiet, stable, almost boring, and they'd all probably done the same. But to Audrey he said, "I hope they're all still alive. Sometimes I think I got off easy."

"What do you mean?" Audrey said.

"It was a wild time, you know? A lot of bad things could have happened. Should have happened, maybe. I was lucky."

She turned away, facing the narrow alley where Roger had made his deals, where Thomas had once kissed Traci and tried, unsuccessfully, to convince her to spend the night. The alley was now piled with cardboard boxes half-rotted from a previous day's rain. Audrey's blood-red sweater, her light hair and clear skin stood out strangely against the sooty stone blocks. "You miss it, don't you," she said.

"Sometimes."

"You're bored with me." He heard the catch in her throat and knew he'd said the worst thing possible. "I'm too dull for you."

"That's not what I meant at all," he said.

"You wish I'd stay out and dance all night."

"No," he said. "I'm finished with all that." He put an arm around her, drew her away from the alley toward a busy avenue roaring with buses and taxis. He remembered the flashing lights, the sweating bodies, the excited charge that began each night, the chill of disappointment with which each ended. "I'm so much happier now," he said honestly. "I'd never go back."

HE TOOK HER TO THE HIGHLANDS, VIA FORT WILLIAM and Glencoe. They climbed Ben Nevis, and he showed her the spot at the base where parts of *Braveheart* had been filmed. It was pure accident that he'd stumbled onto the set just as they were beginning to shoot an evening love scene—he'd been hiking aimlessly down the river when he noticed a strange assemblage of wooden huts on the near bank. Then people in orange vests came running at him, shouting and waving their arms. His first thought was of police—somehow they'd found out about the half-gram of speed he'd stashed in his backpack, the last he'd ever take, he'd sworn to others and to himself. He took off down the river, into a clump of woods, not yet trying to make sense of the cries, "Making a movie! Get out of the way!"

"I probably ruined five grand worth of film," he told Audrey now. She'd heard the story before, but nodded anyway and smiled, slipping off her socks and sticking her small feet into the icy current, watching the clear water bubble over smooth stones, some beige, some purple, some black. The river looked more peaceful now than it had then, but of course his breath had been short and his heart had still been pounding when he'd finally left the woods. And then he'd come upon a pair of vagrants, Glaswegians, camping upstream. They told him about the movie and about William Wallace—a true hero, they said, not an opportunist like Bonny Prince Charlie. Thomas had never heard of Wallace or the Bonny Prince, didn't know how many wars the Scots had fought against the British. The three of them crept close enough to the set to watch Mel Gibson, puny even on his horse, clad in leather and tartan, raging at the cruel world that had stolen his love. One of the Glaswegians whispered to Thomas, "Wallace was a lowlander. He'd never have worn tartan. He probably never set eyes on the Highlands before he died." When the movie came out, Thomas was back in the States, and he told anyone who would listen about the historical inaccuracies, the sentiment-al misrepresentation. He voiced his outrage when it swept the Oscars.

Audrey leaned back against the riverbank, staring up at the mountain they'd just scaled, at the wispy clouds drifting through distant valleys. Even in her hiking clothes—tight white T-shirt, cut-off corduroy shorts—she stood out against the dull earth, an unexpected part of the landscape, far from natural. "You know," she said. "No matter how many times I heard you describe it, it's different than I imagined. Nothing's the way you said it would be."

"Is that bad?" he asked.

She took him in along with the mountain and river, curiously, and then shrugged without commitment. "Just different."

That night they stayed in a secluded bed and breakfast at the end of a soggy, winding lane. Above them stood a solitary peak, gray with streaks of purple, in the unmistakable shape of a woman's breast. He wasn't the first to think so. "Pap of Glencoe," it was called, according to their host, a stooped, white-haired man with a fistful of turkey flesh dangling beneath his chin. Audrey laughed loudly, and laughed again when the old man said, "Most confused country in the world, the United States. Doesn't know what it wants to be." She listened carefully, nodding, as he talked to her about politics, about history. He described the massacre at Glencoe, which Thomas had already told her about on the drive from Fort William. In the car she'd stared absently out the window and responded with vague humming noises. Now the old man's words brought her to the verge of tears. Thomas shifted uneasily in his chair. He didn't know whether she was being sincere or patronizing, and didn't know which he would have preferred. Finally he stood and said, "My back's aching from that hike. I think I'm ready to collapse."

Their room had a peat stove with bricks of dried turf piled beneath. There was an enormous feather bed, a sink with brass knobs, ornate white trim around the ceiling. The last time he'd been here he'd slept fitfully in a hostel room crowded with twenty-three other hikers, cramming a pillow over his head to block out the chorus of snoring, nearly gagging on the sour smell of sweaty socks. He was struck by how much he'd changed in a few short years, how content he'd become with a handful of small comforts, or rather, how he was no longer so easily content without them. Could he have guessed back then what a solid, respectable job he would have now—as an accountant, for godsakes!—or that he would be with a woman who told him daily that she loved him, that she wanted to build a life with him? She was asleep already, in the position that had become habitual, one arm across his chest, the heel of a foot pressing down on his toes, head buried in his shoulder. Not the first time they'd spent the night together but sometime in the first month she'd held him this way, and he was suddenly overwhelmed to realize how lonely he'd been, to know that the terrible longing had left him—he was flooded by the pure relief of it and blurted tearfully, "My God. I'm so lucky. I didn't think this would ever happen for me."

For a moment she didn't answer. When she propped herself on an elbow to look at him, her eyes were cold, even angry. "Don't say that now. Please. Can't you just wait a year or two and then say it?" Of course she saw his stunned, wounded look, and then her face darkened, her lips quivered, and her own tears started. "It's not you, you know that, don't you? You've just got to understand. This all feels so goddamn *familiar*. Even what you just said. I've heard that before. And I'm sure whoever said it meant it as much as you did. But I can't hear it right now. I can't hope anymore. I can't *expect* anymore. Can't we just let things happen?" She turned her back to him, and he held her as she shook. "I'm sorry," she said. "I don't want to hurt you. It's just… Last night I woke up, my hand was on your stomach, and I didn't know who was in the bed. I really couldn't remember. I was afraid to open my eyes."

That was months ago now, and the fear he'd felt that night, the sense of impending loss, had subsided almost entirely. She talked often of their future; she said herself how lucky they were to have found each other, to have broken patterns that had become so deeply ingrained. She occasionally mumbled his name while she slept, no one else's that he could make out. She'd come with him to this place that was a part of him, and his sharpest memories of it now would include her arm draped over his chest, her breath on his shoulder, the soft glow of the slowly burning turf, the wind cutting over the Pap, through the low trees and dense brush, against the thick, impenetrable pane of their window—he would remember the warmth of it, the peace he'd finally found.

THE ISLE OF SKYE WAS JUST AS HE REMEMBERED, DRA-matic, otherworldly, at times a nearly terrifying mixture of bleakness and beauty. They hiked the Black Cuillins and then drove up the Trotternish Peninsula, Audrey remarking every time she spotted an emerald pond, a stone outcropping gnarled like an arthritic finger, a black-faced sheep bounding across the road. The farther north they drove the higher the cliffs rose to their left, the more colorful the grasses became, bright green blending into yellow, edging on purple, fading to brown. When they reached the trail to the Quirang, Audrey said, "Feels like I'm in a dream." He didn't tell her that this was the last place he'd ever dropped acid—clean all these years, the colors still seemed to swirl on the slopes below, and it was no less eerie to step through the cleft in the cliff and feel the wind suddenly drop away, to hear it roaring just out of sight. Inside everything was still, calm except for the chaos of craggy rocks jutting in crazed formations on all sides, the maze of tight passages leading to miniature green pastures atop massive stone pillars.

It was six years ago that he'd been here with Eliza, a Kiwi he'd met at the hostel in Uig. She'd been nineteen or twenty, with a tiny face and sharp jutting chin, her braided hair tied back with a blue bandana. She was the one who offered him the sugar cube, and he shrugged and thought, When will I ever do this again? For a while they wandered the Quirang together, exclaim-ing at every step, "Is this real? I don't believe it." Then he came around the side of a needle-shaped rock, and Eliza was no longer behind him. He called her name and traced his steps backward, but now it was hard to tell where he'd been—the rocks were bending toward him, sprouting tufts of bright green grass before his eyes. He circled, slowly at first, then running, shouting, Eliza's name sometimes echoing, sometimes sounding hollow and voiceless. The passages seemed to wind back on themselves, or else they all looked exactly the same, and he didn't know if he'd ever find his way out. Finally, he made his way to the highest point, where the wind picked up again, nearly blowing him off the cliff. And then he was sure—Eliza had come up here and fallen. Her body was mangled on the rocks below. He didn't even know this person, and now he'd be responsible for calling the police, for explaining the drugs in her system, and whatever else she might have in her pockets. This is how it would all end, this sad adventure he'd created for himself only because he had nothing better to do. What might have happened if someone had fallen in love with him in college, if he'd found a career that interested him, developed a passion for gardening, for collecting old records or rare books? How would his life have turned out if he hadn't been so lonely?

"Hey, mate." She was below him, reclining on a grassy patch atop what looked like a narrow bench perfectly carved out of stone. Her shirt was pulled up to the bottoms of her breasts, her belly exposed to the pale gray sky. "Need a tan," she said.

"I was calling you."

"That was you? I thought it was the wind. Or the fairies."

Soon a thick fog seeped into the cliffs, and the twisting passages filled with swirling mist. Eliza held his hand as they searched for the way out and hugged him when they found the notch in the rock wall. By the time they reached the road the mist had changed to real rain, soaking through his T-shirt almost instantly. They walked almost a mile with their thumbs out, waving hysterically at the few cars that passed, and finally a yellow utility truck stopped a dozen yards ahead. The driver was beak-faced, with wisps of white feathery hair above his ears and only a few teeth at the front of his mouth. Eliza couldn't look at him. She stared out the window and rocked gently back and forth. Thomas sat between them and tried to make conversation. He asked about Skye, how many people lived on the island, which clans were predominant. He forgot his questions as soon as he asked them, and instead watched the burst capillaries in the driver's face wriggle and spread until the whole face was red, the red face of a floppy white bird. He couldn't remember now if they'd thanked the old man when he dropped them off on the pier. "I've got to get a drink, mate," Eliza said. "I've got to come down a little." The barman in the Grand Hotel had a flaring red beard that hung to the start of his chest. They were still a few feet from him when Eliza grabbed Thomas' arm and said loudly, "Jesus. Do you see that?" They backed out slowly. On the street she said, "Did you see it squirming?"

They made their way back to the hostel and huddled together on a narrow bunk, though it was only three in the afternoon. "Help me," she whispered. "Make it stop." Her eyes were ravaged, red and swollen around the gaping black holes of her pupils, and he knew his own must have looked the same. He didn't know what else to do but kiss her, first on the temple, then on an eyebrow, the chin, the lips. He reached for her hair and started to untie the bandana. "I don't even know your name," she said. He knew before she did it that she'd push him away. It was a gentle push, but one that sent him reeling. He settled back against the thin mattress and felt himself sinking into the soft foam. He didn't see her face when she stood up. He stared at the mesh of springs on the bunk above, stared until the coils stopped writhing and became simple coils again. In the morning Eliza was gone.

He didn't want to tell any of this to Audrey as they drove away from the Quirang, on the road to Uig. He didn't want to tell her any more stories—this was the only memory he wanted, no fog or rain, no yellow utility truck, no beak-faced old man. Just he and Audrey driving in a rented car on a breezy summer afternoon, a pair of tourists out to see the sights. "That was incredible," Audrey said. "My head's spinning. I felt drugged in there."

In Uig they went straight to the Grand. "Seems like I haven't eaten for days," Audrey said. The lounge was empty except for two old men at the bar and another playing an electronic trivia game by the door. Audrey took a table while Thomas went to order their drinks and food. It was the same barman he remembered, the same red beard, no less fiery through sober eyes. His expression was no less gruff, his mouth no less fearsome or sneering. "You're back," the barman said.

"Yes," Thomas answered. He was too surprised to say anything else for a moment. "You remember me."

"How could I forget."

"Maybe you're thinking of someone else."

"You've been here before, haven't you?" the barman said. Thomas nodded. "Then it's you I remember."

There was nothing friendly about the words, but he told Audrey anyway. "He recognized me. From six years ago. These people are amazing." He added, quoting their guidebook, "*Hospitality is in their blood.*"

She laughed. "Let's write our own guidebook. *If you go to the Quirang in the morning, be prepared to feel fucked up for the rest of the day.*"

"Are you glad we came here?"

"Are you kidding? Who wouldn't come here. It seems... I don't know, the most ordinary thing in the world to do." She held up her glass. "And my God. This beer. I want to sneak a keg back on the plane."

The barman brought their fish and chips and lingered at the table. Dark red brows arched over eyes that didn't leave Thomas' face. Audrey said, "So you remember this guy, huh? He was quite the wild man back then."

"Is that so," the barman said.

"I've tamed him pretty well," Audrey said.

"Last time," the barman said slowly, "you were in here with a different girl."

Audrey turned to him with a sly, mocking grin. "Is that right?" she said.

"It was nobody," Thomas said.

"An attractive young woman, if I recall," the barman said.

"You little dog," Audrey said.

"Really, it wasn't anything."

"How dare you," she said. She was still smiling. Now she gave the barman a knowing wink. Her bright shirt, her shining hair and open smile, all of it was terribly conspicuous in the lounge's sullen gloom. "Taking me to the sight of a former conquest."

"It was just a girl I met at the hostel," Thomas said. "I only knew her for a day."

"Another pint?" the barman said.

"Sure," Audrey said.

"No thanks," Thomas said. With his thumb he traced a yellowed scar in the dark wooden table until the barman went away.

Audrey was still playful, her toe tapping his ankle beneath the table. "So? Did you sleep with her?"

"I told you it wasn't anything," he said. "I barely remember what she looked like."

"So? I barely remember half the people I've slept with."

"That's you," he said, and immediately regretted it.

Her smile disappeared. She bit a corner of her lower lip. Now she stared at the table, at the scratches and overlapping stains. "Thanks," she said.

"I'm sorry. I didn't mean anything."

"You always do this."

"Do what?"

"We both have pasts," she said. "You get to enjoy yours, and I have to feel like shit about mine."

"You don't," he said. "You shouldn't."

"You did all sorts of stupid things. On purpose. So I slept with people. Most of the time I didn't want them to go away after a week or a month."

"I know you didn't."

"I wanted good things. Normal things. I never set out to hurt myself."

"Of course you didn't," he said. He knew he should stop talking, but went on anyway. "It's just—"

"Just what?"

"I don't know. Sometimes—"

"Sometimes what, goddamnit."

"I just wish I were the only one you'd remember."

Now she was crying. He glanced quickly over his shoulder, but to his surprise, no one was watching. The two old men sat staring straight ahead. The barman leaned against the counter, polishing a pint glass with a filthy cloth. "Well fuck you for not coming around earlier," Audrey said, making no effort to keep her voice quiet. "What was I supposed to do, sit around and wait? For what, ten, twelve years? Was I supposed to have seen you in a dream? Was I supposed to build my whole life around some fantasy? Fuck you."

"You're right," he said, and came around the table, partly to comfort her, partly to block her from view. "Of course you shouldn't have waited. That's not what I meant. It's just—" He stopped himself, thought for a moment, and went on carefully, "Sometimes I just wish I could start all over again. From the very beginning."

He left money on the table and led her from the lounge, staring the whole time at his shoes but feeling anyway the steady gazes of the men pretending not to watch. The trivia player muttered, "Good day," as they passed him on their way out. Thomas followed Audrey down the pier, where a ferry was preparing to leave for Tarbert on Harris, and then on to North Uist. That's where he'd gone the last time, to the farthest islands he could reach, the outer limits, it had seemed then, of the known world. He wouldn't go there again. The freshest memories would end here. Tomorrow they would drive back to Edinburgh, and the next morning they would board a plane and return to their former lives, the quiet bungalow, the bedroom facing the chaos of flowers and weeds. He didn't know whether to look forward to it with relief or with dread. "I'm sorry," he said. "I don't think I was talking about you. I love who you are. All of it. Your experiences. You wouldn't be the person I know without them."

She was staring across the bay, to the outlines of nearby islands shimmering in the haze and spray. Her eyes were dry, her jaw set sternly. "It's really strange," she said. "Why should this seem so magical? It's all so ordinary, just rocks and water and grass."

He had to go on. "It's me," he said. "That's who I was talking about. I just wish I could erase certain things. Not that they're so terrible. I don't think I ever hurt anyone but myself."

A pair of seagulls landed below them, where the concrete slab of the pier ended abruptly and smooth pebbles began to fan out into the bay. "Birds and rocks and water," she said.

There was still anger in her voice. Her stance was rigid. Her flashy clothing marked a stubbornness, a refusal to accommodate to her surroundings. It was stubbornness that kept her from looking at him now. If she saw his face her eyes would go gentle with pity, and she'd throw her arms around his neck. He could feel things, emotions he couldn't name and didn't understand, lurking just below the surface, ready to distort his features and discolor his skin. One of the gulls shrieked at them, while the other pecked at something he couldn't see. "I wish I'd never been here before," he choked.

She didn't answer. At the end of the pier, beside the ferry, sat a yellow utility truck identical to the one that had brought him here six years ago. And coming toward him was the beak-faced driver, wearing the same knit cap, the same oilskin coat and rubber boots, though now the sun was shining and the breeze had nearly died away. His nose and cheeks were as red as Thomas remembered, his hair as glistening white. The whistle on the ferry blew. Men scurried alongside it, unwinding heavy ropes from thick metal cleats. The old man had almost reached them now, and Thomas took a deep breath and stepped forward to greet him. He *had* been here before, whether he liked it or not, and though he'd stayed only three days, he'd somehow made a mark. "Good afternoon," he said, and raised a hand. "Remember me?"

The driver staggered slightly, and something in his face twitched. "Get t' fuck," he said, his voice raspy and pained, his lips and few teeth foamy with spittle. His breath smelled like mud drenched with whiskey, and his huge, withered hand knocked Thomas' arm out of his way. Thomas watched him weave down the length of the pier and pitch forward into the open door of the Grand. The barman was standing outside now, squinting, tugging shyly on the red beard that showed streaks of gray in the sunlight. Audrey still stared out at the water, as the two gulls rose in unison, flapped together briefly, and then went their separate ways.

"I thought he'd know me," Thomas said.

"Next time," she said. "Next time we'll go somewhere neither of us has ever been, okay?"

"Okay," he said.

"You never made it to Greece, did you? I've always wanted to go to Greece."

"That's where we'll go," he said.

He was grateful that she'd even talk about a next time, though now she turned her back on him and started toward the foot of the pier. Her fresh face and red shirt were what they'd always been, bright beacons in an otherwise grim world. But they were more now, too—willful, defiant, a mark of what would always keep them apart. Was he only coming to know her now?

"Ready to go?" she called over her shoulder. Her voice was kinder now, her face beginning to soften with forgiveness. He'd known from the start how cranky she could be in the morning, how depressed in late afternoon. He'd known about the people she'd been with, the life she'd led. He'd known how men looked at her, regardless of his arm around her. He could have run from her then, but his other options had seemed—still seemed—unbearable, not options at all. What choice did he have to but to hurry after her, toward the Grand Hotel and their rented car, back the way they'd come?

Lego

AARON'S SIXTH BIRTHDAY. THE HOUSE WAS FULL OF relatives. Grandparents from Queens, aunts, uncles, cousins from Long Island and Connecticut, old people he didn't know. One woman, with bright pink lipstick and a shrieky voice that belonged in a young girl's mouth, came at him with arms spread wide for a hug. She smelled sickeningly of starch, and he ran from her. She thought it was a game, chased him all over the house, until he found his mother and crouched by her legs, crying. "He must be hungry," the woman said. "I'll get him a hot dog."

He wore his cowboy vest, blue leather with a fluffy cotton fringe. In the living room, his grandfather sat all day in the same chair, chewing the frayed stub of an unlit cigar. He had pouches around his eyes, and his cheeks sagged below his jaw. "Howdy, pardner," he said through his teeth whenever Aaron came close. Aaron raised his fingers, and his grandfather said, "Don't you point those things at me." When Aaron jerked his thumbs and made popping sounds in his mouth, his grandfather flinched and called across the room to Aaron's father. "See what happens when you move to the boonies? Your children become barbarians."

His grandmother wasn't afraid of his fingers. She laughed all the time and combed her hair into a bun that made her taller than anyone else in the room. Now she raised her own fingers and shot at him from the stairway. He dove behind the couch, and fired across the coffee table. They shot and shot, until his mother brought out a tray of pastries, and his grandmother said, "Honey, let's eat and pass the peace pipe."

But Aaron didn't want pastries. They were full of cheese. His grandfather said, "Fanny, don't you think it's time? We'll hit traffic."

"It's Saturday," his grandmother said. And then louder, "It's your grandson's birthday."

Matthew, his brother, not yet two, wobbled through the room waving a soup spoon over his head, singing. The tune wasn't right, but the words sounded like "Happy Birthday," which Aaron had been teaching him all week. He bumped against the coffee table and banged the spoon on the corner of the pastry tray. To keep his mother from scolding, Aaron knelt and called, "Ride 'em horsey!" Matthew dropped the spoon and ran to him, knocking his knees against Aaron's ribs as he climbed. Aaron crawled as fast as he could, his hands growing hot against the carpet. Legs in stockings and creased pants jumped out of their way. Above him, Matthew squealed. The starchy woman said, "Isn't that the most adorable thing you've ever seen?" At the kitchen door, his mother said, "Stay right there," and hurried off to her bedroom. She was gone too long. Aaron's arms began to tremble, and Matthew pulled at the hairs on his neck. "Quit," he said, but Matthew didn't. "Quit, or I'll stand up." Finally, his mother came back with a camera. For a moment the room went white, and then spots of color pulsed in the center of each eye. "Okay," he said. "Get off."

LATER, HE TOOK MATTHEW'S HAND AND SAID, "COME ON. I'll show you everything." He led his brother to the kitchen counter, lifted him so he could see the huge chocolate cake, far enough away so he couldn't touch the icing. Then he fitted the string of a shiny, pointed hat around Matthew's ears, under his chin. He took him to the quiet laundry room, to the pile of wrapped gifts along the wall opposite the towering white machines. He explained slowly, carefully, that he couldn't open them until after they'd eaten their cake. Matthew pointed to his jumper, patterned with boxes and bows. "My," he said, and reached for one of Aaron's presents. He tore a corner of paper from a flat package before Aaron could push his hand away. "It's not your birthday," Aaron said, but it was too late. He saw what was underneath the wrapping—a Lego house with windows and doors on real hinges, exactly what he'd wanted but hadn't dared ask for. His elation lasted only a moment. The surprise was gone. He couldn't tear away the paper and shout his thanks while everyone clapped. He didn't want the Lego house now, didn't want any of his presents. He fought to keep from crying, staring at the row of shoes on the doormat. His father's square, dull black, half the length of Aaron's arm. His mother's narrow and pointed, the wrong shape for a foot. His own with frayed laces and filthy heels from a mud puddle he'd backed into accidentally. And then three pair of Matthew's—tiny blue sneakers with white stripes along the sides, furry slippers, slick red boots tipped over against Aaron's shoes.

He tried to breathe deeply, the way his mother did when she was angry, and turned slowly to Matthew to explain why what he'd done was wrong. But even then he knew—as often happened with his mother—whatever he said would come out as a yell. Matthew had backed away from him, up against the washing machine. His eyes strained, his lips parted slightly. His elbows clanged softly against the white metal. The party hat slipped forward, bounced from his nose, fell to the floor. He's sorry, Aaron thought, and stepped forward to hug him. But now Matthew's arms were flailing, his mouth open in a scream, but no sound. Aaron whimpered for his mother, but couldn't call her. Matthew's face was turning red, and he crashed against the washing machine loud enough to make Aaron cry out. Immediately, his mother's shoes clicked across the kitchen tiles, followed by the heavier clunk of his grandmother's. He felt himself bumped aside, and then stood against a pair of legs, somebody's hands on his shoulders. Through his tears, Matthew's face was far away and purple. His mother said, "My God. Is he poisoned? Aaron, what did he eat?"

She stepped toward him, and he tried to run. But the hands

on his shoulders clamped firmly. They were his father's, and his father's dark eyes stared down on him. He squirmed and cried, "He wanted my presents. I didn't do anything."

His grandmother knelt, grabbed Matthew's jaw in her hand, and squeezed until his mouth opened and held still. Into it she stuck two long fingers with sharp red nails. Out came a soggy bit of blue and white wrapping paper. Matthew gagged, and milky spew splashed onto the floor, onto his grandmother's knees, onto three of the presents lowest in the stack, lowest because they were largest.

WITHIN FIVE MINUTES, MATTHEW HAD STOPPED CRYING and wobbled through the living room with a Tupperware bowl, putting it first into his mouth and then onto his head. But Aaron sat in the corner, chest aching from sobs that wouldn't stop. He watched his aunts, his uncles, his grandmother, even his grandfather wagging fingers at Matthew, pulling lips and eyes into twisted faces to make him laugh. Only the starchy woman crouched beside Aaron and patted his head. "Don't worry, doll," she said. "Your brother's okay now."

He felt better, briefly, when his mother brought out the cake and everyone sang for him. "Congratulations," his grandfather said. "Not everybody gets to be six, you know."

His mother wiped chocolate from his mouth and said, "We'll have to wait on the presents. They need to air out a little."

After two wedges of cake and a glass of milk, he tried to play cowboys with his grandmother, but she had Matthew in her lap, asleep now, both thumbs in his mouth. She put a finger to her lips and then ran a red nail through Matthew's soft hair. Aaron started crying again. The starchy woman said, "Poor little guy. What a fright. He must be exhausted."

He went to his room before most of the guests had gone. In the evening, his mother carried in his presents, all unwrapped, and stacked them near the closet. For a few minutes he wouldn't look at them, but by the time his father told him to brush his teeth and get into bed, Legos were spread across the carpet. "Make sure you pick up all the pieces," his father said. "Matthew might put one in his mouth."

The piece in his hand was blue, two inches long, with six bumps on top and four sharp corners. He closed his fingers over it, the same fingers that had made his grandfather flinch. In the next room, Matthew babbled happily, and his mother cooed in return. The edges of the plastic dug into his palm. He could put the piece in the box, if he wanted, or onto the floor. He could make up his own mind, now that he was six years old.

Rehearsal

ERIC HADN'T SEEN HIS BROTHER IN SIX YEARS. DURING that time they'd rarely spoken, exchanging messages on voice mail every few months, occasionally catching each other running out the door to work or social engagements, both apologizing for not being able to talk longer. Some years they sent birthday cards, never presents, Eric's birthday remembered less often than Josh's. Eric heard reports from his parents, but because they came from his parents he could never be sure to what extent the reports were true. He never forgot that he had a brother, but he was conscious of talking to friends and colleagues as if Josh had died in adolescence and been sufficiently mourned—the pain of first grief had subsided, leaving only a dull, persistent sadness, a nagging regret.

But now Eric was twenty-eight—the older by nearly four years—and getting married. The wedding was to take place over Thanksgiving weekend, in Florida, a white-sand beach outside St. Petersburg, where Melissa, his fiancée, had grown up and where her parents still lived. Along with a natural mix of euphoria and agitation over details, Eric felt a spirit of generosity, of goodwill and forgiveness, and at Melissa's urging, asked Josh to serve as usher. Best man was out of the question, of course, and even groomsman seemed to be going too far. But Eric felt reasonably comfortable with the image of his brother, no matter how haggard and disheveled in the tux he'd have to rent for him, shuffling down the aisle, pointing people to their seats, standing quietly out of the way while the rabbi mumbled prayers. He sent a plane ticket, along with detailed directions from the airport to the hotel and a note that read, "Look forward to seeing you. The rehearsal starts at four sharp."

Josh reciprocated by showing up on time, sober, shaved, showered, dressed in respectable khaki slacks and a blue knit shirt open at the collar. He was already in the hotel lobby when Eric came down from his room, and at first Eric didn't recognize him. He was twenty-four now, his hair short and gelled, skin tan and taut over a prominent chin and narrow, sculpted nose. The last time Eric had seen him he'd still been a boy, really— round face marked with acne, hair in wild ringlets cascading down the length of his neck, a childish slouch to his bony shoulders. Apparently he hadn't stopped growing at eighteen and now topped Eric by two inches or more. He towered over their mother, who'd actually been shrinking over the past few years, the cartilage in her hips and spine corroding prematurely, a visible hump forming beneath her neck. She had to cock her head at a strange angle to gaze up at Josh, and then twisted her whole body awkwardly to face Eric. "See?" she said. "Didn't I tell you he'd come?"

"I never doubted it," Eric said.

"He's a different person now," his father said, coming up behind them and putting an arm around Josh's shoulder. Josh shrugged, whether from embarrassment or false modesty, Eric couldn't tell.

"I'm glad you're here," Eric said.

"I wouldn't have missed it for anything," Josh replied, and Eric was struck by the depth of his voice, so much lower and more resonant than it sounded on his voice mail, with none of the nasal whininess that had made him so impossible to listen to as a teenager. "Thanks for giving me a chance."

Eric put out his hand. Josh grabbed it firmly, pulled him forward to his chest, slapped both hands against his back. Eric patted his brother's shoulders lightly and gave his mother a look he hoped was questioning without being cynical. But she only smiled benevolently, head sagging between curved shoulders, her still-young face floating apart, it seemed, from the body that was quickly growing old. Eric pulled himself from his brother's embrace, leaned back, and looked briefly into Josh's eyes, which were filtered by delicate, wire-rimmed glasses with lightly tinted lenses. "I'm glad you're here," Eric said again, with as much genuine feeling as he could muster. "It means a lot to me."

The last time Eric had seen his brother was on what should have been the weekend of Josh's high school graduation. Eric had been living in Dallas then, working his first job after college, code-crunching for a telecom operation that would, over the next five years, triple in size and then crumble under its own tremulous weight. He took a Friday off and drove all the way back to Jersey in a coughing Ford Escort that needed new coolant every two hundred miles. His parents had offered to fly him up, but they'd done enough already, he'd insisted—they'd put him through school, they'd bought him this car, however slow and rickety it might be, they'd taken care of him for twenty-one years. Now it was time to make his own way in the world, he said, hearing pride swell absurdly in his voice even as he tried to push it away. The Escort's radiator boiled over outside Baltimore, and he made it to his parents' house three hours later than he'd planned, just after midnight. He was surprised to find lights still on, even more surprised to hear voices as he approached the back door. He thought at first that everyone had waited up for him, that they were too excited about his arrival to go to bed, even though he'd called from a gas station in Delaware to let them know how late he'd be. But no one acknowledged him when he came inside. His mother's voice was raised and tearful. "All I've ever asked," she said, pacing the kitchen, arms crossed over her belly. "All I've ever wanted is for you to be honest with us. We're here for you. All you had to do was tell us, and we would have helped you."

His father hunched at the counter, leaning on both elbows. He didn't seem able to lift his head from his hands. "Of course we would have."

Josh slumped at the kitchen table, his bottom hanging off the edge of the seat, hairless shins protruding from cut-off jeans, filthy moccasins kicked up on one of the table's legs. His hands were locked behind his head, fingers lost in the tangled mass of hair. "You would have freaked out," he said. "Just like you're freaking out now."

Eric was confused and surprised to find himself so disappointed that his entrance had gone unnoticed. He'd half-expected a sort of triumphant homecoming, his first time back since he'd gotten the job and struck out on his own. During the long drive he'd pictured it clearly: walking in through the laundry room with his duffel slung across his back, his mother exclaiming about how good he looked, how he must be starving after being on the road all day, his father offering a drink—something adult and manly, gin and tonic, whiskey over ice—Josh asking if he remembered his own graduation from Union Knoll and how many parties he'd gone to in the weeks following. He'd been excited to describe his new apartment, the first he'd ever rented on his own, without roommates or fraternity brothers. He wanted them to hear how he'd learned to cook, how he'd surprised himself by keeping the place clean. He couldn't wait to tell them about the cocktail party he'd thrown for his department, the drunken words of praise his boss—normally sour-faced and taciturn—had heaped on him by night's end. But now he knew he'd have to keep all his stories to himself. "What's going on here?" he asked.

"Why don't you ask your brother," his mother said.

"Why don't you leave me the hell alone already," Josh said.

"Don't talk to Mom like that," Eric said, and his father nodded weakly in agreement.

"Who asked you?" Josh said. "Mind your own goddamn business."

"Hey, asshole, I just drove fourteen-hundred miles—"

"Yeah, well, you did it for nothing."

His father took a long breath and said, "I can't believe it. My son, the dropout."

"I didn't drop out, Dad," Josh said. "I flunked out."

"Jesus," Eric said.

"He's known for two months," his mother said.

Eric slammed his duffel to the floor. "Are you kidding me? You waited all this time to tell us?"

"I'm telling you now, aren't I?"

"Didn't it occur to you I'd have to take off work to drive that piece of crap up here?"

"He doesn't think about anybody but himself," his mother said.

"I only get two goddamn weeks of vacation a year," Eric said.

"I'm sorry I didn't think about your vacation while I was busy fucking up my life," Josh said.

"We already paid his tuition for the fall," his mother said. "It's that pot he smokes," and then, jabbing a finger in Josh's direction, she cried, "Don't think I don't know what it smells like!"

"If you needed help studying—" his father began, but Josh cut him off, kicking himself away from the table, the chair rocking backward, nearly toppling, and then settling against the back of his legs.

"Will you listen already? I didn't need help studying! I could study just fine!"

"He needed help going to class," his mother said, softly now, defeated. "He needed help caring about anything."

Eric was already on his way out of the kitchen, up the stairs, into his old room that now housed a litter box for the geriatric cat who could no longer make it up and down the stairs on her own. He could scarcely sleep for the ammoniac smell of cat piss and the scratchy, starched sheets that hadn't been slept in for a year or more, and woke soon after dawn. His parents were up already—or maybe they'd never gone to sleep—their faces dark and sunken above steaming cups of coffee. He kissed them goodbye, and they seemed barely to notice that he was heading out to his car with the bag he hadn't even unzipped. He was all the way back to Baltimore, he guessed, before Josh even bothered to get out of bed.

Over the next few weeks his parents threw around the words "depression," "therapy," "medication," as if they'd just learned their meanings and now had no use for any others. But then Josh left the house as well, first moving into an overcrowded apartment in Hoboken with a trio of high school friends, and then heading out west to work in ski resorts, Aspen, Park City, Sun Valley, Jackson Hole. Eric heard news of him only after significant delay, his mother keeping unpleasantries from him until they'd already been resolved. First, in Utah, an arrest for drug possession, an expensive hearing, a short stint in rehab. Later, in California, there was some kind of trouble with a girl. A woman, really, four years older than Josh, married and supposedly waiting for a divorce to go through. Beyond this, the facts were murky—the woman pregnant, paternity in question between Josh and the husband. There was a fight, a brawl on the sidewalk of a quiet suburban street that sent the husband to the hospital and Josh on his second visit to jail. It was the husband who'd brought the baseball bat, Josh swore—and his mother swore to Eric—and only by accident had it fallen into Josh's hands. Neither of them made excuses about the white powder the police found in his pocket, and nothing more was said about the baby, if it ever made it into the world.

By this time Eric was living in Connecticut with Melissa, then his girlfriend, tomorrow—he could hardly believe it—his wife. He told her about his brother, but only as an example, a way to illustrate his childhood, to describe the dangers of suburban malaise. "If we ever have kids, I think we should move into the city," he said, though he knew Melissa shuddered at the thought of speeding yellow taxis and screeching subway brakes. "If we stay here, we'll have to be careful." Josh had never taken responsibility for himself, he said. He didn't take his life seriously and had no idea what it meant to forge his own path. But it wasn't only Josh's fault. His parents had babied him. They'd given him all their attention, to the point of disregarding Eric's accomplishments, his successes in school, his independence, his self-sufficiency. But when Melissa expressed sympathy, he shook his head. "I'm not asking you to feel sorry for me. I just want you to know what I was up against. I want you to know how I got to be who I am."

When his four-month sentence was up, Josh disappeared for a time. His mother avoided talking about him altogether, and Eric imagined the worst: Josh's body decomposing on a beach or in an empty trailer deep in some forbidding woods. Melissa was outraged—she went on a tirade about the American prison system, the hypocrisy of "correctional institutions." "They're not about rehabilitation at all," she said. "There's no safety net in place for people when they get out." She worked as a counselor in the VA hospital in New Haven and believed strongly, Eric knew, in the potential for salvation in the most hopeless-seeming souls. He admired her soft heart, her charitable spirit, though he generally avoided talking politics with her. He didn't tell her his own opinion about Josh's chances for rehabilitation—once a criminal, always a criminal—instead nodding and saying, "I've never been able to understand how two people can come from the same place and turn out so differently."

But the worst hadn't happened. Josh had been homeless for the better part of a year, sleeping, it was true, on a beach from time to time, but more often on friends' couches, once or twice in shelters. But he'd also started working, running a drill press in a small, family-owned metal shop, and eventually put together enough cash for a deposit on a studio. In prison he'd taken his GED, and now he was signed up for business classes at the local junior college. Their mother no longer held back any information, instead spending most of their phone conversations telling Eric how surprised she was by Josh's turnaround, how lucky she felt to have been granted a second chance at a happy life. She read a letter Josh had written her and his father, an elegant, heartfelt plea for forgiveness. He was sorry for all the ways he'd hurt them, he said. He wanted them to know he loved them and took full blame for his behavior. He'd make it up to them, he promised. On the phone with Eric, his mother said, weeping, "He already has. I'd go through the whole thing again just to get that letter."

Eric remained doubtful. In his experience, people didn't often change overnight. In fact, they never did. Even if he'd received a letter—didn't he, too, deserve an apology?—he would have continued to withhold his trust until Josh proved himself worthy of it. He listened to his mother praise Josh for only a short while before changing the subject, hurriedly updating her on plans for the wedding, asking for advice on how to handle his pushy future mother-in-law. He waited for the time she would call and not mention his brother at all—then he'd know he'd been right all along, that it was only a matter of time before Josh reverted to old ways and crushed his parents with disappointment.

But it had been nearly a year with nothing but good news. Melissa talked about Josh almost as much as his mother did, with the same misty-eyed, dreamy look she wore when talking about her clients, those grubby, bearded, wheelchair-bound vets who begged for change on freeway off-ramps. "People can just surprise you, can't they?" she said. "It's really heartening." As the wedding drew closer, she pleaded with him to include Josh in the festivities. "It's important," she said. "It'll make you feel better about everything." Did he feel badly? If he did, he'd never told her so. He resisted calling his brother until a month before the big day and was surprised to hear gratitude in Josh's voice when he called back, scratchy and distant as it sounded on the voice mail that never worked as well as his old answering machine had: "Of course I'll be there, bro. I can't wait."

And now here he was, smiling humbly, hugging all the relatives who'd written him off, nodding apologetically to anyone who said how good it was to see him, how terrific he looked, how his parents must be so proud. His hands were behind his back, and he rocked gently as he spoke. "They stuck by me all this time," he said. "Most people would have given up years ago."

Their mother dabbed at her eyes with a handkerchief. Their father thrust his hands deep into his pockets, swallowed visibly, and stared up at the enormous crystal chandelier dangling above them. Eric said, "The past is the past. We're here to celebrate the future." *My* future, he might have said but didn't. Instead he opened his arms wide and tried to sound magnanimous. "It's a new day for all of us."

The elevator doors opened, and out came Melissa, exhausted and jittery, wearing shorts and a tank-top, flip-flops revealing newly painted toenails. Her hair was pinned up hastily, her eyes dark and baggy. Her parents flanked her on either side, her father smiling broadly, showing off his mangled teeth, her mother whispering fiercely about how the flower arrangements were going to look all wrong, how they should have stuck with simple white and red roses, as she'd advised. Behind them was Linda, the wedding coordinator, coiffed and made-up, wearing a lavender pantsuit and carrying a clipboard. "Good morning, Lowengards and Sileskys!" she cried, lifting the clipboard above her head and clapping it three times with her free hand. "Are you ready for a first-class rehearsal?"

Melissa came straight to Eric, took his arm, and said, loud enough for everyone to hear, "Make it stop. They're driving me crazy."

Eric laughed, a bit tinnily, he knew. "You were right. We should have eloped."

His mother frowned. "You never would have done that to your family," she said.

Josh still stood with his hands behind his back, rocking. "You must be Missy," he said in the same humble, sorrowful way. "I always wanted a sister."

When he reached out a hand, his sleeve rode up his arm to reveal a faded tattoo, what looked like barbed wire ringing his bicep. His smile was a small, bright scar in the tanned face. There was puzzlement in Melissa's eyes, apprehension even, until Eric said, "My brother. Josh."

Then her whole face altered, brows lifting, mouth losing its rigid set, lips growing softer, glistening. Here was her hospital look again, the expression she reserved for lost causes, for those clients she believed needed her compassion most, the ones Eric had learned not to judge openly for their choices in life, for the misfortunes he guessed they'd brought upon themselves. She held Josh's hand in both of hers and spoke slowly, exaggerating her sincerity, as if addressing a child. "I'm so glad you made it," she said. "I've heard so much about you."

Josh took off his glasses and wiped his eyes with a thumb and forefinger. "I bet you have," he said, nodding sadly. "I wish I could tell you none of it was true."

Linda clapped the clipboard again, moving now to the brass-handled doors leading to the patio, the pool, the walkway to the beach. "Let's go, everybody! Where's the beautiful couple?"

OUTSIDE, THE SUN BEAT STEADILY, UNOBSTRUCTED, ON the hotel's flamingo walls. At the top of the patio stairs the chupah was half-built, four wooden posts with nothing covering them. A dozen or so folding chairs were arranged in a semi-circle with an aisle down the middle, dozens more stacked on pallets near the pool. The rabbi, from the reform synagogue Melissa's parents belonged to, sat in the front row reading a paperback novel and looking far from scholarly—beardless, not yet forty, wearing a T-shirt that read *Gatorville*. They were paying him two hundred dollars an hour.

Linda bounded up the stairs and down, a frenzy of activity as the rest of them stood waiting. Her coif had already loosened on one side, a clump of hair jumping above her left ear. Her lips were malleable, able to hold a smile even while she barked orders and slapped her clipboard—when the smile began to fade, she forced it back into place. Her teeth were smeared with lipstick. "Bride!" she called. "I need my bride." Melissa stepped forward reluctantly, and Linda snatched her under the arm and dragged her away from Eric, around the pool and out of sight.

"It's not too late," Eric called after them. "We can catch a boat tonight. I hear Cancun's a nice place to elope."

His mother shook her head. His father winked and shrugged in sympathy. Eric was sweating even in his loose clothing, weighed down by the bright rays and moist air. He'd never gotten used to the heat when he'd lived in Dallas, the oppression of a sun that had seemed too close to the ground, and he hadn't missed it for a moment since he'd left. He had a hard time connecting Melissa with this place, despite her stories of growing up on the beach, the pictures of a little brown girl hanging from the railing of a sailboat. When they met she'd already been living up north for six years—four at Wesleyan and another two getting her M.S.W. at UConn—and she seemed to belong to the sharply changing seasons, the small New England towns. Meeting her had seemed a part of his homecoming, a relief from the strangeness of Texan accents and dry, choking summers.

Now he squinted despite his dark sunglasses and had to shade his eyes with both hands. Below, Josh stood with his face to the sky, skin glowing in the fierce light. They had some traits in common, there was no question. Seeing them side by side, anyone could guess they were brothers. They shared their mother's deep-set eyes, more round than oval, their father's solemn mouth, a broad forehead that didn't seem to come from either of their parents but must have been a strange amalgamation of the two. At the same time, there was a different character to their faces, something beyond features, more profound than genetics. Eric's cheeks had begun to fill out over the past few years, partly a function of age, he guessed, partly of lifestyle, but also something less tangible. In the mirror he could see their progression—growing softer with time, sagging, his jaw less sharp and angular whether he dieted or not. His body, too, would begin to bloat and lose its shape, no matter how many push-ups he did every morning, no matter how many hours he spent in the gym. In ten years he would be entirely muddled, indistinct, featureless, while Josh would only grow leaner, more striking, the type of person no one, after the briefest glance, could possibly forget.

Linda came back now, her smile stiff and hideous. "Bridesmaids!" she cried. "Groomsmen! Front and center!" She clapped her clipboard impatiently even as three of Eric's former fraternity brothers—Jim Forhan, Rob Singer, and Rob Morrison—lined up beside him. All three had put on weight in the last year, and both Robs had thrown out their backs, though all they did was stare at computer screens day in and day out. Across from them stood Melissa's best friend from childhood and two of her cousins. All three had dark circles under their eyes, and one of the cousins was green with nausea. They'd had some kind of bachelorette party the night before, much wilder than Eric's bachelor party, though his friends had done their best, taking him to a lap dance club and paying an extravagant fee to have enormous, silicone breasts mashed into his face. When she'd come in last night, staggering, Melissa had refused to describe her evening and begged him not to divulge any details of his own. "Let's let it be our last secret from each other," she'd said, and Eric had agreed, though he wondered briefly what other secrets they had.

The nauseous cousin sniffled, and Linda squealed, "That's the spirit!" She called to the people standing idly below, "She's practicing crying. I knew someone would get into this rehearsal."

Was it strange that he had no family members standing beside him, no one he'd known before he was eighteen? His father was wandering to the edge of the patio, staring out toward the benign waves of the Gulf. His mother had taken a seat beside the rabbi, hunched over and straining to watch, obviously in pain. Josh was sunbathing standing up, his glasses in one hand, face gleaming under the steady glare, peaceful, as if nothing in the world concerned him. Was Melissa lucky to have had her cousins with her last night, on whatever escapades of debauchery they'd found themselves in the middle of? Who in his own family would he have wanted watching while some strange, nearly naked woman ground her thonged bottom into his groin?

"Now," Linda said. "Where's my usher?"

Josh pulled his face from the sun, blinked several times, replaced his glasses, and casually lifted one finger. "I'm your man," he said.

Linda's plucked eyebrows rose and fell. "Are you ever," she

said. "Boy, is it my lucky day, or what?" Instead of gripping his arm the way she had Melissa's, she grabbed him around the waist and pulled him to her hip. "You're the most important piece of the whole puzzle," she said. "You're the gatekeeper, the one who keeps everything flowing." She turned him around and pointed, still talking, Eric could tell, though he could no longer make out any words. Suddenly, she called over her shoulder, "Eric! How come you never told me you had such a charming brother?"

He didn't answer. Linda took a long moment to stare up at Josh, patting the side of her hair, and only reluctantly let him go. Then she was all business again. "Okay," she cried. "It's showtime. Cue the bride." She started humming the wedding march, beating time on her clipboard, though Melissa had chosen her own music for the service, a Bill Evans CD she'd reminded Eric five times to pack the night before they'd left home. Without closing his novel or taking his eye from the page, the rabbi stood and climbed the steps. Melissa appeared around the side of the pool, walking fast, not pretending at all to glide in her long dress. Her flip-flops slapped loudly on the concrete. Dr. Silesky struggled to keep up with her, hanging onto her elbow, a bald, sniveling nebbish of a man, Eric had always thought, wealthy beyond imagination after twenty-five years as a neurologist, but tacky as ever in blue canvas shorts, brown sandals, white socks pulled up to his knees. His wife shouted from the sidelines, "Slow down! Long strides! Long strides!" Melissa's head was lowered as she cruised up the aisle, and Eric couldn't catch her eye. Across from him, the nauseous cousin crouched to the ground and held fingers to both temples. On the lower patio, Josh pulled a disposable camera from his pocket and started snapping indiscriminately, at Eric, at Melissa, at his parents, at the beach, the pool, the hotel's outdoor lounge. Eric stood with his arms crossed, waiting for his bride. No one had given him directions. He hadn't moved at all. They could have done the whole thing without him.

"HEY, BRO," JOSH SAID, WHEN THEY WERE THROUGH. "BUY you a drink?"

Eric glanced around for help. His parents were heading back into the hotel. His fraternity brothers were off to Tampa, searching for an electronics wholesaler they'd read about online, the cheapest hardware east of the Mississippi, they said. Melissa stood commiserating with her bridesmaids. She groaned and said, "Jesus, what were we thinking?" The nauseous cousin had disappeared, and now came back wiping her mouth with the back of her hand. Even Linda was occupied, arguing with the men who'd returned to finish the chupah.

"I figured you probably wouldn't have any time tomorrow," Josh said. "You'll have too many other people to see. Now's our only chance to catch up."

Melissa called to him, "Sweetie? We're going to pass out on the beach for a while. I've got to rest up for tonight."

What was there to catch up on that his mother hadn't already told him? He knew about Josh's promotion at the metal shop—to assistant manager—knew that he would receive his associate's degree at the end of the coming spring term and transfer to the state university. He knew all he wanted to know and more. Maybe his goodwill gesture had been a mistake after all, he thought. Josh seemed to take it to mean more than it did, or something different than Eric had intended. Something was going to be asked of him, beyond what he was willing to give. But he couldn't come up with excuses. "Sure, okay. I could go for a quick beer."

They passed alongside the pool, where a number of out-of-town guests were killing time before the rehearsal dinner. Eric had to stop and shake every third person's hand. Aunt Lucy, his father's sister, said, "It's so good to see you two together like this," and a loudmouth friend of his mother's, a woman he wouldn't have invited at all if he'd had the choice, shrieked, "My God! Your mother told me, but I didn't believe her. I thought you two hated each other."

The outdoor lounge, decorated with strings of pink and yellow plastic flowers, was empty except for the bartender, a ponytailed college girl in a tuxedo shirt and bowtie. Her bored look disappeared the moment Josh leaned on the bar—smiling his humble, apologetic smile, his shirt sleeve riding up again to show off his tattoo—replaced now by an expression that fought between eagerness and forced indifference. She blinked too much while digging in the cooler, her eyelids painted a silver-blue that seemed gaudy to Eric against her olive skin. From here he could see down the beach to where Melissa and her cousins sat on the white sand, oiling their arms and legs, baring their bellies to the sky. She'd stay out too long, he knew, and would regret it to-morrow when her dress chafed the burn. He wanted to go down there and tell her to put on sunblock but knew she'd only laugh and say, "My practical husband. That's why I keep him around." Out on the water a speedboat roared past, followed by a parasail fifty feet behind and above. Even though he could see the rope, the two seemed disconnected, the boat cutting a furious wake, the red and orange parachute billowing placidly against the cloudless sky.

Josh handed him a longneck bottle and frosted mug. In his own hand was a tumbler full of whiskey and ice. He raised it and said, "Cheers."

"You're drinking?" Eric asked. "Aren't you still in A.A.?"

"N.A.," Josh said. "I never had a problem with booze."

Eric nodded doubtfully and poured his beer too quickly, foam rising to the top and spilling over the side. "N.A., right. So how's … Santa Barbara?"

"Santa Cruz. Bay area."

"Right. Santa Cruz. I knew that."

"I'm sure Mom's told you how it is. Straight and narrow. Brand new life."

"We're all really proud of you," Eric said.

Josh ducked his head and let out a quick, bitter laugh. "Cut the bullshit," he said. "I got enough of it this afternoon."

"It's true. We all—"

"You're all just holding your breath until I fuck up again."

"I never said—"

"Everyone's afraid to talk to me like a normal person, like I'll crumble to pieces the second anyone stops being proud of me." He ran a finger along the rim of his glass and then turned it up for a large gulp. "I'm tired of people handling me like a goddamn eggshell."

"Well," Eric said, only then noticing how little air had been moving in and out of his lungs. He was relieved to let a full breath escape, and then had to replenish it before he could go on. "You haven't exactly inspired confidence in people."

"That's better," Josh said. "No bullshit."

"We want to believe in you—"

Josh's glass came down hard on the counter. The bartender, standing with her arms behind her back a few feet away and pretending not to listen, gave a little jump. "Don't. Don't believe, don't be proud, don't do anything. Just let me live my life and be my goddamn brother. Remember? We're supposed to be brothers."

Brothers. What was that supposed to mean, exactly? That he should remember only close, affectionate times they'd shared as boys, playing in the woods behind their house, or at the muddy lake they'd loved until a flock of Canada geese discovered it and blanketed the beach with slick, greenish shit? Why was it easier to recall fights they'd had, or the time Josh stole a stack of *Penthouse* magazines from a hiding place in the back of his closet? Twelve years later the offense still weighed heavily on Eric's mind, the first time he really began to question what kind of person his brother would become. He'd bought the magazines with his own money, passing bills every month to an eighteen-year-old gas station attendant who took a dollar cut and ran across the highway to a cigar shop and newsstand. He spent hours in his closet, flipping through the pages carefully but quickly, as if to pause for more than a moment on an airbrushed brunette sprawled across a bearskin rug meant risking a deeper descent into a world of dubious desires than he was willing to chance.

He'd had them for more than a year before showing them to Josh.
By then he rarely looked at them, but he couldn't help feeling
proud in the role of initiator, pleased with the way Josh suddenly
looked up to him as someone versed in the more chilling mysteries of life. At the same time he was troubled by his brother's
fascination—Josh lingered on each picture, read the captions
beneath, studied the stories in the back pages, tales of secret
encounters that Eric had been afraid to read, with titles like,
"A Night to Remember," "In the Storm," and "The First Glance."
How could he not feel as much ashamed as betrayed when
the magazines disappeared? How could he not worry that he'd
played a role in his brother's corruption?

"Christ," Josh said now. "I didn't ask you over here to talk
about me. I'm sick of talking about me. I haven't seen you in
six years. All I ever hear from Mom is how much money you're
making. Tell me about *your* life."

Until then Eric had been propping himself against a bar-
stool, but now he pushed himself up and crossed his ankles.
What did he have to tell? None of his stories could match Josh's
adventures and misdeeds. There'd been no radical changes
in his life since he'd finished college, just a steady increase in his
happiness, his standard of living, his sense of well-being.
He started talking about the condo he and Melissa had just bought,
a mile outside Old Greenwich, two bedroom, one-and-a-half
bath, a private deck and garage. Before he'd finished, Josh's gaze
had wandered down the beach, to Melissa and her cousins, their
skin glistening along with tiny crystals in the sand. "Commute
into the city's only forty-five minutes," he said. "Most nights I'm
home by seven."

"You and Missy. You've got a good thing going? You're happy
together?"

"We'd better be," Eric said, and let out a brief, uneasy chuckle.

"You planning to have kids?"

"I suppose so. The second bedroom's my office now, but I
barely have time to use it. We could fit a crib in there easy."

Josh raised his glass and held it to his mouth until the whisky was gone and ice bounced against his lips. Eric's mug was three-quarters full, the foam settled now, the frost melted and sweating down the sides. "I loved being a kid," Josh said. "I think about it all the time."

He lifted two fingers, and in a moment the bartender brought them fresh drinks. She flashed her silvery eyelids and said in a high, mousy voice, "Here you go, gentlemen."

Josh took a moment to smile at her again before turning back to Eric. Suddenly his eyes were red around the rims, his nostrils quivering. "Look, bro," he said. "I've been wanting to ask you something."

This was the moment Eric had been preparing for, even if he hadn't known it until now. Josh would tell him what new kind of trouble he'd gotten into and would ask for a way out. He'd want money, more than Eric would want to give. Eric braced himself, ready to do what his parents had never done, what Josh had always needed someone to do—tell him, no, sorry, it was time he took care of himself. He knew how hard it would be, how everyone would second-guess him, his parents, his aunts and uncles, even Melissa, all of them judging him unfairly, believing he had a cold heart. Even as he thought it he felt sorry for himself, and courageous, the only person he knew brave enough to act on his conscience. But now Josh was digging in his pocket. He pulled out a photograph, creased through the middle, rounded off at the corners, with a rough texture that triggered quickly fleeting memories of forgotten sensations: the smell of fresh wax on linoleum floors, the click of his mother's heels, the tremor of an off-balance washing machine behind thin drywall. The photo itself pictured the two of them at Lenape Lake, a few years before the geese took over. Eric was ten, straight hair hanging in his eyes, skinny chest bare, a recent appendix scar visible above the waistline of his bathing suit. He carried Josh piggy-back, his brother's head resting on his shoulder, feet on either side of his hips. Josh smiled clownishly, eyes shut, tongue wagging between parted teeth. Eric's smile was milder, just opening, maybe, or closing. Behind them, the lake disappeared in an orange glare.

"Were we really this happy?" Josh asked. There were tears in his eyes for sure now, and his voice sounded clogged, as if he'd suddenly caught a cold. "Sometimes I don't believe it. I want to, but I can't."

Eric took a drink from his beer and glanced around in embarrassment. The bartender was looking down at her hands. He took the photo, scanned it quickly, and handed it back. "I don't remember it," he said. "I don't think I've ever seen it before."

"I wish I could go back," Josh said, sputtering, wiping his eyes with his knuckles. "I wish I could do it over again."

"You're not a kid anymore," Eric said, immediately filling with an anger and contempt that surprised him and propelled him off the stool. He knew what was expected of him—to reach out and pat his brother's back, to tell him there was still a chance for him to be happy, to make something worthwhile of his life—but he couldn't do it. Instead he wanted to grab Josh by the shoulders and shake him. Why should anyone coddle him? Why should he and no one else be allowed to indulge feelings that were childish and impractical and meant to inspire pity? Eric ran both hands through his hair and said, "You've got to grow up sometime."

He was spared having to say any more. Melissa's cousin, the nauseous one—Carrie or Kathy, he could never keep them straight—was coming up the path from the beach. She seemed to have recovered now, the color returned to her cheeks, though her face was slightly sour-looking even when she wasn't about to get sick. She was the least attractive of the bridesmaids—her lips were full, but her nose was angled upwards, so no matter which way she turned, her nostrils showed. Her forehead was shiny and pocked near the temples. "You two've got the right idea," she said. "Mind if I join you?"

Josh slipped the photo back into his pocket. When he looked

up, his cheeks were blotched, but his eyes were dry, and he managed to smile. He stood and gestured to a stool on his other side. "Get you a drink?" he asked, the humble charm returning, the confident sweep of the tattooed arm, and Eric was sure he could detect a twinge of jealousy in the bartender's new round of rapid blinking as she stepped forward to take the order.

"Have this one," Eric said, handing the cousin his fresh bottle. "I haven't touched it yet. I've got to get going, anyway. I told the banquet manager I'd check in with him before six. Make sure everything's ready for tonight."

Josh nodded and put out a hand for a shake. "Thanks for taking the time," he said.

"Of course," Eric said, taking his hand and quickly letting it go. He couldn't think of anything else to say, so he repeated, "Of course."

Before he reached the lobby doors, he heard the cousin's laughter ring out behind him, shrill and full of suggestion. He took a last look at Melissa, frying on the beach, and at the parachute, far out over the water now, the boat completely out of sight. The air conditioned hallway was a welcome relief, but after being in the sun so long, his eyes had trouble adjusting to the dimness. Everything was green and soft around the edges. The hotel billed itself as Mediterranean-inspired, with keyhole doorways and murals of gondolas and vineyards, but there was still something neon and Floridian about it—mirrored ceilings, Pepto-Bismol diamonds on green carpets, thumping bass and tinkling drumbeats rising up from a basement spa. He followed signs to the Florentine Room, up a flight of gently spiraling stairs lined on either side with runway lights. The banquet hall was a high-ceilinged box with only one narrow window looking out onto the beach. Melissa had made him promise the rehearsal dinner wouldn't outshine the wedding, so he'd chosen the plainest room, the most ordinary food, the simplest decorations. She'd been against having the dinner at all, the same way she'd been against the chupah and the rabbi. "It's what people do," he'd insisted, again and again, until she relented. For a while she'd been against a wedding altogether, knowing how the planning would rattle her nerves, how much grief her mother would give her. "What's the point?" she'd asked. "Why do I need some paper to tell me we're committed to each other?" Eric had argued that it was important to bring their friends and family together, to celebrate their good fortune. "I want to show off to the whole world how lucky we are," he said. What had his real reasoning been? That he was ashamed to tell people his girlfriend didn't want to marry him? Or was he afraid that without some reason to stay, it would be too easy for her to leave?

Inside, chairs were still stacked along the walls, and only half the tables were set. A single waiter, missing his bowtie, his shirt untucked, stood folding napkins and stuffing them into empty water glasses. On the few ready tables the centerpieces were all wrong—cheap candles in burnished glass globes. He'd ordered his own candles, small orange ones, citrus-scented, that would float alongside flower petals in glass bowls half-filled with water. He'd gotten the idea—he would never admit to anyone—from a bridal magazine he'd bought Melissa, which she'd refused to read. "Hey, where are my candles?" he called.

The waiter was a dark runt with a sunken nose and clumsy fingers that worked the napkins with difficulty. He looked up slowly, shrugged, jutted his chin at the nearest table. "What do these look like, man?"

"Where's the banquet manager? Carlos, right?"

With every word Eric spoke, the waiter looked more put out. "Your guess is as good as mine," he said. "Motherfucker's got me setting up the whole room by myself."

"Why don't you go find him for me," Eric said, trying to breathe deeply but finding himself unable.

"Sure, man. You come fold these napkins, I'll go look for Carlos."

He was across the room in six strides. His hands were clenched. He was giddy with rage, with the sudden intention of showing everybody—his parents, Melissa, Josh—that he wasn't immune to the onrush of impulse and emotion. Why shouldn't he, too, spend a night in jail? His fists rose to grab hold of the waiter's shirt, but he stopped them before they touched cloth. They hung in the air on either side of the waiter's head. "I'm getting married tomorrow," he said through his teeth. "The candles are all wrong. You want my fiancée to see this and freak out?"

The waiter tried to keep from cowering, but his posture was beginning to melt. He wound a napkin around two fingers and avoided Eric's stare. "What's wrong with these candles?" he asked.

"Does it really matter? I say they're not right. I say go find Carlos for me."

Only when he'd backed up a few feet did the waiter allow himself to swagger. "That fucking guy," he said. "He always screws something up. I hate folding these damn things anyway," he said, and tossed the napkin to the floor.

When he was out of the room, Eric sat on the edge of a chair and balled his hands in his lap to keep them from shaking.

"WHY CAN'T YOU GIVE HIM A BREAK?" MELISSA ASKED an hour later, from the bathroom of their suite on the hotel's sixteenth floor.

Eric sat on the bed, dressed too early in the black silk shirt she'd picked out and talked him into buying. He knew he'd never wear it again—though there was no official dress code, his office was strictly a white shirt and dark tie place, and when they went out in the evenings he tended toward plaids or thin stripes, sleeves rolled up, the same look he'd had since college. Now he was already sweating, despite the French doors open onto their balcony, a soft breeze coming off the Gulf. The bathroom door was open, too, and from where Eric sat he could watch Melissa rubbing lotion onto her shoulders and arms. She was naked, her skin white where the bikini had been, pink everywhere else. He'd seen her body so many times he often took it for granted, but now it stirred him. Not with arousal exactly—it was more like surprise at the fact of someone baring herself to him day after day, without a thought of turning away in shyness or shame. This was the way he'd felt the morning after their first night together, when she'd pranced around his apartment without anything on, doing her yoga stretches and then making breakfast, not troubled at all to have him glimpse in full daylight the moles on her back, the scar on her thigh from a childhood bike accident, the small bit of cellulite on her ass. He'd tried to act just as casually, parading in front of her, but he couldn't do it without puffing out his chest, sucking in his stomach, his hand moving unconsciously to cover his crotch. After a few minutes he'd hopped into the shower and spent the rest of the morning with a towel wrapped around his waist.

He'd known from their first weeks together that he wanted to marry her. He imagined saying the words, "Let's spend our lives together," long before he'd built up the courage to voice them, before he could conceive of what it would mean to spend a life in someone else's company. The love he'd felt for her then was closer to compulsion than rational choice—it had something to do with her skin, or the way her head moved on her neck, or any number of things he couldn't explain. It was completely out of his control, one of the few things in his life that felt so, particularly because he knew she didn't feel the same. She'd been coming out of another relationship when they'd met—in the laundromat of all places—and wasn't ready to jump into another one. In fact, she hadn't yet cut off the old boyfriend altogether, nor half a dozen other flirtations and casual interests. Eric was one on a list of possibilities—"Laundry Boy," her friends called him—and from the start she warned him not to take things too seriously. She made herself out to be wild and unpredictable, though he learned quickly enough that wildness was a cover for fear and distrust. He played his cards carefully, always appearing nonchalant, relaxed, never raising a fuss when he knew she was out with other men. Eventually, of course, she came around, but not without first making him suffer through months of doubt and rage, on the one hand incredulous that she could even compare anyone else to him, and at the same time convinced he'd never stack up next to guys he could only imagine as everything he wasn't: tall, intellectual, outdoorsy, talkative, constantly professing their passion with rash and utterly convincing gestures. "You were so smart," she told him six months later, after they moved in together and shortly before he proposed. "You let me get all that out of my system. You let me be myself."

Now she stepped halfway out of the bathroom, rubbing lotion beneath her breasts, lifting them and dropping them heavily, something he found less titillating than clinical and strangely troubling, the same way he'd felt at the strip club the night before, with the silent, sullen girl's stiff nipples jabbing into his cheeks. "He's trying, isn't he?" she said. "He's making a real effort."

"I just don't trust him, that's all," Eric said.

"Nobody asked you to," she said. "But that doesn't mean you can't give him the benefit of the doubt."

It wasn't fair of her to argue with him while she was naked, when her skin looked so raw, her bikini lines painfully distinct. What chance did he stand? Anything he said would come off as aggressive and bullying. He tried to calmly describe his conversation with Josh this afternoon, how nervous and unstable his brother had seemed, how the façade of humility and repentance dropped away the moment their parents were out of sight. He didn't tell her about the photo Josh had shown him, or the way he'd bawled out Carlos when the waiter finally brought him back, threatening to call his boss, demanding a refund on all the table decorations. "He's not at all what he seems," he said.

"Of course he's not," she said. "He didn't suddenly turn into some kind of saint. How could he? Who'd want him to?"

"He's got my parents fooled. He's going to break their hearts."

"Your parents aren't so naïve. They know him. They know who he is."

"Maybe," Eric said, though picturing his mother's placid expression, he couldn't be sure how much she really knew. She never

listened to his advice, that was certain, and whatever protective-
ness he felt for her was tempered by frustration.

"What is he, twenty-four?" Melissa went on. "Think about
all he's been through already. Think about how much he's
grown just in the last couple of years. Change doesn't happen
overnight."

"I know it doesn't," he said, hoping the irritation in his voice
would be enough to end the conversation.

But it wasn't. "Look at Kathy. She's a mess. She parties every
night. She's on probation at Lehigh. She'll probably get kicked
out before the semester's through. I wouldn't be surprised if she
ended up in detox or something."

"And?" He was more than annoyed now. He was sweating
through his shirt. They were getting married tomorrow, and here
they were arguing about people they almost never saw. "What's
your point?"

"My point is..." Her voice was raised and brittle. It was a
mistake to have upset her now, when she was already stressed
and anxious. But hadn't she started this? Why couldn't she let him
think whatever he wanted about his own brother? "I don't know.
I guess I just know her. I've known her since we were kids.
I know what she's going through. You and Josh grew up together.
Doesn't that count for anything?"

He stood and went to the balcony doors. The warm breeze
made his shirt stick to his chest. The sound of waves was supposed to be soothing, he knew, but the salt air only added to the
dryness in his mouth. He didn't want to talk anymore. He didn't
want to hope for his brother to change or worry about his parents'
feelings. He didn't want to see any photographs of his skinny
chest or his fresh appendix scar. He'd told the truth when he said
he'd never seen the picture before, but he did remember the
day it was taken. There shouldn't have been anything particularly
special about it, just one of many summertime visits to the lake,
followed by a barbecue at a nearby park. But it had *seemed*
special, the whole family agreed. Something about the light on the

water, the smell of fresh leaves, the comfortable breeze. Everything made them laugh. The burgers were the best they'd ever eaten, the tomatoes the freshest. The ketchup was in a squeeze bottle, the first they'd ever seen, and somehow it made the frozen fries reheated on the grill taste homemade. When they came back the next week, nothing was the same. It was too hot. Weeds had suddenly grown high enough in the lake to tickle Eric's legs when he swam. The cheese melted in the trunk and had to be thrown away. He hadn't been prepared for disappointment, and now it was devastating. He sat in silence on the drive home, refusing to play cards with Josh in the back seat. He wanted to cry but didn't. Why did everything have to change? Why couldn't he count on anything? Why had Josh shown him the goddamn picture?

When he turned around, Melissa had underwear on, her dress halfway over her head. This way her body did arouse him— black cloth sliding over pink skin, hips wiggling to help it along. He wanted to end the argument, to let go of the feeling that cramped his chest, to make her remember why they were here. He stepped forward to kiss her exposed belly, but by the time he reached her the dress had come all the way down. The thin shoulder straps cut deeply into her darkening flesh. "You look fantastic," he said, but when he touched her side, she winced.

"God, I'm an idiot," she said. "I can't believe I fell asleep out there. You'll have to be careful when we dance tomorrow." She turned from him, went to the mirror, started brushing her hair with short, violent strokes. "I can't wait till this is all over and we can get back to our regular lives."

BY THE TIME THEY MADE IT DOWNSTAIRS, THE FLORENTINE Room was already crowded with friends and family. Eric's parents stood at the entrance, greeting guests, his mother craning her neck to see each face, her cheeks flushed from the effort. "Ma," he said. "Why don't you go sit down?"

"I only get to do this once or twice," she said. "It's worth a little pain."

Linda was there, too, making notes on her clipboard. She'd changed her suit—this one was scarlet, with a short skirt and pink hose. Melissa had told her she didn't need to be here, but it was part of her service, she'd insisted, to be available in case of problems. She stepped forward as soon as she spotted them, and Melissa clutched Eric's arm and whispered, "Don't let her touch me."

"Oh, you poor thing!" Linda cried. "You got sunburned! Well, don't worry. Everything's perfect in there. Now, take a deep breath. And remember to eat."

Eric spoke up before Melissa could open her mouth. "I guess everything's under control. We'll see you tomorrow afternoon, right? Thanks for everything." They swept past her before her smile had a chance to dissolve. He muttered, "Don't look back. You'll turn to stone," and for the first time all day, Melissa smirked and pinched his side.

But soon they were separated. Eric's fraternity brothers were back from Tampa, their suits nearly identical, Jim in navy, the two Robs in charcoal gray, all three with faint pinstripes that were visible only from an inch or two away. They crowded around him and clapped his back for the third time this weekend. Tomorrow they would do it again. They told him about the wholesaler, how they'd bought digital video cameras, wireless routers, networking software, all for a fraction of the retail price. These were the same people who'd once chomped peyote buttons and hurled themselves onto a Mardi Gras float, the same ones who'd been arrested for tossing cream-filled balloons from their roof onto passing cars. Eric hadn't participated either time and was glad for it now. It sounded depressing to have to always recall how reckless and carefree he'd once been, after settling into regular routines of work and family.

A glass of wine appeared in his hand. He was passed from person to person, nodding, smiling, repeating details about his job, the new condo, the upcoming honeymoon. He caught a glimpse of Melissa across the room, the swish of her hair, a flash of pink shoulder, but each time he tried to make his way to her someone stopped him and pumped his hand. First the screechy friend of his mother's, with clumping mascara and a wine spot on her cream blouse, who leaned close and said too loud in his ear, "Did you two really make up? Or is this just some kind of truce until the wedding's over?" Nothing he said could convince her that he and Josh had never been enemies. "Come on, now. I've known you since you were in your mother's belly. You can tell me."

Then Melissa's father cornered him near the bar. Three of his front teeth were black in the center, and his breath was rancid. Eric knew how much he was spending on the wedding, but still he'd never be able to like the man. "You'll learn when you have kids," Dr. Silesky said, though Eric had missed what it was he was supposed to learn. "Never take your quiet times for granted."

Finally it was time to sit. Melissa fell into the chair beside him, out of breath. Her hair was already frizzed at the ends, her lipstick worn away. But her eyes were lit up, and she squeezed Eric's hand beneath the table. "Everyone's being so nice," she said. Then, following his gaze to the two empty chairs at the table beside theirs, she asked, "He's not here?"

"Neither's Carrie," Eric said.

"Kathy," she corrected. "They'll be here."

They showed up while most people were finishing their salads. Linda led them in, her arm around Josh's waist again as she scanned her clipboard and pointed them to the right table. Josh wore the same clothes he'd had on this afternoon, the khakis sagging a little now, the knit shirt untucked. His hair had lost its shine. Kathy had thrown on a short sundress and wedge-heel sandals, and Josh's hand rested flat on her bare back. They stopped at the bar, and then tiptoed the rest of the way in, bumping against each other as they walked. Kathy giggled, and Josh put a finger to his lips, though the room was raucous with conversation and clattering plates. "They're hammered," Eric whispered, jabbing a cucumber with his fork.

"They're having a good time," Melissa said, without conviction. "They look cute together."

Everyone was watching them. Eric's mother, pretending to concentrate on her food, stiffened when Josh stooped to kiss her cheek. His father glanced up quickly, a look of helplessness and desperation blearing his eyes, and then went back to nodding idiotically as one of the Robs explained the advantages of wireless networking. Josh squeezed the back of Eric's neck and breathed whiskey fumes into his face. "Sorry we're late, bro," he said. "We got talking and … just lost track of time, you know?" Instead of answering, Eric took another bite of lettuce. Kathy, already in her seat, grabbed a bottle from the center of the table and sloshed wine into Josh's glass and then her own.

How could he take his eyes off them? They drank and whispered and tittered. Their fingers touched, then their shoulders, then their thighs. They were in a world entirely to themselves. There might have been no one else in the room. When Josh dropped a dinner roll onto the floor and nearly fell off his chair trying to pick it up, Eric imagined he heard a gasp rise up from one table, then another, and another, until all sixty-eight guests were holding their breath. Later, when Kathy's hand disappeared beneath the table and stayed there, Eric wasn't the only one, he was sure, who glanced down at his plate in embarrassment. He felt affirmed, all his doubts validated, and wanted Melissa to admit she'd been wrong. But she'd made the mistake of sitting next to her mother, who was hissing about flowers again, and about how she hated the centerpieces. They'd turned out exactly as Eric had seen them in the magazine, candles bobbing among violet petals, a pleasant citrus breeze wafting above their heads. They were the only thing he wanted to remember about the dinner, since the salmon was dried out and the broccoli soggy. But he had no choice—this was the night before his wedding and always would be, and he'd remember all of it, no matter what he might want to forget.

The toasts started before the plates were cleared away. Dr. Silesky couldn't resist being the center of attention, even though his shirt was too big for him, his tie crooked. "Some of you remember how much Jan and I hated the idea of Missy having boyfriends when she was a teenager," he said. "Believe me, it was much worse when we actually had to meet them. Remember the banjo player, honey?"

Melissa shaded her eyes, and her mother called out, "Don't remind me."

"Or the performance artist? The one whose hair changed color three times in one year? You can imagine how relieved we were the first time she brought Eric home. The first thing I thought was, 'I hope this one sticks around. I can't handle another night of experimental dance.'" He paused for laughter, which was scattered and brief. "So here's to you, Eric," he went on, raising his glass. "You saved me from ever having to watch another person crawl around a stage in a diaper and green body paint."

The waiters had finished clearing now and lined up along the far wall, with their hands behind their backs. The dark runt, the one Eric had almost throttled, wasn't among them. Fired, he guessed, and felt a momentary sting of guilt, even though he knew the kid had deserved it, had no place working with the public. Linda lurked beside the entrance, her suit matching the tablecloths so closely Eric wondered if she'd bought it especially for this occasion. It unnerved him to see her there still. He didn't want her hearing about his life, though he couldn't have said why. Rob Singer stood and told about the cream-filled balloon incident, not remembering that Eric had been in his room studying for a comp sci mid-term and found out about it only when he got the call asking him to post bail. Melissa's childhood friend pouted and scolded her for breaking a promise: at ten years old, they'd agreed never to get married—instead they would buy a beach house together and spend their lives getting the best tans in the world. Eric's father got up hesitantly and mumbled something about how wonderful it was to watch a son grow up and go off on his own, but even Eric had a hard time hearing him from across the table, and around the room there were numerous squints and shrugs. He went on too long, and then forgot to take a sip of champagne before sitting down.

Then Kathy leapt up and held her glass above her head. "Laundry Boy!" she cried, and squealed nonsensically, closing her eyes and wiggling her free hand beside her hair. Either she couldn't go on or had nothing else to say. Instead of cringing the way Eric did, Melissa cracked up, slapping the edge of the table, butting Eric's arm with her forehead. Kathy would have kept standing there, laughing and dribbling champagne down her arm, if Josh didn't reach up for her elbow and guide her back into her seat. Eric felt gratitude only for a moment, because then Josh stood himself, a drink in each hand, whiskey and red wine. The dread of anticipation quickly gave way to a pleasurable kind of certainty. This was the moment they'd all been waiting for, and at least it would soon be over. His mother closed her eyes. His father played with a button on his sleeve. Even Melissa thrummed her fingers nervously against her leg.

"I've made a lot of mistakes in my life," Josh said. His smile was loose, his eyes wandering. His whole body swayed. But his voice was even, composed, the same deep, understated tone he'd had this afternoon. Only now he was somehow able to project through the cavernous room, which was suddenly hushed, the silence broken only by the shuffling of a waiter's shoe, and by Kathy's giggling, muffled now in a napkin pressed over her mouth. "But the biggest one was forgetting I had a family that cared about me and had faith in me. Lucky for me, they never let me forget for very long." This speech had been rehearsed, Eric knew, similar to any number Josh had given at A.A. or N.A. or whatever gathering of misfits and lowlifes he belonged to. He wouldn't suddenly break into tears and beg to be a kid again. He wouldn't pull out any sentimental photographs. Eric should have been relieved, but instead he was irate, more than ever, though he couldn't name the reason. Maybe Melissa had been right—he didn't give Josh a break and never would. Anything his brother said was simply wrong, a source of bottomless resentment. "Eric's given me a lot of things over the years," Josh went on. "I think he gave me my first fishing rod, when I was about eight or something.

I know for sure he gave me my first dirty magazine. Don't worry, Missy, he only got them for the articles." There was laughter on all sides now, Kathy cackling loudest and then stopping abruptly, jamming the napkin back over her mouth. "He taught me how to drive when I was fourteen, way before I could get my permit. But this is the best. This beats everything. Bringing me here, giving me a second chance. And on top of it all," he said, making a broad, sweeping gesture with the wine glass and not spilling a drop, "he's given me this whole new family, all these amazing people. Thanks, bro. Thanks for everything."

There was clapping, glasses clinking, shouts of "Hear, hear!" Linda beat on her clipboard with the heel of a hand. Eric's mother covered her face, and his father gripped her arm. Melissa leaned close and whispered caustically, "See?" Her breath was sour with wine, her lips wet with spittle, her eyes crinkled and mean-spirited. She was as drunk as Josh or Kathy, and tomorrow she'd be hung over for the second day in a row. When he didn't answer, she repeated, "See?"

See what? That all these people were fools and suckers? That they were all being duped, believing an utter sham? No— it was worse than that. They all knew a fantasy when they saw it, and went on believing anyway. Later tonight, Eric guessed, Josh would watch as Kathy pitched to her knees and puked up her dinner. He'd pass out on the beach, leaving the two-hundred-dollar-a-night room Eric had paid for empty. In a month, two months, six months, he would be back in rehab or in jail, and these same people would talk about how surprised they were, how they thought he'd beaten his demons, how wonderful he'd been at the wedding. He would go on wrecking his own life and the lives of everybody around him, but it wouldn't stop all these stupid, stupid people from believing in him and hoping for the best.

When Josh sat, no one else stood. Melissa nudged Eric's arm. By the time he got to his feet, he was nearly shaking. Melissa stared up at him with a self-righteous grin, triumphant, as if she and all her scruffy, crippled vets had finally proven something.

Her sunburned face grew redder by the moment. Tomorrow she would be a lobster, and she'd hate all the pictures her father was paying a fortune to have taken, would refuse to keep any of them. Josh leaned back in his chair, a blissful expression on his lean face, one leg crossed over the other knee, a hand on Kathy's shoulder. He believed his own words—for the moment he'd forgotten about the photograph, the lake, his pathetic tears. He was waiting for Eric to say something optimistic and confident, and so were his parents, his mother on the verge of collapse, his father worn out and old. Everyone was looking at him now, expectantly, as if he could tell them what the future would bring. Don't ask me! he wanted to shout. I don't know a goddamn thing! "I guess…" he began, startled and furious at the way each word caught in his throat, emotion welling against his will. It took all his strength to go on. "Thank you. Thanks…for coming. It means so much."

Back in his chair, he wrestled his napkin onto his lap. Melissa had her arms around him, her red face hot against his damp cheek. "Oh, sweetheart," she said, stroking his hair. "Oh, sweetie." He heard movement around him and kept his head down, not wanting to know who was coming to comfort him— his parents, Josh, Jim and the Robs, or worse, Dr. and Mrs. Silesky, Kathy and Carrie, these people who tomorrow would become part of his family. But when he looked up, everyone was still sitting. The waiters, thank God, had started bringing out dessert.

The Headhunter

1.

IF I THOUGHT ANYONE WOULD LISTEN—WHO EVER DOES?—
I might talk sometimes about Howard Rifkin, my neighbor, once
upon a time my friend. Not in order to explain away what
happened between us, or to justify myself, or defend my actions.
I'm not interested in laying blame—or pronouncing my guilt,
either. I just want to make certain things clear, at least the way I
see them. Maybe Rifkin would tell it differently. Or maybe he
wouldn't tell it at all—maybe he hasn't wasted a single thought on
me for the past six months, though who knows what else he's
got to do all day, knocking around in that big silent house with no
work to busy his mind.

That's it at the top of the rise, the boxy brown colonial with
yellow shutters. I have to step out to the edge of my lawn to get
a glimpse of it, but I'm out here anyway, deadheading the last of
the rose bushes, scraping a fresh batch of leaves from the grass
into the gutter. It's a Sunday, early November, not yet 7 a.m. Carol
won't be up for hours still, and since it's quiet and I'm awake,
this seems like as good a time as any to get things done. There's
always something that needs my attention—the dead azalea
in the rock garden, the patch of sod a skunk dug up this summer
looking for grubs, the rusted swing set in the backyard that
no kids have played on for more than fifteen years. But instead of
doing what needs to be done, here I am lingering on the curb,
leaning forward on my rake to get a full view of Rifkin's house,
hoping, maybe, to catch him staring back down the street at me.

If you lived in this neighborhood long enough, you'd get used to seeing that house. Come up either end of Crescent Ridge and there it is, smack in the middle of your windshield, framed nicely now by those enormous pitch pines that were just saplings when I helped Rifkin plant them. I've passed the house so many times I hardly notice it anymore. I go whole days without thinking about it—or about Rifkin for that matter—forget them both the way you forget your own skin unless it itches, or your breath unless it comes up short.

If the house weren't only twenty years old and freshly paint-ed every other year, kids around here would probably take the place for haunted, the way it sits up there all by itself, staring down sullenly on the rest of us. And in a way it is haunted now—by Rifkin, retired for half a year, wandering from room to room with a section of the *Times* tucked under his arm, doing God-knows-what to keep from going insane. Sometimes the house and Rifkin are one and the same to me—or the way I think of them, at least—broad and simple, unadorned in the midst of all these elaborate brick facades and bronze bay windows.

Don't get me wrong. Rifkin's no idiot. He's got a Ph.D., after all. It's just that—I guess I figured a man with so much education would understand a little more about how the world works. I guess, after all this time, he still doesn't make much sense to me.

For one, who buys a piece of property like that, facing north so it never gets a direct ray of sunlight, a lawn so steep it's nearly impossible to cut, the house exposed on the bare ridge to wind and rain and drifting snow? Every Thursday a crew of Puerto Ricans spends three hours up there, with mowers as wide as tanks to keep from tipping over on the slope. During thunder-storms the roof gutters overflow without fail, spilling filthy rainwater into the bedroom windows. Last spring a sudden gust tore the chimney a few inches away from the frame of the house, and now it's teetering there, sometimes leaning toward the living room, sometimes away. Rifkin can only stand and watch which way it'll topple—his insurance won't pay to have it fixed until it falls on its own.

Winter's when I appreciate my lot the most, where the road bottoms out and starts to curve toward Route 10. Facing south, my lawn doesn't keep its snow more than a few hours after the sun comes out. The driveway's flat and easy to shovel. Rifkin's snow lingers well into April, crusty brown drifts wedged against the corner of his garage, covering his wife's flowerbeds. His driveway isn't just steep—it's got head-high stone walls on both sides, and hedges on top of those. To get snow off, you've got to heave it ten feet in the air or else carry it down to the street and pile it on the curb.

I used to get giddy those mornings I'd hear the snowplows and sanders rumble by outside, rattling the windowpanes. Even more than the kids, who held hands and leaned their foreheads together, muttering a prayer to keep school closed. I'd spring out of bed and open the shades onto the white world, blinding Carol, who even fifteen years ago struggled to get out of bed before noon. "Snow," I'd tell her, and she'd pull a pillow over her head and say, "I've got eyes." By seven I was outside with my shovel, no gloves or hat, tearing over my little patch of tar without once looking up. In an hour I was through, and I'd stand and admire the clean black surface, proud of myself for the work I'd done, for the house I'd chosen, for the inconceivable place I'd somehow arrived in my life. I was proud and content even when the kids came out with their backpacks and threw me a bitter, hateful look, despising anyone who worked against the snow that should have kept them home.

Then—when we were still talking—I'd wander up the hill to see if Rifkin needed a hand. He always did. By the time I got there he was no more than a foot or two out of his garage, bundled in a hooded Alaskan parka that drenched him in sweat, scraping a battered shovel over the crumbling blacktop, sliding around in ancient rubber boots whose treads had long since worn away. Here was another thing I never understood about him—he had money, plenty of it, but never thought to replace anything until he was actually using it. He'd lift a shaking shovel heaped with snow, take a deep breath, pause a moment, and then sling it over his head to clear the wall and hedges. If the snow was dry, half of it blew onto his shoulders and neck. The heavy wet stuff would stick briefly to the rocks and slowly dribble back onto the driveway. Afterward, he'd pause again, holding a hand to his chest, and then two fingers to his neck, expecting his heart to give out any minute. I knew he was thinking of Hans Groh, his former boss, who'd been digging in his garden when a sudden jolt sent him reeling forty feet across the backyard into a leaf pile he'd gathered earlier that afternoon. But Hans had smoked two packs a day for thirty years and drank four beers with dinner every night. In all the years I'd known him, Rifkin had never actually finished a full glass of wine. He excused himself from the room whenever I started to light up. His wife trimmed the fat from his steak and roast beef and wouldn't let him eat the skin of her barbecued chicken, which was famous in the neighborhood. Still, he waited until his pulse slowed before leaning over and working the shovel back into the snowdrift he'd barely dented.

I'd watch for a minute before saying anything. He always seemed surprised to see me, no matter how regularly I showed up. Even last December, the first big snow of the season, a couple months before everything started to go sour, he squinted and seemed to take a moment to recognize who was waving from the bottom of the driveway with a brand new, double-width aluminum shovel. "Hey, Dr. T.," I called. "Need some help? Or you want to wait till it melts next July?"

He ran a thick glove across his eyes, not clearing the sweat away so much as pushing it onto his cheeks, where it pooled for a second before streaming along the sides of his nose and over his lips. "That's nice of you, Len. I'd hate to put you out. You've got your own to take care of."

I assured him I had the time, and for a moment he protested without much conviction. Then we both stopped talking and went to work. Our heads lowered and didn't rise for an hour or more. Rifkin forgot about his pulse. Our shovels moved in rhythm, mine smooth as a new razor through taut skin, his making a racket of scraping and grinding but still snaking a quick path from the garage to the front walkway. Rifkin's wife Joan opened an upstairs window and called through the screen, "Howard, don't over-exert. Hi, Len. Can I bring you two some tea?"

By then I was breathing hard. My fingers and the rims of my eyes were numb. I looked to Rifkin, but if he heard his wife at all, he didn't show it. His head was still down, his arms working steadily, his breath steaming. I waved helplessly at Joan and hunched over my shovel. Another hour and Rifkin and I were clearing the last white strip separating the top of the driveway from the bottom. He grunted happily with each stroke. My arms and back ached, and when we finished, I leaned against the rock wall with both hands over my chest. Rifkin pulled off his hood, wiped crystals of snot from his mustache, smiled. His cheeks were bright red, his eyes glistening. Despite the spreading speckles of gray in his hair and the deep creases on his forehead, he looked like one of my kids, fifteen years earlier, at the end of a day of sledding and throwing snowballs through neighbors' windows. He clapped a hand on my sore shoulder. "I owe you one," he said. "Once again."

I couldn't catch my breath to answer. A soft breeze sent a swirl of snow across the cleared blacktop to twist around our feet. The clouds had broken, and now the sun warmed feeling back into my nose and ears. The pain made me shut my eyes. When I opened them, Rifkin was handing me a steaming mug. His gloves were off, and so was his coat. Joan stood beside him, the Alaskan parka wrapped around her bathrobe, her bare feet swallowed in unlaced work boots. "You're too good to us," she said. "I don't know if we deserve it."

I lifted my hand and managed to croak, "My pleasure." Then the coughing started, an icy hack that seared my throat and hurt all the way to my gut. Hot tea spilled over my hand, and I fought to keep from dropping the mug. I reached into my jacket with my free hand and shook a cigarette into my mouth. It was hard enough to hold the lighter steady, and then the wind kicked up and blew out the flame. Joan cupped her hands for me, and I leaned into them. I was careful to blow smoke up over my shoulder. But when I straightened, Rifkin had already backed a few feet away, his cheeks pale again, a hand over his nose and mouth.

MY FULL NAME, IF ANYONE CARES, IS LEN SIEGEL, OF Siegel & Siegel, Pharmaceutical Human Resources. Headhunter. When I first started out in the business twenty-seven years ago, I used to spit that last word out as a challenge, a fact to be wondered at and reckoned with. Then I'd thrust out my hand with a business card sticking up like a blade between the first two knuckles—if you didn't take the card fast enough, its bottom corner jabbed into your palm when we shook. My tactic was shocking people into trusting me, terrifying them with my brutal honesty. But there's nothing too shocking about what I do, and only so much that's honest. I spend my days on the phone or in my car, trying to steal young hotshot biologists from Warner Lambert in order to sell them to Bristol-Meyers or Burroughs Welcome. My livelihood depends on other people's dissatisfaction, impatience, sense of self worth. I court the common belief—or hope, or misconception—that better days lie just over the horizon. I joke and prod, laugh and lie, curse and plead, wheedle, whine, and wail. Three times in my life I've broken down and cried in front of another man—the last two to clinch a deal, the first because I thought my family was headed for the street.

Am I proud of what I do? So I'm not a paramedic, I don't save lives. But I've had my hand in more than a few important careers. The heads of research at Ciba, Squibb, Pfizer—all bench chemists when I found them. The guy who developed the blood pressure pills I take every morning was ready to give up the industry for an academic job until I convinced him he had important things to contribute to—and gain from—a free market society. And it's how I met Rifkin, long before we became neighbors.

The neighborhood didn't even exist back then, in the spring of '73—I've lived in this part of the county all my life, and until twenty years ago there was nothing up here but trees and rocks and a few failing farms on the hill's lower slopes. At the time I didn't even dream of owning my own house, much less living on a quiet street with a hundred yards between me and the nearest neighbor. It was enough if I could pay the rent from one month to the next, and to be honest, sometimes I couldn't. I'd been working for my older brother Barry almost a year by then and still hadn't gotten my feet under me. I also hadn't yet given up the image that first triggered my imagination when Barry had finally agreed— reluctantly, after making me beg—to let me have the job: a browned body in full headdress and war paint, a human bone through my nose and more in my pockets to pick my teeth with. To give myself a boost of confidence after a run of bad luck— did I have any other kind that year?—I'd picture myself slipping through dense jungles on a lonely Pacific island, searching for fresh sacrifices to a greedy god. But I'd already given up any romantic notions about the work itself. I hadn't had a commission in three weeks, and Barry had begun to talk about my "probationary period" being over. Every day he threw around new phrases like "performance reviews" and "disciplinary action." He'd been reading management books in his spare time, though I was the only person he had to manage.

He was just thirty then, three years older than me, already balding and thick around the middle, with sweat-stained collars that cut into the flab around his neck and thumb-width cigars that bulged in his jacket pocket. He didn't seem used to his bulk yet—he made quick, jerky movements with his arms and legs and then glanced around in confusion when his torso didn't follow. His eyebrows didn't quite come together but were linked by a deep crease on the bridge of his nose. He talked in a throaty indifferent voice he'd cultivated since his days as a high school greaser, when he'd discovered how to intimidate other kids by pretending not to care whether they were intimidated or not.

He'd never taken an interest in my life when we were growing up—somehow he managed to ignore me completely even though we shared a tiny bedroom in our parents' single story bungalow—but now he suddenly had something to say about everything I did. "When you planning to buy some decent clothes?" he'd mutter, waving a hand at an embroidered shirt I'd paid good money for, even with an employee discount, when I'd worked as an apprentice tailor in the department store a few doors down the street. His own suit was cheap and too tight and frayed at the cuffs. "You look like a goddamn gypsy." If I ever complained about my family—Carol was pregnant for the second time then, bloated and rashy, and Katie, not yet two, never slept through the night—he said, "Cut 'em loose," and snipped an invisible string with two chubby fingers. "Look at me. What have I got to worry about? Where's all my money go? Right into my pocket."

The only things that marked us as brothers were our small eyes that tended to water easily and the loose set of our teeth, spread apart in our mouths a bit like stretching toes. Otherwise, I was wiry and nervous, my cheeks already sinking between my jaws, a deep hollow forming at the base of my throat. My own hair, several shades lighter than Barry's, was just beginning to recede along the hairline, but I kept it brushed back in a careless wind-blown way, as I had ever since riding in a convertible for the first time, at seventeen. I wore rose-tinted sunglasses indoors and out and a hip-length leather jacket in all weather, well-oiled and honey-colored, with six-inch lapels and a wide belt that flapped around my knees.

We were called Siegel & Siegel even then, but I was nothing like a full partner—Barry just liked the snappy sound of repetition in the name. We worked out of an abandoned storefront on Spring Street, flanked on one side by a pharmacy and smoke shop and on the other by a liquor store advertising Meister Brau and Piels and Old Crow on brightly colored construction paper cut out in the shape of stars. Rents were cheap downtown now that most lucrative businesses were moving to the first of the strips

on Route 46, just half a mile away. Our plate glass had been painted black, the front door shaded by heavy floral oilcloth once used
to cover a picnic table. Inside, exposed pipes and beams stuck
out from the gutted ceiling. Wires and cables dangled head-high.
Two bare bulbs flickered and buzzed intermittently, sometimes
blinking off altogether until one of us pounded a fist against the
pressboard paneling directly above the switchbox.

There were two phones, but only one desk. My papers, my
handwritten scraps with leads underlined or circled depending
on how reliable I considered their source, the stub of pencil that
disappeared whenever I needed it most, all of it was piled on
an overturned cardboard crate that had once held seventy-five
grapefruits our parents had sent from their new home in Pom-
pano Beach. I watched enviously as Barry leaned back in his swivel
chair, kicking his feet onto the spacious top of the mahogany
pedestal desk he'd inherited from our Great Uncle Al, with its four
large drawers and built-in pen holder. The old man had left me
a crystal chandelier, which of course I couldn't have hung in my
rented apartment and wouldn't have anyway—I pawned it too
quickly for too little cash.

It always troubled me to see how leisurely Barry could talk
to complete strangers, never stumbling over his words, never
showing any emotion. My fingers started to tremble even before I
picked up the receiver. I blamed the cardboard desk, the metal
folding chair that forced me to sit stiffly upright. How was I supposed to relax? I stared at the phone for ten minutes, shuffling
my scraps to make myself look busy. Behind me I heard Barry
arrange two appointments and confirm a placement he'd made
the week before. I wrapped the phone cord around my knuckles
like boxing tape and bounced my fist against my knee while I
listened to the dial tone and worked up the courage to go through
with a call. I should just give up, I told myself. Give up the job,
the family, any expectation I had for a meaningful life. I would just
hand myself over to the hopelessness I fought off with less and
less energy day after day.

But in the end I dialed. There was only one ring and a click on the line. Then a long sigh. "Sweetheart, you have to stop calling every five minutes," said a young voice, tired and slightly nasal. "What's he done now?"

"Dr. Hummel?" I said. "Dr. Hummel, this is—"

"Wait a minute."

"Dr. Hummel, I know you're tired of hearing from me, but if I could just take a moment of your time—"

"Hold on—"

"If you'll just listen for a minute—"

"I'm not Hummel."

"Excuse me?"

"I'm Rifkin," he said. "Howard Rifkin."

"Rifkin?" I could feel Barry behind me, though I didn't dare turn around. He was laughing or shaking his head, the sweat in either case dripping from his neck into his collar. "Who the hell is Rifkin?"

"Who the hell are you?"

"Jesus Christ. You think I have time for this? Where's Hummel?"

"Beats me. I'm not him."

"B.R. Hummel. I've called him four times this week. This is his number."

"This is my number," the young voice said. It still sounded tired but not annoyed. It sounded as if it could go on this way all morning. "I've never talked to you before in my life."

"I don't have time for this," I said. "Just give me Hummel's extension."

"Never heard of a Hummel. Never met anyone named B.R."

"For christsake. Isn't this Squibb, oncology department?"

"Reinhardt DeLouche, quality assurance."

Now Barry was laughing for sure, a scratchy, disappointed chuckle. "Maybe I don't need two Siegels in the name after all," he muttered.

I rummaged through the scraps on my crate until I came up with the right one. "Howard Rifkin?" I asked.

"That's right."

"Of Reinhardt DeLouche?"

"Like I said."

"Quality assurance. Organic chemist. Ph.D. from Rochester."

"You got it."

"You looking for a job?" I asked.

"I've got one."

"Want a better one?"

"Who doesn't?"

I leaned back in my folding chair and carefully propped one foot on the edge of my crate. Barry stood with his arms crossed, his sweaty frog face turning red. The light bulbs flickered but didn't go out. "Now you're talking," I said.

I DIDN'T KNOW ANY BETTER THAN TO HAVE RIFKIN MEET me at the Firelight, a low-ceilinged, smoky bar across the street from the office. Or maybe I did know better, but I was stubborn and determined to sabotage myself every chance I got. Why should I have to change for anybody? Why should I put on a suit and go to some gray-walled sterilized office full of thick journals I couldn't understand, just so some egghead in horn-rimmed glasses could look down his nose at me and tell me to get lost? If I never expected to gain anything, what could I lose? In either case, Rifkin didn't object to the Firelight—he only asked if he could get onion rings there, and then mumbled something about not telling his wife about them, how he'd never hear the end of it if he didn't have an appetite for dinner.

I stopped into the Firelight most nights on my way home, and I'll admit, sometimes I didn't make it out of there before midnight. The place catered mostly to vets recently back from Southeast Asia, and though the draft board had excused me from service—heart murmur, same as my father—I sat at the bar and imagined myself in their ranks, haunted, pissed off, drinking only to numb the unbearable pain. I tried to remember names from TV reports I'd watched, Khe Sanh, Quang Ngai Province, the

Iron Triangle, but it was all just dense jungle in my mind, scattered with rice paddies and grass huts. Hadn't I been through tough times, too, in the last few years? I'd had almost a dozen jobs before I started working for Barry, some promising ones among them, but failure crept up on me wherever I turned. The department store where I trained as a tailor went out of business after JC Penney opened a branch in Rockaway. The owner of the roofing crew I spent the summer with, breathing tar into my lungs, working ten hours a day under the broiling sun as my shoulders and arms burned, peeled, and burned again, let me go to make room for his nephew, a clumsy nineteen-year-old who ended up tumbling from a garage and breaking his wrist. By then I was selling cars on the Chrysler lot in Morris Plains—or trying to sell them without much luck. After a month with no commissions the manager told me to take a hike, but I didn't budge until he threatened to call the cops.

I know I should have felt guilty sitting in that bar while Carol carried her enormous belly around the one-bedroom garden apartment on Route 46 and New Road, cooking and cleaning for me, chasing down Katie who kicked and howled whenever anybody tried to change her diaper. But I couldn't face the bleak expression she'd greet me with, her stoic attempts not to ask whether or not I'd made a placement, her eventual tentative questions. I couldn't watch how she'd flinch when I snapped at her and then sit in sullen silence for the rest of the night. I couldn't spend more time than I had to in that cramped apartment with upstairs neighbors who walked around all night in heavy boots and downstairs ones who left stinking trash on the landing. The longer I sat at the bar, the less likely I was to leave. Drink has a way of turning guilt into bitterness and resentment—the second I started to question how I might be hurting my family, a long list of justifications rose to my mind. I wouldn't stay out all the time, I reasoned, if Carol and Katie didn't make me so miserable when I was home. Or if Carol would let me invite friends from the Firelight to come drink in our living room. Hadn't they fought a war for us? Didn't they deserve our hospitality?

Tonight I showed up half an hour earlier than I'd told Rifkin to meet me. On the first two stools sat Jeff Green and Brett Hoffer, as they did whenever I came in. Green worked mornings at a service station far out on Diamond Lake Road and made it to the bar by noon—Hoffer didn't have a job and, except to go to his classes at County, wouldn't have left at all if the place didn't close from two to ten in the morning. In high school the three of us had considered each other best friends, though I knew without them ever acknowledging it that Green and Hoffer considered each other better friends than either of them considered me. If the day called for fishing in a two-person boat, I was the one left on shore. They both dropped out of school at the same time, signing their letters with a dramatic flourish right on the vice-principal's desk. I found out only later that afternoon, and when I went to turn in my letter the next morning, the vice-principal just shrugged and told me to give it to the secretary. Instead I stuck it in my pocket and decided to ride out the last few months to my diploma. A few weeks after graduation, Green and Hoffer were arrested for shoplifting—socket wrenches of all things, to work on the hopelessly broken motorcycle Green's cousin had given him— and when I drove them home from jail, after harassing Barry into letting me borrow his car and shelling out $150 in bail, all they could talk about was how close they'd come to getting out of the store, how that clerk must have been a psychic, how next time they'd stick the wrenches in their pants instead of their shirts. Not one word of thanks, not a single explanation of why they hadn't invited me along. After that I decided to give them up altogether, and I would have, too, if they hadn't gotten drafted at the end of the summer.

Now they had one up on me by being vets, though neither had actually made it all the way to Vietnam, much less into combat. While they were away I followed the newspapers, trying to picture the terrible things happening to them, the bullets whizzing overhead, the booby traps exploding without warning, the deceitful communist hookers slipping drugs into their drinks. Neither of them sent letters, of course, so all I could do was imagine. I used to read articles to Carol when we first started going out, trying to sound concerned rather than envious, though once she pushed her coffee cup away and said, "You'd rather be off killing people than be here with me." I don't know how long she'd been crying, but when I looked up from the paper her face was streaked with tears. It was the first sign of her sulking, and maybe I should have known then what was coming—the silences that would last for days, the unexpected twitches every time I asked a question, the bitter laughter that would burst out of her at odd times, in response to nothing.

Green came home with a finger-length pink scar on his neck and a story about dragging a wounded buddy through a swamp in heavy fire. The scar could easily have come from a tracer, as he said it did, but Hoffer took me aside one night and told me the truth: Green had been showing off with a straight razor instead of the army-issued safety and nearly clipped his jugular. After that the army left him at a desk in Seoul for the rest of his tour. "He made me swear I'd never tell anyone," Hoffer said after he'd already let it slip. "He'll never talk to me again if he finds out." Another time, while Hoffer was in the can, Green said, "You've got to promise not to let him know I told you. Did you believe him when he said he got dysentery? How many people you know get dysentery while they're still in basic training? It was the nervous shits, plain and simple."

I agreed not to tell, partly because they let me sit and drink with them even though I'd avoided the draft, and partly because they played the roles of grizzled, damaged soldiers so well. Green rubbed thoughtfully at his scar and talked in a slow lilting voice about all the things he would do to the next woman who made the mistake of coming home with him. Hoffer smiled and nodded in silence for a while, until the right balance of whiskey had mixed into his blood. Suddenly his mouth opened and out came a string of precise hatred and abuse directed at whoever happened to catch his eye. "You wear all those tattoos to make up for your tiny prick," he told the burly bartender with the waxed, shiny scalp.

To Green he said, "Why don't you quit rubbing that goddamn scar and go whack off." Me he only stared at in bewilderment and disgust. "You," he said. "I'm not even going to waste my time."

Hoffer had thick yellow farm-boy hair that hung in fringes over his eyes. Orange freckles covered most of his face. Only his nose looked less than benign, blunt and spud-like, cocked a little to the left. He was still smiling by the time I came in tonight, but he had a shot and a beer in front of him, so I knew the smile wouldn't last long. "It's the cannibal," he said, rapping his knuckles on the sticky countertop. "Get the man a drink before he eats everyone in here."

The waxy-headed bartender was twice Hoffer's size, but his big body seized up whenever Hoffer opened his mouth. The dragon tattoos on his arms did look like big green and red pricks, and I wondered if Hoffer hadn't pegged him exactly right. He seemed to have a knack for seeing into people's souls and pointing out the black spot at their centers.

Green glanced up and said dreamily, "That girl behind the counter at Gerald's? Not the drug side, the smokes." His head bobbed as he spoke, loose ringlets bouncing over his ears. His hands were covered in engine grease, and so was his scar now that he'd been rubbing it. Another silver-black streak shimmered on his chin when it caught the light. "You seen her? She's trying for that free-love, hippy look, you know, with a flower over her ear. She gave me the eye the other day and did that thing where she sucks her lip between her teeth. She doesn't know what she's in for."

I knew Rifkin the second he walked in. Not only because he still wore his white lab coat beneath his windbreaker, with cheap plastic goggles sticking out of the front pocket. It was the confused way he glanced around the bar, squinting through the haze, the slouching shoulders that somehow matched the voice I'd heard on the phone. His hair was hugely bushy, and his mustache ended in sharp points on either side of his chin. He looked like someone trying out for a motorcycle club, soon to be turned down. I let him stand there a second, turning from side to side, jumping a little every time balls collided on a pool table in the next room. The bartender leaned over the counter and called, "Can't use the can unless you buy a drink."

Rifkin shrugged and smiled, his mouth closed, his eyes squinting further. "Sorry to bother you," he said, and started to back toward the door. I was off my stool and after him before he could take another step. What did he see charging at him down the length of the bar? A thug in a leather jacket and pork-chop sideburns, with a hand thrust forward. Maybe also his own bludgeoning and violent death. He froze, shoulders raised to his ears, hands in front of his chest. "Len Siegel," I said. "Of Siegel & Siegel—"

Before I could finish he let out his breath, relaxed his arms, and said, "I know all that already. You told me on the phone." He plucked the card gingerly from between my knuckles and then shoved both hands into his pockets so I couldn't shake them. "I can get onion rings in here?" he asked, sniffing the air and surveying the dismal room.

Behind me Hoffer called, "Take a look. Siegel's applying for a new job. Lab rat."

"Why don't you have a seat," I said. I put a hand on Rifkin's back and guided him to the table farthest from my friends, but the place was narrow, and there wasn't far to go. "You want a beer?" I asked. I was already sweating by the time I got to the bar, and I thought of Barry laughing and crossing out the second Siegel from the handwritten sign on our office door. All the doubt I'd felt that morning came rushing back. Give up, I told myself again. Send this guy packing and go back to the much easier task of destroying your life. I forgot to order myself a beer and had to go back to the bar, and then went back a second time because I'd forgotten to put in Rifkin's order for onion rings. Hoffer said, "A little side dish for your feast? You going to eat him plain, or you want some ketchup?"

"I really should get back soon," Rifkin said when I finally sat. "My wife, she's a little bit sensitive about her dinners. Once I told her I didn't like her meatloaf. Big mistake. You'll help me eat the onion rings, won't you?"

"Sure," I said. My hands were shaking. I suddenly had no idea how to make small talk. Instead I reached into my jacket pocket for the job portfolio I'd put together in a hurry, no binder, no plastic dust covers, just six sheets of paper folded over twice. "You want to see what I've got?"

Rifkin still flinched at every crack of the billiards, and I flipped through the papers too fast. The jobs were all lateral positions, nothing very exciting, and I knew it. I'd thought I'd be able to talk him into one, but now I could hardly talk at all. He shook his head at each listing. "More quality assurance," he said. "I've had enough of that already. Don't you have anything in research?"

"You know how hard it is to find research jobs?"

"Why do you think I'm sitting here?"

There were no more listings. I pictured Carol on her back, scratching furiously at the rash spreading across her chest. I saw Katie's face, twisted and red and howling. Give up, I thought one more time. Out loud I said, "Give me a break."

"I'm sorry," Rifkin said. He slid his chair back and started to stand. "I should really go."

"What about your onion rings?" My voice cracked. My throat started to burn, my eyes itched, my nose was suddenly clogged. This was panic, desperation, the first time I'd really felt it. What was a person's life supposed to be about? What was I supposed to hope for? I had no idea. "Don't you want them anymore?"

Rifkin settled back into his chair. "Maybe just a few," he said. He leaned forward and reached out a hand as if to pat me on the back. Then he seemed to think better of it and tapped the folded job listings instead. "Why don't you show them to me again," he said. "I'm a little distracted tonight."

I wiped my eyes, swallowed hard, and unfolded the papers again. Behind me I heard Green describing a pair of thighs, wistfully, like a man who's just spent thirty years in prison. Hoffer cackled maliciously. I smoothed down the first sheet and made an effort this time to describe the position, the company, the salary and benefits, my voice for some reason catching every time I came to the words "pension" and "retirement." Rifkin listened carefully now, nodding as I spoke, then pretending to consider for a moment before saying, "Sounds like an interesting job, but I don't think it's right for me." We came to the end of the stack once more, and he said, "I'm really sorry. If it was the right opening. You know." Tears came to my eyes again, but even I could tell they were forced—this time they didn't keep Rifkin from standing up all the way. "I don't mind if you call me again," he said. "If anything comes up."

The bartender came to the table then and dropped a steaming basket of onion rings in front of us. They weren't bad ones either, to my surprise as much as to Rifkin's—the freshly battered kind, oil still sizzling around their rims. Rifkin sat down for the third time. "Maybe just a few," he said, again.

The smell caught Hoffer's and Green's attention. They crowded around, pulling up chairs on either side of Rifkin. "Good to meet you," Green said before I had a chance to do any introductions, putting out a grease-smudged hand. Rifkin shook it politely and then held his own hand in the air a second before wiping it off on a corner of his lab coat. Hoffer sent two fingers diving straight for the basket and came up with the biggest ring they could find. Steam was still coming off it, but he stuck the whole thing in his mouth without blowing on it or letting it cool. He chewed once, and his eyes bugged. He tried to suck air into his mouth and at the same time let out a hooting noise. Finally he just leaned forward and let the mess of onion and batter fall into his lap. "Save it for later," he said, and bared his yellow teeth at Rifkin, who only smiled with his mouth closed, squinting and nodding, as if this were the best idea he'd ever heard. "So you're doing experiments on this guy?" Hoffer asked. "Making him run around a maze?" Rifkin looked puzzled, but Hoffer didn't give him much time to think. "You should be careful around him," he said. "He eats people's livers for lunch."

"You married?" Green asked. Rifkin nodded. "Got a picture?"

"She's expecting me," Rifkin said. "I really ought to be

going." He pushed his chair back and reached for an onion ring at the same time. He didn't seem anxious to leave. He was still smiling and squinting and surveying the room as if he belonged here, or wished he did. The crack of billiards didn't seem to bother him anymore. He spoke with his mouth full. "She's been taking care of the little one all day. Our son. He's a bit of a handful. And she's a good cook, really. She will be. She's trying. I shouldn't miss dinner."

"Ball and chain got the balls on a chain," Hoffer said.

"You sure you don't have a picture?" Green asked.

"Some men do what they want with their lives," Hoffer said.

"Can't you describe her?"

Rifkin had onion rings in both hands and alternated bites from each. "She's making some kind of chicken. It didn't turn out so well last time, but she's getting much better. She's learning. I got her a cookbook."

"I'll find you a new job," I said. "A good one. I swear."

"I bet she's got nice hair," Green said. "Long brown hair. Down to her shoulders."

Hoffer said angrily, "Some men can take care of themselves."

"It's been a pleasure, gentlemen," Rifkin said. He shook hands all around and wiped more engine grease onto his lab coat. He smiled at me and said, "Hope we can do it again."

"I'll give you a call," I said. "If anything comes up."

He hooked another three onion rings onto his pointer finger, gave a little wave, made a couple of turns as if he'd forgotten where the door was, or was pretending to have forgotten, and then made his way to it in a stiff-legged, reluctant way. The celebratory mood I hadn't even recognized at our little table until now faded almost immediately. Hoffer was sneering at a shaggy-haired kid setting up a behind-the-back shot at the nearest pool table. Green traced a pattern of scored grooves in the wooden tabletop. I picked up Rifkin's beer—he'd taken a sip, maybe two—and finished it in one extended swig. Mine was long gone.

I STAYED UNTIL THE FIRELIGHT WAS CLOSED. THEN GREEN and I carried Hoffer to his car, where he'd spend the night, and somehow I made my way to my own. Route 46 was a blur of lights and black pavement. I had no hope of driving past the apartment as I wanted to, past the exit for my childhood home, past the campuses of all the pharmaceutical firms that were supposed to provide my living, never once looking back. I could barely get out of the car, which I parked crookedly across two spots, and then couldn't make it the last few feet to the bedroom. Instead I threw myself into a creaking second-hand armchair and sat staring at nothing. Above me the boots stomped, a hobnail army. A siren wailed down 46, lights flashing through the useless translucent drapes. The smell of rotting trash seeped into the apartment even with all the windows closed. The bedroom door was open a crack, and I focused on the darkness inside. Who knows what I was thinking? Bitter, shameful thoughts about how I'd never really wanted a family, how this wife and kid were sucking all my money away, how they were keeping me from the life I'd always dreamed of. But what life was that? The one Green and Hoffer pretended to have lived, scarred and terrorized halfway around the world? The one Barry claimed to love, sleeping alone and growing fat in a studio above our office?

The door swung open wider, and Katie wobbled out. Her hair was no more than wisps above her ears and neck, and she wore pink pajamas with the feet built in. She was a beautiful toddler, round and soft, all eyes, not angular and hard-looking the way she's grown up, too much like her old man, I think, to be called pretty. She could say only a handful of words by then, and I was sure she was retarded, though Carol insisted she was just a slow developer. She held a stuffed monkey by the finger and dragged the rest on the ground behind her. It didn't occur to me to wonder how she'd gotten out of the crib. Her eyes were puffy, her cheeks cut with the imprint of a creased blanket, the few wisps of hair sticking up in back. I scowled down at her, trying to convince myself of my own meanness. It's hard to admit, but I'll tell you the truth—I hoped she *was* retarded, so I could feel sorry for myself, so I'd have a justifiable reason to hate the world as much as I wanted to.

Katie's eyes were half closed, but her mouth suddenly twisted into a hideous little grimace. Her head lifted, and her nostrils flared. I was drunk, it's true, so who knows what she really said. But I heard, "Jerk," and I swear to God she pinched the skin above my knee.

"What was that?" I asked with all the fury and insult I could muster, but already I could feel my anger draining away, replaced by some kind of creeping dread. "What did you say to me?"

Her eyes were closed all the way now, her head leaning to one side. She was asleep when I picked her up and held her to my shoulder. I didn't plead for forgiveness or shake with guilty sobs, if that's what you think. What good would it have done? She wouldn't have heard me anyway. I carried her back to her crib and stared down at her in a sort of bewildered and anxious way, as that dread kept spreading through my chest and right into my heart, with its pathetic, blubbering beat, not fit for the army or anything else. Carol snored once and rolled to her side, hugging her gigantic belly—protecting it from me, I thought. Even while she was asleep I could feel her judgment. I'd felt it since we'd first gotten together, when she used to return my intent and—in my mind, at least—passionate gaze and then burst into giggles, saying, "Lighten up, will you? You look like you just killed your own mother."

From the beginning I'd been waiting for her to drop me, to recognize, as I always had, that she was too good for me. She'd gotten her teaching degree at Montclair State and had supported us for two years before getting pregnant with Katie. Why did she stick around? So she could laugh at me, so she could feel superior. I saw men on the streets, the ones she really belonged with, and sometimes I wanted to point them out to her—lawyers and accountants, tall men in suits and ties and wingtips, with pomaded hair and chiseled jaws.

Now I resented her for not leaving when she'd had the

chance, for making me prove to her day after day that I wasn't worthy of her, that I would only ruin her life. I couldn't even bring myself to lie down beside her. I went back to the living room and dropped into the battered armchair again, the only place I belonged. Katie had left her monkey behind. It wasn't much of a toy, a flaccid crocheted thing without much stuffing, long limp arms and legs, frayed red lips, plastic eyes. "Jerk," I said, and shook it. I squeezed its neck, trying to make those empty eyes pop off. "Jerk," I said again. I twisted its arms, pinched its toes, punched it in its idiotic smiling mouth.

I don't know how long I wrestled with that monkey in the dark, but I was hugging it to my chest when I woke up. Carol and Katie were already moving around, ignoring me. Carol didn't make any comment about me sleeping in the chair in all my clothes, and she didn't seem to register any change in my expression. Maybe there wasn't one—I'd slept only a few hours and must have looked as haggard and bloodshot as ever. She carried her heavy belly into the kitchen and started banging pots and pans louder than she needed to, repayment, I guessed, for the hobnails upstairs. Katie was back to her nonsensical babbling, not a clear word in all those syllables, no memory, it seemed, of coming out to see me the night before. I handed her the monkey, which looked untouched, the same sagging bag of stitching it had always been. She took it by the finger and dragged it, face down, over the kitchen's scuffed linoleum floor. I swallowed something sour and salty and had to turn away.

2.

LOOK, I'M NOT TRYING TO SAY RIFKIN SAVED MY LIFE OR showed me the error of my ways. I didn't suddenly stop frequenting the Firelight or drop Hoffer and Green as friends or start going to Friday night services like my mother. It was another three years before the thought of not drinking even entered my mind and another two before I quit for good. But this was the beginning of something, a new stage in my life, if you want to put it that way, and Rifkin happened to be in the picture. I can't help but associate him with the good things that came to me from that point onward, even if they had nothing to do with him.

I didn't manage to place him until two weeks after our first meeting, but he never seemed to mind my calling every couple of days to offer a job I knew he wouldn't want. He always took his time before saying, "Well, Len, it's tempting, but I don't think that's the right move for me at the moment." Then he'd ask after my friends and say he hoped he'd get to see me soon. Finally I landed him at Elistra, running a lab in the new diabetes department directed by Hans Groh, who I met entirely by accident, in line at the liquor store next to the office. Barry was crazy with envy. He'd been trying to break into Elistra for months and so far hadn't had any luck. But how much could he complain? He took half of all my commissions.

Rifkin couldn't show enough gratitude. He called three times in one week to thank me. He took me out to lunch. He sent a bottle of champagne and a note that read, "I owe you one. Let me know if there's anything I can do for you." He didn't know how much he'd done already, and I didn't tell him. I doubt Barry would have fired me, but now he had no room to talk about performance or discipline or probation. Suddenly he'd lost his claim as the only recruitment authority in the office, and I stopped listening to his advice. He had a strict theory about why we should never get to be friends with a candidate, even after we'd placed him. "Conflict of interest," he said. "Someday he might get canned, and you'll have to fill his position." But I decided it was good business to keep in touch with Rifkin. I called a few weeks after he'd started at Elistra to ask how the job was working out, and then once a month or so I'd take him out to lunch and inquire gently if he had any openings in his lab, or if he knew anyone who did. Why not, if he really wanted to show his gratitude? He told me everything he knew. Once I casually suggested that if he ever wanted to slip me a copy of his company directory, I wouldn't object at all. But then he got very serious and reminded me of

Elistra's confidentiality policies—they were written into his contract, which he'd signed in triplicate. "Sure, sure," I said, shrugging. "I was only joking. You don't have to lecture me."

We'd talk shop for only a few minutes before moving on to our families. Rifkin's kid Seth was completely out of control— he loved to pull records out of their sleeves and run his toy trucks against the grain of their grooves. Katie, I told him, had suddenly turned shy to the point of neurosis, throwing wild, flailing tantrums whenever a stranger glanced her way. Joan was pregnant, too, a month behind Carol, and we laughed about our wives' mood swings—though I admit, Joan's moods sounded much funnier to me than Carol's, which seemed to swing in only one direction. We talked about getting everyone together, and even made plans for a barbecue, but when the time came Carol—no surprise— developed a headache, and I canceled, more than a little relieved. When lunch was over and the check came, Rifkin always insisted on paying. "Put that wallet away," he said. "You've done too much for me already." I'd feel only slightly guilty coming away with a full belly and an inside line on Elistra.

For a while I was surprised every time I heard from him. I'd gotten him the job—what else could he want from me? When he invited me to play tennis or racquetball, I suspected some hidden agenda and waited for him to ask for more favors. I kept reminding myself of Barry's cautions, though I was less concerned about conflicts of interest than about looking like an idiot. Sure, he was grateful for the placement, but what would happen when his gratitude ran out? Sometimes I returned his calls, sometimes I didn't. Either way I usually paced in front of the phone for half an hour, making up my mind. "Why don't you just send him flowers," Carol said once, watching me with an unfamiliar, teasing grin. She was pleased with herself for a second, but then her smile faded. She glanced down at her bony hands and said, "Of course, you didn't need them with me."

We'd known each other a year before finally bringing our families together, a Sunday outing to the Turtleback Zoo. I was twenty minutes late as usual, getting Katie calmed down from a screaming fit and Brad, a bruiser of a baby, with a body like Barry's, strapped into his car seat. Carol tried to back out at the last minute, as I expected she would. "I'm allergic to elephants," she said.

"Yeah? When did you figure that out? On your first African safari?"

"I've been to the Bronx Zoo," she said.

"And you survived."

"I had to go to the emergency room."

"Well, lucky for us there aren't any elephants at this zoo," I said. "The biggest thing there's a black bear, and she's skinnier than me."

Rifkin was sitting on one of the stone turtles in the picnic area when we showed up. I'd somehow expected him to be wearing his lab coat and goggles, but instead he was in plaid slacks and a sweater that hung past his hips and gave him wings when he lifted his arms to wave. He'd trimmed his mustache, but his hair was bushier than ever, standing a good three inches from his scalp, perfectly still in the stiff breeze. He perched awkwardly on the angled turtle shell, his feet splayed to keep him from sliding, his back bent and arm outstretched to rock a stroller that held a runt of an infant with a full head of black curls. An older boy ran between two picnic tables, sliding his feet along the dirt so clouds of dust swirled around him and blew into his mother's face. Joan was a pudgy little woman who looked like she could have been sixteen despite her well-trimmed linen dress and tightly permed hair. I didn't blame the kid for ignoring her as she stood with her hands on her hips, calling, "Seth, honey, that's enough. Mommy doesn't like it when you ruin her makeup. Howard, will you please talk to him?"

Rifkin left the turtle and came down the path to meet us. "So glad you could make it," he said, as if he were ushering us into his own home. He knelt to tickle Brad under the chin and came away with fingers covered in drool. Katie was hiding her face in

Carol's crotch. "I won't look at you, don't worry," Rifkin told her. "I was shy, too, when I was your age."

"I'm allergic to bears," Carol said before he could shake her hand. He paused a second, wondering, maybe, if she was making a joke about his hair, of if she'd somehow mistaken him for a grizzly. "Can't you make a pill for that?" she asked.

"I'll work on it," he said.

Joan's hair was covered in dust, and she had to cough for a minute before she could tell us how nice it was to meet us, and comment on how beautiful the kids were and how lovely Carol's blouse was, a lime-green flower pattern I'd just bought her, one of a dozen or so gifts I'd given since I'd finally started to make a living. "Where'd you get it? Was it on sale?" Joan talked in a breathless rush, touching her cheeks and the ends of her dusty hair, not giving anyone a chance to answer her questions. "Let me ask you," she said, looking straight at Carol. "Do you use cloth diapers or plastic?" Carol glanced quickly between her legs, where Katie's head was still buried, and her face flushed. "Oh, not you, not you!" Joan cried, waving her hands next to her face, trying, it seemed, to fan away her embarrassment. "For the baby, I mean. We've been taking a poll of all the people we know. Haven't we, Howard?"

"It seems to be the question of the hour," Rifkin said.

"We've always used disposables, but little Evy gets a rash twice a week. I'm at my wits' end. Tell me, do you use cloth?"

Carol's face was still red. Any second I thought she'd turn around and head for the car. But she managed to mutter, "Pampers," and reached behind to smooth down her slacks over her rear.

Seth came charging at us, a cloud still billowing out behind him. He stopped short at the sight of Katie, who let herself peek at him with one half-closed eye. His arms went behind his back, his feet shuffled, and he made a squishing sound in his mouth. I waited for Katie to start shrieking and kicking at Carol's shins— part of me hoped she would, so we could just be done with this quickly and go our separate ways. But she only put the end of her thumb in her mouth and nibbled. "What a flirt," Joan said. "Don't they make a cute pair?"

"Arranged marriage," I said. "I like that idea. I won't have to worry about kids with hard-ons sniffing at my door fifteen years from now."

Joan's smile was rigid and terrified. Rifkin said, "Sounds like the monkeys are chattering up a storm." I heard a couple of bird noises but nothing else. "Why don't we go take a look?"

We walked between a pair of chicken coops where emaciated, mildewed birds pecked at specks of food I couldn't see on the dusty ground. Rifkin and I hung back, letting Joan and Carol get a few yards ahead with the strollers. Seth took off running from cage to cage, throwing himself against the bars and sometimes trying to squeeze through. His arm swung at a pair of sleeping bobcats until Joan pried him away. Katie followed tentatively, staring with her huge eyes as he hissed at a pointy-eared owl. Rifkin didn't seem bothered by any of it. "It's nice to get a break, isn't it?" he said. "I almost never get to relax anymore."

I nodded, though I couldn't have felt further from relaxed. I fumbled for a cigarette and patted all my pockets before I found a lighter. I had no idea what I was doing here. What did I have to say? I had to clear my throat a couple of times before I could ask, "Things going okay at work?"

"Not bad," he said, and then sighed heavily. "Some days I have no idea what I'm doing." He looked up at me then and shook his head. "That's not to say I don't appreciate being there. I still can't thank you enough for getting me the position."

Instead of waving off his gratitude, I said, "It's just my job."

"Well, I owe you," he said. "And really, it's thrilling. Most of the time. There's a lot of potential. Nobody's really done much with Type II." He paused and glanced at me again. "That's non-insulin-dependent."

"I know that," I snapped. "You think I found the job in the classifieds? I do my research."

"Of course you do, of course," he said in a hurry, flapping the loose arms of his sweater. Then he went on to tell me exactly what he was working on, the challenges and pitfalls, not sparing any technicalities. I understood less than a quarter of what he said, but what was clear was the excitement that grew during the telling, the way his brows arched and beads of sweat formed along his hairline. When he was finished he took a long breath and said, "It's nice to have someone outside the lab who understands what we're trying to do. Joan doesn't even pretend to take an interest."

Ahead of us, Joan was pushing the stroller with one hand and hanging onto Seth's straining arm with the other. She was talking rapidly to Carol, who nodded and smiled—genuinely, I thought. To her right a black bear paced a five-foot by ten-foot patch of concrete, but only Katie seemed to notice, shrinking back against her mother's leg. Maybe it hadn't been such a mistake to come here, I thought. Maybe I'd finally done something right. I calmed down enough to start telling my own stories about work, the way Barry mistreated me, how he wouldn't share information about clients, how he refused to buy a new desk even when I'd brought in higher commissions three months and counting. "He says I haven't proven myself yet," I told Rifkin. "Anyone can have a good run, he says."

"It's criminal," Rifkin said. "There are laws about that sort of thing. You should talk to someone."

"Yeah, well, he's my brother," I said.

"What does that matter?"

"He'll come around."

"He'll come around faster if you sue him," Rifkin said, growing excited again, sweater flapping.

"He's my brother, and he'll come around," I said. "What do you care anyway? What business is it of yours?"

"None," he said softly. "Sorry."

We made it to the petting zoo, and Joan let Seth loose again. He went straight for the nearest sheep and started yanking on its wool. A pair of llamas came bounding at us, until they were standing nose to nose with Rifkin and me. I was ready to haul off on the one with its face in mine, but Rifkin said, "They just want to smell our breath." The big nostrils constricted, the rubbery lips sputtered. The llama's breath smelled like a wet dog who'd rolled around in rotting meat. My fist was still cocked, but then the ugly thing turned its nose up and trotted off to sniff another family coming in behind us. Joan was calling, "Seth, honey, animals don't like it when we kick them," and then came a blistering scream. I knew right away it was Katie's. A gray goat, no taller than my knee, with knobby horns half an inch long and a pinkie-length snarl of beard, had her sleeve in its mouth. The sleeve was empty—for a second I thought the goat had eaten her arm, and I stepped forward to throttle it. But then I could see the arm's outline inside her shirt, which was bunching on one side and stretching around her neck. The goat kept munching, the sleeve disappearing between its jaws. I managed to get my fingers between its gums, but even then its eyes strained with pleasure, its teeth grinding, unable to stop itself, I guessed, even if it wanted to. Katie screamed right in my ear now, and I winced with pain. Carol and Joan both circled around us, trying to make comforting noises and petting Katie's hair, but mostly getting in my way. The babies were both wailing now, competing from their separate strollers. Rifkin knelt beside me and offered advice, his voice maddeningly calm. "Maybe if you could wedge your finger against its tongue? What about the roof of its mouth?"

Seth was the only one of us with any sense. He yanked on the goat's tail until it gave a yelp and let go of the sleeve. Even now Katie didn't stop screaming, and Joan and Carol didn't quit making cooing noises. I wanted to scream myself. For the first time in months I wished for my old life back—the irresponsibility of failure, the ease with which I could convince myself not to care about anything. But beside me Rifkin was chuckling quietly. "Relaxing, didn't I tell you?" he said. Katie's sleeve was soggy and ripped in several places. I tore it off at the elbow and flung it at the goat, who quickly snatched it up and gobbled it whole. Katie refused to put her arm back through what remained of the sleeve. Her mouth was still open, but the only sounds coming out were stuttering sobs and wheezes. "That's it for her," Carol said. "We'd better get out of here."

"We'll have to do this again," Rifkin said. "Only without the animals. Maybe without the kids."

"You'll come over for dinner, won't you?" Joan asked.

"Sure, we'd love to," I said. Carol moved her head in what might have been either a nod or an attempt to get the hair out of her eyes.

Both kids were asleep two minutes after we got them into the car. I'd finally started to breathe normally, when Carol said, "Don't ever do that to me again."

"What did I do?"

"Those people," she said.

"What's wrong with them?"

"Snobs."

"What do you mean, snobs?" I asked. "Did you see that sweater he was wearing? Joan used to be a teacher, too."

She mimicked Joan's frenetic, dizzying voice. "Not every teacher's got a master's in early childhood education."

"She liked you," I said. "You could be friends. You could get out of the house more."

"She thought I wore diapers." She crossed her arms and stared out the window. I tried arguing, but nothing I said could convince her otherwise. After a few minutes I just shut up and drove.

OUR CAREERS TOOK OFF AT THE SAME TIME. SIX MONTHS after I'd placed Rifkin my list of clients had doubled, and I'd compiled a backlog of candidates three pages long. Within two years I came to Barry insisting on partnership or a parting of ways. He held out for a few weeks, telling me how ungrateful I was, asking where I would have ended up if he hadn't taken me in. He even brought up the time he'd saved me from drowning on a family vacation down the shore when I was eleven. "I should have let you sink," he muttered, but when I started packing up my notebooks full of leads—I'd finally given up the scraps of paper— he relented. "Sixty-forty," he said, wiping the sweat from his forehead with a grimy shirt cuff. I agreed, first because he was my brother, and second because I knew it would only be a matter of time before I managed to wrangle out the extra ten percent. We moved our offices into a plush suite on Route 10, not far from Elistra's campus, and after another year we hired our first employees, a secretary who quit after a week of Barry's badgering, and a part-time bookkeeper who's with us to this day. Soon I was making enough money that Carol could stop fretting over whether or not she should go back to work, and when Rifkin called to say there were new houses going up in his neighborhood, I spent only one day telling myself that something was terribly wrong, that I didn't deserve a happy, successful life, before making an offer and forking over a downpayment.

At the same time, Rifkin turned out to be a star in the world of diabetes research. He registered two dozen patents in his first four years. He was invited to give talks at conferences around the world. Three of his compounds made it all the way to clinical trials, though each ended up too toxic to pass FDA standards— two enlarged the liver, as Rifkin suspected they might, and the third sent a man's sperm count into a mysterious, irreversible plunge that he couldn't for the life of him explain. But when Hans Groh kicked off, raking those leaves in the fall of '79, Rifkin was a shoo-in for department director, the youngest in company history. He flew out to Basel to meet with the CEO and board of directors, and when he came back I called to congratulate him. "Hey, Turkey," I said. "You still talking to lowlife headhunters now that you're such a big shot?"

There was a long pause on the line. "Excuse me," Rifkin said slowly. I hadn't meant my question seriously, but now I went cold. I should have expected this moment—I should have been waiting for it all along, and now I was furious with myself for having let my guard down. "That's *Doctor* Turkey to you."

Most people considered it a strange friendship, and maybe it was. What did we have in common? Sure, our kids were almost exactly the same age, and our wives had both been teachers. We were fairly competitive on the tennis court, though my net game was a notch above Rifkin's. He could usually take me in the second or third game of racquetball, when I was so winded I started to get dizzy.

Most of the time I tried not think too much about our differences. For years Rifkin would show up in my backyard on Sunday afternoon, when I was feeling cranky after having spent the last day and a half with Carol and the kids and already itching to get back to work. He'd wave and smile his closed-lip smile and plop down in the most uncomfortable lawn chair we owned, the one with aluminum bars that cut into your thighs and upper back, and almost immediately I'd start to let go of that clenched, persecuted feeling that had been building all day. We'd talk about the weather for a minute or two, and then he'd start rambling in his monotonous, eggheaded way about some reaction he was planning for Monday morning, or the structure for a compound that was eluding him, which was enough to send Carol inside and the kids off to find trouble elsewhere in the neighborhood. Then I'd talk about a client who was giving me a hard time, or an argument Barry and I were having over office decorations, and suddenly the afternoon had leaked away to evening.

Sunday was Joan's night off from making dinner, and Carol had quit cooking for good as soon as the kids were old enough to boil hot dogs and fix macaroni and cheese. When it was warm enough, Rifkin and I would grill a couple of steaks, Rifkin drinking half a beer while I put down a six-pack of O'Douls—out of sheer habit—or else we'd head out to one of the dozen or so pizza joints in the strip malls on Route 10. By eight or eight-thirty, Rifkin would check his watch and fake a yawn. I knew he wasn't tired, only thinking about the Sunday *Times*, which he read cover to cover, even scanning the classifieds, fascinated by how much apartments were going for in the Brooklyn neighborhood where he grew up and by how much people thought they could get for a used refrigerator. I'd clap him on the back, and he'd stick out his hand for a formal shake. "It's been a pleasure, Len," he'd say, and then start trudging up the hill in that strange way he had, arms stiff at his sides, head lowered so far he seemed to be counting not only the cracks in the sidewalk but the blades of grass between them.

Otherwise I saw him only when something on his house needed repair, and even then I had to prod him to tell me when he could use my help. "Well, there's nothing pressing," he'd say. "It's just that the roof of the porch is starting to sag. I don't think they put enough beams in when they built it."

"I'll be over in an hour," I said.

"Oh, I don't mean to put you out," he said. "I can call a carpenter. I've been meaning to, really."

"By the time you get around to it, you'll be buried under half a ton of wood. I got that new ladder last month. Might as well make use of it."

He claimed not to know how to fix anything, but before I even showed up he'd already figured out the exact angle we needed to wedge the beam and where to place the bolts to avoid cutting the wires to the ceiling fan. I took the first turn on the ladder, twisted awkwardly against the top rung, drill in one hand, heavy beam in the other, sawdust spilling onto my sweaty face and sticking there. I didn't listen to Rifkin's offers of help or Joan's of a glass of lemonade until the first two bolts were in and the beam was hanging. Then I let Rifkin take over and stepped off the porch to smoke. I watched him through the wire screen, humming to himself, surprisingly limber on the ladder and handy with the drill he claimed not to know how to use. By now—this was maybe '86 or '87—he'd given up the plaid pants for a pair of black jeans he didn't know any better than to fold like slacks when he put them away, making white creases down the center of each leg.

But even in the middle of summer, unless he was standing direct-ly in the sun, he still wore the straw-colored sweater that hung to his knees, ragged now, frayed at the hem, with holes in each armpit. "I guess this isn't so hard after all," he said. "But I never would have tried it on my own. I swear, Len, I'd be in serious trouble without you."

The sight of that sweater unraveling thread by thread filled me with the strange sensation of time having sped up—days, weeks, months zipping by even as Rifkin stood still on the ladder and I stood still in the backyard. It was impossible to believe that thirteen years had passed since I'd made that mistaken phone call, almost ten since I'd bought my house. What had happened in all that time? Nothing. That was the point of a quiet, stable life, and here was the price: in a blink it would all be gone.

It didn't help when Rifkin's kids came outside. I still wanted to see them as toddlers, but they were teenagers now, Seth fifteen, short but broad-shouldered, with a few dark hairs already growing on his chin. He had Rifkin's smile, close-lipped and squinty, but his manner was jokey and confident, even a little bit arrogant. "Hey, Len," he said from the porch steps, where he sat to thread black laces into his high-top sneakers. "You got an extra smoke for me?"

"Don't you dare," Joan called from the kitchen, her voice carrying over the sound of the drill.

I didn't know if she was warning Seth or me, but I felt guilty enough to drop my butt in the grass and grind it out with a heel. "Another three years and you can smoke all you want," I said.

"Over my dead body," Joan called.

"Three more years," Seth said, holding up either end of a lace to make sure he'd threaded it evenly. "That's how long I have to stick around this goddamn place. Might as well be forever."

"It'll be over before you know it," I said, and meant it.

Evan was still dark and undersized, half his brother's weight. He never said a word to me and kept his distance whenever I was around. He was the only one in the family who seemed to question my presence and doubt my good intentions. Now he stood at the far end of the lawn, tossing a wiffle ball into the air and swinging at it with a long yellow bat, missing mostly, the plastic making a huffing noise in the humid air whenever the drill went silent. "Hey, why don't you let me throw a couple for you," I said. He held the ball a second, staring at the holes in the plastic, and then tossed it to me without looking up. The ball landed at my feet. Evan stood with the bat at his waist, his knees locked. "Come on," I said. "I'm not messing around here. Give me a real stance." He crouched a bit and propped the bat on his shoulder. "Elbow up," I said. He did what I told him, and finally I went into an exaggerated wind-up and gave him a high, arching lob. He connected this time, popping the ball straight up, and slightly behind him. It curved to the left, hit the roof, rolled into the gutter, and stuck there. "Hey, not bad, not bad," I said. "I'll get it down after your old man's done on the ladder." Evan stared after the ball for a second, then gave me a look that startled me— there was no surprise in it, just disappointment, as if all his expectations had been confirmed. He propped the bat on his shoulder and without another word walked back into the house.

Seth's shoes were laced and tied now and he lifted each foot in the air to admire the job he'd done. Then he stood and came up to me. This time he whispered, "Sure I can't have just one for the road?"

"Get lost," I said.

The drill stopped. Rifkin said, "Well, that's one done. Only two more to go. You want to get the next one started?"

When we were through, the two of us stretched out on deck chairs, Rifkin popping one knee and then the other. "You're a lifesaver," he said. "How about I take you out for Chinese." He said it lazily, half-yawning. On the floor beside him was today's *Times*, still folded and stacked. He eyed it and said, "You up for a bite?" He didn't want to take me out, I knew. He wanted to sit under the newly reinforced roof of his porch, read his paper, and eat whatever food Joan put in front of him. I was hurt that he didn't mean his thanks as genuinely as he usually did and angry that he thought he still had to go through the motions of thanking me, that we weren't close enough by now to forget all that.

"Carol and I have plans," I said, though I couldn't remember the last time we'd done anything together but watch TV from opposite ends of the couch. I stood up quickly and brushed sawdust from my shirt onto the floor. "Maybe another time."

"You're not going already?" Rifkin said. Now he was the one who sounded hurt, but his eyes were half-lidded, and one of his hands was already drifting toward the newspaper. "At least stay and have a beer. I've still got your O'Douls in the fridge."

"Another time," I said again.

"Well, I owe you," he said. "I won't forget."

I folded up the ladder and wrapped the drill in its power cord. I was halfway down the hill before I remembered Evan's ball still on the roof. By then I was no longer angry at Rifkin—instead I was furious with myself for not taking him up on his offer. Who cared if he really meant it or not? What would I do with the rest of my night now? What if he never offered again? I made a U-turn in the middle of the street and tore back up the hill. "Carol's not feeling well," I said as I raised the ladder against the side of the house. "You still in the mood for chow mein?"

THE TRUTH IS, OUR BEING FRIENDS STRUCK ME AS STRANGE mostly when other people were around to watch. Carol would sometimes hang around the edges of our conversation on Sunday afternoon, looking from one of us to the other, trying to figure out what strange creatures had invaded her backyard. I'd suddenly hear myself talking and wonder, too, who had taken over my voice—it was softer than usual, the accent leveled out, no edge to it. Carol was jealous, I guess, the same way she had been when I'd started staying at work until eight o'clock or when I'd played golf with Barry three Saturdays in a row. "You never ignore *him*," she'd say when I finally came to bed on Sunday night, after Rifkin had gone and I'd spent an hour or so cleaning the grill, finishing my O'Douls and a last cigarette. "You never tell him you're too tired to talk."

Sometimes Barry dropped by as well, and he didn't even try to hide his hostility. He answered Rifkin's questions with grunts, and interrupted me whenever he thought I was talking too much about the business. "That's not information for public consumption," he'd say when I mentioned an opening we were trying to fill at Mennen. Once, when Rifkin headed home for the night, he asked, "You having trouble sleeping?"

I shrugged. "No more than usual."

"Then what the hell are you doing, keeping that guy around. He's the dullest person on the planet. You need to sleep, I'll get you some pills. I've got a good connection at Smith-Klein. You can tell Rifkin to bug off."

He thought I was crazy to let someone on the inside know any secrets of our trade. But he'd also thought I was crazy to get married, to have kids, to buy a house, to live any life at all, it seemed. He still rents the dump above Gerald's pharmacy downtown, the same place he's lived since we had our first office there. The rooms are barely furnished—couch, bed, TV—and the only views are of a brick wall and a parking lot. I don't know where his money goes, except into his stomach—and he's made plenty of it over the last twenty-five years, believe me. Secretly I fantasize he's drawn up a will with my kids as sole beneficiaries. Katie and her soon-to-be husband can probably get by without it, but God knows if Brad'll survive without a little help—he calls once a month, from California, from Nevada, from Colorado, and I've become expert at using Western Union. But I could easily imagine Barry forgetting a will altogether, though he needs one sooner than later—he can't be long for this world with all that weight and the cigars to boot. Most likely when he goes, all the cash he's buried away God-knows-where will end up in the pockets of some clerk at the IRS.

I usually tried to keep Barry and Rifkin apart, but a few years ago, on a whim, I invited Rifkin into the weekly nickel-ante poker game in my basement. For years there'd been six of us: along with Barry and me were two other headhunters from our office, Ron Levinson and Teddy Gacialla, plus Hoffer and Green, who by then had dropped the damaged vet act and become functioning members of society— Green co-owned a busy service station on the corner of Hanover and Speedwell Avenue, and Hoffer, if you can believe it, was an art history professor at Fairleigh Dickinson. I knew Rifkin would stand out in that crowd, but who among us didn't stand out in some way? Levinson lived in a shack up in Boonton—money flew out of his pockets as fast as he made it, and he usually had to borrow a few bucks to stay in the game. Gacialla? Goes without saying—even though he was fair-haired and pale-skinned, we called him Meatball; we asked when his wife was going to make us pasta, even though we all knew her maiden name was Purdy; we joked that we'd better let him win a hand or two, or we'd all end up sleeping with the fishes. Green hadn't touched an engine in years—now that he was boss he only did the books—but he still smelled of motor oil, his hands permanently stained, his forehead as pimpled as when we were in high school. Sometimes he still talked about women in a dreamy, sick kind of way while rubbing his scar, even though he'd been married for more than ten years. Hoffer was married, too, with three kids, and had as many degrees as Rifkin. But I still sometimes caught that twitch above his right eyebrow after his second or third beer, that sneer that started in one corner of his mouth, and before long he'd say to whoever happened to be sitting next to him, "You know what your problem is?"

Barry was an easy target, the tub—he got bigger every year, spilling over the sides of any chair he sat in. "Keep your fingers away from Barry's mouth if you want to keep them," Green would say. "He hasn't always been single, you know. He was married twenty-four hours. Poor girl. Tried to kiss him. Big mistake. She got slurped up like Coke through a straw."

And don't think I was immune just because it was my house and I bought the pretzels and beer I didn't even drink. They called me "Mr. Bones," or for a while when our kids were watching *He-Man* cartoons, "Skeletor." It was true, the more weight Barry gained, the more I seemed to lose. "I think I hear the wind whistling through your ribs," Levinson would say. "Does Barry sneak into your bedroom and gnaw on you when you're asleep?"

If Rifkin stuck out among the rest of us, he didn't seem to know it. He came down to the basement that first night with a chilled bottle of Chardonnay, which he presented with a little formal bow. He was dressed in the same tweed sports coat he wore to most of our weekday lunches, with corduroy pants that matched too closely. "Evening, gentlemen," he said, and shook hands all around.

"No onion rings here tonight," Hoffer said.

Rifkin slapped his flat belly. "That's all right. I'm not allowed to eat them anymore."

"You wouldn't want to reach for one anyway, not with Barry around," Green said. "You might lose a thumb."

"Are we playing cards here, or what?" Barry asked.

Rifkin pulled up a seat between Barry and Meatball, but only Meatball slid his chair over to make room. Rifkin had to sit with his shoulders hunched to keep from brushing against Barry's flab. Right away I began to wonder what I'd been thinking in bringing him here. Was I trying to prove something about our friendship? Was I trying to show off to these people I'd grown up with that I'd moved beyond them now, that I'd become smarter, more sophisticated? Barry reached into his jacket, pretending not to notice that he jostled Rifkin, and pulled out an enormous Honduran, thicker than his fat finger. His first two puffs drifted straight into Rifkin's face. Rifkin's nose wrinkled, his eyes blinked, and he waved a hand discreetly beneath his chin. "Anyone else want one?" Barry asked. He was ordinarily as miserly with cigars as he was with money or compliments or affection, but tonight I knew he was trying to smoke Rifkin out of the house. Levinson, the beggar, immediately reached for one, and so did Green. I'd planned to hold off smoking until we took a break and I could sit out on the deck, but now Rifkin reached into his own jacket and pulled out an old wooden pipe, a small cherry bowl on a gently curved stem. He took his time tamping down the tobacco, then puffed twice before laying the pipe on the table.

With this we all loosened up. I dealt quickly. Meatball and Hoffer shouted about hockey stats, a game I never cared about one way or the other. "Talk about American sports, or move to Canada," I said. Rifkin patted his hand into a neat stack, and then spread it into a fan one card at a time. He studied the cards, then rearranged them, patted them into a stack again, and spread them once more. This went on three or four times. He didn't notice Barry clearing his throat or Meatball tapping his foot. He stroked his eyebrow, absently pulling at one or two long hairs. "Elistra planning to make pills that get people to move faster?" Barry asked.

Rifkin glanced up and answered seriously, "Not that I'm aware of." He spread the fan again and said, finally, "I think I'll take three this time around."

He won the first hand, the second, the third. He smiled and squinted and rubbed his eyes raw in the swirling smoke. He didn't join the conversation much, though to my surprise he did have his own opinions on hockey teams. The Devils, he said, would always be second-rate, the same as the Nets—who could get excited about teams housed in the middle of a swamp? After four or five hands, without any warning, he turned to me and said, "Remember when we were talking the other day?" He reminded me of what he'd been saying about a new class of compounds he was working on, how they seemed to mimic natural stimulators, though he couldn't understand why. For five minutes straight he went on in the same monotonous, eggheaded way he did on Sunday afternoons, talking about chemical structures and the function of the pancreas. Everyone else glanced from one of us to the other, in utter confusion. Normally I could follow what he was saying, but tonight it was pure gibberish. I couldn't wait for him to shut up. When he finally did, all I said was, "Whatever you say, Dr. Turkey. You dealing, or what?"

He blinked twice, glanced around, and did some strange thing with his lips, as if he were trying to swallow back everything he'd just let out. Levinson said, "You know, my grandmother died of diabetes. Went blind and everything. I hope you find a fix."

"I'm trying," Rifkin said quietly.

Later, when he went upstairs to find the bathroom, Barry stretched his arms out and said, "It's so goddamned cramped in here."

"You'd be cramped in an empty warehouse," I said.

"We had a perfectly good game going. Why'd you have to bring in another person?"

"Hell of a card player," Green said. "Best bluff I've ever seen."

"That's because you've never played with anyone but us," Hoffer said.

"Chemistry," Barry said. "Jesus. Don't you think I hear enough about that all week long?"

"You should be grateful," Levinson said. "If anyone's diabetes material, you're it."

"We don't have enough room for seven," Barry said. "This basement's too small."

"We could play in Meatball's basement, except that's where he stores all those dead bodies," Hoffer said.

"Why don't you go do some arts and farts," Meatball said. "Professor Fairly Ridiculous."

"We don't have enough pretzels, either," Barry mumbled. "Did you see him hogging the bowl?"

"You're really wasting away over there," Green said.

"My grandmother was almost as big as you before she got sick," Levinson said. "By the time she died she looked more like Len."

"He thinks he's better than us," Barry said.

"He's better than you for sure, you fat fucking turd," I said. "Now shuffle the goddamn cards."

When Rifkin came back no one spoke. Again he didn't seem to notice that all of us were looking down at our hands, or that

Barry made a disgruntled snorting noise as he shuffled. "Is Carol sick?" Rifkin asked.

"Probably," I said.

"She was sitting in the kitchen with the lights off. She didn't look well."

"She's fine," I said.

We played a few more hands before Rifkin checked his watch, yawned conspicuously, and stretched his arms above his head, careful not brush against Barry. "Well, gentlemen," he said. "It's been a pleasure." He gathered up his winnings into a pile and shoved handfuls of change into his jacket pockets. There wasn't much left to play with. He stood for a moment, nodding at each of us, and I didn't think he'd leave unless I showed him out. At the front door he shook my hand as usual. It was a mistake to bring him into this, I knew it, and as much as I felt sorry for him, I was angry, too—angry that he couldn't see for himself what a mistake it had been to come. It was painful to watch him drift through life without really knowing what people thought of him. He never tried to adapt to his surroundings. Didn't the rest of us have to do it all the time? Didn't I drop the Jersey tough guy act when I went into a meeting of executives? Didn't I talk their talk and try to make them feel as comfortable as I could? I suddenly questioned whether Rifkin was really incapable of reading people's reactions to him or simply unwilling—I couldn't help feeling there was a kind of stubbornness in the way he refused to accommodate to anyone else's way of being. And as much as it infuriated me, I think I admired it a little, even envied it.

"Appreciate the invite, Len," he said. "I really enjoyed it."

There was the gratitude again—as much as it annoyed me, I'd been waiting for it all night. "Glad to have you," I said. "Same time next week."

"Yeah? You sure I'm not intruding?"

"Don't be ridiculous," I said. "We need a chance to win our money back."

"Well, thanks again," he said. "I'll look forward to it."

A little wave, and off he went, up the hill to the house perched precariously on the rim of the ridge. I wanted to shout after him, to warn him about all the trouble he'd find in the world, but instead I closed the door and went back to the game.

3.

CHARLIE'S CHOO-CHOO SITS ON A BLUFF ABOVE ROUTE 10, just out of sight of the road. It looks like a classy place from most angles, a cluster of freshly painted railroad cars—three freight, one caboose—marked by a discreet wooden sign. Until the early '80s, the cars housed a family restaurant famous for its prime rib. Charlie's still serves one of the best burgers around, though now no one comes for the food or the imported beer or the satellite dish showing sports from around the world. I know all the girls by sight and almost all by name—most are young, beautiful, moderately intelligent, working their way through Montclair State. It's not a bad set-up for them, I suppose. Charlie's is strictly go-go—bikini tops and thongs stay on, unless the girls choose to give private peeks for tipping tables. Most are smart enough to keep their distance when I'm closing a deal, and I leave big tips on my way out the door. When I'm alone they don't bother strutting by—I never even reach for my wallet. Sometimes, during their breaks, they'll sit with me and smoke, talking about their boyfriends or about school. I can't help wondering if Katie ever resorted to a job like this at Penn State, those occasional months I was short and couldn't send a check for extra living expenses. I don't know that she would have made much with that hard knobby body, boyish hips and not much chest. The men here prefer the curvy, breasty ones—no imagination, I think. More than one of the girls has asked if I'm a homo, even when my wedding ring's in plain sight. I don't mention Carol or Katie. Instead I say, "I don't pay for anything I can't touch. And anyway, I'm working."

I've done a lot of business at Charlie's over the past fifteen years—nothing takes down a man's defenses like the full length of a woman's leg—and even when I'm not with a client or a candidate,

I'm listening to the talk at surrounding tables. The place is always filled with Elistra employees, who work less than a mile down the road. Some are from sales, some from marketing. Manufacturing takes over the pool room after five. Research lab technicians claim the two tables in back on Wednesday afternoon. Middle managers come for lunch on Friday. Executives poke their heads in between two and four, blinking in the smoky dimness to make sure none of their underlings are around before taking their seats. I sit back and listen for signs of bitterness, resentment, malaise. I wait for news of department shake-ups or expansions. I crane my neck to make out the words "downsizing" and "acquisition."

Elistra has treated me well over the years, thanks in part to Rifkin and in part to Charlie's. I've always taken a special interest in the company, not, I'll admit, because of its good reputation among the Swiss firms for things like worker satisfaction and environmental sensitivity, but because I like its atmosphere. Its grounds are rolling and green, the lawn mown twice a week, brick paths winding between sandstone-colored buildings, rows of tall pines blocking views of the highway and the appliance megastore on the opposite side. Its gates are wrought iron, molded in floral patterns, and the security guards look more like tour guides in their maroon and mustard uniforms. Labs and assembly lines are carefully hidden out of sight, no more than a few wisps of smoke visible from the windows of the executive suites. Walking from one office to another, I'm always reminded of the first time I visited Katie's college campus, and the feeling I get is similar—a wistful kind of pang that's less like regret than a longing for some life I didn't get to live.

Compare that to Reinhardt DeLouche, which doesn't try to hide its true nature. It sits in full view of traffic on Route 3, a sea of cars in the parking lot at all hours, a two-story fence topped with barbed wire, smokestacks spewing menacing white clouds, a rubbery, choking, evil smell. Back when I started working for Barry, I thought it was my duty to get as many people out of there as possible—I imagined myself freeing Rifkin from an unimaginable, torturous fate. But of course we're equal opportunity recruiters—wherever the money comes from—and now I'll gladly fill any position that opens up at Reinhardt.

The trouble at Elistra started last winter, and because of Charlie's I knew about it before Rifkin did. First there were rumors about a new CEO for the U.S. division, an import from Basel, with that notorious Swiss sternness, precision, and love of efficiency. Then came whispers of restructuring, a workforce reduction of a quarter or more. Rifkin dismissed them. "We've had record profits four years in a row. Why would they want to change anything?" A month later he came to me with that look of confusion and hurt on his face, an expression I would come to know well. "They're crazy," he said. "They think we're inefficient, that we can do the same work with half the people. They're out of their minds."

Over the next few months he flew back and forth to Basel eight times, making his case that diabetes research was necessary at all, that there was a significant market for the drugs he was trying to discover. "They're Europeans," he said. "They don't understand. I tell them, 'Come to the States if you want to see some fat.' Do you see the way people here eat and sit around all day? Well, you know, look at Barry. In ten years there'll be an epidemic, you better believe it." The new CEO doubted whether Rifkin could ever develop a workable compound. He referred to the disappointing results of past clinical trials and seemed personally offended by the drug that killed sperm.

I should have been sympathetic, I know. On the outside at least, I sided with Rifkin, nodding and grunting to encourage him. But secretly I was giddy. It makes sense, doesn't it? New prospects on the market, real talent up for grabs, and the probability of new positions opening up at Elistra once the dust settled. It's my job, after all, to care about such things—maybe by now it's in my blood. Beyond what all this would mean in terms of the business and my checkbook, there was the pure chaos of it, the upheaval that thrilled me. Barry took it all more calmly, shrugging his blubbery shoulders, puffing cigar smoke at the ceiling.

"Spoils of war," he said, and nothing else. Again, I wondered what he did with all his money, why he was in this business at all. He had no family besides me, no real friends beyond the people we played poker with. I had no idea what he did those evenings and weekends he wasn't at my house. True, my kids were gone by then, Brad in Montana last I heard, Katie engaged, but they were still in my thoughts. And maybe Carol talked to me once a day if I was lucky, but still she was in my bed every night, and we were surrounded by the walls of the house I'd bought with my own money, and those walls were hung with pictures of the kids we'd raised. Barry had nothing. I couldn't think about his life for more than a few minutes before it chilled me.

In early March, Rifkin called me at work and said he needed my help. His voice sounded fragile in a way I'd never heard before. A sob hung at the edge of each word. I thought he must be sick, or else Joan was, or one of the kids. "Anything," I said. "You name it."

It turned out his department was being reduced, not enormously. "I've never given pink slips before," he said. "I didn't sleep at all last night." He wasn't worried about most of the staff he was cutting—a few were old enough to take early retirement, one had a wealthy husband, another was incompetent and should have been let go years earlier. But there was one kid Rifkin couldn't bear to tell. Kevin Tucker. I'd been hearing about him for almost a year now—how gifted he was, how he ran his reactions as if he were conducting an orchestra. "He's got a little boy," Rifkin said. "Two years old. His wife's pregnant. He's just like I was when you found me in that Reinhardt dungeon." He didn't want to let the kid know he was canned until I agreed to try to place him somewhere else. You want to know what I thought? Why not let the kid fend for himself, the way the rest of us had to? But I kept my mouth shut. How could I turn Rifkin down when his voice quavered like that, when he was so close to pleading?

I told the kid to meet me at Charlie's two afternoons later. It was a good place to do business with the young married ones, who felt guilty about looking at other women while their wives were home taking care of the kids, or out working to help pay the mortgage—they didn't care so much what kind of job I offered, so long as it made them feel worthy of being fathers and husbands. Today, Charlie's was boisterous, echoing with whistles and cat-calls. It was Thursday, almost five, and most tables were taken up by Elistra's sales team, the only group not affected by the shake-up. They were celebrating—second quarter figures had come in, and sales of the newest anti-psychotic had exceeded all projections. They toasted schizophrenics and gave three cheers for bipolars. They called to the girls who danced between their tables, "Hey, are you delusional? Paranoid? Hearing voices? I've got the perfect thing for you."

I sat at my usual table in the corner, far enough from the crowd to stay inconspicuous, but close enough to catch conversation all around. I watched the door, expecting a young Rifkin to walk in, complete with lab coat and goggles, bushy hair and pointed mustache. A wave of nostalgia came over me, for the disaster my life had been twenty-six years ago, for the almost blissful feeling of having no idea where it would take me. I wanted to indulge the memory but was quickly distracted—by the shouting salesmen and the girl they were cheering on. She was new, and younger than most, probably right out of high school. Her body was nice enough, but her eyes were too close together, and her teeth were long and narrow. She wore a leopard-print bra, a leopard-print thong, leopard-print boots, and a leopard-print hair tie that let her toss her ponytail over her head. She was doing a big gaudy show up on the bar, slithering along the beer stains, baring those long teeth, pretending to claw and hiss at the men who waved bills at her. "Cat Scratch Fever" blared out of the speakers. Not very original, but the salesmen loved her. They paid her to do a private dance on their table, pounding their glasses to the beat of her clicking heels.

I was disappointed with the manager, who hired all the girls personally and usually had taste. I knew him well enough to tell him so, but before I spotted him, the girl started toward me. Not walking, either. She crawled over that sticky floor scattered with cigarette butts—half of them mine—making some kind of roaring noise and thrashing her claws again. Her nails were long and sharp and painted with leopard spots. Her eyes were so close together I wasn't sure if she could see straight. "Beat it," I said, when she was still a foot from my knee.

"You gotta pay extra for that," she said, and laughed. Hers was the least erotic voice I'd ever heard—high, whiny, childlike. She got up off the floor and started in on her routine, first bending one way so I could see the leopard strap of her thong between her cheeks, and then the other way, so I could spy her belly button through the gap between her tits.

"Get lost," I said. "I'm working here."

"What do you think I'm doing?" she asked.

"Look, maybe the other girls told you about me. I'm Len—"

"Sure, honey. They all said what a great lover you are. Now why don't you find something to stick in here." She pulled the front of the thong away from her waist, far enough that I caught a quick glimpse of hair, a thin dark strip of it, perfectly squared, before I could turn away. You think I'm a prude? Trust me, there's nothing appealing about that kind of peek, and anyway, when I'm working I can't think about anything else. I would have felt the same way about a fifty-dollar steak—save it for later.

"You Len?" a voice said beside me. I hadn't seen the kid come in, but I wouldn't have recognized him anyway. He looked nothing like Rifkin—a tall, sandy-haired goy, clean-shaven, with shining, tanned skin. He wore khakis and a white shirt with two buttons undone, a tuft of curly golden hair visible on his chest. He smiled and then winked. "Who's your friend?"

The girl hissed again. "I'm Sheila of the Jungle," she said. She was still holding her thong open. Standing, the kid must have seen all the way down.

"She's just leaving," I said.

"You wanna put something in here before it gets cold?" the girl asked.

"Sure, why not." The kid fished for his wallet. He had a gold watch on, and a pair of rings, an ordinary wedding band and beside it a bulky college keepsake with a raisin-sized red stone. The girl started moving her hips again. I realized now why her teeth seemed so long—they didn't have enough gum around them, and seeing her smile was like getting a glimpse of her skull through a hole in her face. The kid held up a bill—a twenty—and lowered it slowly, starting at the girl's ribs. All three of us watched its movement, swirling as it dropped, slightly out of rhythm with the girl's dancing. The bill didn't stop at the top of her thong. It kept going in, until it disappeared completely. The kid's hand followed, the rings going in first, then the watch—it stayed there for a second and came out just as slowly.

"Thanks, doll," the girl said. Her voice was supposed to be husky now, but it sounded more like the crackling of a pubescent boy.

"My pleasure," he said.

To me she said in her ordinary whiny voice, "See how easy it is to be nice?"

"I'll be nice as soon as you get the hell away from my table," I said.

She walked off awkwardly, her legs spread apart—for a second I wondered what the kid had done with his hand down there, with that big red stone, until I remembered the twenty-dollar bill stuck against her crotch. The kid pulled out a chair and dropped into it lazily, feet in polished brown lace-ups thrust out in front of him and crossed at the ankles. He surveyed the room before turning to me, and ran a hand through his hair—the same hand that had just gone fishing in the girl's thong. "So?" he said. "You got something for me?"

"Well, Dr. Tucker," I started, but before I could go on he laughed and shook his head.

"You don't have to give me that formal bullshit. Not in this place. Call me Kev."

"I might have a few possibilities for you, Dr. Tucker," I said deliberately. "But first I'd like to hear what it is exactly you're looking for."

"Jesus, I think I'd like your job," he said. "Staring at snatch all day long. Not bad."

"Of course I'll need to look over your résumé, and hear more about your experience," I said. Already the calm was going out of my voice. I was gripping my job binder to my chest, the plastic edges digging into my palms. The leopard girl was back on the bar, dancing now to "Ape Man." One of Elistra's salesmen had his tie off, snapping it at her like a whip.

"Rifkin said you were going to hook me up," the kid said. "Didn't he talk to you about me?"

"Dr. Rifkin—"

"Dr. Turkey, right? Isn't that what you call him?"

"Dr. Rifkin," I said through my teeth, "told me you've got some skill in the lab but that you don't have much experience supervising technicians."

"That guy," the kid said. "He's a piece of work." Either he didn't notice my growing irritation or didn't take it seriously. He ran a hand through his hair again and then shook down his bangs. "You know, three people in his department were making designer drugs on their off-hours. Ecstasy, crystal meth, you know? He never had a clue. Just thought they were working overtime. He gave one guy a promotion."

"I'm sure he knows a lot more than you think," I said, though I doubted my own words. I felt myself filling with rage, at Rifkin for being so blind, at the kid for pointing it out.

"You know how he pulls on his eyebrows when he's nervous? All you've got to do is kiss his ass a little and he thinks you're the best chemist on the planet. Okay, Howard. Thanks, Howard. Great idea, Howard." He leaned forward and said, "I'm that guy's wet dream."

My hands were on his collar before I could stop myself. The binder crashed to the floor. The kid's mouth twitched, but no sounds came out. "You're talking about a close friend of mine,"

I said quietly, my nose an inch from his. I could see the faint freck-les beneath his eyes, and the pores on his cheeks. "Do you understand? We go way back. We grew up together." Who knows why I said it? Who cares? In that moment it was true. We were as close as I wanted us to be. I might have told the kid we'd been in the war together, too, if I thought he would have believed it—but Rifkin had been in grad school until '68 and then in Europe doing his postdoc. "He saved my life once," I said. "Our families were on vacation down the shore, and I got caught in an under-tow. Rifkin dove in and pulled me out. I would have *drowned* if it weren't for him."

I stopped talking. My breath came out fast and hard in the kid's face. My heart, weak and sputtering as it was, pounded furiously behind my ribs. I don't know if he believed me—did he know Rifkin couldn't swim?—but by then it didn't make a dif-ference. His collar was still bunched in my fists, his straining face only inches from mine. "I'm sorry," he said.

"He's my friend."

"I didn't mean anything. I like Howard. I'm sorry."

I loosened my grip a little but didn't let him go. "I want you to go home to your wife and kid," I said. "I want you to quit stick-ing their money down other women's crotches."

"But you—" he started, and then stopped himself. "Okay," he said. "All right."

I pushed him gently back into his chair and dropped a busi-ness card in his lap. "Give me a call when you grow up," I said. "Maybe then I'll find you a job."

He put the card in his pocket, stood up, and smoothed down his shirt. "I'm a good chemist," he said.

"I'm sure you are."

He left without taking another glance at Sheila, the leopard girl, but her act was almost finished now anyway. She waved goodbye to the salesmen, stuffed wads of cash into her purse, and brushed loose bits of pretzel from her ass.

RIFKIN AND I HAD A RACQUETBALL GAME SCHEDULED during our lunch hour the next day, and I considered canceling. I didn't want to tell him what the kid had said, but I didn't think I could keep quiet about it, either. In the end, I decided to go and let him down easy. I'd only tell him how the kid had thrown away his family's money on that idiot girl in the leopard thong, and he'd realize how mistaken he'd been and forget the whole thing. But when I got to the Y, he was already pacing in front of the entrance, one hand deep in a pocket, the other clutching tightly to a paper shopping bag—in all the years I'd known him he'd never bought himself a proper gym tote. That impenetrable mass of hair that never moved seemed messy somehow, wind-tossed. He didn't notice me until I was almost on top of him, and then he jerked up, looking stunned and desperate, dark veins bulging beneath his eyes. "Well," he said. "Did you find him something? Please, tell me you did."

I should have told him the truth then, but I didn't. What I wanted to do was turn around and head back to my car. "It's a tough market," I said. "I'm working on it."

"But you will find something, won't you?"

"I said I would, didn't I?"

"You know how much I appreciate it," he said, but he didn't look reassured. He would have gone back to pacing in front of the doors if I didn't open one. Inside I had to nudge him to take out his membership card. I came in as his guest every week, even though it cost me more in the long run—I couldn't see myself being a member of the Young Men's Christian anything. There were better courts at the new JCC on Route 10, glassed-in, with lacquered hardwood floors and pouches on the door to hold your wallet and keys, but Rifkin insisted on playing at the Y. He'd been a member for twenty years, and besides, he said, he found glass courts disconcerting, knowing there were people behind him watching as he served. It had never occurred to me before, but now I wondered if there was another reason, too—maybe he was one of those Jews who tried too hard to make gentiles like him, as if he wanted to show he had no hard feelings for all the years of persecution. Is that why he creamed himself over Kevin Tucker? If it was true I wanted to feel sorry for him, but mostly I felt disgusted.

In the locker room Rifkin started right in talking about the kid, telling me for the fifth time how he was the most promising chemist to cross his path in the last ten years, how he was humble and honest and willing to take risks when there was little chance of gain. The more he said, the faster I tore things out of my bag. He couldn't see my face because I kept behind my locker door to change, but even if he did see the anger rising in it, I don't think he would have shut up. He wasn't normally the type to prance around nude, but today he was talking so much he forgot to pull his shorts on. "His wife," he said. "A real catch. So sweet, but smart, too. She was a social worker before they had their baby. Not the stay-at-home type, but they decided it was best for the boy if she did."

He would have kept going until our court hour was up, so I finally slammed my locker shut, looked past him to the row of empty shower stalls, and said, "We playing a game today, or what?"

"Sorry," he said, dressing quickly now, nearly tripping over the leg of his shorts. "I'm so preoccupied. I can't think about anything else."

"Good," I said. "Maybe I'll finally take all three games."

I'd hoped to lighten things, to make him laugh, but he didn't take what I said as a joke. He just nodded and shrugged. "I don't know how well I can play today."

The Y's courts were a wreck. The finish had worn off the floor in most places, the walls marked with the skids of hundreds of balls, the service line hardly visible. Two of six light bulbs were burned out, leaving the front corners—where I liked to place my kill shots—dim and shadowy. Here was how our games always went. I'd start out on a tear, all power, my serves unhittable, the first twelve points locked up before Rifkin had a chance to get in the game. He'd just try to hang on until my wrist tired a little and my heart sped up, and then he'd make his move. His game was all about placement—he served to my backhand, easing the ball gently along the wall, so even if I could get to it, the best I could do was flick it back to center court. He stayed in the same spot all game, just back of the service line, feet planted lightly, anticipating the ball's ricochet seconds before it hit. He hardly broke a sweat, but still he stopped for a full minute between rallies to let his pulse slow to normal. Me, on the other hand, he had running from one end of the court to the other, sending me to the back wall with a ceiling shot, and then making me dive to the floor to reach a dead ball just inches from the front wall. Most weeks I scraped through the first game with a two- or three-point win, but by the time it was over my breath couldn't come fast enough and my eyes stung. More than once I'd bloodied my knees and elbows on the floor's rough spots. "Good hustle," Rifkin always said, and then stood casually waiting for my serve.

But today he couldn't stand still. He rocked from his heels to the balls of his feet. He fiddled with his goggles and adjusted the racquet's strap around his wrist. He let my first three serves go by without even taking a swing. After the fourth, which he swung at but missed, he said, "I mean, you really are going to try, aren't you? To find him something?"

"I said I would, didn't I? How about getting your head in the game here."

"What about Smith-Klein? I thought I heard about some things shaking up over there."

"Do I tell you how to do your job?" I said.

"No, I just thought—"

"I'm serving, whether you're ready or not."

This time he sent the ball dribbling past my feet. "It's just that I don't see how I could live with myself, knowing he had nowhere to go."

"Five-zip," I said. "I might as well be in here by myself. Only then it'd be quieter."

"I know he'll get unemployment, but with two kids and a house? It's nothing."

My next serve wasn't much more than a lob, but all he could do was send it straight back to my forehand, a quick kill. The pop of rubber against the cement wall ordinarily gave me a little jolt of energy, but now it only felt like insult. "Look, Howard, you didn't ask for layoffs. None of this is your fault."

He might not have heard me at all. "The worst part is wasting all that talent. Just imagine if he's out of work six months, a year. Think about what he could have gotten done in that time."

"Six-oh," I said, and gave the ball a few quick bounces before serving, a perfect shot hugging the wall. I heard Rifkin's racquet connect, then a whooshing sound, a slap behind my right ear, and I was on my knees. My eyes went blurry and snot leaked out of my nose. "Jesus Christ!" I shouted, loud enough for all the Christians at the front desk to hear. I stumbled to my feet and tried to throw my racquet, but the strap was still around my wrist and instead of flying, it swung back against my shin. Rifkin flapped around me, far enough away that I couldn't grab him, muttering apologies I couldn't hear through the buzzing in my ear. "I'll get the kid a fucking job, okay?" I said. "Just lay off."

"You don't think I meant it, do you?" he said. "I just can't concentrate. I'm really sorry."

I stomped around for another minute, cursing and kicking at the walls. When I finally calmed down, I went to the door, rubbing the sore spot, waiting for the lump to rise. "We'd better call it quits for today."

"No, no, let's finish," he said. He flexed his knees and took a couple of practice swings, and then chased down the offending ball. He reached out cautiously to hand it to me, but I waved it off.

"You're too dangerous when you can't concentrate."

"I'll pay attention. Really."

"And anyway, I've got work to do," I said. "I've got to figure out where to place Kevin Tucker, God's gift to chemistry."

I left him standing in the middle of the court and headed to the locker room. He didn't come in while I was changing. On my way out I flung my visitor's pass at the skinny Christian girl behind the front desk. She only flipped her hair around, showed me her braces, and said in a maddening singsong, as if she'd never encountered rudeness in her life and didn't recognize it now, "Thanks for coming in. See you next time."

I FOUND THE KID A JOB AT ELI LILLY IN INDIANAPOLIS, as far away as I could send him. I was furious even as the paperwork came through for my commission—at Rifkin for having been so naïve, at myself for having carried through with his request. I could have found half a dozen other candidates suitable for the Lilly job, but what then? Rifkin's baggy eyes, his shrug and squinting smile, his mumbled words, "Thanks anyway for trying." Or worse, another blow behind the ear, followed by urgent and sincere apologies.

I made the mistake of telling Barry what had happened, all except for the racquetball. He shook his head sadly, as if I'd let him down. "He's taking advantage of you."

"The man's just clueless," I said. "He thought that kid worshipped him."

"He's playing you like a grand piano," Barry said.

"He wouldn't know how to play someone if he wanted to. It's not in his nature."

"He knew you wouldn't turn him down. He knew you'd do exactly what he asked."

"He's a friend. I can do him a favor every once in a while."

"What's he ever done for you?"

In my anger I couldn't think of anything. Not the house he'd helped me find, not the inside tips he'd given me, not the steady, comforting presence he offered every Sunday afternoon. Now I saw only an unbalanced transaction, the thing I'd learned to scorn above all during the course of my career. "What do you care?" I asked Barry.

"He owes you," Barry said. "He owes the business. I care about that."

Rifkin said the same thing the next time I saw him. He

showed up in my backyard on Sunday, the same time as always, but today his consistency only irritated me. Didn't he have a spontaneous bone in his body? Couldn't he for once in his life be unreliable? I was on my knees at the edge of the lawn, digging flowerbeds where they didn't belong—they'd be easy pickings for the deer that fed in the narrow strip of trees behind the house, all that was left of the woods that had covered the hill when I was a kid. "How's your head?" Rifkin asked, swaying above me, hands in his pockets. Keys and change jingled as he spoke.

I touched the spot. There wasn't much of a lump, and my hearing had returned to normal. "I'll live," I said.

"I can't tell you how sorry I am," he said. "I hope you'll forgive me."

"What's to forgive? It was an accident, right?"

"I spoke to Kevin yesterday," he went on. "I can't thank you enough. It's such a huge load off my mind. I don't know if my conscience could have taken it, just cutting him and his family loose, with nowhere to go." I jammed the eight-inch blade of my hand-shovel into the ground, turning up mostly rocks. "I owe you, Len. Really. I mean it this time. What can I do for you?"

I didn't pause to think. All day I'd known exactly what I'd ask for. "The directory."

I didn't look up, but Rifkin's battered tennis shoes shuffled in the dirt. "Excuse me?"

"The Elistra directory," I said. "You can get me a copy."

He laughed uneasily. "You're kidding."

"You asked what you could do. That's it."

"You know I can't do that," he said. I speared the shovel into the ground, and this time metal against rock made a spark. I smelled smoke. "It's against company policy," he went on after a moment. "It's in the employee handbook. Grounds for dismissal. Possible prosecution."

"No one would ever know," I said.

"They'd find out. I'd be on the street."

"It would never get back to you. I'd be completely discreet."

"People know we're friends. They'd make the connection."

"You don't trust me," I said. I could hear the injury in my voice, but even now I couldn't tell you whether it was put on or not. "That's what you're really saying."

"Of course not," he said, his feet shuffling again, raising small clouds of dirt. "Of course I do."

"You're afraid I'll screw you."

"Of course not," he said again, squatting now beside me. "I trust you completely. It's just—" He took his hands from his pockets and scratched both sides of his chin at once. "These corporate bastards. They're ruthless. You've seen how they've cut my department without a second's thought. You saw how they would've let Kevin and his family starve."

I would have relented, I swear. I'd only been testing him, though I might not have known it at the time. But mention of the kid brought back the full depth of my anger. I pictured his family, his pregnant wife, his toddler in diapers, waiting in the cold as their heat was shut off, while the kid stuck twenty-dollar bills down a leopard-print thong. I attacked the rocky ground, dusting Rifkin's shoes. "Forget it, then," I said.

"Really, Len, you've got to understand—"

"I said forget it."

He sighed. "You know I appreciate everything you've done for me."

"Sure," I said.

"Can I help you with that?" he asked, gesturing at the mess of dirt and rocks at my feet. The trench I'd dug looked more like a place for a sewer pipe than a garden. I already knew I'd have to fill it back in by the end of the afternoon.

"I've only got one shovel," I said.

Carol came out on the deck then, the first time I'd seen her all day. She was in her bathrobe and socks, hair wild, face looking sallow even from across the yard. When she spotted Rifkin, she started to back away. But then Rifkin straightened, one knee popping and then the other. He stretched each leg in front of him and shifted from foot to foot. "Well," he said. "I guess I'll leave you to it." He shifted some more, cleared his throat, clucked his tongue, stuck his hands in his pockets to jingle his change and then took them out. I knew he was waiting for me to shake, but I didn't look up from the scarred lawn. "Well," he said again, but this time he had nothing to add. I didn't watch him walk away, but when I looked up, Carol was lying back in the lounge chair, the bathrobe hitched to her knees, her face turned up to the hazy sky.

TWO DAYS LATER RIFKIN CALLED ME AT WORK, LATE IN the afternoon. I had my feet up on my desk—a steel wrap-around with built-in file cabinets and three-shelf storage units on either side—and my eyes closed. I'd finished all my work for the day, but I wasn't ready to go home yet. This was when I used to meet Green and Hoffer at the Firelight, and I'll admit, at times I missed being able to piss away my nights in a blind stupor. There were too many hours before I'd come back here the next morning, and I didn't know how I would fill them. Everyone but Barry was gone. His office was across the hall from mine, his door closed. I had no idea what he was doing in there, but I knew he wouldn't leave before eight. Some mornings I came in to find pizza boxes or Chinese take-out cartons in the trash. Occasionally he was wearing the same clothes he'd had on the day before, and I knew he hadn't gone home at all.

When the phone rang—my personal extension, not the switchboard—I figured it was Carol. "I'll be there when I get there," I said.

"You can come get it from me tonight." Rifkin's voice was a faint whisper, hardly more than a gasp.

"Get what?" I said.

"You know," he said. "Come up to the house at eight."

He hung up before I could turn him down. If he'd given me the chance I would have said, "Thanks, Howard, but you don't have to do this." I could have called him back, it's true, but by then I was overtaken by curiosity. This was a test, of our friendship, of

Rifkin's trust in me, and I had to see how far it really extended. I left the office then, without knocking on Barry's door to say goodbye, and went straight to Charlie's. Even with the music blaring and the girls dancing, the mood inside was glum. At the nearest table a group of lab technicians talked about severance packages, unemployment benefits, health insurance extensions. The more upset they sounded, the happier I felt. I couldn't help it—this was my livelihood after all, and really, didn't they need me now more than ever? Wasn't I going to help them? Not all of them, sure, but as many as I could. I handed out two dozen cards that night, and stayed longer than usual—partly because I didn't want to go home before stopping at Rifkin's and partly because I was enjoying myself, celebrating, even. I put down three O'Douls and treated myself to a burger and fries, though I knew my doctor would throw up his hands in frustration the next time I went for a check-up. When Sheila came out in her leopard outfit, I clapped along with everyone else, and even flicked a dollar bill across the table as she strutted by.

When Joan opened the door at a quarter past eight, I smiled sheepishly and crossed my arms. She didn't seem surprised to see me. But she didn't seem angry, either, and for a moment I was relieved. Joan was no longer as plump as she'd once been, and her hair was thinning and obviously dyed, but she still had that way of talking at you as if she were continuing a conversation broken off a few seconds earlier. "Just in time," she said. "The cookies'll be ready in a minute."

"I don't know if I can stay," I said, following her into the foyer.

"Then I'll send some home with you. Carol likes butterscotch, doesn't she? She does, I remember." I couldn't imagine when Joan might have learned Carol's tastes, but I shrugged and nodded. "Evan's coming home this weekend," she went on. "He'll eat as many as I leave out. But until then the smell's going to drive Howard wild. I'll have to put a lock on the cupboard." She gestured at the stairs. "He's in his office. Go on up."

I couldn't help feeling guilty walking through the house

unaccompanied, but even more I was annoyed with Rifkin for not telling Joan why I was here. He should have spent the whole afternoon bad-mouthing me. I took the stairs slowly, putting as little weight on my heels as possible, to keep the wood from creaking. Less than a quarter mile away, my house couldn't have been any more different from Rifkin's. I'd spent thousands of dollars bringing as much light in as possible, putting in picture windows and skylights, painting the walls white and eggshell, replacing old Formica countertops with stainless steel. Rifkin's place had a dark, Old World feel, with gray wood paneling in the living room, a velvety wallpaper along the hallway, a spidery crystal chandelier above the dining room table. The ceilings were high, but no window was as wide as my arm span. I'd never felt entirely comfortable in this house, and to tell the truth I hadn't been inside all that often—maybe twenty times in as many years, and then mostly to make repairs. More often I sat on the back porch, or stood smoking on the lawn, talking to Rifkin through the screen. He'd been happy to have me in his neighborhood, but that was close enough. Since then he'd kept me at a distance. He wanted me to get jobs for his friends, but he didn't invite me to dinner parties with his Elistra colleagues. I knew when they were going on, even if he didn't tell me—from my driveway I could see cars lined up on the street, lights on in rooms he didn't normally use. True, Carol would never have come if we had been asked, and it would have been awkward for me to be there alone among all the couples, eggheads and their wives and husbands. But still, would it have been so hard to invite me? Didn't I call him to join the poker game even when I expected him to turn me down? By the time I reached the top of the stairs all my guilt was gone. I was just here to collect what was owed me, what I deserved.

Rifkin sat in the near dark, a single dim reading lamp turned on above his recliner. There was a book in his lap, a good six-inches thick, dictionary-sized. Even before I came into the room I could tell he wasn't looking at the pages. The only other chair was stacked with magazines, so I stayed standing, hovering above him. I could almost feel my shadow cast behind me, looming from floor to ceiling—the image was part troubling and part comical, like a scene from a 1930s horror flick, Dracula menacing but also papery and clownish. "You've got something for me," I said, aware even as I spoke of the cinematic sound of the words. I think I cracked a smile, though Rifkin didn't return it.

He said, "I really do appreciate everything you've done for me."

"I know you do," I said.

He reached underneath his chair and pulled out an enormous binder, thicker than his book and heavy—he needed both hands to bring it up. As he held it out to me I thought I saw his arms trembling—either from the weight or the proximity to my grasp—and immediately the guilt came back, sharper than before. I should just wave it away, I thought. He'd passed the test, hadn't he? I wanted to say something about our friendship, something neither of us had ever said before. What could I tell him? That we'd shared an important time, even if we hadn't grown up together or fought side by side in a war? I could have said something about our kids growing up—how once, when I caught Brad picking on Rifkin's younger son, chucking clods of dirt at him in my backyard, I flew off the deck in a sudden rage and smacked my boy across the jaw. Or a couple of years later, the time I came down to the basement to find Katie and Seth wrapped up in each other's arms. They were both fifteen, their mouths mangled with braces, and their kissing sounded like dogs slopping up water. They didn't hear me come in. If it'd been any other kid, I would have kicked both their asses around the block, but now I crept back upstairs as quietly as possible. In the kitchen I played out a fantasy of a neighborhood wedding, my family linked with Rifkin's. Even the idea of Katie pregnant and dropping out of high school didn't scare me then. Wasn't I hoping for a reason to feel as close to Rifkin as I did to my own brother? Whatever romance there was didn't last the year, but until Katie called to say she was engaged, I still held out hope that she and Seth—a lawyer now, living somewhere near Boston—would reconnect and discover something they had in common. I could have said any number of things, but it was Rifkin who spoke first. "Just…use discretion, will you, Len? I can't…No one can find out about this, okay?"

I blinked and swallowed to fight off a mild pain in my chest. Then I tucked the binder under my arm and nodded curtly. Before I left the room I turned to face my shadow—it was narrow, skeletal, slicing through a print of a Van Gogh landscape, bending into the crook of the wall and ceiling before disappearing into a shapeless darkness above Rifkin's desk. I hurried out without another word.

Joan stopped me on the stairs. Without thinking, I hid the binder behind my back. She held out a plate of cookies, heat waves visible above them, and all I could think was how far she'd come since I'd first met her, when everything she cooked smelled like burnt toast. "You've got time for one, don't you?"

The sweet smell made my eyes water. I sniffed hard, swallowed again, and shook my head. "Blood pressure," I said. "You know what the doctor says. Probably not such a good idea."

"Neither are those cigarettes," she said, but as soon as I was outside, I propped the binder between my feet, reached for my pack and lighter, and took a long, long drag.

AT NINE THE NEXT MORNING I OPENED THE BINDER TO the first page and didn't stop calling until noon. I'd planned to be discreet. Really, I had. I was going to show Rifkin how he'd misjudged me, how his lack of trust had damaged our friendship. But faced with those hundreds of names and numbers, I couldn't help myself. If you were in my profession, you'd understand. You have to know the value of a phone number, a name and title. You have to experience one slow month with no new clients and no new candidates, the mortgage envelope waiting to be mailed. You get the taste of desperation on your tongue once, it never goes away. All the headhunters I've told the story to have nodded, shrugged, and said, "Of course. What did he expect?"

When Barry knocked on the door to ask what kind of sand-
wich I wanted from the deli next door, I shoved the binder under
some papers. He didn't see it but asked anyway, "What's the
matter with you? You got a fever?" I felt my face. I was flushed. I
wanted to laugh out loud. I couldn't hide something so important,
not from Barry, who would understand what it really meant. I
scattered the papers onto the floor and held the binder over my
head like a trophy. "Is that what I think it is?" he asked. "How'd
you weasel it out of him?"

My excitement dampened, but only for a second. "He gave
it to me," I said. "We're friends, remember?"

"Well?" Barry said. "Are you going to hog it, or what?"

I popped open the binder's rings, pulled out a third of the
pages, and shoved them into his fat fingers. He forgot all about
sandwiches. We made calls for an hour and then congregated in
the little hallway between our offices to exchange news of
possible leads. Elistra was in chaos. Everyone seemed ready to
jump ship. There was real pleasure in Barry's eyes, deep as they
were in the surrounding puffs of flesh. I remembered a summer
when we were kids, nine and twelve, fishing for perch in the
muddy lake near our house—there were days when you couldn't
stick your worm in the water without getting a bite. No skill to
it at all, but that didn't matter. Tug after tug, each one more thrilling than the last, even when the tug was on Barry's line and not
mine. We'd shout encouragement to each other from a few yards
down the bank and trade compliments when we started home
with our haul.

By the end of the day I was exhausted in a satisfied way, my
voice scratchy, my neck sore from cradling the phone. I heard
Barry slam down his receiver and shout, "Bag it!" In a minute he
leaned against my office door and said, "Hell of a month we've
got ahead of us. Thanks for sharing."

Sweat drizzled from his temples to his ears. His nostrils
flared. The few strands of hair left on his head were long and
plastered to his scalp. Again I found myself wondering what it was

he lived for, what drove him to get up each morning and come to work. What did he have to get excited about? "Rifkin's gonna be pissed," I said.

"His own damn fault," Barry said. "Why'd he give it to you if he didn't want you to use it? Come on, I'll buy you a drink. I'm meeting a pair of pill pushers down at Charlie's at six. Half an hour to watch some tits and ass."

Rifkin called first thing the next morning. This time his whisper was so faint it took me a second to figure out anyone was on the line at all. "What are you trying to do to me?" he asked.

"Don't worry," I said. "No one'll know it was you."

"They'll find out. People know you're my friend."

"That's right," I said. "I'm your friend. Trust me."

"You've got to give it back."

"I can't do that."

"Please," he said.

"Look, I'll ease up a little, if that makes you feel better."

"Please," he said again.

"I've got to go, Howard. I'll see you at poker tonight."

Did I stop making those calls? Did I slow down for a minute? I couldn't have if I'd wanted to. And I certainly couldn't have stopped Barry, who had no concerns whatsoever about Rifkin's feelings. But I didn't even try. By this time I was possessed, blind to anything but names and numbers and commission percentages. I'm not saying this to excuse myself—don't think I'm trying to plead insanity or anything close. It's just that this was what Rifkin never gave me the chance to explain. But maybe he wouldn't have understood anyway, never having given himself over to impulse, the pure thrill of it, the freedom. When he showed up for poker, his face was drawn, the skin around his eyes darker than before, his hair, I thought, speckled with more gray. I made a big show of everything being normal—maybe too big a show—calling, "Hey, Dr. T., ready to lose some money?"

Barry nodded to him with his usual offhand iciness. Jeff Green said, "When you coming in for those new brakes?"

"Soon," Rifkin mumbled. "I need to. I will."

He hardly glanced at his cards. He didn't pat down the stack or make a fan or rearrange the order. Still, he won the first two hands. Barry lit a cigar, Hoffer and Levinson pulled out cigarettes, but Rifkin didn't reach for his pipe. He couldn't have looked more crushed if one of his kids had died in a car wreck. Barry said, "The game's more interesting now, don't you think?"

"How so?" Green asked.

"Now that we've got a criminal in our midst. Besides Meatball that is," he said, and patted Rifkin on the shoulder. "A real criminal."

"Jesus, Barry," I said.

Hoffer laughed and asked, "What'd you do, steal a test tube?"

Rifkin took a sudden interest in his cards, holding them close to his face. "He didn't do anything," I said.

"Not according to Elistra's employee handbook," Barry said. He leaned back in his seat, satisfied, his blubber settling comfortably around him. I wanted to strangle him. I would have thrown him out of the house right then if he didn't turn to me and wink, as if we were sharing a joke. I was so confused I could only reach for a cigarette and take a swig of O'Douls. Did he think I wanted this? Did I? Beneath my anger was something like relief, it's true. For a long time I'd been tired of feeling like I had something to lose. Better to be done with it, I often thought, and move on. But now that the moment had arrived it was the last thing I wanted. I didn't really believe the damage I'd done was irreparable. Twenty-six years of friendship couldn't fall apart so easily.

No one spoke for the next few hands. Rifkin checked his watch half an hour earlier than usual. He didn't bother yawning this time. "I'd better…" he started, but his voice trailed off. He stuffed his winnings in his pockets, nodded quickly all around, and headed for the stairs.

I stubbed out my cigarette and followed. "Don't forget to kiss your girlfriend goodbye," Barry called, but no one laughed.

Rifkin didn't face me until we'd reached the front door.

When he did, I was taken by surprise. His eyes weren't full of tears as I might have expected them to be. His lips weren't trembling. Everything about him was still and dry and composed. "Look," I said. "I'm sorry. He's an asshole. I never should have let him know about the goddamn binder."

"You've got to stop," he said.

"It's not criminal," I said. "I don't believe that for a second."

"People are talking."

"What's the big deal, anyway?" I asked. "So I got a few names and phone numbers. So I made a few calls."

"I'm asking you," he said.

"The place is a disaster. They won't bother with you. And anyway, they should be happy. They wanted to make all these cuts. I'm taking people off their hands. Think about all the money they'll save on severance packages. They should be grateful."

"This is my life," Rifkin hissed, the harshest sound I'd ever heard come out of his mouth. He reached into his pockets, pulled out handfuls of poker change, and raised fists on either side of his head. "It's my life," he said again, and I waited for all that change to come jangling down on my front stoop. But his fists didn't open. They lowered slowly and disappeared back into his pockets.

"All right," I said. "Okay. Look, don't worry. It's finished. No one'll know a thing."

His face didn't relax the slightest bit. Nothing in his countenance changed. "Thanks for having me," he muttered, and started walking briskly up the hill.

Back in the basement, Barry was chuckling hoarsely, while Green waved his arms and said, "She was! She was! I'm telling you!" Levinson was eyeing my money, and I wondered how much he'd already swiped. Meatball picked his nose behind his cards. Hoffer's whiskey glass was empty, his eyes wandering. I hated these people. I wanted them out of my house. The poker game was over as far as I was concerned, tonight and forever. I was through with all of them, even if they were supposed to be the people closest to me in the world. Why should I care about any of them? Just because we went to high school together, or because we worked together, or because we were raised by the same hapless, long-dead parents?

My mouth was sticky, and my chest throbbed. I massaged my ribs through my shirt. Hoffer set his bleary eyes on me and started to sneer. "You," he said. I blinked and worked hard to breathe. He was going to condemn me, to point out the rotten blackness at my core. But tonight I didn't care. He couldn't tell me a thing about friendship, not a goddamn thing. The minute he opened his mouth I'd start talking about straight razors and dysentery, all the things I'd kept inside for so long. I'd let him and Green figure out what to do with their betrayals. I'd let them decide what it would take to break their bond. Hoffer picked up the deck and started to shuffle. "You need to ante." It took me a second to understand what he'd said. Part of me still wanted to send them all home, to close myself off from everyone, but already I'd begun to wonder how I'd make it through the week if I didn't have Thursday nights to look forward to. I sat down and tossed in my nickel.

4.

SUNDAYS, I'LL ADMIT, HAVEN'T BEEN EASY FOR ME LATELY. It's almost eleven now, and I've finished with the rose bushes. All the leaves are raked and bagged. I trimmed a hedge that didn't need much trimming, and now all that's left is a tangle of prickly twigs. The swing set will stay for today, until I can decide whether I want to try digging up the huge concrete blocks holding it in place or just hacksaw the four legs. The sky has lightened since I came out, but somehow it's also grown colder, and the breeze has picked up. My hands are starting to ache. Up the hill there hasn't been a single movement, not a flutter, though I've checked every ten minutes without fail. Back inside I hear Carol stirring upstairs, earlier than usual, so I grab my car keys from the kitchen counter and head to the supermarket. I pass Rifkin's house on the way, but all the windows are dark, no sign of life at all. I'd guess that they've taken a vacation, except that Joan has to teach tomorrow morning, and whenever they do go away Rifkin always sets timers on lights in the front rooms, to scare off burglars. It occurs to me that in all the years I've known them they've never once asked me to watch their house while they're gone, to water their plants or feed Joan's fish, that the whole time someone else must have had a key. And once again I try to tell myself that it's best this way, that now at least we're on equal ground.

Let me be clear: Elistra didn't take action against Rifkin for giving me the directory. No one even confronted him about it, just as I'd expected. But still, he didn't show up at my house the Sunday after the poker game or the Sunday after that. He didn't call me to play tennis or racquetball. In two weeks Barry and I made more than twenty-five placements. Our commissions were through the roof. Between us we called nearly every listing in the directory. News of our talent pool spread, and in the last six months our client roster has doubled. We've hired two new re-cruiters and another secretary. We could probably sell the business and retire in a year or two, though neither of us has even brought up the possibility. Barry, I'm sure, is set on dying at his desk in the middle of a phone call or halfway through a meeting with an important client. And me? What would I do without the work? Buy a sailboat and take Carol on a cruise around the world? And then what?

A few weeks after that last poker game—the last for Rifkin, not for the rest of us—I heard at Charlie's that the diabetes depart-ment was being merged with lipids, and all senior management fifty-five and over had received strong encouragement to take early retirement. Rifkin made the cut by two months. I called him as soon as I got back to the office. "Hey, Doc," I said. "I just heard."

"Afternoon, Len," he said. "How are you?"

His politeness stung deeper than any show of anger would have. Why couldn't he curse me, shout my ear off, tell me I'd ruined his life, even if it wasn't true? "I'm really sorry," I said.

"Not your fault," he said. "They're out of their minds."

"I know," I said. "All these fat people. Like Barry."

"In ten years there'll be an epidemic," he said.

"You going to take the package?"

"What other choice have I got?"

I hadn't planned this before I dialed, but now I said, "Maybe I can help. I've got an opening." I paused for a moment, but Rifkin didn't answer. There was barely any sound at all, no rustling from Barry's office, no noise from the street, just the faintest hum on the line. I took my feet off the desk slowly and leaned forward, both elbows on the cold steel surface. Maybe there was still a chance to start over, to wipe the slate clean—all past favors and requests erased, all debts forgotten. "Reinhardt," I said. "Your old stomping grounds. V.P., quality assurance. Cushy job, big bucks."

Rifkin's exhale whistled over the phone line. "Thanks," he said. "But I'll have to pass. You know me, research or nothing."

"Sure," I said, struggling to keep the dejection out of my voice. "I'll keep my eye out for something."

"Thanks," he said again. "I guess retirement doesn't sound so bad. More time to—I'm sure I'll find something to do."

We haven't talked since then, and even though I drive past his house every day I haven't seen him once. His last day of work was in May, and if there was a retirement party, I didn't hear about it. No one at the poker game has asked about him, not a single mention, and sometimes I have the strange sensation that he never existed at all, that I just dreamed him up, and now, through a failure of my imagination, he's simply disappeared from the world.

But on my way home from the supermarket, there he is, standing in his front yard, hands on his hips, head tilted back, eyes raised to the wobbling chimney. He's already wearing the Alaskan parka, and maybe he needs it. It's even colder and truly windy now—some leaves lift out of his roof gutters and others fall in. There's a chance it could snow soon, and I doubt the chimney can carry the extra weight. I pull to the curb, roll down my window, and call, "I don't think staring at it's going to make it fall. Why don't you let me take it down for you?"

He turns slowly. It takes him a second to recognize me. From this far away his hair looks completely gray, his expression hollow and confused. A sudden sickening feeling comes to me—maybe more time has gone by than I've realized, and now Rifkin is an old man, senile and passing quickly out of this life. Finally he shrugs and says, "The insurance."

"I know, I know," I say. "But I'll make it look like it came down on its own. They'll never have any idea."

He turns back to the chimney and seems to consider my offer. Then, without looking at me, he calls, "It'll fall soon."

"It might hit the house," I say.

"It might not."

"If you change your mind—"

"Appreciate it," he says. His back is stiff, his feet planted firmly. He won't turn around again, I know.

I put the car in gear and roll slowly down the hill. Carol is already downstairs when I come in, showered, dressed in jeans and a sweater, drinking coffee in the kitchen. I know better than to show my surprise. "I picked up some sirloins," I say, and she answers, "I might have half one." Later in the afternoon I stick the steaks under the broiler, and we sit down to watch an overdue video, some sappy drama about a brother and sister who were orphaned as kids and then can't seem to get along as adults. I have a hard time paying attention, but when Carol sniffles and dabs at her eyes, I reach across the couch and rub her elbow. She doesn't pull away. This isn't such a terrible way to spend a Sunday, is it? I remind myself of all the things I can look forward to—Katie's wedding next summer, for one, and then waiting for the grandkids. And the day I still hold out hope for, when Brad finally decides to make something of his life. I put my hand on the back of Carol's neck, and she leans into it. I try to relax and only occasionally find myself tapping my foot or fiddling with a button on my shirt.

But before the movie's over, Barry shows up, as he has every

Sunday for the past few months. He roots around in the fridge and cracks open a can of Coors Light, left over from a recent poker game. "What's this crap," he says, jutting his chin at the TV.

"You'll really slim down with those things," I say. "Why don't you try Pizza Light, while you're at it?"

Carol stops the tape, pops it out, and goes up to the bedroom to watch the rest. I wrap her half-steak in foil and stick it in the fridge. Barry eats the other half, along with a whole one of his own. By the time he finishes, he's gone through most of a six-pack as well. "Jesus," I say. "You trying to eat yourself to death?"

"You should talk," he says, waving at my cigarette. "What's your blood pressure these days? A thousand over six hundred?"

"Those steaks cost twelve bucks each. How about kicking in?"

"So now you're nickel-and-diming me. Christsake, after all I've done for you?" He starts on the same rant I've heard dozens of times before, how he gave me a job and took me under his wing, how I would have been in jail if it weren't for him, or in a grave. "You are one ungrateful sonofabitch," he says. But now I'm not listening. Instead I'm thinking about Rifkin's chimney—there'll be bricks in the living room by the end of winter, I'm sure of it—and the way he suddenly looked so old. It's strange to think that I can't help him anymore, that he wants nothing from me. Whether I could fix it or not, the swaying chimney still haunts me, almost as much as the blank look Rifkin gave me.

Soon Barry's talking about how he took care of me when we were kids, and how I never thanked him for it. He once beat up three punks who'd cornered me in a playground and tried to make me eat mud. Don't I remember that? "Or that time down the shore?" he asks.

"Here we go again," I say.

"You would've drowned if it weren't for me."

To be honest, my own memory of the day is hazy. At eleven I was already pigheaded, that much I know—I didn't listen when my parents told me to stay close to their blanket. Instead I drifted toward a wooden pier where the biggest waves came crashing in.

I can recall a few vague sensations—water pounding over my head, salt in my eyes, a drag from below. Then, more clearly, an overwhelming desire to give in to the pull, followed by the bitter disappointment of finding myself hacking and puking on the sand.

"Jesus," Barry says. "I almost shit myself when I saw you go under. I don't think I've ever been so scared in my life." He takes a long swig of beer before going on. "Dad kept yelling for a lifeguard, but no one came. He didn't see me go in. I was up to my neck in three steps." He couldn't have been much of a swimmer even then, so it's hard for me to imagine him fighting the waves, catching me around the waist, hauling us both out. "I don't know how I did it," he says. "No idea. I just kept thinking, Get him out or go down with him." He tilts his head back, blows air out of his bloated cheeks, and closes his eyes. "Get him out or go down with him. I meant it, too. I would've rather been dead," he says, and as much as I might not want to believe him, after a slow minute I do.

Hawthorne Books & Literary Arts
Portland, Oregon

Current Titles

At Hawthorne Books, we're serious about literature. We suspected that good writers were being ignored and cast aside as a result of consolidation in the publishing industry, and in 2001 we decided to find these writers and give them a voice. We publish American literary fiction and narrative non-fiction, although we won't turn down a good international title if we find one. All of our books are published as affordable original trade paperbacks, but feature details not typically found even in casebound titles from bigger houses: acid-free papers; sewn bindings which will not crack; heavy, laminated covers with French flaps and built-in bookmarks. If you like to read, we think you'll enjoy our books. If you like to write—well, send us something. We're always looking.

Core: A Romance

Kassten Alonso

Fiction
208 pages
$12.95
ISBN 0-9716915-7-6

FINALIST, 2005 OREGON BOOK AWARD

THIS INTENSE AND COMPACT NOVEL crackles with obsession, betrayal, and madness. As the narrator becomes fixated on his best friend's girlfriend, his precarious hold on sanity rapidly deteriorates into delusion and violence. This story can be read as the classic myth of Hades and Persephone (Core) rewritten for a twenty-first century audience as well as a dark tale of unrequited love and loneliness.

Alonso skillfully uses language to imitate memory and psychosis, putting the reader squarely inside the narrator's head; deliberate misuse of standard punctuation blurs the distinction between the narrator's internal and external worlds. Alienation and Faulknerian grotesquerie permeate this landscape, where desire is borne in the bloom of a daffodil and sanity lies toppled like an applecart in the mud.

JUMP THROUGH THIS gothic stained glass window and you are in for some serious investigation of darkness and all of its deadly sins. But take heart, brave traveler, the adventure will prove thrilling. For you are in the beautiful hands of Kassten Alonso.
    TOM SPANBAUER
    Author of *In the City of Shy Hunters*

KASSTEN ALONSO takes the reader on a wild ride inside the mind of a disturbed man as he descends into madness and violence. A beautifully written book. Impossible to put down.
    JAMES FREY
    Author of *A Million Little Pieces*

KASSTEN ALONSO'S AMAZING Core will startle you. A fierce story that taught me to read it as I went deeper and deeper—it's as if this book is written in a rich, beautiful language I'd once known and somehow forgotten. I'm happy and terrified to have it back.
    PETER ROCK
    Author of *Bewildered*

Decline of the Lawrence Welk Empire

Poe Ballantine

Fiction
376 pages
$15.95
ISBN 0-9766311-1-3

"IT'S IMPOSSIBLE NOT TO BE CHARMED by Edgar Donahoe [*Publishers Weekly*]," and he's back for another misadventure. Expelled from college for drunkenly bellowing expletives from a dorm window at 3:00 am, Edgar hitchhikes to Colorado and trains as a cook. A postcard arrives from his college buddy, Mountain Moses, inviting him to a Caribbean island. Once there, Edgar cooks at the local tourist resort and falls in love with Mountain's girl, Kate. He becomes embroiled in a love triangle and his troubles multiply as he is stalked by sinister island native Chollie Legion. Even Cinnamon Jim the medicine man is no help. Ultimately it takes a hurricane to blow Edgar out of this mess.

I'M DRUNK AS I WRITE THIS and I wish I would've never left San Diego. San Diego is PARADISE. Billings, Montana is a PIMPLE ON MY BUTT. Edgar, Edgar, I loved you, why did you run away to a desert island? And why didn't you take me with you? I would've fought by your side. I would've drank with you all night and waited tables at that hotel. Jesus, the booze there is cheap. When I called your parents they said you'd gone to New YORK. How was I going to reach you? And why didn't you mention me more than once in your new novel about love and betrayal in the jungle? I thought I was your best friend, Edgar. I feel so bad about Bev. Oh, Edgar, Edgar, please forgive me (and put me in your next book, OK?). **BIG PAT FILLMORE**

YOU'RE LUCKY YOU RAN OFF to that island, Edgar, you *pinche pendejo*. *Chingada*, I'm still pissed and if you ever show your face around here again I'll kick you in your *pajarito*. My husband is gay and it was your fault. I'd still like to know what you did to him. **CHULA LA RUE**

I'M FAT NOW, EDGAR. I'm a blimp. I married this navy guy, do you believe it, and we're living at my mom's house on Mt. Helix. I see you're still drinking too much. And then you fall off a cliff and I can't stop crying. I'm so unhappy. Adrian told me about Bev. It wasn't your fault. Why do we have to grow old? Why can't we have another chance? **NORMA PADGETT**

God Clobbers Us All   Poe Ballantine

Fiction
196 pages
$15.95
ISBN 0-9716915-4-1

SET AGAINST THE DILAPIDATED halls of a San Diego rest
home in the 1970s, *God Clobbers Us All* is the shimmering, hysterical, and melancholy story of eighteen-year-old surfer-boy
orderly Edgar Donahoe's struggles with friendship, death, and
an ill-advised affair with the wife of a maladjusted war veteran.
All of Edgar's problems become mundane, however, when he and
his lesbian Blackfoot nurse's aide best friend, Pat Fillmore,
become responsible for the disappearance of their fellow worker
after an lsd party gone awry. *God Clobbers Us All* is guaranteed to
satisfy longtime Ballantine fans as well as convert those lucky
enough to be discovering his work for the first time.

A SURFER DUDE TRANSFORMS into someone captivatingly fragile, and
Ballantine's novel becomes something tender, vulnerable, even sweet without
that icky, cloying literary aftertaste. This vulnerability separates Ballantine's
work from his chosen peers. Calmer than Bukowski, less portentous than
Kerouac, more hopeful than West, Poe Ballantine may not be sitting at the table
of his mentors, but perhaps he deserves his own after all.

SETH TAYLOR
San Diego *Union-Tribune*

IT'S IMPOSSIBLE NOT TO BE CHARMED by the narrator of Poe Ballantine's
comic and sparklingly intelligent *God Clobbers Us All*.

PUBLISHER'S WEEKLY

GOD CLOBBERS US ALL SUCCEED[S] on the strength of its characterization
and Ballantine's appreciation for the true-life denizens of the Lemon Acres
rest home. The gritty daily details of occupants of a home for the dying have a
stark vibrancy that cannot help but grab one's attention, and the off-hours
drug, surf, and screw obsessions of its young narrator, Edgar Donahoe, and his
coworkers have a genuine sheen that captivates almost as effectively.

THE ABSINTHE LITERARY REVIEW

Things I Like About America

Poe Ballantine

Non-fiction
266 pages
$12.95
ISBN 0-9716915-1-7

THESE RISKY, PERSONAL ESSAYS are populated with odd
jobs, eccentric characters, boarding houses, buses, and beer.
Ballantine takes us along on his Greyhound journey through small-
town America, exploring what it means to be human. Written
with piercing intimacy and self-effacing humor, Ballantine's writ-
ings provide entertainment, social commentary, and completely
compelling slices of life.

IN HIS SEARCH FOR THE REAL AMERICA, Poe Ballantine reminds me of
the legendary musk deer, who wanders from valley to valley and hilltop to
hilltop searching for the source of the intoxicating musk fragrance that
actually comes from him. Along the way, he writes some of the best prose I've
ever read.   **SY SAFRANSKY**
                                   Editor, *The Sun*

BALLANTINE NEVER SHRINKS from taking us along for the drunken, drug-
infested ride he braves in most of his travels. The payoff—and there is one—
lies in his self-deprecating humor and acerbic social commentary, which he
leaves us with before heading further up the dark highway.
                    THE INDY BOOKSHELF

POE BALLANTINE REMINDS US that in a country full of identical strip malls
and chain restaurants, there's still room for adventure. He finds the humor in
situations most would find unbearable and flourishes like a modern-day Kerouac.
With his funny, honest prose, Ballantine explores the important questions
about being an American: Do I have enough money to buy this bucket of KFC?
Can I abide another sixteen-hour Greyhound bus trip? Did my crazy roommate
steal my beer again? It's a book to cherish and pass on to friends.
                    MARK JUDE POIRIER
                    Author of *Unsung Heroes of American Industry*
                    and *Goats*

Madison House

Peter Donahue

Fiction
528 pages
$16.95
ISBN 0-9766311-0-5

WINNER, 2005 LANGUM PRIZE
FOR HISTORICAL FICTION

PETER DONAHUE'S DEBUT NOVEL chronicles turn-of-the-century Seattle's explosive transformation from frontier outpost to major metropolis. Maddie Ingram, owner of Madison House, and her quirky and endearing boarders find their lives inextricably linked when the city decides to re-grade Denny Hill and the fate of Madison House hangs in the balance. Clyde Hunssler, Maddie's albino handyman and furtive love interest; James Colter, a muckraking black journalist who owns and publishes the Seattle *Sentry* newspaper; and Chiridah Simpson, an aspiring stage actress forced into prostitution and morphine addiction while working in the city's corrupt vaudeville theater, all call Madison House home. Had E.L. Doctorow and Charles Dickens met on the streets of Seattle, they couldn't have created a better book.

PETER DONAHUE SEEMS TO HAVE A MAP OF OLD SEATTLE in his head. No novel extant is nearly as thorough in its presentation of the early city, and all future attempts in its historical vein will be made in light of this book.

> **DAVID GUTERSON**
> Author of *Snow Falling on Cedars*
> and Our Lady of the Forest

MADISON HOUSE TREATS READERS to a boarding house full of fascinating and lovable characters as they create their own identities and contribute to early 20th century life in Seattle. Every page reflects Peter Donahue's meticulous and imaginative recreation of a lively and engaging moment in American history. I loved reading this novel and sharing in the pleasures and labors of the diverse and authentic inhabitants of a remarkable city.

> **SENA JETER NASLUND**
> Author of *Four Spirits* and *Ahab's Wife*

So Late, So Soon

D'Arcy Fallon

Memoir
224 pages
$15.95
ISBN 0-9716915-3-3

THIS MEMOIR OFFERS AN IRREVERENT, fly-on-the-wall view of the Lighthouse Ranch, the Christian commune D'Arcy Fallon called home for three years in the mid-1970s. At eighteen years old, when life's questions overwhelmed her and reconciling her family past with her future seemed impossible, she accidentally came upon the Ranch during a hitchhike gone awry. Perched on a windswept bluff in Loleta, a dozen miles from anywhere in Northern California, this community of lost and found twenty-somethings lured her in with promises of abounding love, spiritual serenity, and a hardy, pioneer existence. What she didn't count on was the fog.

I FOUND FALLON'S STORY FASCINATING, as will anyone who has ever wondered about the role women play in fundamental religious sects. What would draw an otherwise independent woman to a life of menial labor and subservience? Fallon's answer is this story, both an inside look at 70s commune life and a funny, irreverent, poignant coming of age.
　　　　　　　　JUDY BLUNT
　　　　　　　　Author of *Breaking Clean*

PART ADVENTURE STORY, part cautionary tale, *So Late, So Soon* explores the boundaries between selflessness and having no sense of self; between needing and wanting; between the sacred and the profane. Sometimes heartbreaking, often hilarious, Fallon's account of her young life in a California Christian commune engagingly illustrates the complexities of desire and the deeply-rooted longing we all feel to be taken in, accepted, and loved. Shame, lust, compassion, and enlightenment—all find their place in Fallon's honest retelling of her quest for community.　　**KIM BARNES**
　　　　　　　　Author of *Finding Caruso*

Dastgah: Diary of a Headtrip

Mark Mordue

Memoir
316 pages
$15.95
ISBN 0-9716915-6-8

AUSTRALIAN JOURNALIST MARK MORDUE invites you on a journey that ranges from a Rolling Stones concert in Istanbul to talking with mullahs and junkies in Tehran, from a cricket match in Calcutta to an S&M bar in New York, and to many points in between, exploring countries most Americans never see as well as issues of world citizenship in the 21st century. Written in the tradition of literary journalism, *Dastgah* will take you to all kinds of places, across the world ... and inside yourself.

I JUST TOOK A TRIP AROUND THE WORLD in one go, first zigzagging my way through this incredible book, and finally, almost feverishly, making sure I hadn't missed out on a chapter along the way. I'm not sure what I'd call it now: A road movie of the mind, a diary, a love story, a new version of the subterranean homesick and wanderlust blues – anyway, it's a great ride. Paul Bowles and Kerouac are in the back, and Mark Mordue has taken over the wheel of that pickup truck from Bruce Chatwin, who's dozing in the passenger seat.

WIM WENDERS
Director of *Paris, Texas*; *Wings of Desire*;
and *The Buena Vista Social Club*

WIDE-AWAKE AND SENSUOUSLY LYRICAL, Mark Mordue's *Dastgah* gets in behind the shell of the familiar, reminding us that the world is vast and strange and that everything is—in case we've forgotten—happening for the first time.

SVEN BIRKERTS
Editor of *AGNI* and
author of *My Sky Blue Trades: Growing Up
Counter in a Contrary Time*

AN EXTRAORDINARY AND DAZZLING VOYAGE across continents and into the mind. Mordue's book is almost impossible to summarize — reportage, reflection and poetry are all conjured onto the page as he grapples with the state of the world and his place in it.

GILES MILTON
Author of *Nathaniel's Nutmeg: Or, the True
and Incredible Adventures of the Spice
Trader Who Changed the Course of History*

The Cantor's Daughter   Scott Nadelson

Fiction
280 pages
$15.95
ISBN 0-9766311-2-1

IN HIS FOLLOW-UP to the award-winning *Saving Stanley: The Brickman Stories*, Nadelson captures Jewish New Jersey suburbanites in moments of crucial transition, when they have the opportunity to connect with those closest to them or forever miss their chance for true intimacy. In "The Headhunter," two men develop an unlikely friendship when recruiter Len Siegel places Howard Rifkin in his ideal job. Len and Howard buy houses on the same street, but after twenty years their friendship comes to an abrupt and surprising end. In the title story, Noa Nechemia and her father have immigrated from Israel to Chatwin, New Jersey, following the death of her mother. In one moment of insight following a disastrous prom night, Noa discovers her ability to transcend grief and determine the direction of her own life. And in "Half a Day in Halifax" two people meet on a cruise ship where their shared lack of enthusiasm for their trip sparks the possibility of romance. Nadelson's stories are sympathetic, heart-breaking, and funny as they investigate the characters' fragile emotional bonds and the fears that often cause them to falter or fail.

THESE STORIES ARE RICH, involving, and multi-layered. They draw you in gradually, so that you become immersed in these characters and their lives almost without realizing it. An enticing collection.
DIANA ABU-JABER
Author of *The Language of Baklava* & *Crescent*

NADELSON, A TIRELESS INVESTIGATOR of the missed opportunity, works in clear prose that possesses a tremolo just below the surface. His narratives about contemporary American Jews are absorbing and satisfying, laying bare all manner of human imperfections and sweet, sad compensatory behaviors.
STACEY LEVINE
Author of *My Horse and Other Stories* and *Dra—*

Saving Stanley: The Brickman Stories

Scott Nadelson

Fiction

220 pages

$15.95

ISBN 0-9716915-2-5

WINNER, 2004 OREGON BOOK AWARD
WINNER, 2005 GCLA NEW WRITER'S AWARD

SCOTT NADELSON'S INTERRELATED STORIES are graceful, vivid narratives that bring into sudden focus the spirit and the stubborn resilience of the Brickmans, a Jewish family of four living in suburban New Jersey. The central character, Daniel Brickman, forges obstinately through his own plots and desires as he strug-gles to balance his sense of identity with his longing to gain acceptance from his family and peers. This fierce collection provides an unblinking examination of family life and the human instinct for attachment.

THESE EXTREMELY WELL-WRITTEN and elegantly wrought stories are rigorous, nuanced explorations of emotional and cultural limbo-states. *Saving Stanley* is a substantial, serious, and intelligent contribution to contemporary Jewish American writing.
DAVID SHIELDS
Author of *Enough About You: Adventures in Autobiography* and *A Handbook for Drowning*

SCOTT NADELSON PLAYFULLY INTRODUCES US to a fascinating family of characters with sharp and entertaining psychological observations in gracefully beautiful language, remini-scent of young Updike. I wish I could write such sentences. There is a lot of eros and humor here – a perfectly enjoyable book.
JOSIP NOVAKOVICH
Author of *April Fool's Day: A Novel*

THERE'S A CERTAIN THRILL in reading a young writer coming into his own. The nuances of style, the interplay of theme and narrative, the keen and sympathetic eye for character—all rendered new by a fresh voice and talent. Scott Nadelson's stories are bracing, lively, humorous, honest. A splendid debut.
EHUD HAVAZELET
Author of *Like Never Before* and *What Is It Then Between Us*

The Greening of Ben Brown

Michael Strelow

Fiction
272 pages
$15.95
ISBN 0-9716915-8-4

FINALIST, 2005 OREGON BOOK AWARD

MICHAEL STRELOW WEAVES THE STORY of a town and its mysteries in this debut novel. Ben Brown becomes a citizen of East Leven, Oregon, after he recovers from an electrocution that has not left him dead but has turned him green. He befriends 22 year-old Andrew James and together they unearth a chemical spill cover-up that forces the town to confront its demons and its citizens to choose sides. Strelow's lyrical prose and his talent for storytelling come together in this poetic and important first work that looks at how a town and the natural environment are inextricably linked. *The Greening of Ben Brown* will find itself in good company on the shelves between *Winesburg, Ohio* and *To Kill A Mockingbird*; readers of both will have a new story to cherish.

MICHAEL STRELOW HAS GIVEN northwest readers an amazing fable for our time and place featuring Ben Brown, a utility lineman who transforms into the Green Man following an industrial accident. Eco-Hero and prophet, the Green Man heads a cast of wonderful and zany characters who fixate over sundry items from filberts to hubcaps. A timely raid on a company producing heavy metals galvanizes Strelow's mythical East Leven as much as the Boston Tea Party rallied Boston. Fascinating, humorous and wise, *The Greening of Ben Brown* deserves its place on bookshelves along with other Northwest classics.

CRAIG LESLEY
Author of *Storm Riders*

STRELOW RESONATES as both poet and storyteller. In creating inhabitants of a town, its central figure and a strong sense of place, he lays on description lavishly, almost breathlessly ... The author lovingly invokes a particular brand of Pacific Northwest magic realism, a blend of fable, social realism, wry wisdom and irreverence that brings to mind Ken Kesey, Tom Robbins and the best elements of a low-key mystery.

HOLLY JOHNSON
The Oregonian

Soldiers in Hiding

Richard Wiley

Fiction
194 pages
$14.95
ISBN 0-9766311-3-X

WINNER, 1987 PEN/FAULKNER AWARD

TEDDY MAKI WAS a Japanese-American jazz muscian from Los Angeles trapped in Tokyo with his band mate and friend, Jimmy Yakamoto, both of whom are drafted into the Japanese army after the bombing of Pearl Harbor. Thirty years later Maki is a big star on Japanese TV and wrestling with the guilt over Jimmy's death that he's been carrying since World War II.

This edition of *Soldiers in Hiding* includes both an introduction by Nobel Prize Winner Wole Soyinka, and a new preface from the author. *Commodore Perry's Minstrel Show*, the prequel to *Soldiers in Hiding*, is due out from the University of Texas 2007.

A rich and ingenious novel that succeeds brilliantly.
THE NEW YORK TIMES

Extraordinary...a feat of the imagination rendered with surprising skill...you'll remember this book for a long time.   **CHICAGO SUN TIMES**

Intelligent and interesting...daring and entirely convincing.
THE WASHINGTON POST

A mature novel...the spirit of Graham Greene is here.
KIRKUS REVIEWS

Wonderful...Original...Terrific...Haunting...Reading *Soldiers in Hiding* is like watching a man on a high wire.   **LOS ANGELES TIMES**

A work of exceptional power and imagination.
PUBLISHERS WEEKLY

Admirable, smooth, dispassionate...for an American to write from a Japanese standpoint, regardless of how long he has studied their culture, is an act of extreme literary bravery.   **CHRISTIAN SCIENCE MONITOR**

September 11: West Coast Writers Approach Ground Zero

Edited by Jeff Meyers

Essays, Poetry, Fiction
266 pages
$16.95
ISBN 0-9716915-0-9

THE MYRIAD REPERCUSSIONS and varied and often contradictory responses to the acts of terrorism perpetrated on September 11, 2001 have inspired thirty-four West Coast writers to come together in their attempts to make meaning from chaos. By virtue of history and geography, the West Coast has developed a community different from that of the East, but ultimately shared experiences bridge the distinctions in provocative and heartening ways. Jeff Meyers anthologizes the voices of American writers as history unfolds and the country braces, mourns, and rebuilds.

Contributors include: Diana Abu-Jaber, T. C. Boyle, Michael Byers, Tom Clark, Joshua Clover, Peter Coyote, John Daniel, Harlan Ellison, Lawrence Ferlinghetti, Amy Gerstler, Lawrence Grobel, Ehud Havazelet, Ken Kesey, Maxine Hong Kingston, Stacey Levine, Tom Spanbauer, Primus St. John, Sallie Tisdale, Alice Walker, and many others.

Baudrillard and his ilk make one grateful for Harlan Ellison, the science-fiction novelist, who tells a story in *September 11: West Coast Writers Approach Ground Zero.*
THE NEW YORK TIMES

A remarkable anthology.   **THE LOS ANGELES TIMES**

Physical distance doesn't mean emotional or intellectual remove: in Seattle poet Meyers's anthology of diverse voices, 34 writers from the left coast weigh in on September 11 in poems, meditations, personal essays and polemics. New and vociferous patriots beware: many of the contributors share criticism as strong as their grief.   **PUBLISHERS WEEKLY**

[*September 11: West Coast Writers Approach Ground Zero*] deserves attention. This book has some highly thoughtful contributions that should be read with care on both coasts, and even in between.
THE SAN FRANCISCO CHRONICLE